TREACHEROUS

A RISE OF THE CHARIOTEER NOVEL

BOOK TWO

SUSAN LASPE

ALSO BY SUSAN LASPE

Rise of the Charioteer Series

Sorcerous

Treacherous

To Mark, for his geekiness, love, and patience.

CAST OF CHARACTERS

Aeron Drefan: Knight of Chaddesden in Derbyshire

Alice: Cousin of Brynwen and Talfryn

Brynwen Masson: Healer and midwife-in-training from Derbyshire, twin sister of Talfryn Masson

Byron Keen: Knight of Chaddesden in Derbyshire

Circe: Roman goddess of sorcery

Danallis: Naiad (water nymph)

Douse: matron of the infirmary in Cataractonium

Eliva: Dryad (wood nymph) in Cataractonium

Gregorio Fiori: Italian tutor of Padric, teaches Latin and Greek

Helius: Roman god of the sun, father of Circe

Herman: knight from Nottingham; has winged shoes

Isemay: companion of Miriel Wilmot, of Chaddesden

Jarod: Worker in Cataractonium, specializes in glass and jewelry

Leowyn Masson: Knight of Chaddesden in Derbyshire, cousin of Brynwen and Talfryn

Miriel Wilmot: Daughter of Baron John Wilmot, of Chaddesden

Nalini: Dryad (wood nymph) in Cataractonium

Padric de Clifton: Lieutenant knight of Chaddesden in Derbyshire

Rhetia: Naiad (water nymph)

Ranulf Rawlins: Sergeant, knight of Chaddesden in Derbyshire, friends with Padric since childhood; goes by Rawlins

Roana: Sibylline Oracle from Nottinghamshire, gave Padric the prophecy

Serill Whitehead: Knight of Chaddesden in Derbyshire

Talfryn Masson: Farmer from Chaddesden in Derbyshire, twin brother of Brynwen Masson

Thimble: Dryad (wood nymph) in Cataractonium

Ulysses: Also known as "Staggy"; servant of Circe; half stag, half bird

Warin Ingram: Lieutenant knight from Nottingham; rival of Padric

ORACLE ROANA'S PROPHECY

Ut heberes aurigae quondam feres maledictum
Auri repete obscurissimae amuletum
Noctis ut deleas immemoratae vis telum
Et liberes illos cuius petis priusquam
sol suum consequitur verticem altissimum.

As the heir to the charioteer of old
Thou wilt bear a curse of gold.
Reclaim the amulet of darkest night
To destroy the weapon of untold might,
And rescue those of whom you seek
Ere the sun attains its highest peak.

PART I
CHARIOTEER

"Some things you will think of yourself...some things God will put into your mind."
— **Homer,** The Odyssey

CHAPTER 1

May 27, AD 1356
Unknown location

*B*rynwen awoke with a start.

What happened? Her chest tightened as her brain tried to work. Why was she frightened? Nothing immediately came to mind, but her body knew something was wrong.

She thought of her brothers Talfryn, Samuel, and grandfather Eduard, sleeping near her. Were they in trouble?

Opening her eyes, she lay in an unknown location, plagued with a searing headache. Blinking back the pain, her muddled mind tried to discern her surroundings, but the single candle did little to help make out anything with clarity in the dark. After a few heartbeats, other figures formed in the dimness, their light snores and whimpers creating the music of the night. And yet, they sounded strange.

No, she thought with a pang. *This isn't home.*

Flecks of memories spotted her mind, but nothing she could definitively grasp.

Reflecting on it, she thought the noises were not so different from her life with her brothers and grandfather in the little cottage. Could one of those people be her twin brother, Talfryn? If he was here, their cursed knight friend, Padric, could not be far away.

Padric and Talfryn! she thought in alarm. Her chest seized as she frantically tried to remember what had happened. She must have been captured and taken to the lair of the huntsman Drogo, who had hunted her and Talfryn down, along with his followers. Or maybe she had been taken by the hooded man who had, for a short while, donned Padric's cloak and pretended to be him.

Though he never spoke a word, she found out soon enough what the hooded man was after. Images rushed through Brynwen's mind of him; his face shadowed by the hood, strong shoulders heaving, edging toward her with his knife, holding out his other hand expectantly for something.

He had kept her from saving her brother from the murderous hands of Drogo. Had plunged a knife toward Padric's chest.

Was he still here? Hands shaking, she peered at every shadow, every cranny, expecting him to leap out at her. Could he hear her heart crashing against her ribcage?

But after a few strained moments, nothing happened. Did she dare hope he had gone?

As her mind cleared, Brynwen could not fathom the wonderful fortune that her captors had failed to bind her hands. Shifting her legs, she realized she lay neither on the rough forest floor nor on the stone of a dank cave, but in a room with walls and windows. On a cot with clean linens. Cloth drapes covered the windows, blocking the room from the light of the moon and stars.

And Nessie?

The bird, she discovered with relief, slept in her domed cage on a little table by the cot. It was the same cage they had found her in, hanging from the ceiling of a secret room below the mausoleum of a long-deceased legionnaire in the ruined fortress of Mamucium. The amulet of obsidian had been sitting at the bottom of the cage when they retrieved her. Through the dim light, Brynwen could make out dents in the cage's wiring, proving an arduous journey.

The memory surfaced.

She fell from a great height...a cliff. Air rushed around her, whipping at her dress, her hair. Nessie's cage tumbled with her, the little bird inside bashing against the metal bars. Brynwen stretched an arm toward the cage. Missed. Lunging again, this time curling two fingers around a thin bar. Then Brynwen twisted her body to see where they would land: large jagged rocks and the rushing river; each heartbeat bringing them closer and closer to their doom.

And then...

A loud snore nearby startled her back to the present.

Then what happened?

Brynwen played the memory repeatedly, trying to recall what occurred after that. How did she and Nessie survive, and how did they end up here—wherever here was?

Her eyes now adjusted to the darkness, Brynwen had a better sense of the room. Two rows of cots, ten on each side of the long room. Her cot was near the center of the room, with lumps occupying the three beds to her right. The rest remained empty, their white sheets ghostly in the candlelight. A dormitory or an infirmary, if she had to guess.

Talfryn and Padric. She had to find them—or what happened to them—if she could, and then they would escape together.

Her stomach clenched again. What if they weren't here?

One thing at a time, she reminded herself.

With careful movements—the cot yielding only the slightest squeak—she alighted onto the floor. Her bare feet slid along cool stones. The sensation both refreshed and grounded her.

Please, Lord, let Padric and Talfryn be here.

With a stealth she could only hope to possess, she crept to the first manned cot. Snuffling and snorting noises came from the figure lying there. Getting as close as she dared, they were almost nose-to-nose when the figure's sour breath choked the air out of her throat. Gagging, willing herself not to heave, she pinched her nose and examined the figure more closely. Upon a second glance, she thought maybe she still dreamed. She blinked several times, but each time, the vision was the same.

A pig lay on the cot.

This is absurd! I must be dreaming.

She had to stop herself from laughing in hysterics and shuffled away from the creature to the next occupied cot.

The blanket of the owner on the second cot covered its owner's head. The person was small, perhaps a child. There was only a slight chance that Padric or Talfryn lay beneath the blanket, but she had to be sure. Peeling back the coverlet, she discovered the creature beneath was a badger, its black hide and white stripes clear in the candlelight. And were those bandages around its foreleg? She scratched her head at that one.

She was leaning over the last occupied bed, inhabited by a disheveled hare which muttered in its sleep, wondering what sort of crazed place this was, when the scuff of shoes on stone startled her. Without thinking, she dropped to her knees and slid under the hare's bed, banging her knee on its wooden leg. Heart pounding and biting her lip till she tasted coppery blood, she waited, berating herself for not escaping sooner.

The faint glow of the single candle multiplied into brighter illumination. More people had arrived, whispering to one another. One was much louder than the others—voice high-pitched, as though she was ill-practiced in the art of quiet talk.

It was three maidens. They sounded young, not much older than herself. She wondered if they could be slaves. Why else would they be among Drogo's band of murderers? Perhaps she could talk them into letting her go. Or escaping with her.

After further thought, she decided to wait until they left the room, then dash out the front door by herself.

But she couldn't leave altogether. Not until she found out if Talfryn and Padric were here somewhere. And then there was the matter of Nessie and her cage.

She let out a quiet huff, impatient for the maidens to leave, when—

"She's gone!" one maiden said.

"What?" said another. "Where could she go?" Her voice was quieter.

"She was fast asleep," said the loud maiden.

"You were supposed to keep watch, Mir," the quiet one scolded.

"I am sorry, Isemay. I closed my eyes but a moment." Then she yawned.

"Come on, we have to find her," a third voice chimed in. "I fear she will get hurt out there alone, in her condition." This last voice sounded familiar.

"If she went outside—"

"Where would she go in the dark?"

"She is resourceful—let's go check. Miriel, stay here in case she returns."

The breath caught in Brynwen's throat. Miriel and Isemay? Could they really be the same Miriel Wilmot, the daughter of Baron John Wilmot, and her companion Isemay, both of whom Padric was searching for? The evil sorceress had kidnapped them weeks ago. What sort of ruse were these people trying to pull on her?

Their steps retreated, then a door opened and closed. The loud maid, whom she thought to be Miriel, muttered and paced two turns around the cots, coming incredibly close to Brynwen's hiding place, then disappeared into a little room off to the side. All was still.

Wasting no time, Brynwen scooted out from under the cot and dashed to the door, veering to her cot and snatching up Nessie's cage on the way. But, as she pushed the latch down, the door opened of its own accord. A maid stood there with a candle in hand and flaming red hair, barring Brynwen's and Nessie's escape. The bird chattered with great excitement.

They stared at each other, equally startled.

"Please, Miss, we don't want to harm you." The maid raised her hands placatingly. "'Tis a dangerous place at night."

Brynwen spun on her heel, but the loud maiden, Miriel, appeared from the room off to the side, blonde hair shining in the candlelight. "Be quiet, Isemay," she hissed. "Can you not see these ill men sleep?"

What ill men? Brynwen only saw animals.

Brynwen worried her lip. How could she get around them? "I wish to leave peaceably. My friend here and I ask for no trouble."

"Nay, you can't. Truly," Isemay said, her eyes sad.

Another person appeared behind Isemay. The woman's weary features flickered in the candlelight and Brynwen's knees nearly buckled. Her blonde hair may have been a little longer, and her stomach rounder, but Brynwen would know the sight of her anywhere.

It was her long-lost cousin, Alice.

CHAPTER 2

"Brynwen!" Alice exclaimed, almost bowling over Isemay in her rush to get to Brynwen. She launched into Brynwen's arms, squeezing the unsuspecting maiden so tightly she thought she'd die of asphyxiation. Then Alice's rotund stomach bumped into her.

"Alice!" Brynwen came to herself, tears flooding from her eyes. "You are alive!" Alice, who was among the first who had disappeared in December, over six months ago. Her new husband had looked high and low for her, being most anxious about her and her condition. Two years her senior, Brynwen's cousin Alice, was like a sister to her. The loss had hit everyone hard, but especially Alice's husband and Brynwen.

She couldn't believe it. After all this time, Alice lived here, safe.

Isemay lowered her voice. "Please, there are sleeping patients. Can we move this joyous reunion to the herbarium?"

Too elated for words, Brynwen could only nod. Alice took her by the arm and led the way, beaming all the while.

Passing the cots, they turned right into the room Brynwen had seen them come out of earlier. The moment Isemay closed the door to the small room lined with shelf-upon-shelf of herbs and remedies, Brynwen burst. "How I missed you so, sweet Alice. And the baby..." She broke free to lay her hands with love on the swelling stomach. "She is almost here. How do you and she fare?"

Miriel's eyebrows furrowed. "How do you know it is a girl?"

"Brynwen has good hunches about these things, being a midwife-in-training," Alice said, winking at her cousin. "We are fine, though as time goes on, I feel less and less comfortable. I'm practically waddling like a duck now."

Yes, Brynwen thought. She was about eight months along now. And to think, the last time they had seen each other, Alice was only three months along, barely showing, if at all.

Alice's expression became serious. "Tell me, how is Jack?"

Brynwen's smile faltered. "He is worried sick about you. I haven't seen him smile once since you vanished. He searches the notices in Chadd every week for news of you, though." She didn't want to tell Alice how initially people had blamed her husband Jack for her disappearance. Some townsfolk called him a murderer, a wife-killer. But there was no evidence. Then other people vanished, and then more, and soon any blame toward him stopped. No, Alice need not know any of this. Instead, she squeezed Alice's hand and gave what she hoped was an encouraging smile. "But he will be so relieved when you come home. And with a new addition to your family."

A tear slid down Alice's cheek. "I miss him so. But I'm glad he's as well as can be. I dream this will end soon, and we can go home to have my baby, away from this place. I don't feel it's safe to have her here." She fell silent.

"We will find a way home, I promise," Brynwen said, although she did not know how to fulfill her promise. Not without Padric and Talfryn. In fact, she began to wonder if she was a captive of Drogo or the hooded man at all.

"Where are we?" Brynwen's fingers scrunching her skirt until her knuckles turned white. "How did I get here?" The answers to these questions were very important.

"Dear cousin." Alice laid a hand on Brynwen's arm. "We're in a place called Cataractonium. Where that is, I can't tell. Ulysses brought you here the night before last. You gave me such a fright when you arrived, unconscious from a head wound and lying still as death—I feared the worst!"

Isemay nodded, her wild red hair bouncing around her head. "You slept the whole of yesterday."

"I see. Who is Ulysses?" Brynwen asked.

"He is the Mistress's servant. Some call him a spy, though no one knows for certain. He comes and goes all the time."

"He is quite the mysterious creature," Miriel said. "Beautiful antlers that stretch over everyone's heads, long, graceful wings, and a long bird tail."

Mistress? Spy? Antlers? Padric had mentioned a stag that followed him for weeks, all starting the same day he received a prophecy from the oracle Roana, and then again, the day the sorceress cursed him into becoming a mythical creature—a faun, with goat legs and little ivory horns atop his head, sticking out above dirty-blond curls.

Brynwen licked her lips, realization slowly dawning on her. *Animals sleeping in beds.* And Miriel's words: *"Can you not see these ill men sleep?"* The sorceress had shrunken Padric's fellow knights to the size and shape of animals.

Her heart picked up the pace as she opened her mouth to phrase the next question, though she already knew the answer. Her shaking voice came out barely above a whisper. "Who is this Mistress?"

The face of each maid became solemn, their mirth suddenly gone. It was Alice who finally answered.

"She is a great, powerful sorceress. I've only seen her twice, but she is exquisite. Her father is here, too."

"They are Roman gods," Miriel added with wonder.

Circe and her father Helius. They are real, and they are here.

Brynwen sat still for a moment, thoughts swirling. This Ulysses had rescued her, only to be brought to Circe's lair, the very place Padric had been trying to find. A sudden excitement filled her. *If Nessie and I are here, what of the others?*

Miriel cocked her head. "When most people first come, they are awestruck. But you do not seem surprised. Why is that?"

But Brynwen didn't hear as she launched into her next question. "Pray—did Talfryn, and a knight named Sir Padric de Clifton, arrive with me?"

Alice shook her head. "Nay, you and the bird were the only ones."

"Oh," Brynwen said, her shoulders sagging along with any of her hope.

But Miriel's face twitched at Brynwen's question. "Padric de Clifton? How do you know him?" She was almost angry with the question until she remembered Padric mentioning Miriel's fiery personality.

"He has been looking for you, Isemay, and the men from his unit. My brother and I chanced upon him a short time after he fell afoul of Circe, and we have searched for you these last weeks. But," her stomach whirled, "we became separated." Her throat caught at the implication. *They might be dead now, all because of me.*

Hot tears filled the edges of her eyes.

Alice lay a gentle hand on Brynwen's arm, her eyes moist. "Bryn, I'm sure they are fine. Talfryn is strong, and Sir Padric, from what I remember of him at home in Chaddesden, seems to be a capable fellow. Mayhap they became detained and are on their way now."

Alice drew Brynwen into another hug, rubbing her back to calm her down. *If I didn't make Padric find food...if I didn't leave Talfryn...if I didn't follow the cloaked man...Could the prophecy be wrong? Could their journey have all been for nought? Please Lord, please let them be alive.*

Padric's prophecy was the whole reason they had left Chaddesden—to find the missing people, to find and retrieve the amulet of obsidian, and to stop a dangerous weapon from destroying the world.

"You cannot blame yourself for everything."

I can, and all for a blasted amulet!

The amulet. Pulling away, Brynwen slid a hand along her skirt, only to find she wore different clothes than what she wore the other night, a light blue dress where before she had a cream blouse and a blue skirt. How hadn't she noticed this before? Her head shot up. "My clothes and satchel—where are they?"

"The dryads washed and mended your clothing and placed them in the drawer next to your bed," Isemay replied. She left the room and returned a minute later with a pile of clothing, freshly washed and folded, and handed them to Brynwen. "This is everything that came with you."

With eager fingers, Brynwen placed the short stack on the workbench and rummaged through it. She knew when Isemay brought it in that pile was too short to carry all her things.

The skirt pocket where the ring had been now had a new brown patch sewn with careful black stitches. But the skirt pocket was empty. Blood rushed to her ears as she felt every inch of fabric, every stitch. The amulet of obsidian, a gold ring with an obsidian stone, was gone. *It must have fallen out when I tumbled off the cliff!*

Retrieving the amulet had not been easy. In Mamucium, she, Talfryn, and Padric had fought a succubus and were nearly trapped inside a mausoleum. A band of deadly woodsmen had vied for it. The cloaked stranger had threatened her life for it. And now it was missing.

"My satchel is gone," she announced forlornly. Unfortunately, she couldn't mention the amulet for fear of its being discovered in the wrong hands. Did the cloaked man end up getting his hands on it? It was clear the silent, hooded man wanted the amulet, but why did he seek it? Who knew they had it? Her stomach twisted into knots. Padric needed that amulet to save the world by the solstice. What would he do if she couldn't find it?

Alice winced and grabbed her belly.

All other thoughts vanished as Brynwen caught her cousin's arm.

"Alice, you must let me examine you. Your time is coming." Helping Alice might assuage some of the guilt and remorse she felt. Being an apprentice midwife since she turned fourteen, Brynwen sometimes examined expectant mothers without the supervision of the experienced midwife. Now she would have no one to consult should something go wrong. *Nothing will go wrong,* she admonished.

The mother-to-be beamed. "Of course. If we get ready quickly, you can examine the baby before I need to head to the kitchens."

Brynwen started and peered to her left out the window. Was it nearly dawn already? How long had they been talking?

Isemay moved away from the workbench. As if for the first time,

Brynwen noticed the herbs and jars filled with colorful medicinal mixtures. She'd been so preoccupied with Alice and her own fears, she hadn't noticed the wonder that was the herbarium. Now she looked at it with appreciation. If only she could have something like this at home.

Isemay glanced at Miriel. "We have to see to the patients now."

The blonde maid sighed. "Yes, yes, I'm coming." Miriel lifted a basket of rolled bandages from the shelf behind her and slung it over her other arm. It was then Brynwen noticed that Miriel and Isemay were aged sixteen years, the same as her.

"May I help?" Brynwen asked, taking a step forward. "I have some healing knowledge."

Isemay smiled warmly, the freckles on her nose standing out. "We would be happy of your help. There is always so much to do."

Miriel nodded enthusiastically.

Alice patted Brynwen on the arm. "Bryn, mayhap you should rest a little more. You've only just awoken, and need to gain your strength."

"I am fine, truly." The headache lessened with each minute, and moving around would help with that much faster than lying back down.

"Well then, I would be happy to put in a good word for you with the matron, Douse."

"Thank you, I would appreciate that very much." Brynwen returned the smile.

"We would be delighted to show you around the fortress and our dormitory." Isemay's eyes were bright. "It is a snug fit, but we will gladly find space for you."

All was not lost on Brynwen. She had come to Circe's lair without her comrades, without the amulet, and yet, she felt she needed to be here, with Alice and her unborn child, no matter what else came. Even if the world ended in a few short weeks.

Later that day, she moved into the dormitory and began work at the infirmary. As she entered a routine, it amazed her how large Cataractonium was, and how it could remain hidden from the rest of the world for so long. Circe's magic seemed to know no bounds.

Brynwen knew not what tomorrow would bring, but it ate at her with each passing day that Padric and Talfryn did not appear at Cataractonium's gates. Each day she glanced at the horizon, hoping they would march down the hill. But they did not come. Each evening, a hole of despair grew wider and wider in her stomach.

Where could they possibly be?

CHAPTER 3

2 June, AD 1356,
    Cataractonium, England

*P*adric and Talfryn followed the sorceress Circe as she led the procession down the hill into Cataractonium. The bruises and ichor, the blood of the gods, leaking cuts on her arms along with the rips in her blue dress, were evidence of her scuffle with the two men a few minutes before. Despite this, her golden hair remained impeccable atop her head as she marched confidently down the hill with staff in hand. Less impeccable but still imposing, the two nymphs, Nalini and Eliva, marched directly behind her, one curved-bladed shaft, or polearm, between them. Behind them, the winged stag named Ulysses, formerly known as Staggy, proceeded the four fearsome animals that ushered Padric and Talfryn down the hill, the wolf and tiger in the lead, with the lion and bear in the rear. Padric was little fond of the lion and bear marching behind him where he had limited sight of them. It would require little provocation for them to show their great strength and sharp claws on his person.

Padric's head still reeled from the information Circe had related to him only moments before. Nothing was as it had seemed. The goddess Circe was only a pawn in the disappearance of hundreds of people. Not only that, but she and Helius were Padric's relations. His many-great-grandparents, sixty generations removed, to be exact.

And Brynwen, whom he thought to be dead for the past week, was, in fact, very much alive. His heart thrilled at this most welcome knowledge, and he held onto it with everything he had. It was part of what drove him down the hillside despite his exhaustion and wounds. That, and the giant lion and bear loping behind him.

Their descent down the hill was precarious at best. Padric spent much energy dodging stones and holes in the ground with deceptively long grass, which threatened to swallow his faun legs whole if stepped into. Even in his worst days as a knight, never had he felt so depleted. After fending off two nymphs and a goddess, being nearly eaten alive by a carnivorous bramble bush, and still recovering from a knife wound, his strength waned quickly. He wondered if he would make it to their destination without collapsing.

Once their feet, paws, and hoofs alit on even ground, Padric peered up to notice the city for the first time. He took an intake of breath and even Talfryn's mouth fell open at its grandness. "We are here. We made it."

"I think I'm in heaven." Talfryn's eyes roved hungrily over the entire compound. "This architecture is to die for. Look at all the columns and arches." He let out a loud whistle of appreciation. A few heads nearby turned in his direction. "Let me get my hands on a chisel, and I'll have this place looking like New Rome in no time."

"Forgive me for not thinking of putting one in my pocket," Padric replied. After everything, he found himself chuckling. "Do you even know what Rome looks like?"

Talfryn gave a cheeky grin. "Not a clue, but it can't be that hard to duplicate, right?"

Talfryn may have been amazed at the architecture, but Padric was startled by all who filled it: the missing people. The quantity was even larger than he had imagined. Both men and women walked about, unhindered, unchained. Everyone was active with an occupation, whether carrying a bag of wheat or sliding a building stone. Some stopped to stare at the group as they passed. Padric forced his eyes straight ahead but could feel the gazes of all those around him, making him uncomfortable. He wondered how many, if any, had been led into this place with such an intimidating escort as theirs was.

The strange group entered Circe's compound, what was once the great Roman fortress called Cataractonium, and down the old fortress's main road. This was what Mamucium must have looked like when it was in use by Roman Legionaries: all built with the same sandstone, buildings of one and two stories, some with two and three pillars adorning the outsides. Walls and roofs decorated in reds, blues, yellows, and white—the colors abounded throughout the place.

Mamucium, the place where he, Brynwen, and Talfryn had nearly been killed by a succubus named Lilith, where they found the amulet of obsidian; the key to defeating Helius's great weapon and fulfilling the Oracle's prophecy.

If only Gregorio could see this. He would love it.

Mamucium had also been the place where his friend, Gregorio Fiori, was kidnapped from his own campsite. Padric missed his aging Italian tutor, the man who had taught him Latin, Greek, and ancient Roman mythology. Still, he wondered if the huntsman, Drogo, had anything to do with Gregorio's disappearance, but it was too late to question him now. The vile man and the rest of his group were last seen miles away.

Padric's faun hoofs click-clacked against the white stones as they traversed the well-kept road, each stone laid straight and even, their presence drawing the attention of many of the people going by.

"Do you see anyone we know?" Talfryn asked. He looked around in every direction. "I had no idea they'd taken so many people."

"Not just from Derbyshire, to be sure." Padric, too, turned his head this way and that, hoping to catch a glimpse of his best friend Rawlins, Talfryn and Brynwen's cousin Leowyn, or the other knights from his unit. He cast anxious glances at each maiden's face for a sign of Brynwen, Miriel, or Isemay.

Dare he believe Circe spoke the truth? Did Brynwen actually live?

He had not had time to drill the sorceress much about Brynwen's whereabouts. His heart lifted at the prospect of seeing her again, even if only from a distance.

As they marched along the streets, the crowd behind them grew, whispering to each other and scrutinizing the newcomers. It was all Padric could do to ignore them. He had never replaced his cloak about his shoulders, and now everyone had a full view of his legs and the small horns atop his head. He berated himself for not questioning Circe about why he could not become fully human again. That was the least of his worries now, but something he needed to ask her, and soon.

To his consternation, Talfryn waved at the people with great enthusiasm, his hands still bound with the green and black snakes. "I saw my friend Charles. I didn't even know he'd disappeared."

After a time, Circe and the nymphs headed left down the major thoroughfare, the prisoners and their guard following, then halted at the edge of a set of large stone steps leading up to a dais, and bowed their heads. Two thrones made of the same white stone rested at the top in a regal fashion. The crowd gathered around them on both sides of the dais.

As they approached, Padric wondered about this god, who had been known to his worshippers as an all seeing witness, and invoked in oaths, including weddings and contracts.

The man sitting on the larger throne was not at all what Padric had expected. He knew the mythologies, but according to Circe's description of the sun god Helius, he should have been an old, crazy man. But this person before them appeared young, perhaps only a couple of years older than himself. Golden curls surrounded his handsome face, and purple robes flowed around him. Sitting with one leg crossed over the other, his Roman sandals adorned long feet, the straps creeping up his ankles like golden snakes. A pagan god, he reminded himself. Nothing like Christ and the one true, all-knowing God.

Yet the most astonishing thing about the man was his eyes. The same sapphire eyes as Circe, but more piercing and imperious, clever and...something else. Padric gaped. What did he have to offer this man in exchange for the people of England?

Helius continued to scrutinize his new pets with evident delight. When at last he spoke, it was in the voice of someone used to giving orders and getting his way. "Daughter, it is so good of you to join us, and thank you for bringing our latest visitors."

Circe bobbed her head. "M'lord, I caught these two sneaking over the outer hill into our home. I have brought them to you to do with as you will. This is the one who dared to escape me and stole some of my magic," she indicated Padric. The slightest sparkle lit in her eye. "And this one is his meddling friend." Her head swiveled in her father's direction with a sweet smile. "What will you do with them?"

Bile gurgled in Padric's throat. Again, he regarded Circe. Had he misjudged her? On the hill, the goddess had explained how Helius had made her swear on the River Styx—no light oath—to aid him in the building of his temple, not knowing at the time that she would be his pawn in kidnapping people throughout England and turning them into slaves. She had later discovered the prophecy and the dangerous weapon her father was creating, one that could destroy half the world. It was the reason Padric was here, to stop it from happening, and freeing the slaves in the process. She had sworn him to secrecy about their clandestine meeting at the hilltop, but now he began to doubt their agreement to stop Helius. Whose side was she really on?

"Daughter, please, show some restraint. Ah yes, Sir Padric de Clifton and Talfryn Masson of Chaddesden. We have been waiting for you two. I trust the trip was not a taxing one?" He regarded their rumpled and bloody selves with a raised eyebrow.

"How does he know our names?" Talfryn whispered.

"Mayhap because he is a god," Padric replied.

Helius smiled at the display. "I have followed your exploits for quite some time, anticipating your arrival."

Padric cleared his throat. It took patience to ignore the hissing snake twisted around his arms. "M'lord," he began, "how is it that you have come to follow us a'tall?"

Helius chuckled. "Daughter, will you remove those bonds from these gentlemen? They are distracting to me, and I do not think our guests will try to escape just now."

Circe snapped her fingers and the snakes uncurled themselves from their captives and slithered down their legs. A tingling sensation ran along Padric's skin as it made its way to the ground.

"To answer your question, a number of instances come to mind." He tallied each on his fingers. "You made yourselves known when you first spouted my name; your escape from my daughter Circe; even your newfound abilities. You have piqued my curiosity, young man. I hear all, as you must be well aware by now."

"Yet others have spoken your name. We are not the only ones to speak it."

"Of course. Scholars. Readings of so-called ancient texts. But you—" he pointed a manicured finger at Padric. "You and your friends have drudged up old stories of our family, which should have been locked away eons ago. Cursing my daughter's name, making threats to her wellbeing, to our home. You threatened to tear down all we have accomplished and take away those who worship us. How could I possibly ignore that?" Helius cocked his head to the right. A bit of jewelry caught the sunlight by his ear. "Indeed, you two are plotting to thwart my plans. I am still pondering as to your deserved punishment."

"You could give them to me to play with." Circe spun to look upon her captives for the first time. Then she moved in their direction as a panther ready to strike. Padric tried his best to keep an impassive expression as she stopped directly in front of him, raising a forefinger to rest on his chest. "How I adore new toys. My lions love treats. We could make a sport of it in front of all our servants. An entertainment as an encouragement to work harder. Yes?" With a slow motion, she strolled around Padric, gently tracing her finger along his chest, bicep, then finally his back, until she faced him again.

Padric spoke around the goddess, mustering all his authority and strength. "Lord of the Sun, I entreat you." At that, Helius perked his ears. "You must release all whom you have wrongfully taken."

The sun god grew impatient. "Lad, I can do as I please. I am god of the sun, with all of its strength on my side. Why should I bow to the likes of a mere mortal?"

"You have always been known as a man of honor, always true to your word."

"This is true. But what of it?"

"I am your many-great-grandson. You would not willingly kill your own family." *Not after what happened to Phaethon.*

Phaethon, the mortal son who begged his godly father Helius to allow him to drive the sun chariot around the world for a day. A foolish error on Helius's part, for Phaethon did not survive the ride.

Helius smiled, but it did not reach his eyes. "And how came you to this conclusion?"

"I have my resources."

"I see. What a coincidence that you should come this day." Helius leaned back in his throne and made a pyramid with his fingers. "You are not the first claimant as my heir."

Padric started. "M'lord?" What was Helius up to? He and Talfryn exchanged a glance. Even Circe's shoulders tensed, but he could not see her face. Did she know?

"It may or may not be a surprise that you are not my only descendent. It has recently come to my attention that I have another potential heir in this very place. A cousin, of sorts, to you." He waved his hand in a lazy gesture.

From around the bottom of the dais, a tall young man with broad shoulders and a shock of wavy brown hair walked up with purpose. A collective gasp went up from the crowd.

Padric frowned when he recognized the man: a well-known knight from Nottingham. "Warin Ingram."

The Nottingham knight halted within two paces from Padric, a grin plastered on his face. He towered over Padric by almost a head's length. "Well met, de Clifton." Warin's eyes rose up to view the horns atop Padric's head, then wandered down to Padric's legs. His eyebrow twitched, causing Padric to feel even more mortified.

What confidence Padric's plan had contained moments before now faded like an old flag left out in the sun. When first leaving Chaddesden with the twins to find Circe and the missing people from Derbyshire, it had occurred to Padric that he would encounter the other missing knights here. He had hoped—no, *expected*—cooperation from them in a unified front against Circe and Helius. But Warin's presence changed that.

"So, you are the other heir." Warin smirked.

"Does that surprise you?" Padric's stomach soured at the thought that they could be related, even if only via distant godly parentage instead of by blood.

"Not at all." But Padric noticed the edge in Warin's voice.

"Ah, good," Helius interrupted. "I see you two are already acquainted. That will save us some time."

Time...

The oracle Roana's prophecy rushed through Padric's vision, the intense image of the earth being consumed in fire and people screaming crushed his spirit. He had no time for this. The *World* had no time for this.

"Warin Ingram. I've heard of him, too," Talfryn said. "He once fought five robbers at once."

Padric glared a warning at his friend.

"Now, unless we have more claimants?" Helius peered around the gathered crowd. "...I propose a competition between you two to decide who shall be my heir. Prove your worth to me. Show me you can overcome everything I throw at you. Together, we will take back the sun and rule the skies, as is our right." His visage became wistful, as though thinking of a fond memory.

"Is that necessary, my lord?" Circe asked. "I do not think—"

"It is so," proclaimed Helius, his voice ringing through the air.

Padric's chest tightened at this, his fears of the past few weeks coming to a head. It was just as Circe feared: Helius planned to go after Apollo with his weapon and blast him from the sky. A two-fold strategy to both avenge the death of his mortal son Phaeton by Apollo's father, Jupiter, and to ride the skies once again as the sun's charioteer. Unfortunately, it sounded like Helius wished for his new heir to assist in carrying out this despicable plot. An eye for an eye, after all these millennia. The very thought gave Padric indigestion.

But what did that mean for the winner? Padric raised his voice. "M'lord, what becomes of your heir once the skies are reclaimed?"

"The winner will remain here, of course, and will claim recognition with the gods of Olympus. This includes becoming the general of my great legion."

> *As the heir to the charioteer of old*
> *Thou wilt bear a curse of gold.*

If he won against Warin, he would remain here, away from everyone and everything he knew. *What legion?* Padric wondered. He imagined a legion of fierce nymphs like Nalini and Eliva.

Sparing a glance at Warin, Padric spied the large knight's eyes twinkling. *Ah, that is his goal. To be on the same playing field as the gods, if not to become a god himself.*

"May we, as competitors, add to the terms of this competition?" Padric asked.

"And those are?"

"Should I agree to this pledge and became your loyal servant...in exchange, would you release all of your slaves?"

Aghast, the god's face dropped. "*All* of them?"

How many slaves does he have?

Warin regarded Padric, his face unreadable, then peered up at the god, apparently curious for the answer.

Padric clarified, "Yes, m'lord, all. Those are my terms."

Helius's smile weakened. He drummed his fingers together. "*Slave* is a harsh term. I prefer bound servant or retainer."

"Sir Warin," Circe said, "do you agree to these terms or have any of your own?"

Warin gave a slight nod. "I agree with these terms."

Helius huffed. "Oh, very well, you may have them all should you win at the conclusion of the competition."

The tightness in Padric's chest lessened a tad. At least whoever won the competition would be allowed to set the slaves free—if Warin went along with it. Yet, according to the prophecy, Padric had to win. There was no other way around it. Another pang struck his chest as he realized that if he fulfilled the prophecy and releasing the slaves, all his friends would return home, and he would remain here, virtually alone. He could not care less about recognition with the Olympic gods—he wanted his old life back, away from gods and magic. But to save everyone, he would do this thing. There was no other choice.

His thoughts drifted to Brynwen for a moment, but he shook them away—she did not need him, and he had no reason to believe she held any feelings for him.

"Good, M'lord," Padric replied, hiding all signs of his reluctance. "Of what shall this competition comprise?"

Helius tapped his fingertips together, and a spark of silver jewelry near his ear nearly blinded Padric. He blinked twice to clear the spots from his vision.

"There will be three trials of my choosing which you both must partake in," Helius said. "The ultimate winner will be named my heir." Then he glanced at Talfryn as if just now remembering he was there. "And you, young man, may contribute your time and muscles with the rest of the servants building my glorious temple."

"Huzzah," Talfryn said with all the enthusiasm of anyone on tax-day.

Averting her face from Helius and the crowd, Circe's sapphire eyes flamed with anger, but she hastily contained it without losing the rest of her composure and resumed her sweet smile.

"You shall hand your life over to servitude until your death?" Helius asked.

Padric sensed Talfryn's body stiffen beside him.

"I shall," both contestants replied.

Satisfied, Helius nodded affirmation. "Then so be it. The winner shall be bound to my service for the entirety of their mortal life. You shall both come to me tomorrow morning to find out the terms of your first challenge. Circe will take you to your quarters in the guest residence."

Warin gaped at the god for a moment before bowing deeply. "You are most gracious, M'lord."

Padric bowed, pulling Talfryn down as well. "As you command, M'lord."

As Warin straightened, he locked eyes with Padric, a wicked grin growing on his face.

Padric's chest constricted at the chilling sight.

It was the tourneys all over again. But this time, Padric was deter-mined to win. He *had to.*

❦

THE SHADOW WATCHED the proceedings with curiosity. No one would notice an extra shadow lurking near the purple-clad god's dais. Back when he mattered, Helius was well-known amongst all people. They prayed and sniveled to him. But these weak mortals knew nothing of his once-greatness—nor did they care. They were only here to do a task.

Which was why the Shadow dared enter Cataractonium through the secret way.

When first it learned the cursed lieutenant Padric de Clifton yet lived, the Shadow was greatly vexed, and thought to berate its myrmidon, who failed to kill and retrieve the amulet over a week before. It should not have been so shocked at the news, for this lieutenant and his farmer friend seemed quite resilient.

Now, though, the Shadow saw an opportunity. Its tour of the grounds of Cataractonium proved most enlightening, to say the least.

Helius's acceptance of a second challenger was another welcome kink in the lieutenant's plans.

This will be most interesting. And beneficial to our cause.

The Shadow scanned the crowd for the myrmidon.

Ah, there he was. Close enough to the front to see all, yet far enough back to avoid catching the eye of the lieutenant. The dark eyes of the young man, a trained knight, followed the cursed lieutenant and farmer as they departed from the gods' presence, a shadow passing over his eyes like a cloud covering the sun. Then the knight's body stilled, and he turned to peer directly at the Shadow. He nodded. After another few minutes, the crowd dissipated, including the knight. They would meet up later to discuss matters. The solstice was nigh, and they had much to do before then.

Now, to get to work.

CHAPTER 4

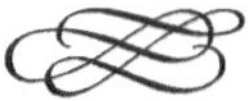

2 June, AD 1356

"**I**s that everything?" Brynwen asked.

On the edge of the garden, still completely enclosed by the fortress's wall, Brynwen and her matron, Douse, collected herbs for the infirmary's stores. Brynwen browsed the rows of herbs and vegetables for anything she or Douse may have missed. The fruit trees and bushes were farther down, but she didn't think they'd need anything from there now.

Brynwen had been in Cataractonium for just over a week, helping in the infirmary with patients and mixing up ointments, tinctures, and even her Miracle Mix. It was the best part of being here. It was hard work, but despite being a captive, life was not so bad. Apart from a handful of places, she was free to roam around the compound as she pleased, and she could put her midwife and herbalist skills to good use. She could check on Alice regularly as well.

Despite this, the amulet of obsidian remained lost. There was no way she could search for it within the compound—if it was here at all—

without arousing suspicion from Circe's nymphs or nosy workers. They were now one week closer to the solstice—one week closer to the world's destruction.

Now, sifting through a basket of rosemary and hyssop to ensure she had enough, she heard a commotion and glanced at the sky.

"That is strange," Douse said, pointing to the west.

Brynwen followed suit, her eyes perusing the cloudless sky toward the large green hill, which was said to be an edge of the property.

Two birds glided in the cloudless blue afternoon sky.

"What is so strange about them?" she asked.

"Look closer," the matron said.

Another glance, and her eye fell on their great wingspans. Eagles—or could they be Stymphalian birds? Padric had mentioned their trying to pluck Miriel from his horse's back. She imagined the heavy talons required to lift a human into the air and fly away with it. Circling in the sky, the creatures watched something on the hill.

Heart jumping, Brynwen said, "Mayhap we should go see what it is," and took a step toward the hill.

"Come along," Douse said, halting her with a hand. "Whatever it is, I dare say word will come to us soon enough." Her stern gaze penetrated Brynwen's resolve, and she followed the matron to the infirmary.

As they walked, she kept her ears perked for information. Two of Circe's green-skinned servants dashed around in their sheer blue and brown skirts, speaking another language. She thought she detected a few words in Latin, tidbits she had captured at Mass on Sundays:

"*Interventores capti sunt. Duo eorum.*"

They had captured intruders. Two of them.

Her heart raced. Was it them? Could it be Talfryn and Padric? Before she knew it, her feet carried her away from Douse toward the hill.

"Where are you going?"

With a sigh, Brynwen halted in her steps. Where *was* she going? She had to be patient.

"Forgive me, matron."

They walked on toward the infirmary, the slow pace Douse set taking all the patience Brynwen could muster. When they reached the last turn before the street with the infirmary, a loud commotion took place on the main road—the one leading from the hill.

It's them! I can feel it.

"So sorry, matron. I will return," Brynwen shouted over her shoulder, nearly dropping the basket of rosemary and hyssop in her haste.

Her legs couldn't move fast enough; her apron straps flailed freely about. Dodging men and women, many whispering about the new arrivals, she made her way back to the infirmary where she had left Isemay, Miriel, and Alice.

They were already standing and talking with another group of young maidens, all with wide eyes.

"It's them," Brynwen cried, out of breath.

Isemay started to ask, but Miriel cut her off. "Padric?" It was all Brynwen could do to nod.

They ran all the way through the streets, past columned buildings and dozens of unhurried workers and carts, to the dais and plunged into the crowd.

It had been a long time since Brynwen had been inside a multitude of people, when she would sell crops at the Chaddesden market. It was almost like being at home. Except she wasn't. The smell of sweaty, unwashed bodies assailed her nose to remind her of her present location.

She had never seen Helius before, so the appearance of him atop the dais surprised her. The god appeared no more than a youth with golden hair, sitting proudly atop his throne of stone. The light breeze swished at his purple robes as he conversed with someone at the bottom of the dais.

Brynwen rose on her tiptoes, but the crowd was too tall and vast. For a time, she waited for the tiniest break so she could see. She tapped the shoulder of the young man standing in front of her. "Excuse me, but may I pass?" He obliged. Following this, she started shoving her way through, apologizing as she went along.

"Bryn, come back!" Alice, Isemay, and Miriel called. Brynwen did not look back, did not care at the moment.

Then the sun god dismissed his prisoners, and again Brynwen raised herself on her toes, but was still too far away. How could she ever get close?

She gave up moving forward, and instead shimmied to the side, hoping to catch up with them as they exited the crowd.

"Wait, please wait." She prayed she was not too late.

Finally, a break opened, and she leaped out and rushed toward the retreating group: two men surrounded by four large intimidating animals. She caught sight of Talfryn's strong shoulders and Padric's curly, dirty-blond hair. Her heart leapt with a joy she had not felt in a long time.

Images of Padric with a wide smile and green eyes dancing as they beheld her made her stomach flutter. Talfryn's goofy grin as he hugged her tight.

"Talfryn, Padric!" Picking up speed, she sought to overtake them. She called their names, but they did not hear her, did not turn around. In her desperation, she had not thought of a plan of approach.

Suddenly, a large cat-like creature pounced into her path, nearly bowling her over. She stopped in her tracks with a yelp. Eyes wide in terror, she gazed at the long black stripes adorning the strange creature's yellow and tan side. Its razor-sharp teeth and claws extended as it roared at her, and she wondered how much it would delight in ripping her to shreds. The irresistible desire to flee passed through her mind. But her feet refused to move, as though ankle-deep in mud.

"I..." she said, barely above a whisper. "I only wished to see them."

It snarled, and with narrowed eyes, dared her to pass.

Perspiration trickled down her neck as Brynwen watched the animal warily. Daring a quick glance up, her eyes followed the other strange animals leading Padric and Talfryn away. They turned a corner and disappeared. There was no chance of catching up to them now.

With a heavy heart, she retreated one slow step. Then another. *Please don't follow, please don't follow, please...*

To her immense relief, the enormous cat held its ground. Then a strange feeling came over her, as though a cold blanket had been thrown over her head. She shivered and turned, her eyes sliding up the dais to Helius's throne.

The sun god stared directly at her. The breath caught in her throat. Even from afar, his intense sapphire gaze made her entire body freeze in place.

The beautiful woman in blue stood at the bottom of the dais, also looking her way. Not in superiority or anger, but in curiosity. Brynwen stared back. *Could this be Circe?*

Isemay caught up to her and put her arm around her friend. "Come on, Brynwen," she said, breathless. "We must go. Nice kitty." With a gentle hand, she helped Brynwen slowly back away from the fierce creature. It didn't strike Brynwen until later just how strong the normally timid Isemay truly was at that moment.

They were halfway back to the infirmary before Brynwen's brain began to work again. She'd never been so close to death from an animal. "What was that creature?"

"'Tis called a tiger," Isemay explained. "They are strong and fierce, and you do not wish to tangle with one of them."

"Certainly not." She grimaced, imagining what might have happened if the tiger had attacked. "How do you know so much about them?"

"Miriel's brothers enjoyed frightening us with stories of wild creatures when we were younger," the redhead said with a wistful smile. "They borrowed books—their term—from their tutor, many with the most frightening tales about all sorts of dangerous animals and creatures, to read in their spare time. Some of those pictures and details *still* give me gooseflesh."

As they traversed the streets, Brynwen did not pay the slightest bit of attention to where they headed, nor that Alice and Miriel had caught up to them. She had been so close to holding her brother and seeing Padric's handsome face. She had missed them so much.

"They are alive. My boys are alive."

The tears she had been holding for over a week finally flowed down her face. But instead of fear or loss, she found herself crying with relief.

Alice held her close. "Of course. Those we love are more resilient than we give them credit." Sometimes, Alice had words beyond her eighteen years.

CHAPTER 5

"*D*id you hear something?" Talfryn asked. They hadn't gotten far from their interview with Helius before he heard the voice. His heart was still hammering in his chest, certain they had barely escaped a brush with death, not once, but twice in the last hour. But they still had a bit of distance to go before being out of the god's sight—when Talfryn might breathe a little easier.

He started to twist his head back, but the bear growled at him.

"What?" Padric asked, his eyebrows furrowed.

"I thought I heard my name." He shrugged. *My overactive imagination again. Grandfather said it'd get the better of me someday.* "Never mind. So, what's with Sir Warin? He doesn't seem to like you. Come to think of it, you didn't seem particularly thrilled about seeing him, either. I've seen him at the tourneys against Nottingham." Yearly tournaments held between Derby and Nottingham that consisted of games, jousts, and sparring. All knights and squires participated, including Padric and Talfryn's cousin, Leowyn. Talfryn and his family made it to most of the events, eager to root Leowyn on.

Padric chuckled. "Ah yes, the tournaments. Then you know Sir Warin's ruthlessness at winning."

"Aye, he was a bit...rough with the competition." Talfryn recalled the burly knight's antics at the last tourney, having no apparent qualms about breaking his opponents' weapons, armor, or bones. He winced just thinking about some of them.

"Precisely. Last year, I turned eighteen and was eligible to take part as a knight for the first time. I witnessed Warin win every match he competed in. Few of our knights match his size, but one fellow in my unit, Byron, gave a one-on-one match with him a go. Both Rawlins and I were in other tournaments and came back just in time to see Sir Warin give Byron an appalling battering." The knight's lips tightened into a line.

"And?"

"Byron nearly lost his arm. It was over two months before he could swing a sword again. I should have prevented it."

I don't know this Byron, but he might've fought him anyway, Talfryn thought. "What'd you do about it?"

Padric ran a hand through his hair. "His bullish behavior had gone too far. Their superiors meant the tournament as a fun exercise, and Warin made it his personal mission to maim and embarrass the knights of Derby. *My friends.* Thus incensed, I confronted Sir Warin about it, how unsportsmanlike he was acting. In my crossness, I may have called him a..." The knight's cheeks flushed and he turned his gaze straight ahead.

"A what?" Talfryn asked, eyes shining with mischief. "Please tell me it was something brilliant."

"I called him an uncultured barbarian."

"Ohhh. That's a low blow. Come to think of it, he *does* swing his sword around and bellow a lot."

"Huh! He might have run me through with his sword had both our captains not rounded the corner the next moment. Warin vowed retribution for my words."

Talfryn recalled Warin's smirk as he answered Helius's challenge. "And now is his chance for revenge. That was a shocker, him being your godly cousin and all."

Padric scrunched his nose in distaste. "Please never say that again. It leaves a foul taste in my mouth. But no, I had no notion of that. It might explain his great size and strength—almost like Hercules." Padric clenched his jaw, and Talfryn wondered what memory the faun had conjured up. "Circe even seemed surprised by the announcement, and I begin to wonder if she has played me for a fool."

"Well, then she's a good actress, 'cause she looked pretty stunned to me, too."

"We shall see, I suppose," Padric replied. He furrowed his brow, deep in thought.

Talfryn hoped his friend didn't try to shut him out again. Padric had asked him to be his eyes and ears in this place—no one cared about a poor farmer. But once Padric rescued his knight friends from Chaddesden, would Talfryn be kicked to the edge?

A knot formed in his stomach. *No, Padric wouldn't do that. Would he?* Having not known Padric long, he couldn't honestly say. His cousin, Leowyn, was loyal to his commander, and was convinced of Padric's returned loyalty. Talfryn knew he needed to give him the benefit of the doubt.

Speaking of family, he hoped to see Leowyn and Brynwen soon. His excitement grew knowing they were nearby.

Wait, the voice that called to him a few minutes earlier, just outside the dais…*was it Brynwen?*

"I have to go back," he announced.

Nalini and Eliva spun around, bringing the group to a halt.

"Why?" Nalini asked, bewildered.

My sister is back there. "I…left my sock back there." Talfryn pointed toward Helius's dais. *Really? That was the best excuse you could think of?*

Both nymphs looked down at his feet.

"But you are wearing boots," Eliva said. "How did you lose a sock?" She crossed her arms.

Talfryn noted how tightly she held her polearm and gulped, trying and failing to avoid her gaze. It burned deep holes in his head. She hadn't wiped all the blood—his blood—off the weapon, which made it that much more intimidating. *This could hold so much more of your blood on it,* her eyes seemed to say. Not a lot of blood, but enough to sting when he moved around. After Eliva's whopping of him up on the hill and thrusting him into the carnivorous bramble bush, he felt certain she'd wish to finish the job she'd started. She was a much better fighter than him, and she knew it.

"Oh, well," he miraculously kept his voice even, "they scrunch up and then they just kind of *squish* out of the boot. You know how boots do that sometimes."

He looked at Padric. *Help me out here, mate!*

Padric nodded slowly, as if understanding. "It has happened to me many a time. When I had feet," he added hastily.

Both Eliva and Nalini furrowed their eyebrows. Talfryn looked down at their feet. Their very bare, green feet.

He really hoped they didn't see the deep flush creeping up the back of his neck and heating his face.

"Well, you can *imagine* how uncomfortable it is. So, can I go get my sock?"

"I have tried them," Eliva said.

"I beg your pardon?" Talfryn asked, his voice a high-pitched squeak.

"I tried wearing boots once."

"And?"

"I tore them off and threw them to the lions. They enjoyed ripping them apart."

Noted: never give a nymph a pair of boots.

"I am sorry about your sock," Nalini said, "but you are expected at your new job. We cannot delay."

"Surely they can wait a few minutes," Padric pleaded on his behalf.

"We have strict instructions, Sir Padric. Please, we must hurry."

"Fine," Talfryn said. Brynwen probably left already anyway. *I'll find her later.*

Periodically, bystanders stopped and stared at the newcomers surrounded by the nymphs and big animals, sharing whispered conversations with each other as they passed. This did not make Talfryn and Padric feel uncomfortable *at all.*

Stuck in his own thoughts, Talfryn nearly crashed into the tiger when the animals stopped moving. He found himself standing amid an enormous construction site, with scaffolding and men toiling all around. The half-finished building at their center radiated a grand magnificence, the pillars in the front thicker than many of the trees in the forest. Yet it was also daunting, imperious. It must be the temple of Helius of which Circe had spoken. The very thing the sun god had dragged so many people away from their homes to build.

Padric nudged Talfryn's arm and looked upward. Talfryn followed the faun's gaze to the top of the temple. "Wha…oh."

Be my eyes and ears, and find out all you can about our friends.

Padric's words came to his mind, his last instructions after Helius sent the large animals to capture him and Talfryn and bring them into Cataractonium. Yes, according to Circe, that was where part of Helius's weapon was located: his new chariot, the one he needed to destroy Apollo, and therefore, Jupiter. There were probably guards watching it too. With all her magic, Circe couldn't get to the top of the temple to disarm the weapon. What made her or Padric think Talfryn could?

Be my eyes and ears…

Well, if nothing else, he would find out what he could about it, then see about accessing it. Start small, then work big.

"You are the new recruit?"

Talfryn's thoughts were broken by the sudden gruff voice at his side.

The two large cats had parted, and a young man, around thirty years of age, stood in their stead. Brown hair and a short beard covered his chin. He seemed unaffected by the sharp teeth and claws of the animals, as he undoubtedly saw them every day.

Talfryn nodded. "Hello."

"I'm Cyp. You must be Talfryn."

Word spread fast. "I see my reputation precedes me."

Without missing a beat, the deadpan Cyp said, "Come along."

With a slight hesitation, Talfryn started to follow him, but Padric remained, the animals barring his way. "Cyp, what about my friend here?"

The bearded man merely shrugged. "Another assignment, mayhap."

Padric's eyes glistened. "I fear they have something else in mind for me."

A sudden fear of being alone struck Talfryn. "But we have to stick together." He looked to Padric and then the nymphs. Eliva seemed to enjoy his unease.

"Later," Padric said. His eyes sent encouragement and a request to remember what they had spoken of earlier.

The lion, bear, tiger, and wolf began clawing at the ground with impatience. A growl came from the wolf. As Talfryn drew back, Padric said one last thing: "Find her."

Still pondering that last remark, gaped at the grand, partially built stone house covered in Roman arches.

"Time's a'wasting." Cyp waved Talfryn to follow him.

Sighing deeply, Talfryn obeyed.

THE MIDSUMMER HEAT did its best to choke all the moisture from his body as Talfryn toiled in manual labor along with the other lads. He hacked at stone. Lifted stone. Carved stone. Carried stone. Hauled stone in a wagon. Lay stone down. Climbed stone. Flipped stones over.

There was a time when his greatest dream was to be a stonemason. Now, if he never saw another stone again, he would be content.

By the time the break bell sounded, he was grateful for the respite. A water carrier came by with a pail and scoop. No more than sixteen, the scrawny youth, Simon, ran around serving the workers drinks all day, never seeming to take any breaks himself.

Talfryn splashed the ladle full of water over his head, then the lad was off to the next man in need of a drink. Then the next.

The few men he knew from Chaddesden worked on the other side. He had spied them from a distance, but no sign of his cousin Leowyn yet. Nor Brynwen, though she would not likely be working with the builders.

Find her.

If he knew his sister, she would be aiding the healers. Some of the men obtained minor wounds while they worked and were instructed to head to them. He was determined to follow one at some point soon. He hoped she still had the amulet of obsidian, but he worried their captors might have found and confiscated it, like they did his hatchet and Padric's weapons. If Helius had it, what would happen then?

A man with cropped, light red hair and fuzzy eyebrows scrutinized Talfryn. "You're new around here, aren't you?" His hair gave off tints of actual orange when it caught the light just right. A relatively new scar adorned his left cheek.

"Yes, I arrived today. I'm Talfryn."

"Ah. So, you're the one everyone's making a fuss over today. That's two pieces of excitement in just over a week. Jarod Brown, at your service."

"Talfryn Masson." Talfryn leaned over to lift the heavy white stone. "What else happened?"

"Part of the wall from the tower collapsed while we were working. Several wounded. It was a right mess. The Master was none too pleased and has had us working overtime to reconstruct what fell down. We've hardly had any breaks."

"Is that where this is from?" Talfryn asked, pointing at the scar on Jarod's face.

"Aye."

"And the Master?" Talfryn questioned. "Helius?"

Some men working nearby paused in their work and eyed Talfryn warily.

Jarod peered around and lowered his voice. "Don't go around spoutin' the Master's name too often, lad. He's likely to hear you and send someone over to 'inspect' things."

Talfryn saw the man's discomfort. "Right, then. I will keep that in mind." He shifted the stone. "That's why even Simon is running himself ragged."

"Aye. One of the other water boys, Walter, was injured in the collapse and is still limping. Simon's picking up the slack."

Talfryn nodded in understanding.

"How long have you been here, Jarod?" Together they hefted the large piece of rock to the larger pile closer to the temple.

"Oh, nigh on three months, I reckon. I started out making glass for the temple, and the Master has me making a special project with a crystal. But since the accident, I've been helping here. I don't mind the change for at least a little while. The forges are hotter than the midsummer sun!"

Talfryn didn't doubt the older man's words. He wondered what the special project was and asked about it.

"Don't rightly know, and no one will say. But the Master gave me specific measurements and dimensions for the crystal. It has to be perfect. It is a large piece, and 'twill go on a chariot the Master is having built specially." He raised his gaze to the top of the temple. Men climbed around the scaffolding and ledges. "Right up there," he pointed.

Outwardly, Talfryn only nodded and didn't miss a beat of work. Inwardly, he danced. He couldn't believe his luck at finding Jarod and getting some helpful information on the first day. They'd be saving the world in no time. *Look out, prophecy, Talfryn is on it!*

Talfryn took clandestine glances at the temple and pondered the chariot and crystal. He wondered how he could get up there. How he and Padric could destroy it. They only had until the solstice to figure it out, just over two weeks away.

The next bell came none too soon. Immediately, the men stopped what they were doing and started putting their tools away. Talfryn looked around, confused. The sun was still shining, would be for at least another hour or so, so why had everyone stopped?

Together, everyone started walking toward the center of Cataracto-nium. Jarod bid Talfryn follow, and he stepped in line.

"Time for the evening meal, then back to the barracks."

"Why is everything ending so early? There's plenty of light left."

Jarod's eyes shifted. "It's hard to explain...You'll see soon enough." Talfryn was uncomfortable with what the glassmaker didn't say. He didn't look forward to finding out.

After everyone finished eating bowls of stew and chunks of bread, the food washed down with mugs of watery mead, they were led to the men's barracks. By this time, the sun was starting to go down. But the place they were led was not any kind of barracks he had imagined. It was not even a building.

"Meet your new 'bedroom,' Talfryn," Jarod said, throwing his arms wide. Talfryn waited for the man to laugh, but Jarod's face betrayed no signs of a jest.

Before them were a dozen or more chest-high pens constructed with the same white stone used to build the temple. In fact, except for Circe's home, which had trace amounts of marble, everything in the Roman fortress was constructed with the same kind of stone.

Talfryn slowly moved with the crowd, noting the passage of the setting sun as they crept forward. Every single man went into the pens. He pivoted amid a group of men and boys toward the open gates, an uncomfortable feeling creeping up his skin as he walked into the first available structure. Once everyone was inside, and without anyone touching them, all the gates closed simultaneously, iron hooks catching the wooden doors in place.

And that was it.

What made Talfryn more nervous was how everyone appeared relatively calm, despite being placed in animal quarters.

Panicking a little, Talfryn pushed his way to Jarod's side. "Are we to be sacrificed and led to slaughter after a hard day's work?" He gulped.

"It won't be as bad as all that, I assure you."

He crossed his arms. "Then what?"

"It's hard to explain what happens. Just wait a few minutes. Follow the sun."

As requested, Talfryn waited, expecting large tigers and bears to come out and murder them all with their razor-sharp teeth and claws.

The crowd shuffled and parted just enough for Talfryn to see into the other pens.

His eyes widened and heart skipped as he found a familiar face not far away.

"Leo."

The cousins' eyes locked, and Leowyn mirrored Talfryn's surprise, then nodded greetings.

It was just for a moment, then the sun said its farewell for the evening. Everything grew dark in a rush.

Murmurs filled the pens. "I hate this part," came from nearby.

Sweat covered Talfryn's brow. *Now what?*

A sudden cramp started in his side, then a tugging at his stomach. The tugging intensified, and he thought he would be sick. An unseen force bade him double over in pain, just as others did the same. A jolt sliced through his limbs, and he found himself on his hands and knees, crying out. Right in front of his eyes, his hands curled and shrunk. Fur grew—*so much fur*. He tried to stand up but couldn't. He attempted to call for help, but all that came out of his mouth was a squeal. Another squeal escaped his lips to cover the last one. Bolting forward, he slammed into the hide of a small animal. A mole. He attempted to apologize, but it came out more like a pathetic bark. The mole merely gave him a bored glare. Frightened, Talfryn ran around, looking for any way out. Most of the other animals lay down, as though nothing was wrong, while others dashed around in circles. No people, just animals.

His mind was so muddled. None of his thoughts made sense. He wanted to run. He needed to dig a hole. He wanted to cuddle up to the warm-looking dog in the center. He was sleepy. He needed to get help.

Help.

Yes! I need help...to...to find a comfy place to sleep. Aha!

He waddled around in a circle. Lay down. And endured fitful and terrifying dreams of being a hedgehog.

CHAPTER 6

*P*adric was led directly from the gods' throne on the dais to their homes—two mansions. By all standards, one was a modified castle, made by master hands. The white sandstone intermingled with white marble to perfection. The largest building boasted three stories with two balconies on the top two-story windows. Next to it, the smaller building had only two stories, but was just as grand as its neighbor.

From what he could see, both homes comprised columns all around the front, with intricate artwork of laurel leaves and partially hidden animals carved in relief along the bottom of each. The animals reminded Padric of *The Odyssey,* where Circe turned humans into animals to capture the hero Ulysses. He mused whether the goddess loved animals or humans more, or if she had turned people into animals out of sheer enjoyment. In the myths, she appeared to love it. But after speaking with her on the hill, he was not so sure.

A large, three-tiered fountain separated the two buildings, spouting water into each tier with graceful arcs that reflected the sunlight.

Talfryn, Padric knew, would kill to lay his hands on the stonework. Baron John Wilmot, Miriel's father and owner of the largest mansion in Chaddesden, would marvel at this architecture.

The nymphs, lion, tiger, wolf, and bear stopped at the front door of the second house, which was more the size of the Wilmot residence. Nalini smiled somberly and led Padric inside a wide door displaying the likeness of a sun with golden rays on the door knocker.

He glanced back to see three of the large animals and Eliva remained outside the door, while only the wolf followed them inside. The tiger let out a growl for good measure. Having disposed of their charge, Eliva scratched behind its ears, and the beast emitted a low purr of pleasure, and...*was that a smile?*

"Good lad," Eliva said as Nalini closed the front door.

The foyer was spacious, full of smooth cherry wood—the first wood he had seen since entering the compound, other than the living trees outside.

"Welcome to Circe's guest residence," the green maiden said. "Come this way."

Guest residence?

Padric followed Nalini in a rush of flowing translucent sky-blue skirts and bare feet through a wide entryway. She dropped off the polearm near the staircase, then ushered Padric up the grand oaken staircase which curved around the foyer. The gray wolf continued to follow.

"Pet of yours?" he asked.

Nalini kept a straight face and continued walking. "He goes where he is needed." She stopped abruptly in front of a wooden door and opened it. She followed him inside, but the wolf stayed in the hallway.

Padric examined the Romanesque furnishings. Two consecutive walls were covered from floor to ceiling in Roman artwork, which for all appearances resembled brick masonry in alternating browns, blues, yellows, reds, and greens. Each row held to the patterns. The third wall was architectural style. It was truly mesmerizing; differing perspectives, with pillars and windows and outdoor scenery that looked so realistic, he desired greatly to take a glance out the window. Gregorio had described this artwork in detail, but nothing compared to a glimpse of the real thing. In fact, he had described this same wall once. *Strange...*

A grand candelabra ablaze with candles stood tall at one end of the room. The low dining table near the balcony was surrounded by colorful cushions instead of chairs. Lastly, a plush maroon couch with fluffy cream-colored pillows sat in the middle of the room before a matching, thick Persian rug.

"This suite is yours, and will remain so for the rest of your stay."

A suite. No cell in the basement to keep him locked up. No chains to clamp around his wrists and ankles. He was half surprised Helius's offer of staying in his guest residence turned out to be true.

"Does Sir Warin get a suite as well?" he asked, refraining from grimacing.

Nalini opened the scarlet drapes, letting sunlight splash in from the window that spanned almost the entire wall.

"He does. He will be down the hall."

Perfect, no privacy from any of my nemeses.

She gave him a tour of the suite: a living space, a large bedroom, the bed covered with fresh scarlet and cream sheets, a small lavatory, and five wardrobes.

"Five wardrobes?" he mused. "What could I possibly need five wardrobes for?"

"I am sure you will find a use for them," the warrior-turned-serving maid smiled sweetly. Almost as sweet as Circe's manipulative grin.

"We have been preparing for your arrival for some time."

Padric nearly choked. *Has everything I have done been anticipated?*

"My sisters and I run the house."

"I see." Her sisters. He had noticed her and Eliva, along with a few other green skinned maids milling about Cataractonium. *How many of them are there?* "I hope you do not mind my asking, but I have never seen someone like you in Derbyshire. From whence do you hail?"

"I suppose I do look different than the English maids you are used to. I am a wood nymph known as a dryad."

Ah. Memories of reading Roman mythology in Signore Gregorio Fiori's study came flooding back to him. "Ah, yes. I have heard of you—your kind, that is. Do you not customarily live in the forests? And are all your kind warriors as well as servants?"

"We customarily do live near trees, yes. There is a forest nearby where we congregate on occasion. That is partly why we chose this island of Britain to inhabit. There are so many lush trees." Her face beamed as she spoke. "But we are not all warriors. The goddess Diana trained some of us, and every so often we gather with her for a hunt, mostly for wayward monsters. In fact, we are always looking for new sparring partners." She gave him a meaningful look before turning her gaze out the window, where the sun was quickly reaching the horizon. "Oh my, look at the time! You are to be ready first thing in the morning to meet the Master for your initial trial."

"Is it a difficult trial?"

Nalini thought for a moment. "It is hard to say. The Master comes up with the most elaborate schemes sometimes, so we shall see what he has in store. But after hearing all you have accomplished, I do not doubt you will be victorious." Another smile lit her lips.

"What about Sir Warin? Should you not be more neutral in this matter?"

"Mayhap, but, well, I am not yet sure what I feel about him. I have not fought him as I have you. As my mother says: 'Do not trust anyone until you meet them in combat.'" She fluffed a pillow. "I believe you will be here a good long while, if my sisters and I have anything to say about it."

"How many of you and your sisters are there?"

"There are fourteen of us. We all serve Circe. She protects us and vice versa." Another smile, laced with a warning. Padric was glad she left her polearm downstairs. "If you should need anything, do not hesitate to pull the rope in the corner. The evening meal will be brought to you shortly. Do make yourself comfortable."

She padded toward the door, closing it softly behind her.

Immediately, Padric rushed to the door and tried the handle, jiggling it a few times. "It is locked from the outside," he muttered. He sighed and turned around, leaning heavily against the door. "It was worth a try. It appears I am a prisoner after all."

Padric plopped down on the couch, falling into its softness, immediately dissipating the tension in his shoulders. He let out a satisfied breath. This was certainly most lush, considering he was a prisoner. He wondered how Talfryn fared. Padric felt guilty knowing his friend had been sent to work right away, while he himself was allowed to rest in a luxurious suite. Doubtless Rawlins, Byron, Serill, and Miriel's two servants were working to the bone like Talfryn.

And what about Miriel and Isemay?

And Brynwen.

Per Circe, she lived, and was here. Longing filled his heart. Since their parting, he dearly missed her presence, her bright eyes, her smile. The way she twisted her braid between her fingers when she was nervous. Their conversations about healing herbs and ancient mythology. If only he could see her, even for a moment. A glimpse would be enough. When Circe gave the news on the hill, Talfryn seemed less surprised than Padric was. *Had he suspected she was alive all along?*

Padric took a moment to pray and thank the Lord that her life was spared. And that he and Talfryn had made it with relative safety to Cataractonium as well. It was strange, praying to his Christian God, when he found himself coming face-to-face with two living, breathing pagan gods. If Christ appeared to Padric right now, he could only imagine what He would have to say about it.

Next, he considered the reason he was there. *As heir to the charioteer of old.* Try as he might, Padric could not get over the fact that Circe and Helius were his many-great-grandparents. How many people could claim they had personally met their ancestors who lived thousands of years ago? It was certainly something to mull over. That, and having Warin as a long-lost cousin, whom he would never wish to claim.

The evening meal, when it was brought, was exceptional compared to the gruel he and Talfryn had been scraping by on for the last few days of their travels. The scent of freshly baked bread and sweetmeats made his mouth water. He also relished the display of green vegetation, fruits, and orange cheeses. A grand meal for a prisoner. He ate his fill, then got up to walk around the suite.

A small bookshelf lined the wall connecting to the bedroom. He perused the titles, coming across a few dating back hundreds of years. There was even one on Greek and Roman mythology, which greatly resembled the books his old tutor, Gregorio Fiori, owned. It made him wonder what became of his tutor, and a stone of guilt grew in the pit of his stomach. The man had disappeared from Chaddesden two months ago. While searching for the amulet of obsidian at the ruined Roman fortress of Mamucium, Padric and his friends had found the tutor's abandoned campsite, with evidence of a struggle scattered throughout. Yet for all that, Gregorio had left Padric a clue to the location of the amulet, hidden within a Roman Legionnaire's tomb.

How would he ever be able to save Gregorio from his unknown captors? And for what reason did they kidnap him? Neither he, Brynwen, nor Talfryn ever found any more clues to his whereabouts, or if the woodsmen who attacked them were also involved in his tutor's kidnapping.

After an interminable time of being all-too alone with his thoughts, he became restless and walked to the balcony, swinging the glass door inward on silent hinges. At least *this* door remained unlocked should he need a quick escape. About a twenty-foot drop extended to the ground with another balcony around halfway down. Padric had never tried leaping down so far as a faun, and thought it unwise to try it now. But between the lower balcony and stones, climbing down appeared to be a viable option. Perhaps he was not as much of a prisoner as he had thought.

With the sun's repose into the west, the night was quickly advancing. The view of the compound was exquisite. However, this place was quite different from Chaddesden. Even in the dark, some people would be roaming around, especially knights and squires on duty or running errands. Padric expected to see people continuing to run around as they had earlier, but not a soul moved about anywhere close to the house. Nor farther out. He strained his ears for any sounds, but besides the owls, insects, and night creature noises, there was nothing. Odd. For such a big place, there should be at least some noises made by people. Something was wrong.

As the sun set behind the distant hills, he heard a strange sound. With the last rays of daylight came the moans and cries of men from a short distance away.

Fear gripped Padric's chest. *What in the world is that?* He craned his neck in the gathering darkness, but could see no one. The sound lasted a few minutes, then as abruptly as it began, it all stopped. Still wary, he pricked his ears to catch anything else amiss, but he heard only the noises of animals. Woodland and farmland animals intermingled with the roars and growls of Padric's animal guard.

He sent up silent prayers to his Christian God that everyone in the fortress was safe, wherever they were. Nevertheless, to his great consternation, small thoughts tapped at the back of his mind and wrestled with his prayers. The knowledge of mythical gods being real and roaming around England freely while his God resided in heaven kept coming to mind. *But God is everywhere,* he reminded himself.

A shiver ran down his spine. Circe still harbored secrets, explaining that he would understand in good time. *But when was that to be?*

Heavy of heart and tired in mind and body, he blew out the candles and went to bed for a restless night.

CHAPTER 7

The morning sun reigned brightly in the sky. Not a cloud could be seen for miles. The June heat sweltered, and each step was a chore. The same four animals, sans snakes, flanked Padric and Warin as Nalini led them from the guest house through the streets to the arena.

Padric's usual green cloak had been taken, presumably to be washed. It would not be welcome in this weather anyway. He and Warin donned light tunics along with sets of tailored leggings that were even able to fit his faun legs. However, without his cloak, he was certain to endure further scrutiny.

Sure enough, despite the ferocious animals, several men and women followed the group down the road, their whispers heightening as more joined them. Padric glanced behind to see perhaps a hundred people following from a distance. When they passed by the temple workers, Padric strained for any signs of his friends, but could find no one he knew well. From what he could see of their work, though, he did not envy their positions in the slightest.

Having Warin walk beside him proved difficult to ignore.

"How was your room, de Clifton?" Warin asked.

"It is quite fine, Warin, with a wide view of Cataractonium. And yours?"

"Quite nice. Although not as grand as my home in Nottingham."

"Ah, 'tis a pity." Padric nodded. Through his father, he had learned Warin's family owned an extensive estate in Nottinghamshire. "Mayhap if you win, Helius will grant you a larger home." *...for your ego*, he wished to add.

"Mayhap," Warin responded, thrusting out his chest. "I suppose if you win, you will require a larger stable."

Padric fumed, half expecting steam to emanate from his ears. Instead, he laughed, perhaps too harshly.

He mulled over a witty rebuttal when Nalini announced, "We have arrived."

The arena was a large, circular building, the outside made completely of the same white stone as everything else in Cataractonium. Built to resemble the Colosseum in Rome, the framework consisted of the main load-bearing platforms, upon which rested the facade, then rose three levels higher. Symmetrical arches were framed by columns on each level.

The lion and wolf guided them through a door, and they traveled down a long stone tunnel lined with shadowed doors and pillars. One of the first hallways led to an upward staircase where all the captives ascended to the arena seats. Other hallways led to training and preparation rooms. Then the hallway continued, spilling out into the dusty arena. Thousands of people took in the morning's spectacle. He wondered if the Roman Colosseum heralded such grand size.

The animals halted at the far end of the arena floor. Directly up, about halfway, sat Helius, wrapped in another set of purple robes, residing imperiously on his stone throne in the emperor's box. Circe sat at his right in a blue dress similar to the one she wore the day before. Her expression was impassive, revealing no sign of their conversation from yesterday. Padric was beginning to think it had all been imagined.

Helius raised his arm, and the audience quieted. "Welcome to the Arena, Sir Padric de Clifton and Sir Warin Ingram. Approach."

Padric squared his shoulders, moved forward, and bowed. It would do no good to disrespect the god now. Helius beamed as though thrilled at the command he held over the mortals.

Warin spoke first. "We have come to receive our first trial, m'lord."

"Very good," Helius said with a grand smile. "Your first of three trials is this: A competition between two teams. You shall each assemble teams of your choosing. The object of the competition will be to retrieve a certain item belonging to my daughter Circe. Whichever team succeeds in bringing the item before me shall be declared the victor."

Padric looked from one god to the other. "We need only retrieve the article and return it to you, here, m'lord?"

Helius smiled, his lips curling inward, almost cruelly. "A simple retrieval, yes." Circe's eyes betrayed a flash of worry, but she quickly masked the emotion.

Padric did not fail to miss the note of glee Helius bestowed when emphasizing the word "simple." He was much too excited about it. Padric fully expected traps to be set for him and his comrades, whomever they may be.

"Indeed. You may train with your teams however you deem necessary. Three days from now, the trial will begin."

"And what is the perimeter of our training area?" Padric asked. "I assume we must stay within the boundaries of Cataractonium."

"You may go anywhere within the compound. The training fields lie just beyond the arena to the west. But you must be finished training before the sun sets at the close of each day."

Padric furrowed his brow in confusion. *Why before dark? Curious.*

Warin must have been in the same frame of mind, as he asked, "What of our teammates' duties? Surely, they cannot be expected to work all day and then train until sunset."

"An excellent question. The teams you pick shall be exempt from their duties for the duration of this trial. Once the trial is over, and a team is made victorious, everyone will return to work." That seemed reasonable—as much as could be expected given the circumstances—and Padric nodded agreement.

Helius turned to the audience. "All will attend the trial as entertainment."

A deafening cheer erupted from the crowd.

"What number of teammates may we have, m'lord?" Padric asked.

Helius thought a moment, a shimmer catching the light by his ear. "Seven seems a fair number. Now go out and choose your team. That is all."

So many for a simple retrieval? Padric took a breath. He would have to make do, and could only wonder at how big this operation was to be.

"One final thing," Circe boomed. Padric pivoted on his hoof to see Circe stand up, dress rustling in the hot breeze. "Your escort of four is no longer required during the day. But they will keep an eye on you from a distance." She waved at the two large cats, wolf, and bear. Free of their charge, the animals wandered to the tunnel as a group and disappeared through the opening.

Relief flooded through Padric as the animals left. There was one less thing he had to contend with, at least.

"See you in the arena, de Clifton," Warin said with a wide grin. Without waiting for a response, he lumbered off in the opposite direction.

Padric froze. That grin held more meaning than he thought possible. Even after a year, Warin had not forgotten.

The memory came back vividly. He and his friend Rawlins were too late to stop their colleague, Byron, from fighting in hand-to-hand combat with Warin in last year's tourney. Padric's confrontation with Warin and calling the larger knight a barbarian were only the beginning of their troubles. What happened after that turned any hope their captains had of reconciliation impossible.

Nalini stepped up to his side, jarring the memory away.

"Will you stand here all day?" she joked.

"Of course not," Padric frowned, his mind already moving to the next task. *Forget Warin. There are more important things to consider.*

The fiery words of the prophecy flashed before his eyes: the amulet, the weapon, and the Earth's destruction by fire by the solstice.

"Off you go," she replied soberly, moving toward where Warin exited the arena.

Padric's eye caught movement in the retreating audience as they proceeded down to the lowest level instead of up and out the inner stairwell. His heart leaped as he spied his friend Rawlins in the stands with arms crossed and his familiar scowl, Byron and Serill standing next to him. Alas, there was no sign of the twins or Leowyn, nor any of the other knights from Chaddesden who had gone missing in recent months. Padric inclined his head to indicate meeting them outside. The knights nodded in understanding and headed back up toward the exit.

Padric picked up his pace to meet the men from his unit. At last! A light in the darkness.

❦

"Oy, so you finally found yourself here in this pit?" Rawlins smirked. "You've missed out on the merrymaking for weeks."

Padric grinned. "So I see. I have had adventures of my own." They stood near the arena entrance, in the building's cool shade.

"So *I* see." Rawlins noted the horns and faun legs with interest.

"Is that what she done to ya, Sir?" asked Byron.

"Yes, and it is positively tiresome to get around cities this way."

Byron's eyes grew wide. "You can't change back, Sir?"

"Alas, I cannot. But I can manage to change into another part-animal form. Now, enough about me," he said, noting their inquisitive faces. "How fare you fellows? Are they treating you well here?"

Serill chimed in, "As well as can be expected, I s'pose, Sir. They make us work to death, and the food's decent. But the nights..." He shivered.

Rawlins jabbed Serill's arm hard with his elbow. "Can it, will ya?"

Serill rubbed his arm vigorously. "I was only explaining—"

"Hush. If we complain, we'll hear all about it later from them." He nodded toward the large animals lumbering by a shade tree not fifteen yards away.

"What are you refraining from telling me?" Padric asked.

With care, Rawlins peered around to make sure no one was listening and lowered his voice. "Look, there are ears everywhere. Ye'll find out in due course, I imagine." He left it at that.

After a moment of intense glaring, Padric ceded. If Helius could see

53

far and hear much when he wanted to, he might not think highly of his servants and slaves complaining about him behind his back. There might be other servants with great hearing sneaking around as well.

"I see." He changed the subject. "Now, about this trial business, retrieving the object against Sir Warin and the team of his choosing. Would you three join me? It has been too long since last we stood together on the field, but I am confident we can manage."

Rawlins gave a silent nod, his arms folded over his chest. His only betrayal of angst against Warin was the clenching of his jaw.

Byron huffed and rubbed his arm. "What I wouldn't do to win against that blasted man. Honestly, though, I was hoping the Master would suggest playing bandyball. I do love a good game of bandyball."

"Aye, don't we all," Serill said with a wistful gaze. "There's a chance Sir Warin might not know how to play that one."

"Mayhap," Byron said, "you could mention it to the Master, Lieutenant. Ask to play that instead."

"I doubt very much he will change his mind."

"Mayhap just nudge him toward it?"

It was all Padric could do to keep a straight face. He knew how much the knight loved the game. It was all he spoke about in Chadd, both on and off duty. "Byron. We are retrieving Circe's most beloved item. When we return home, you may play all the bandyball you wish on your days off. I am sure no one has taken your bandy stick." The others snickered.

Byron grinned sheepishly. "Aye sir."

"Another question, lads. Have any of you seen Leowyn about?"

"Yes, sir," Rawlins affirmed. "He has the early shift today, cutting stone. We can go find him now. Aeron is here, too, but I'm not sure where."

"What?" Padric asked, stunned. "Aeron Drefan is here?"

"Yes, sir. His position moves around often," Byron said.

"I see," Padric said, dismayed. *Another one taken.*

"Let us hope to find him today as well. Lead on to Leowyn." He waved for his fellows to head toward Helius's temple. *Perhaps we will find Talfryn working in the same area.*

They walked a short distance before Padric stopped in alarm. He thought he spied a familiar figure disappearing around one of the other buildings. Byron, who had taken to walking directly behind his lieutenant, bumped into his back. "What is it, Sir?" He regarded Padric's face. "You look like you've seen a ghost."

Padric rubbed his neck. "I thought—I was positive I saw..." He shook his head. "Disregard. 'Twas nothing."

Those shoulders....it was the cloaked man.

His gut wrenched and he yearned to pursue the figure. The man who had donned Padric's cloak and lured Brynwen to her near death off the cliff. For over a week, Padric had grieved her loss, believing her dead and lost to the river forever. Every time he thought about it, his blood boiled. If it was the cloaked man, he could confront the scoundrel once and for all. He would not be allowed to hurt anyone Padric cared about ever again. *But why would he be here, and how could he have gotten into Cataractonium? Perhaps I should go after him anyway.*

"Sir Padric?" Rawlins asked.

With regret, Padric remembered his current mission. "Ah, yes, lead the way." Even if it was the cloaked man, he had already disappeared into the city.

Lost in his brooding, he paid no attention to the turns they made to arrive at the construction site. The sight before him quickly pushed his other thoughts away. Glancing upward, he was astonished at how much the temple had progressed since he had seen it only yesterday. The last pillars had been lifted and placed in their respective places. *Quite impressive.*

Returning his eyes to ground level, he spotted a familiar face and blonde head, working diligently with a pick on a large white stone.

"Leowyn!" Rawlins shouted, completely disregarding the glare of the human foreman only a few yards away.

The young man froze mid-swing and looked up. "Lieutenant!" Upon seeing Padric, Leowyn tossed his pick to the ground and rushed to the group of young men with a toothy grin.

"Leowyn." Padric smiled and grasped the knight's arms. "You appear to be in one piece. Your mother worried you had been stolen off by bandits."

"Well, she wasn't far off about that."

Padric laughed.

"I'd heard you'd arrived," Leowyn said, "and would have gone to the arena this morning, but I had to work. My sincerest apologies, Lieutenant." Leowyn peered down sheepishly, then up again, eyes wide. "But sir! What has happened to your legs?"

This is going to be a long day, Padric thought with a sigh. "It is an extensive story, which I will gladly regale you with later. For now, have you seen your cousin Talfryn? He arrived with me yesterday." *And his sister*, Padric wanted to add. "I need to find him."

"Talfryn?" Shock was the best way to describe Leowyn's reaction. He ran dirty fingers through his ruffled blonde hair. "I thought I was dreaming when I peeked a glance at him last night. Was—is he really here?"

"Yes, and when we parted yesterday, he was headed to work on the temple."

Leowyn scratched his chin. "Really? There are a lot of workers, so I suppose it wouldn't be hard to miss him. Certainly, I'll keep an eye out for him. But," he glanced around, "I should be getting back to work before I get lashes instead of supper."

Quickly, Padric and the other knights explained the trial. Leowyn agreed to participate without hesitation, and grinned. "It would be great to get away from this for a while."

"Splendid. We will see you first thing tomorrow for training," Padric said. *Not quite like it used to be in Chaddesden, but I will take what I can get.*

Leowyn returned to work, the overseer giving the knight-turned-stone-layer an angry eye.

Padric turned back to the men from his unit. "We must locate Talfryn and Aeron, but I trust you need to return to work soon as well."

Rawlins snorted. "They won't miss us."

Hiding his grin, Padric eyed his sergeant. "Return to work. If you happen to see Aeron and someone named Talfryn Masson, urge them to come with you and Leowyn to the evening meal. I will join you then, and we shall strategize."

Rawlins, Serill, and Byron saluted as one. "Aye, aye, captain."

The lieutenant rolled his eyes. "You get a few days leave from home and spend it making horrible jests." He shook his head, feigning disappointment. "Now off with you lot, before I make you meet Circe face-to-face again."

"You don't have to tell us twice." Rawlins rushed the other two away to their duties.

Padric chuckled. If there was one thing he could count on regarding the men in his unit, it was that, on any given day, he might threaten to throttle them one moment, then laugh with them later in the tavern.

Left to himself, Padric decided to scout out the compound to get an idea of what he was up against. He would worry about Warin later.

Journeying around the perimeter, he studied the walls, roads, and landscape, well aware of the large brown bear following him from a distance. Like the buildings, the wall was built of old, sturdy white stone. He wondered if Circe and Helius had managed to keep the whole of the old fortress in the same shape as it had been when the Roman legions roamed England hundreds of years ago.

The training fields were quite large, the grass a lush green. For some reason, the grass reminded him of Chaddesden and Derby. His heart lurched. How he longed to return home. Alas, he had made an oath to remain, and was honor-bound to keep it—if he won the trials. A deep breath loosed from his chest. *If* he won, *if* he defeated the weapon, *and if* Helius kept his word and allowed everyone to return home, Padric would be left here, alone. All of his friends would be gone.

The shriek of a Stymphalian bird—he would never forget their cries—rang in his ears, releasing him from his reverie. Resembling eagles, the birds' feathers and bronze beaks were as deadly as a freshly sharpened blade. They were among the first mythological creatures Padric had encountered, directly before Circe changed his unit into woodland animals and himself into a centaur.

Glancing up, he spotted the bird of prey swooping over a clump of trees near the edge of the property. The sound seemingly awoke the inhabitants of the tree . Raucous squeaks and barks shook the foliage of the trees, causing great arm loads of leaves to ruffle out and flutter to the ground en masse. The Stymphalian bird dove once, resulting in a wider panic in the trees, and the great winged creature flew off with a small creature wriggling in its talons.

Entranced by the sight, Padric stayed to observe anything else unusual. However, after a couple minutes the cacophony withdrew until the world was silent.

With renewed caution, he scrutinized the fields for the better part of an hour. The high ground, the low ground, searching for a mode of escape in case the worst happened.

After collecting all the information he could muster, Padric turned at the wall to search the rest of the compound. He had barely rounded the corner by the baths when he spotted the cloaked man sitting with his back to him. Although cloakless, his strong shoulders gave him away. This time it was not his imagination. Steam rolled over Padric's body, heart pounding as he approached. Oh, how he wished his sword was at his side to avenge the pain and heartache this man had caused Brynwen, Talfryn, and himself.

Taking two steps closer, he halted in shock. It was not the cloaked assailant.

There was no mistaking the raven hair and neat attire of one Aeron Drefan, knight of Chaddesden.

CHAPTER 8

"Aeron?" Padric asked in shock.

An undignified yelp tumbled from Aeron Drefan's lips as he jumped nearly a foot off the ground. He plopped back onto the gnarled stump of the ancient tree he had been sitting upon, then rushed to his feet, pulling his arms behind his back, and breathing hard. He struggled to swallow the gasp stuck in his throat.

"I thought that was you skulking about." Padric's eyes shone in pleasant surprise. He was relieved it was not the cloaked man. "Rawlins said you were here."

Aeron's face turned ashen. "L-lieutenant," he stammered. "How are you here? When did you arrive here?"

Padric smiled at the knight's bafflement. "I imagine I came the same way as you—via the golden-haired goddess Circe, only yesterday."

"Yes, of course. Her. How else?" He shrugged. "Yesterday, you say? But you disappeared weeks ago. When you and the others did not return from Nottingham, the baron's eldest daughter sent a worried note. We searched the whole of the countryside for you. And then, poof, she got me."

"Only you?"

"Only me."

Padric's chest constricted as guilt wracked him. He ran a hand through his hair, grazing a small curved horn, wondering why Circe took him at all. "At least the others in Chaddesden are safe. Indeed, I am aggrieved this happened to you. Nonetheless, I have a plan to deliver us from this mess. The men from our unit are all in on it. I would ask for your aid as well."

"Of course." Aeron gave his cocky grin. "And that is?"

"Helius has set three trials for me to face against Sir Warin. If I succeed, everyone will be set free."

Aeron mused. "Three trials, and that is it?"

"That is it. The first trial requires two teams for a retrieval, of sorts."

"A retrieval? Of our meals?" He smirked.

"Ha ha. In truth, a certain item belonging to the Mistress Circe."

Aeron's eyebrow rose. "Ah, a treasure, then."

"Quite. What say you? Will you join us? We can use another member on the team."

"Another member...Who else is on this team? Did you not just arrive yesterday?"

Padric rattled off the other members of the Chaddesden unit who were playing, along with their plan for the evening meal.

"Good men, that lot. Count me in, Lieutenant. I'd be proud to play on your team." Aeron put out his hand, and Padric shook it.

"See you first thing, Aeron."

"Aye, sir."

Padric turned to leave. "Oh, and Aeron?" The guard spun around, eyes wide. "What is your position here? Are you a stone worker?"

Aeron smiled widely. "Yes, that's me. A stone worker. Love the old stones. I was just gathering some more." He gestured to an old wooden cart which stood nearby. It did not appear sturdy enough to hold much weight, but who was he to judge?

"I will leave you to it then. See you at the evening meal."

He turned on his heel to resume his observation of the grounds, half wondering at the knight's odd behavior.

❧

THE MIDDAY MEAL OVER, Brynwen, Miriel, and Isemay made their way through the streets back to the infirmary with the other women.

Absently, Brynwen's hand hunted around the empty space at her side for the strap of her satchel. With a pang, she let out a sigh. *Right, it's still gone.* It was the bag in which she had carried her herbs and medicines; where, as a child, she had carefully placed interesting things she found outside while helping her mother and father. Its patches had been carefully stitched and restitched from constant use.

For perhaps the hundredth time, her brain sought desperately to remember the instant it left her shoulder the night the cloaked man had captured her. It was there when she had dangled the Saint Christopher medal on a chain in front of her adversary, hoping he'd believe it was the amulet. The amulet had been safely sewn into her pocket—until it fell through a blasted hole and was lost. She was sure the satchel was there when she fell off the cliff. If it came off as she fell, it was lost to the river forever. The knot in her stomach tightened. *How could I have so utterly failed that night?* She hoped that if anyone did find it, they would have no idea of its importance. *Who knew what would happen if it ended up in the wrong hands?*

Brynwen walked in silence next to Isemay. In front of them, Miriel struck up a conversation with a group of maidens walking beside them, carrying large laundry baskets piled high with clean, folded laundry.

"Why," Miriel said to the closest maid with light hair, "Sir Padric and his knights are the bravest people in the world. I should know, Sir Padric is my very good friend."

Since the knight's arrival the day before, Miriel had told everyone she encountered of Sir Padric being her very good friend. Along with all the reasons why they were friends: they had known each other all her life, he was friends with her brother, he was kind, etcetera.

Brynwen and Isemay exchanged looks. *Here she goes again,* they mentally said to each other.

However, this time, before Miriel could relate why she and the knight were friends, a maid with straight brown hair trailing down to her waist scrunched up her nose. "I don't know, I've heard Sir Warin is the best. They say he won tournaments five years in a row, while Sir Padric won none."

Warning bells passed between Brynwen and Isemay. Clearly, these maids were not from Derbyshire. They both tried to interject before the fiery blonde could lash out. It had happened once yesterday when a maid laughed in Miriel's face. "Mir—"

"Oh, no." Miriel pushed both of her friends out of the way. Her face red and crowned with yellow hair, much resembling a flame, she clenched her fists. "Sir Padric won his share of tourneys. It is Sir Warin who cheats. He-he..." Miriel was about to explode.

"Sir Padric is the most skilled and gallant knight," interjected Brynwen, giving Miriel the behave yourself look. "I will grant you, Sir Warin may be nice to look at, but he will not best Sir Padric this time." *I hope.*

"Then why," the dark-haired maiden asked, "if Sir Padric is so wonderful, why can't he become fully human? The other men change back in the mornings, so why can't he change back, too? Is there something wrong with him?"

Miriel shook a fist. "There is nothing wrong with him. He is cursed."
Oh no...

The laundry maid frowned, looking every bit unimpressed. "You're not helping your case at all, you know."

"Cursed knights are even worse," another with raven red hair replied. She and some of the others moved two steps away, as though Miriel were cursed by mere association.

"Regardless," Isemay said, "cursed or not, Sir Padric has our full support. We have been acquainted with him for years, and know him to be kind to all and brave of heart."

Brynwen grinned. She couldn't have said it better herself. But alas, by the undaunted looks of the other maids, it wasn't enough to sway them to their cause. Padric needed more support. Perhaps she couldn't give Padric the amulet of obsidian, but she could help in this. She thought for a few moments, then the obvious came to mind:

Lilith.

Remembrance of the succubus left a bitter taste in her mouth. She, Talfryn, and Padric had barely survived their encounter with her. *But would it be enough?* Brynwen cast a glance over the skeptical maidens, eager to complete their laundry task. *Only one way to find out.* She cleared her throat. "Sir Padric defeated a demon weeks ago. I was there to witness it." In truth, the succubus had seduced him and Talfryn, and they would have killed each other if Brynwen hadn't arrived in time. She threw holy water on the creature, then Padric cut off her head.

All the maidens stopped short and turned their heads toward Brynwen. One maid nearly spilled the contents of her basket.

Brynwen did her best not to smile. *Aha. I think we've finally turned some heads Padric's way.*

❦

AFTER MEETING his teammates at the evening meal in the workers' dining hall, Padric returned to Circe's guest residence.

The meeting with his friends had concluded to everyone's satisfaction. Leowyn had successfully found Talfryn. Aeron joined them last, and they were all in agreement to start practice directly after dawn on the morrow.

Talfryn had indicated having something to tell Padric, but they did not have a chance for a private word before he needed to get back to his barracks. They decided to talk the following day before their first practice. It confused Padric when, as they were leaving, Talfryn's body tensed when Rawlins announced they needed to all head to bed. *Why was that?*

In fact, now that he thought about it, every single man and lad cleared their tables and left the dining hall at the same time. A few women came in to clean up.

The sun waned fiercely when Padric stepped into the lit foyer of the guest residence. No sign of Warin. He hoped he would not encounter the other knight, for he was in no mood for insulting banter.

Padric placed a hand on the ornate stair banister when a shadow moved to his left. He spun around, heart hammering in his chest. With no weapon at hand, he clenched his fists, ready to challenge his assailant.

"Forgive me for startling you, Sir Padric," Nalini's voice spoke from the darkness. A candle came to life, illuminating her figure in half shadows. "I came to see if you needed anything."

"Nalini…th-thank you, no," Padric said hastily, unclenching his fists. He turned so she would not see his burning face. "That will be all for tonight." Then he bolted up the curving stairs, heart thundering.

Once in his suite, he crumpled onto the couch and combed his hands through his hair. Seeing what he thought was the cloaked man twice today was getting to him. Between him and Warin, Padric thought he might go mad. Taking deep breaths, he shoved down those thoughts—they would do him no good, and he had to focus on something he could control: training for the first trial and figuring out a way to stop Helius's weapon, the chariot on top of the partially-constructed temple.

The Oracle Roana's prophecy rushed through his mind. Its constant reminder of death and destruction for much of the world if he was unable to destroy Helius's weapon by the solstice haunted him.

Padric needed to retrieve the amulet from Brynwen to destroy it, but more than that, he wanted to see her. Foolishly, when he first entered Cataractonium, he dared to hope she would be among the first people he would see, but in the end he was disappointed. *Is it a good idea to seek her out? Would being around her put her in danger from Helius's machinations?* He would have to tread lightly.

Padric's ears perked. The accentuated hearing he had acquired from his faun abilities caught every inflection, the sounds of men floating through his open balcony doors—moaning and crying out in agony, just like the evening before.

Padric rushed to the balcony, hands gripping the stone. "Not again." The grounds were completely devoid of people. Whatever was going on outside, he needed to find out more.

Taking hold of the stone balcony rail with one hand, he jumped and twisted, hoofs landing flush on the ledge. Calculating the descent, he jumped to the next balcony. A hoof scraped the ancient stone and slipped off. His heart pounded as he scrambled to grab a hold and made it. He continued the descent, not pausing long enough to catch his breath.

At last, he plopped to the ground and made a mad sprint around the corner toward the noises. A roar followed him as his tiger guard rounded the house and gave him chase. He raced around two clusters of buildings, stopping short at what he saw. The tiger scrambled to a halt a pace away.

There were pens and pens, some made of stone, others assembled with wood, all grouped together. *How did I miss this on my tour from earlier today?*

The view was made from nightmares—the bodies of both man and animal twisting and screaming. Shrinking. Deforming and reforming. Hair on heads receded, while simultaneously the amount of hair and fur increased all over their bodies. Every single man and boy in the pens was affected. Padric's stomach roiled and his knees buckled, but he could not rip his eyes away from the horror.

At last, the shrieking stopped, and only animal snorts and squeals remained. He crept over to the edge of the first pen and peeked in. Woodland animals of all shapes and sizes filled the space, some walking and crawling around, others lying down, while some had fallen asleep straight away.

Cursed. They are still cursed.

Memory of the first set of encounters with Circe flashed through Padric's mind, how she transformed Rawlins, Byron, Serill, and Miriel's servants into writhing animals as Padric became a centaur and fell into the river, which swept him away. Agony gripped his chest at the memory of his helplessness to save them then, and he felt just as helpless now.

The nights. Serill had physically shivered at that statement. *They must change every night. At sunset.*

Padric traveled to the next pen, then the next. The larger animals had been assembled into taller pens so they would not escape. Something about the pen in the middle caught his attention. Something—a creature—stared at him. He approached and beheld a red fox, ears long and straight, staring directly into his eyes. Trying to communicate something.

"Rawlins?" Padric knew not why, but it reminded him of his dark-haired, stoic sergeant.

The fox stared back, unflinching. A quick flicker of its nose told Padric the fox had understood.

"Why am I not surprised she would turn you into a fox?" Despite his rising anger, he smirked at his furry friend.

How much sway did Helius have over Circe to curse every single man in the compound? Except for myself—why are Warin and I excluded? And what of the women—are they in other pens?

The pens were filled with men, along with some lads barely old enough to wield a sword. *Did the men's changing of form keep the women from trying to escape?* It seemed a foolproof plan. The maidens could not hope to conspire escape with the men, for they would change with the coming of night. *Was it the pens that caused the men to shift forms, or just being a man in general in Cataractonium?*

Rage boiled in his blood. Even if Circe was not completely to blame for all of this, she would never hear the end of it. Not when he could do something about it. He would free his friends and all the people of England, if he had to fight Helius with his bare hands.

He felt her before he could react. The wind died abruptly, and the buzz of power electrified the very air to tickle his skin.

"It will not help, you realize," said Circe from behind him.

CHAPTER 9

"What?" Padric spun around. He should have been accustomed to people popping in unannounced by now.

Circe scratched the tiger's chin, releasing a loud purr from the giant cat. "Freeing your friends from the pens. They will retain their animal forms the entire night."

"From dusk till dawn?"

"Of course. It is the best way to keep them calm at night. No silly notions of running. You pitiful humans get it in your heads to long for things you do not begin to understand. Alas, freedom and hope are only thoughts of the mind. But the hope of every dawn and the chance of life begins anew. Nay, it is survival. Survival, my dear grandson, is the key to human existence. Living another day. Making it to tomorrow. You would do well to remember that."

Survival. Padric curled his fingers into fists at his sides. "Men have survived much longer than the Roman gods have been around. They survive because they must. Because losing is not an option. They fight for what is right, to protect, to fight for others who cannot. Why chain these men to animal forms and keep them in pens? Why not only enchant the barriers so they cannot escape?"

"Because, dear Padric, where would be the fun in that?" Though she hid it well, the toll of the shifting drained much of her reserves. He could practically see the essence of her magic flowing toward the pens of animals. "Also, the pens are to prevent them from accidentally hurting themselves or others. When they are in the pens, they are subdued. But free to roam, they become territorial. Let us just say...the first few weeks were arduous. Lessons were learned."

Jaw clenched, Padric took a step forward. "Why do I not shift at dusk as they do? It would keep me restrained and under your control."

"But my boy, as you have already learned, I have no hold over you. Twice now, you have broken my spells. Curses, at least from me, are useless against you."

Padric stared at her for a beat. "What do you mean, you have no control over me? You have had every control over me from the beginning. How do you think I landed here in the first place? You even admitted to taking my friends for the explicit motivation of getting me to act."

Circe shifted uncomfortably. "That is true, I have moved things along to get you here. But whether because of our blood ties or some other force, it is a fact that you break my curses with little more than your own rational thought. My father knows this and wants you on his side."

"He would bribe me with glory."

She nodded.

"And what of Sir Warin? Would Helius bribe him as well?"

"He has already done so, I fear," Circe said. "Sir Warin has his own set of skills which my father desires. Either of you would make worthy allies."

That was an interesting admission, Padric thought. *Did Helius really not care which of his two potential contestants became his rightful heir?* "I see. M'lady, I need you to be candid with me. Did you know about Warin's claim as Helius's heir prior to my coming?"

"No," she replied, but her eyes shifted.

"Circe."

She huffed, and her nose scrunched. "The truth is that when my father introduced Sir Warin as his second potential heir, I was just as astonished as you. When I brought Warin here months ago, he quickly became popular with the people, and rose to be a sort of leader. Yet, to be honest, he showed no signs of overthrowing my father or becoming his heir—if he even knew his relationship to us. My dryads watched him carefully, and they found nothing untoward."

"That is interesting, for if Warin has been more accommodating than me all this time, why would he not be the logical choice as the heir in the first place? Why have a competition at all?"

"That has been on my mind as well."

Crossing his arms, Padric leaned back against a stone pen and let out a breath. "Is it not curious how much your father is keeping from you, try as you might to undermine his motives?"

"Indeed, it is quite vexing." She looked at the pens, then away. "You should get some rest, for tomorrow will be a long day for you and your friends." Then she peered at him. "Come to me the day after your first trial. I have a few tactics that may help you expand your shape shifting abilities."

"What makes you think I need help?" Padric asked, standing to his full height.

Circe grinned, showing her teeth. "I have been watching you, remember?"

"I know full-well how much you have watched me these last months." The pit of his stomach lurched. The goddess had even sent her winged spy, Ulysses, to whittle its way into his and Talfryn's good graces.

"Then trust me on this. If you wish to win the trials, you will come to me. Let me know your answer when you decide."

The goddess's gaze shifted to the north. "Padric, you must not beat yourself up over things out of your control. Know your strengths and the weaknesses of yourself and others. Use that as your guide."

With those words, she spun around and sauntered away gracefully, blue robes flowing around her legs.

Padric shivered. The night had suddenly grown cold, but that could have been the bitter stone resting in the pit of his stomach. *If I have no one to blame but myself for my inability to change back, how can I continue?* Everything he had known in the past few weeks had been turned upside down.

CHAPTER 10

June 4, AD 1356
The following morning

"You do not want to be late for your first day of training." Nalini held Padric's suite door open with one hand, her polearm in the other. Her body was poised, but he could see the humor in her eyes as she followed his movements. *As long as she does not throw her polearm at me again.*

"Lead the way," Padric said as he fastened the last belt loop on his new leather jerkin, courtesy of his very-great grandmother. *Will I ever get used to that?*

He very much doubted it.

Just yesterday he considered her an evil sorceress. Now...he wanted to believe she was on his side, but after all he and his friends had been through, getting used to the idea of her helping them threw him off that much more.

Nalini would guide Padric to his first practice with Talfryn and the knights, whether because she thought he could not remember his way there or she felt she needed to keep an eye on him, he could not say. Nor could he say if it was up to Circe or Helius whether Padric had a shadow or not. His animal escort was gone, but it felt like he would never be free to roam around again on his own, even after freeing the kidnapped people from this place.

They barely stepped into the front courtyard of the guest residence when he glimpsed Circe, her back to him, sitting on the lowest part of a three-tiered stone fountain in front of her home. Water cascaded from the top tier down to the second and landed in a pool at the bottom. Circe conversed with someone hidden behind the fountain. As he and Nalini passed by, Padric nearly tripped over his own hoofs as he spied who the sorceress spoke to: a stag with long, intricate antlers and white wings, and a red mark on its chest.

Of course, it would still be here, Padric thought.

Padric's skin itched at the sight of Staggy. That had been Talfryn's endearing name for the creature. Never had Padric quite put his trust in it, but he had wanted to give Talfryn the benefit of the doubt. However, yesterday, Circe had called it Ulysses, like the Roman hero. He had wondered all day why she would name the creature after her former lover, who had died a painful death centuries ago. *Then again, maybe she wanted to remember him?*

Seeming to notice the angry green eyes staring at him, Ulysses turned his head and set his gaze directly on Padric.

Glancing away, Padric tried to hold down his seething feelings toward the winged stag. It may have rescued him and Talfryn over a week ago, but its abrupt departure from them as they recovered from their wounds had troubled Talfryn, and that act did not sit well with Padric.

When they were safely off the property, Padric relaxed his shoulders slightly.

"At last," Nalini said, her eyes remaining forward. "Your body was as rigid as a statue."

The remark took Padric aback. "I beg your pardon?"

Nalini laughed. "I am a warrior, remember? I have come to notice these things easily. Living a long life helps, too."

A long life? She looked no older than him. Before he could stop himself, he asked, "How old are you?"

"Do they not teach knights manners these days?" asked Nalini with a dramatic scowl.

Padric rubbed his face, mortified. "Forgive me, I am not myself this morning." He must work on keeping his outer emotions in check.

She nodded. "It is none of my business, but what exactly happened between you and Ulysses?"

"Correct, it is none of your business. But all the same, was it that obvious?"

"The whole of Cataractonium probably noticed it. Yesterday, the moment he came up the hill, you glared at Ulysses, as if wishing he burst into a million pieces. No, do not become stoic again. I promise not to stab you with my polearm."

Padric had to smile. "I appreciate that. I think."

Hesitation struck him in telling her. He respected Nalini as a warrior. If women were allowed to be knights, he might consider her for a position. But Padric barely knew this dryad and did not know if he could trust her. He could only imagine his father's reaction at allowing a woman—let alone an exotic woman—to become a knight. However, would there be any harm in letting out a little of his frustration?

Nalini waited patiently.

"Ulysses followed me for weeks, popping up here and there," Padric explained. "I knew he was a spy for Circe, but I never had a good chance to capture him. Not until the night Drogo's woodsmen attacked us. We nearly drowned, and Ulysses rescued us. Talfryn said he even protected us whilst I lay injured, so we could both rest. He stayed during our recovery, and Talfryn grew close to him." Padric had tried to warn his friend, to no avail. "Talfryn lost his sister the night Ulysses rescued us and needed someone solid to piece him back together. The Lord knows I was in no shape or mindset to help him. But then..."

"Then?" Nalini encouraged. She pointed her polearm to the right, and they moved that direction. The buildings lessened, and the training fields came into view.

Padric took a long breath. "Once I healed enough to travel again, we thought he might lead us to Circe. Instead, he disappeared. Talfryn was devastated. First his sister, then his new friend. He tried to hide it, but I have been around him long enough to see how much it affected him."

"And you cannot forgive Ulysses for this?"

"Nay, I cannot. We knew he was working as her spy, but hoped he might have changed heart and become our ally instead."

"Hmm," she said. "And his saving you and staying a few days left you confused. Vulnerable."

"Aye." Padric shuddered. He hated to admit it, but that was true.

"Well, I know Ulysses a bit, and he was quite stunned at your reaction to his presence. He is too proud to show it, but he was shaken also."

Cynicism built up in Padric's mind. *I knew the creature had human or near-human intelligence, but how much does Ulysses have in the way of human emotions?*

"Would you believe me if I told you how loyal Ulysses is?" Nalini asked.

"Loyalty?" Padric could not begrudge its loyalty to its mistress. After all, what was a knight without loyalty? But still, leaving them, leaving Talfryn, was a deep blow. Losing Brynwen had been horrible enough, but when this new friend deserted them—that crossed the line.

"Aye," she said. "Ulysses has been with the Mistress a long time. Since saving his life, he has always been by her side. But with you...let us just say he was torn. You will need to ask him and Circe about that.

Torn?

"Does Circe ever lie?"

A pained expression took over Nalini's face. "Not frequently. And if so, always for a good reason. But she would never lie to you about Ulysses. Of that, you can be assured." She turned her head and hissed under her breath. However, she did not expect Padric's enhanced faun hearing as she whispered, *"Dissimilis illi bifronti deo."* *Unlike that two-faced god.*

Two-faced god? What does that mean?

"Here we are."

They had made it in seemingly no time. Padric wanted to ask more questions, but had no chance. His six teammates for the first trial waited for him in front of the playing field for their initial training session, and it would be a full day.

They trained all that day and the next, practicing drills as though they had never left Chaddesden, or encountered magic and sorceresses. Talfryn's training had paid off, as he got into the groove of things within the first few hours, impressing both Padric and the other knights to no end.

CHAPTER 11

June 6, AD 1356
Two days later

The seven members of Padric's team waited outside the white stone arena, appearances rumpled, as though they had slept in their clothes. Padric looked at each man in turn, every single face a reflection of how he felt inside. *We would feel more confident if we knew exactly what we are up against. What Warin will do. But Helius being Helius...*

A smile pulled at his cheeks. "Cheer up, fellows. 'Tis a game, not a sentence to life imprisonment."

"It is if we lose," Rawlins said crossly.

"Then let us not lose, shall we?" He shoved his friend in the arm and ushered the others into the tunnel.

Changing quickly in the room reserved for them, they spent their time hovering over a metal rack filled with blunt wooden weapons consisting of clubs, mallets, and staffs.

"What kind of weapons are these?" Aeron demanded. "There is nothing of real use here. Nothing with pointy ends."

"Can we keep them?" Serill asked with hopeful eyes.

Padric shook his head. "I am afraid not." He swiped up a staff and studied its thickness and range, making a few practice arcs. Talfryn picked up a mallet, then the rest chose from the remaining arms.

From somewhere outside rang the sound of a gong. They marched down the torch-lit tunnel in twos, with Padric and Rawlins in the lead.

"This will be the swiftest of trials," Serill said with a wide grin to Aeron in the rear. He was already anticipating a large reward for passing the trial.

"Serill," berated Padric, "how often must I tell you..." He stopped short at the arena entrance and Byron and Talfryn nearly collided into him and Rawlins.

Collectively, they gaped in awe at the arena's complete transformation. It was as though it had been picked up overnight and dropped in the middle of a woodland, swamp, and prairie. Obstacles of all sorts covered the area, including sand pits, small ponds, and ten-foot trees with long vines hanging from their branches. Strategically placed boulders stood near clusters of tall grasses. In the epicenter of the arena stood a single eight-foot column, similar in appearance to the columns in front of Circe's home. That was what they could see from the arena's entrance.

Who knows what lay beyond the barrier of trees? Would Helius have taken away precious resources from his temple to create this field, or did he use magic? The dryads could have aided as well, Padric supposed. Whatever the reason, it was spectacular. The scent of wood and leaves, as well as pond water, wafted to him, reminding him of home. It was all so real. He had to wonder at the power of the magic used to create such a playing ground for the trial.

The other team, composed of six armed men no older than themselves, prepared at the other end of the field, each wielding their own equally blunt weapons. Some knights Padric recognized from the Derby-Nottingham tourneys. Their leader, Warin Ingram, with his tall stature and broad shoulders, stood with confidence.

"They don't look so tough," Byron sneered. He would not forget nearly losing all use of his arm because of Warin at the previous year's tourney.

No sooner had he spoken than a male lion—half a hand taller than the one in Padric's personal animal guard—sauntered out from behind the opposing team. *Leave it to Warin to locate the mightiest creature in all of Cataractonium to join his ranks.*

"They have a lion?" asked Aeron with a scowl. "How is that fair?"

"Oh," Talfryn said. "I wasn't aware we could bring pets, or I would've brought my dog Finn along."

Padric grinned. "To be sure, he could lick our opponents into submission." He recalled Helius's wording and had to laugh. "Come to think of it, Helius did not specify that only men could compete in the trial..." *Why did I not think of that?*

Rawlins smirked and twirled his club. "We could have brought your pet bear or tiger, Padric."

"They are hardly my pets."

"So you say." He shrugged, then moved away to study the other team further.

Talfryn moved next to Padric and watched the spectators take their seats, eyes scanning the crowd.

Padric placed a reassuring hand on his friend's shoulder. "I am confident she will come—she would not miss this for the world," he said, although his own emotions with regards to Brynwen were in similar turmoil. Beyond anything, he hoped to detect her beautiful face and bright eyes watching from somewhere in the audience; yet at the same time, he had to admit to an embarrassing anxiety in making a complete fool of himself in front of her.

Great clouds of purple and blue smoke filled the emperor's box, surprising several slaves in nearby seats. In dramatic fashion, Helius and Circe emerged from the clouds, faces alight with anticipation for the upcoming event.

Lordly in his violet robes, the youthful-looking Helius stepped forward and projected his voice without effort. "Welcome, my subjects, to the first of the three trials. Champions, approach." Padric and his group as well as Warin's team, stepped forward and stopped at a line traced on the ground. The crowd roared to life, clapping and cheering, the majority of the voices for Warin.

He has been here longer, Padric told himself, attempting to keep his expression neutral. *That is all.*

Helius continued, "The rules of this trial are simple: you must locate and collect the object, then bring it back to the drawn line before you within the hour. The time will be kept via the sundial located directly in front of you. The object which you seek is a hair comb belonging to my daughter Circe. Not merely any comb, mind you, but one enshrouded in enchantment. You may use the blunted weapons provided to you, or anything upon the field, but nothing sharp. Excepting the lion's claws, of course," he grinned, "which it has vowed to keep detracted during the trial. There will be no killing. This is a fair competition, so you will have the tools to defend yourselves. And now...to your places."

A trickle of sweat ran down Padric's forehead. *Why do I feel like we are being drawn with Daniel into the lion's den?* Taking a deep breath, he led his friends forward to take their starting positions at the edge of the playing field.

Helius waited a beat, then arms raised in the air, announced, "Begin."

It took but a moment of eyeing the field for Padric to decide on a plan of action. He shifted easily back into a military role as he dispatched his teammates in quick succession. He had a suspicion the comb hid at the top of the column—the most difficult location to infiltrate. Yet it was too risky to gamble everything on one location, so he sent his men out to search the entire field. After seeing everyone off, he moved forward. Likewise, Warin's team took up their positions. In no time, men on both sides peeked under boulders and wove through grasses.

Meanwhile, Padric made a zig-zag pattern toward the center of the arena, through a thick copse of trees, toward the column. Every so often he crossed paths with a teammate of Warin's or his own. After skirting a handful of holes in the ground and carnivorous bramble bushes, he emerged out of the trees and into a spacious round clearing. A large pond took up much of the area, and at its very center stood the white column. It was thick, at least four feet in diameter, with a five-foot platform at the top. How was he to get up there to search for the comb?

Warin had a similar idea, for he emerged from the trees at the same time not ten feet away, towing two men whom Padric recognized from the previous year's tourney between Chaddesden and Nottingham.

Padric gripped his staff, ready to fight if needed. He was outnumbered, but he would do his best against them. "I must say, Warin, your team is in fine form today."

"Only the best for me." Warin winked. "I would be happy to show you some pointers."

Padric grinned. "Thank you for the kind offer. I shall think about it. And now I am finished thinking about it."

A loud, frightened shout came from close behind Padric. A moment later, a terror-stricken Talfryn darted out of the trees, swinging his mallet in wild arcs. The lion came charging after him, roaring at the top of its lungs. Padric and Warin dove out of the way as the two barreled in between them.

From the ground, Padric watched in horror as the huge cat chased Talfryn across the clearing and around the water. With every step, its claws drew dangerously closer to its quarry's back. Leowyn tore into the clearing after them, brandishing a club.

All thoughts of Warin and the comb vanished as Padric got to his hoofs and bounded after them.

Talfryn continued running around the perimeter of the pond, until a paw sent him swerving into the water. Lucky for him, the lion skidded to a halt on solid ground. It growled in annoyance, curling its toes in to prevent any water from touching its paws.

Talfryn stopped at waist-height about six feet from shore, holding his mallet in the air. "Nice kitty. You wouldn't wish to eat me, no—all gristle."

The lion roared as if to say, "I would enjoy it immensely," and pawed at the air, reminding its prey how sharp its claws were.

Talfryn gulped but remained resolute as he and the lion shared a staring contest.

Padric halted by Leowyn, a dozen feet away from the spectacle. "What happened?"

"Tal stepped on the lion's paw." Leowyn noticed the incredulous look Padric gave him. "I don't know how it happened, either."

Padric loathed the idea of switching places with Talfryn and becoming lion bait, but something had to be done.

"Do we flank it, Sir?" Leowyn asked.

"My thoughts exactly. Let us see if it likes being boxed in."

Before he could move, he spotted something in the pond. The water closest to the column, about fifteen feet behind Talfryn, began to bubble. At first it was a few sporadic bubbles. Then the frequency and number increased, at the same time moving closer to Talfryn.

Something lurked in the water. Padric feared it to be much larger than a minnow, or a lion.

The lion saw it too. It sniffed the air, scrunched its nose, then began backing away with a wary growl.

"Talfryn, get out of the water," Padric warned.

The farmer looked at his weapon in wonder. "Well, this mallet must be more intimidating than I thought. I'm switching out my hatchet for this."

"That's not it," Leowyn replied. "There's a—"

A huge fountain of pond water exploded into the air not five feet from where Talfryn waded. The impact thrust him forward, submerging his whole body. Up through the center of the fountain emerged an enormous serpentine head, its mouth open in a deafening roar, boasting long rows of sharp teeth. With a loud whine, the lion spun on its tail and dashed into the trees in terror.

"Talfryn!" Padric called, but his friend's head had not popped up above the water yet. It was all Padric could do not to panic. Talfryn could not swim and had nearly drowned over a week before. At least this time it was a pond instead of a fast-moving river.

Padric turned to call for Warin, but the large knight and his two teammates were already heading at full speed toward the far side of the pond—away from the pond monster. Scowling, Padric's dislike for the knight increased with each step he moved away. *And he calls himself an honorable knight.*

The rest of the monster became visible as the water fell away, revealing dark green scales lining the sides of its sleek, fish-like body. Its body had criss-crossed scarlet scars all over it. A giant fish tail whipped into the air behind it and made another great splash as it came down.

Padric's insides turned cold at the sight of the terrifying creature. *We must get past that to reach the comb?* He shook his head to dismiss his stupor. "Come on, Leowyn. Talfryn needs us."

"Yes, Sir. What is that thing?" Leowyn eyed it warily as they moved towards where Talfryn had last been seen.

"It is a Cetus—a mythical sea monster." Another creature Padric had learned about in his Latin mythology studies under the tutelage of the Italian, Gregorio Fiori.

"Doesn't look very mythical to me," Rawlings said, joining them.

Startled, Padric's heart nearly hurdled out of his throat. "Where did you come from? Never mind." He never knew why he bothered to ask that question whenever Rawlings snuck up on him, which was most of the time.

At last, Talfryn's head emerged from the depths. Immediately, he sputtered out the water he had swallowed during his dip. He wiped away the excess water from his face, missing the piece of algae that had entangled itself in his hair. The mallet was gone.

"Get out! Hurry! It is coming!"

Talfryn regarded them in confusion. "But the lion's gone."

A loud, gargle-sounding bellow emanated from the creature. Leowyn shuddered at the sound, but Rawlins seemed unmoved by it.

It set its beady-eyed sights on Talfryn.

Talfryn's eyes grew as wide as saucers. "Oh. I don't suppose that's a bear." His body jerked back when he tried to move. "Well, slight problem. My foot's stuck."

The Cetus lumbered forward. *Anytime now,* Padric presumed, *it will strike. Of course.*

"We are coming," he called, already splashing into the pond, his staff brandished. His heart darted around his ribcage. Rawlins and Leowyn followed close behind. *Where is everyone else?*

He spied his opponent and most of his party standing on the opposite side of the shore. Warin, flanked by two men, waded into the water. Padric knew what they were doing. While their opponents were distracted with the sea monster, they would get to the column first. It was a smart move.

A giant fin shot out of the water not five feet in front of Warin and wrapped around the man on his left. It dragged the screaming man below the water in a spray of bubbles and foam. Warin and the other knights retreated in a frenzy. To Padric's great surprise, a blond-headed youth took to the air from the shore and latched onto Warin's tunic, pulling him back onto dry land.

So, there are at least two sea creatures in this pond. And who is that lad who can fly?

Padric and the two knights reached Talfryn just as the creature hissed and plunged at them, brandishing row upon row of razor-sharp teeth. As it came down, the scholarly part of Padric's brain wondered how fast it could swim when fully submerged.

CHAPTER 12

"*E*xcuse me. I beg your pardon. Forgive me, I didn't mean to step on your foot." Brynwen sighed with both relief and annoyance as she finally sat down in one of the last empty seats in the arena stands, their backs against the outer wall of the vast structure. Searching for any better seats would take time, and they were already late enough as it was. Alice and Isemay settled contentedly on either side of her, while Miriel gave a pinched expression.

"We are so high up, my nose shall bleed. And it will be all your fault, Alice."

"I said I was sorry. Scrubbing porridge pots with an ever-growing belly isn't easy."

"Don't listen to her, Alice," Brynwen said with an encouraging smile. "You clean those pots better than anyone in those kitchens." Unfortunately, the last few weeks had been harder on Alice, with the baby pinching a nerve, her back aching all the time, and her feet swelling. And yet, she did everything with a smile and worked as hard as anyone else in the compound. Her husband Jack would be proud. That was what Brynwen loved so much about Alice, and had always looked up to her as a child. She just wished her cousin would take it easier.

Today was no different for Alice's chores, and it took her almost twice as long to finish up and meet them at the arena.

"Fact," Isemay seconded.

From so high, the arena floor seemed very far away. But as Brynwen took in the amazing scene before her, she marveled at all the plants that had been placed there in the last three days. A ring of forest surrounded a large pond with a tall stone column in it. There were darker areas that someone near her remarked was a swamp. *It must be magic.*

Fortunately, they only missed a little bit, as Helius had just instructed the participants to begin the trial. Unfortunately, the contestants were on the other side of the arena, hidden by all the foliage. She imagined them disbursing into the trees. *Who knew what happened in there until they came out the other side?*

As they waited, Isemay turned to Brynwen. "What do you think is inside the forest? I heard there were traps."

"As did I," Brynwen replied. "Someone mentioned seeing carnivorous plants being brought in for the trial." Thinking about it made her shiver. She did not envy anyone who came into contact with the dangerous vegetation and hoped it to be only a myth.

Then she remembered where she was. Myths became real before her eyes every day, especially with a sorceress-goddess in charge. She could imagine her brother sitting against a tree only to discover the moss trying to munch on his leg.

Isemay nodded. "They also said—" She paused. Her eyes flicked to the window behind her, then grew wide.

"What is it?" Brynwen strained to swivel her neck around to view whatever caught Isemay's attention.

"I thought I saw a…there it is again! It has wings!"

What is that supposed to mean?

Brynwen shifted until she was almost on top of Isemay before she spotted it. At first, she only saw a black blur, but then it slowed down, revealing a black horse running across the sky at a canter.

In the sky with wings!

Transfixed, they both watched as six more joined, four large and three smaller ones all together. They danced around the sky, over all the compound, racing each other, doing flips, and shaking their manes. It was easy to get lost in the grace of their movements.

Since arriving in Cataractonium, Brynwen had thought she'd seen everything, but every day she learned something new about the place, about the magic within. Her whole world view had been turned upside down like a pot turned over to dry. And now this. *How can I have missed these winged horses before?*

"I never imagined I would ever see horses with wings. Where do they come from?" she asked breathlessly.

"I don't know, but they are magnificent," Isemay replied, her expression filled with wonder. *Well, if even Isemay hadn't known about them, and she'd been here almost a month longer, then this must be a rare sighting indeed.*

Alice leaned over, her voice incredulous. "Horses with wings, did you say?"

"Yes, just outside."

Alice tried craning her neck for a better view out the window, but could not shift enough to do so.

"It is all right." Brynwen patted her hand. "I'm sure we'll see them again later."

Brynwen was still ruminating about this rare sighting when Miriel gasped and stood up, pointing toward the pond. A lone figure came out of the trees, followed by three more twenty yards away. "Look, there's Padric."

As Brynwen spotted the dirty-blond faun, his shoulders high and confident in a leather jerkin and short trousers, a lightness came to her chest. Despite her efforts, this was the first glimpse of him she'd had since their unexpected parting two weeks ago. Even from a distance, he looked well.

She watched intently as Padric and Sir Warin had a confrontation no one in the stands could hear. Then a shout came from the forest, and Talfryn dashed between them, a gigantic lion speeding after him.

"Talfryn!" Brynwen shouted, getting to her feet. She didn't care if anyone stared, that was her brother, about to be mauled by a lion. He splashed into the pond, and from that moment, she was sucked into the trial, all thoughts of magic and winged horses lost to the spectacle unfolding on the arena floor below.

CHAPTER 13

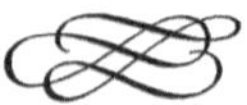

$\mathcal{P}$adric and Rawlins yanked Talfryn's arms. They dove to the left, while Leowyn dove to the right. Even through four feet of water, Padric could hear the *shhhlup* of mud as it released Talfryn's foot.

The Cetus's head came crashing down where they had just vacated.

Water engulfed Padric. He spun in the water, his sense of direction lost. Something grabbed his arm. On impulse he yanked it back—but then realized it was a hand, and let it drag him up.

He coughed up revolting pond water. Then he and his three friends rushed to the shore, Talfryn trudging between them. Miraculously, the Cetus had caught none of them. A quick check over his shoulder showed the creature had recoiled back onto its haunches, ready for a second strike.

In quick succession, their feet and hoofs reached the shore, and they crumpled to the ground in a heap of ragged breaths and beating hearts. The monster did not follow them, but remained ready for another round.

By this time, the rest of the team appeared: Byron, Serill, and Aeron. Byron and Serill were scratched and dirty, as though they had fought in a pit filled with feral cats. Padric wondered if they had an encounter with any carnivorous bramble bushes. They stopped in amazement at the scene before them.

"What did we miss?" Serill asked.

"All the fun, it looks like," Byron replied.

"Great job fellas, I didn't even lose my boots," Talfryn proclaimed.

"How do we get past that thing?" Rawlins asked. Padric could feel the zeal of battle emanating off his friend's body, ready to attack the beast, but waiting on Padric's word.

Padric replied, "Even if we get past it, we will need a way to climb up the column."

"Look." Aeron pointed past the Cetus to where Warin's group stood.

Warin argued with the flying youth, who hovered above the ground. They both pointed at either the column or the first monster, no doubt debating over strategy. Finally, the lad seemed to give in, for he gracefully descended to the ground and sat down, removing the footwear from his feet.

Padric had no time to worry about Warin. He had to figure out a way onto the column without dying by either of the Cetea. Its meal gone, the Cetus paced back and forth, daring—or welcoming—any other foolish creatures to enter its domain.

"He's putting on that lad's shoes." Byron was incredulous, still watching Warin's team.

"That's Herman. Why's Warin doing that?" asked Serill. He placed a hand on his forehead to shield his eyes from the bright morning sun for a better view.

"Because he wishes the glory for himself." Padric scowled. *I should have known. First a lion, now a lad with flying footwear.* Padric felt inadequately prepared for this trial.

"Umm, Lieutenant..." Byron said, his eyes wide. "Now he's in the air."

"I would take him down if I could fly," Rawlins said, his eyes dark with anger against Warin.

Talfryn and Leowyn shared a whispered conversation, until Leowyn raised his voice. "No. It's too far." He shook his blond head.

Talfryn nodded excitedly at his cousin. "I know he can make it."

"Who can make it?" Padric asked.

"You can jump."

Padric considered Talfryn's idea and glanced over the pond, past the Cetus, at the column more than ten feet further away. *I could not make even half that distance. Yes, I had leapt to the top of a ten-foot mausoleum in the ruined fortress of Mamucium, but never this far or high.*

"Yes, you can," Talfryn replied. "You're our best chance. Use the monster as a halfway mark."

"You can't be serious," Rawlins muttered.

"Wait," Padric said. He looked again to the creature and made mental calculations. "Perhaps it could work…but I would need a distraction."

Rawlins glared at Padric, then nodded. "That, I can do." *You better be careful,* he seemed to say through his glare. Then with a sharp command, he gathered Talfryn and the other knights to make noise on the shore twenty paces away.

While Padric prepared for the jump, they shouted names and called the Cetus things not even its mother would bear to hear, while Padric waited for the right time. Aggravated by all the noise, the Cetus gave a growling roar and pivoted to glide in their direction. Their noise only grew louder as it approached.

There!

Halfway from the shore to the column, the creature had angled itself away from Padric so he would not accidentally leap anywhere near its deadly mouth.

Not more than eight feet above the water, Warin slowly gained on the column, but it became clear he struggled to control his flight. His arms stretched straight out, fighting for balance, and his body dipped every so often. It was as though he were an acrobat, on the verge of tumbling from a great height. He would be there in less than a minute.

Now is the moment.

Bending his knees, Padric took off, pounding at the earth with his hoofs toward a cluster of stones piled at the pond's base. Less than a foot from the water, he bounded into the air, willing his body and the wind to go with him. His hoofs hit the slick fish scales and slid down until he found hoof- and handholds in its scars. The Cetus grumbled and quaked at the contact, jarring Padric's footing. He slipped and fell against the monster's back, and scrambled for a new handhold before he could slide into the pond water and get stomped on or eaten—or both.

The staff he carried fell into the dark water. Heart pounding in his chest, Padric tried to figure out his next move. The plan to get to this point was solid, but he had not counted on the creature moving so fast.

The Cetus did not enjoy having anyone on its back. It roared and spun in a circle, whipping its tail fin to and fro in wild arcs. Each movement threatened to loosen Padric's hold on the scales.

Daring a glance down, Padric noticed the fin. *The way its tail fin moves, I might get enough leverage to leap into the air once again, as long as it flung him the right direction.* Or risk the probability of being eaten.

Bracing himself, he let go. Keeping his goat legs bent, he landed flush on the tail. The monster roared and flipped Padric up, up, up—toward the column. Wind whistled past his ears, flinging hair into his eyes.

The power of the fin somersaulted him in the air twice before he stretched his arms out on his way down. His fingers clasped ahold of the column's square top. The action broke his momentum, and his body smashed against the column hard, jarring his bones. His hip took the brunt of the crash, although his arm also ached with the impact. Clenching his teeth, his hoofs slipped on the smooth stone, but after a couple attempts, they caught on a crack in the column.

He spotted Warin not more than six feet from the column. Padric had almost forgotten about him. The knight had troubles of his own. Face flushed, he fended off the second sea monster, another Cetus, with his feet and a club.

Now that they were closer, he could see the flying footwear commandeered from Herman. It was more wondrous than Padric could have imagined: birds' wings flitted at the sandals on his feet, keeping him aloft; white laces rose from the sandal heels and wound halfway up his calves, haphazardly tied at the top. They reminded him of the Roman God Mercury, but Warin's issue with them made Padric think of the mythical inventor Daedalus and his ill-fated son Icarus.

Reaching for a better hold, thousands of tiny suns seared through Padric's vision. Averting his eyes in shock, his right hoof and hand slipped. His breath hitched as his palm sliced open on the column's sharp edge and his hoof caught on another imperfection in the stone.

After blinking several times, his vision cleared, and he smiled. The object which had blinded him was an ornate metal hair comb with gold prongs and an embellished flower, its petals made from tiny metal violets and blue crystals. Strips of green metal twisted into three realistic leaves.

Circe's comb!

As he hauled himself up, he wondered how Warin fared. He glanced around, but saw no sign of the large knight. Had the Cetus defeated him? Padric could still hear both monsters moving around amidst the shouting of men on both sides of the pond.

Thwap!

"Ahh!" Padric cried out in surprise. Biting pain shot through his shoulder and arm.

"It's mine, de Clifton!" an angry Warin shouted. "I am the rightful heir." *Apparently, the Cetus had gotten on his bad side.*

Fighting to keep a hold on the column with an injured arm, it was all Padric could do to keep his hoofs steady. That gave him an idea. He kicked off the column and aimed a hoof at Warin's shin. The knight bowled over in pain, screeching curses about Padric's parentage.

"Forgive me," Padric said, "sometimes my legs have a mind of their own."

"You will pay for that." A rush of air passed Padric as Warin flew around him.

"To me, it would seem we are even."

Without landing, Warin jerkily reached down and grabbed Circe's comb. It shimmered at his touch, but when he continued to fly away, it remained in the same place.

"What?" cried Warin, enraged. "How can this be?"

Padric was likewise stunned. With a grunt, he pulled himself up onto the column and took two deep breaths before studying the comb. He reached for it with his good hand, but like Warin, his fingers passed through it, emitting the same silver shimmer. "'Tis enchanted," he said under his breath. This was unexpected, and yet he felt he should not be surprised. He chuckled, imagining Helius's amusement at pulling this trick on his potential heirs. The sun god might be losing his mind, but no one could say he was without a sense of humor.

Even if I do retrieve the comb, how am I to get down? The monster likely will not be fooled into a second ride. Warin still held the advantage of the winged shoes, which bulged dangerously around his too-large feet, ready to burst. Padric doubted the sandals' owner would be pleased if Warin broke his special footwear.

Warin set his winged feet on the ground with all the grace of an intoxicated man, nearly toppling backward. However, he regained his footing just in time. The strings holding the tight-fitting sandal on his right foot had loosened.

Padric wondered at the winged shoes. *Who is this lad Herman whom Warin took them from, and wherever did he get such winged apparel? Could he be related to Mercury, the Roman god of good fortune and thievery, as well as the messenger of the gods?*

Padric snickered. It was too cramped for two people atop the column.

"What is so funny?" Warin asked warily.

"You had to steal magical footwear from one of your men for a prize no one can have."

"We are a team, and he agreed to it."

"Not happily, I would gather. What did you threaten him with?"

Balling his hands, Warin shoved his fists in front of Padric's face, ready to knock him off the column.

Ignoring Warin, Padric concentrated, recalling his history studies with his old tutor Gregorio. "The ancient Romans," he finally mused aloud, "often made sacrifices to their gods."

"What?" Warin asked, looking up.

"The ancient Romans normally sacrificed food from their harvests, or livestock, to appease their gods." *Why am I explaining this to him? What did he study growing up?*

The knight regarded Padric with a wary expression. He remained squatting, his weapon in one hand and his other ready to snatch the enchanted comb. "Neither of us have any food or animals to sacrifice."

"No," Padric agreed. He clenched his cut hand, its biting sting increasing with each beat of his heart until he thought he might swoon. "But they did have blood sacrifice." His hand opened slowly. A shallow, dark red well of warm blood pooled in his palm, threatening to seep between his fingers to stain the white stone of the column. Quickly, his hand hovered over the comb and trickled three drops of blood onto it.

Before Warin could act, Padric slid his fingers around the comb. No shimmer of enchantment passed through his hand. He could feel the cold metal of the petals and leaves against his palm, the tongs brushing against his fingers.

It worked.

He lifted it without effort, its magic released by blood. A wide grin lit his lips at this small victory. It was Gregorio he needed to thank for countless hours spent studying ancient Roman and Greek lore and mythology. Over three months ago, he never would have believed this knowledge to be helpful for anything other than debate with his old tutor or the bard of Chaddesden.

Warin's eyes widened. "How did you do that?" He lunged for the comb but stumbled as Padric rose to his hoofs.

"See you at the finish line." Padric pocketed the comb and leapt over the edge.

CHAPTER 14

*B*efore jumping, Padric had looked down to find no Cetea around. *Likely, they gave up once their waters became calm for the time being. If clever enough, there is a good chance they waited underwater directly below the column, ready for a surprise attack.*

Unfortunately, Warin was faster than he appeared. Before his shoulders passed the top of the column, Warin seized Padric's tunic and wrenched him up, scraping his back painfully against the corner of the support.

"Not so fast." Warin's face leveled with Padric's. "Hand it over, and I'll settle you down gently."

"Gently into the pond?" Padric presumed. He could feel Warin's wide grin as he imagined dropping Padric into the monster-infested pond. Trapped in Warin's huge hands, Padric's hoofs dangled uselessly. He cursed himself for not moving sooner. *There must be a way to get loose. But how?*

An idea came to him. "Warin. Listen, we could share the win. I beg you, do not sacrifice me to the Cetea."

"The what? Never mind," Warin said, shaking Padric. A shot of nausea swam through Padric's stomach at the thought of being dropped and eaten by the sea monsters. Perhaps this was not one of his best ideas.

"Helius would be displeased to end the trials so soon," Padric pointed out.

As he spoke, he kept one hand in full view, while the other slowly unhooked the tethers of his leather tunic. The comb still sat in the pocket of his under-tunic.

"He said nothing of the sort," Warin chided. "Now, do you give up?"

"I think not."

The last tether came loose, and Padric slipped through the tunic. He reached out and seized one of the loose straps of Warin's right sandal as he fell.

The weight of Padric's body dragged the large knight's foot out from under him. "Gahh!" Warin cried as he slid off the column. His free hand caught the edge of the stone.

The sudden stop jarred Padric's arm and teeth. Nevertheless, he kept hold of the sandal string even as it unraveled.

"Let go!" Warin's foot wriggled and kicked, which only helped to loosen the sandal further.

With a final twist of the string, Padric found himself falling, with the winged sandal in his hand. He slid down the mostly smooth stone column, wincing when a few jagged, imperfect pieces of stone tore into the flesh of his palms and legs. Just before nearing the bottom, he pushed off with his hoofs. They slipped from the smooth surface, but he managed to gain enough power to launch a few feet across the water.

A dark shape rose to the surface beneath the swirling water. *There it is.* He braced himself, preparing to meet the water and the submerged Cetus head-on, but instead of crashing down, he retained a steady altitude. The wings of the sandal beat furiously, as though it also expected another terrifying brush with a sea monster. Padric could not help but wonder if it was sentient. Unfortunately, having only one sandal, the going was no faster than a walking pace, and the large, ominous shadow beneath him grew larger.

Another shadow came from above in the form of Warin, jerking around in his final piece of footwear. Of course, one missing winged sandal had not deterred the knight from chasing after the comb. One thing Padric could say about Warin—he never gave up. *He just usually served his opponent "justice" in the form of a pounding.*

"Can we go faster?" Padric prodded the sandal, whose lace he still held. "Please? Avoiding the monster and the scoundrel would be preferable."

As if in answer, the wings flitted faster, propelling Padric away from his adversaries at the pace of a light jog, then a run. *Perfect.* Padric stared up at the sandal in amazement. Perhaps it shared his opinion of Warin. After all, it had to live a few minutes too many engulfing his overlarge, stinky feet.

Not to be forgotten, the water bulged. The sea monster's scaled green head broke the surface. Though it did not make as intense an entrance as the first time, its appearance made Padric's stomach pitch.

A curse came from Warin, and he urged his own sandal faster. The second Cetus arose from the depths to target him.

Both knights raced toward the shore, now only a few feet ahead of the monsters. The creatures were slow when only half submerged, which was to Padric's and Warin's advantage. Perhaps their only advantage. At the pond's edge, Padric's team jumped up and down in a frenzy of weapons and warnings. "Hurry! It's almost upon you! Look out!"

The stench of standing pond water and sludge engulfed Padric. He nearly gagged, and thanked Mercury for not giving the winged sandals a nose, for it would sure as not swoon from lack of breathable air.

The Cetus snapped at Padric's backside. A shiver of revulsion traveled up his spine as something smooth and slimy touched his faun tail and legs. *It's teeth.*

A rush of desperation clawed at Padric, urging him forward. *No, it cannot end here.* He shoved off the creature's closed teeth with his hoofs, causing the wings to adjust their flight plan.

Rawlins, Leowyn, Talfryn, and the others rushed to the edge of the water, shouting and pointing their weapons at the Cetea as Padric and Warin flew over them.

Once over their heads, the wings of both sandals immediately went limp, and Padric and Warin fell the last seven feet and crashed in heaps on the grass.

Padric lay on the ground a moment to catch his breath and calm his belaboring heart. *That was incredibly close.* Lying forlorn on the ground, the sandal now appeared worn and wrinkled. "Many thanks, my friend," he said to it. "You are a worthy companion. I hope your owner appreciates you as much as I do."

Foiled for a second time from their meal, the Cetea retreated into the depths of the pond. Still animated from the ordeal, Padric's team moved from the pond's edge to help pick Padric up from the ground. They completely disregarded Warin as he lay on the ground catching his breath. However, he made a point of glaring up at Padric for several uncomfortable seconds.

Shouts came from further down the pond, where the remainder of their opponents assembled to make chase on them. Down two teammates—the one who was taken by the second sea monster as well as the frightened lion—Warin's team was outnumbered, but they pursued them anyway. It was easy to spot the youth who lent Warin his winged sandals. He had the deepest scowl of them all. Padric wondered if his anger stemmed from wishing to aid Warin or to retrieve his winged sandals.

"We have to go," Padric announced with raised voice, watching their opponents approach. They had to leave immediately or face off with the others and potentially lose the comb. "The top of the hour draws nigh, and we still have to face the traps in the woodland and swamp."

Talfryn, Rawlins, and the others nodded.

Warin was just getting to his feet when Padric and his team disappeared into the trees.

The last to enter the woodland, Talfryn waved as he passed by the large knight. "Graceful flying, by the way. Top marks for the landing."

As they sped away, Warin cried "Stop them!" with more rage than Padric had ever heard before.

CHAPTER 15

*P*adric and his team made their way through the woodland, circumventing the carnivorous bramble bushes and traps. Talfryn avoided them like the plague. How could he forget? Both he and Talfryn still held a few scars from their previous encounter with a particularly unfriendly bush a few days before.

Rawlins took the lead and pointed out other plant- and man-made traps. Mainard nearly fell into a well-hidden pit filled with long-legged spiders before Byron and Serill caught him by the arms. Aeron kept to the rear to hide their tracks from Warin's team as best he could.

"I still don't trust that the lion's given up entirely." Rawlins's eyes swept from one potential trap to the next.

"Nor do I," Padric replied. "Unfortunately, we have no way of knowing where the animal ended up once it left the pond."

"I'm pretty sure it was scared of my mallet." Talfryn shoved a tree branch out of his way as he skirted yet another bramble bush.

"I'm pretty sure it wasn't," Leowyn replied, rolling his eyes at his cousin. "Besides, you lost your deadly mallet."

"Well, it wasn't my fault the pond wanted to keep it."

"Right."

A light noise caught Padric's attention, like the sound of shoeless, pattering feet. He held up his hand, signaling the group for silence. *Did they catch up to us?* he wondered. Warin, he knew, would be disinclined to leave the trial without the comb. If in his boots, Padric would do the exact same.

Everyone looked around in confusion and knit eyebrows. Their eyes skirted from left to right, straining their ears for more sounds. When nothing happened after a couple minutes, Padric began to relax. *Perhaps it was nothing.*

"I hear voices," Aeron announced in a whisper. "Not far behind us."

"We need to hurry, then," Rawlins said.

"Hurrying will only cause them to hear us. We need to hide if we can," Padric decided.

They split and ducked behind trees and tall bushes. After another minute, Warin and his team passed, miraculously noticing none of Padric's men.

Padric released his breath in relief. *That was too close.* They decided on a slight course change.

A blur of gold bolted silently out of the trees. It careened into Talfryn and knocked him to the ground with a loud growl. Talfryn was too stunned to cry out as the huge lion rested its massive paws on his chest and roared at its highest volume.

All became an uproar as the knights ran to Talfryn, but paused an arm's breadth away. Weaponless, Padric shoved his way to the front, in case the lion went after anyone else. Rawlins shoved Padric back a step, holding up his gnarled club between them and the enormous cat.

"What do we do?" Serill asked with white face.

Padric licked his lips. *Good question.* He had to somehow get a handle on the situation. "We calmly and carefully—"

"Hand me the comb," Warin demanded, hands on hips, emerging from the trees. His band of friends appeared behind him and surrounded Padric's group.

All the blood rushed to Padric's face. *It was a trick.*

"You can't be serious," Leowyn said, picking up a defensive stance.

"I am very serious," the knight replied. He sneered at Talfryn and turned his gaze onto a seething Padric.

"The comb is in our possession, Warin," Padric said, working to control his irritation. *How is Warin always one step ahead? It seems the only thing he had not been prepared for was the type of enchantment over the comb.*

"If you wish for your farmer friend to keep all of his appendages, I suggest you hand it over."

The lion growled threateningly into Talfryn's face. With eyes clenched as though his life depended on it, the farmer's face paled. Lion saliva dripped from his nose, chin, and hair as he shivered beneath the creature.

"He's bluffing," Rawlins muttered to Padric. "He can't kill him." He gripped his club until his knuckles turned white. Leowyn and the other knights agreed.

"I wish I could say for certain he were. Warin is not known for holding anything back." This last he said under his breath. A cold feeling seethed into his blood as he made a realization. "The Master said there would be no killing, but he never mentioned anything about maiming."

Padric cast a glance at Byron as he unconsciously touched his previously injured arm, his face red with hatred. Even after a year, his heart went out to the brown-haired knight. No, Padric would not allow another of his friends to be harmed at the hands of Warin ever again, but that did not mean he would give up without a fight.

"How do I know you and your lion will not maul Talfryn or us once you have the comb? What is your word worth these days?"

The knight's shoulders lifted in a shrug. "Believe me or not, but your friend over there might start crying at any moment."

One final look at the distressed Talfryn did more for Padric's anger than it ought. He clenched his fists to keep from punching Warin's smug jaw. "Your word?" he repeated, fixing his gaze pointedly at his adversary.

Something in the Warin's eyes shifted. "You have my word," he finally replied and held out his hand.

Padric dug the comb from his pocket, the metal still surprisingly cool despite having been close to his body. Warin snatched the comb out of Padric's fingers, then flipped it over and over to verify its authenticity.

"Let him go," he instructed the lion.

The lion gave a farewell roar at the shivering Talfryn. Then, with a final shove to his chest—to which Talfryn's eyes bulged nearly out of his face—it sauntered away and into the trees, followed by Warin and his cheerful, taunting teammates.

"He tricked us again," Rawlins growled. He punched the nearest tree trunk next to him as though it somehow offended him. "We need to go after him—" He took a step, then sank into a hole and tumbled headlong into a bramble bush.

PADRIC and his team exited the woodland slowly. Rawlins, hobbling and with one arm around Leowyn and Byron, looked as bad as everyone on his team felt.

"Champions, approach the dais," Circe announced once Padric and his team exited the forest portion of the trial.

Circe stood at the fore of the emperor's box, Helius sitting regally on his throne, a grin of pride spreading from ear to ear. The goddess's cerulean dress swayed with the cooling breeze as she regarded the seven victors. The dozens of gold and silver bracelets on her wrists clinked as she raised her arms.

"Well done, Sir Warin and your fellow champions," Circe beamed at the winning team. "You have retrieved my comb, intact, and completed the first trial. Take pride in being the first victors Cataractonium has seen in nearly one thousand years."

The chest of every man in Warin's team swelled with pride.

Not for the first time, a feeling crept up on Padric. He feared he had lost any chance he might have had at fulfilling the prophecy.

When Circe's speech ended, keeping their heads low, he and his friends made a beeline directly to the exit.

CHAPTER 16

*S*till reeling from the loss of the first trial, Padric followed Nalini through the home of Helius and Circe, not paying attention to the priceless artifacts from the second century before Christ or the ornate Roman archways and statuary. They paused outside the garden door to wait until being summoned. It seemed another blow, having to wait for his grandfather to see him and berate him for his failure.

I should be with my men. Another bout of guilt struck his chest. As much as he disliked the circumstances, his duty to Helius overrode any duty he had to his knights and friends. Playing Helius's game until he could destroy the god's weapon and save everyone to fulfill the prophecy was his top priority.

At this moment, Talfryn and the knights were making their way to the infirmary to address their wounds. He would have gone as well—but Helius summoned him to his garden for a post-trial chat. This might have been his one opportunity to see Brynwen, if only to ensure she fared well. Until he saw her again in person, he would forever hold the last view he had of her, falling over the cliff those many days ago. His heart still shuddered at how close she had come to death that day. He had no idea how she had survived at all.

He carried dread, wondering if she could ever forgive him for letting her fall. If not for the cloaked man, she would not have nearly died. But if not for Padric, she would never have been in danger in the first place. *No, it is better I stay away. My presence can only make things worse for her.*

His own men were injured because of his bitter rivalry with another knight. *How had everything gone so completely wrong in so short a time?*

Thoroughly aware of his own stench from the heat and action of the trial, Padric stood next to the open window in the sitting room and waited. When asked, Nalini refused to allow him to take a quick bath next door before seeing the god.

At last, the door to the garden opened. Padric stood up. He should not have been surprised when Warin stepped through the door into the sitting room, his teeth set together in a self-satisfied smile. He paused when he saw Padric, then grinned ever wider.

It was the same grin he bestowed the day he and Padric became true nemeses. Warin and his men had humiliated the squires on the second-to-last evening of the tourney the previous year. They had dared the lads to drink ale until they could no longer stand. In the morning, the squires were too sick to do anything but lay in their cots the entire day instead of assisting the knights with their competitions. Warin laughed off the incident as nothing more than showing the lads a good time— and too bad they could not keep up with their elders.

It was all Padric could do not to knock that smile off the knight's face. "Sir Warin."

"Ah, Sir Padric." Warin placed his hands on his hips. He ignored Nalini altogether. "Come to congratulate me on my victory?"

"Hardly."

"Two days' training is never enough time to form a cohesive unit. My team, on the other hand, has been training together for months. I would be happy to show you some pointers."

How did Warin have time to train with the strict regimen of work, sleep, and mealtimes? Something does not add up.

"Thank you for the kind offer." Padric kept his voice level with great effort. "But I believe my team performed admirably today. It was a very close match, if you recall." *Despite being tricked by a traitorous knight.*

"Indeed, it was." He took a few meandering steps, seemingly to admire the antique vases and mosaics. Then he asked in a thoughtful voice, "There *is* something I have been wondering."

Crossing his arms, Padric raised an eyebrow. *Now what else must I endure? Where is Helius?*

"Does all that fur keep you warm at night? I can imagine all the pretty young maids appreciating such a feature in a—"

"Sir Warin!"

"Oh, come now, don't let your fur get all ruffled. It does not become you."

"It is good to see some things remain the same: you gather a team around you, train them, then take the win and all the credit."

"That may be, but *you* take all the blame for losing." He grinned and pounded Padric on the back as he walked past him toward the door. "And tell your pet farmer to take a bath—he smells like a pigsty."

Seeing red, Padric's body shook as he made to follow him. "This ends now."

Stepping in front of him, Nalini barred his path. "The Master is ready for you, Sir Padric. Now."

"He can say whatever he wishes of me, but I will not allow him to speak that way about my friends."

"You will have time to best him later."

"There are only two more chances before…"

Nalini must have seen the panic in his face, for her mouth trembled. "Before what?"

"Before Helius decides the winner," Padric said quickly.

Nalini stared him in the eye, the dryad unrelenting in her resolve. After another moment, his anger deflated. *Why does Warin's presence always provoke me so much?* He took a deep, calming breath.

"I suppose you are right. There is still time." *But not much.* The prophecy made his stomach lurch as its red and gold text traversed across his vision. *Fire. Death.*

"Plenty of time," Warin agreed and made his exit before Padric could get another word in.

"Is Sir Warin always this pleasant?" Nalini asked, moving toward the door to the garden.

"From what I gather, yes." Padric knew little about Warin Ingram before becoming a knight. Rumors had spread that he only grew in stature, strength, and self-confidence once he was knighted, five years before, the same time Nottingham started winning all the tournaments. The thought had never occurred to him before—*could it be a coincidence?*

❧

THE MOMENT PADRIC entered the garden, nature assaulted his sinuses, stopping him in his tracks. Earthy scents of plants and trees flooded his nostrils. He took another step inside, and floral aromas took over. All other thoughts faded as he took in the magnificence of the place. White marble statues stood at intervals along a winding path carefully laid with rounded red stones. Ranging in size from ankle- to shoulder-height, an arrangement of flowers in reds, violets, yellows, and oranges lined the path which branched out in five directions. Behind those, rows of three shades of greenery. Beyond those, random plots of flowers, green plants, and bushes filled the rest of the space, blending together perfectly. Padric did not know what he expected to find, but it was not this.

In the center, a three-tiered stone fountain spouted a ring of water spouted into the air and arced down to the first tier without splashing. Around each tier and the base were detailed carvings depicting creatures, gods, and heroes of Roman mythology, painted in rich colors. Padric recognized a manticore, Jason and the Minotaur, Hercules facing the Nemean Lion and Stymphalian birds, and Perseus fighting Medusa.

The hint of lavender drifted around him, reminding him of Brynwen. A slight smile lit up his face as he pictured her wandering around and naming all the plants for him. *She would love this place. Perhaps someday I can bring her here.*

Then Padric remembered why he was here, and his smile faded. His friends were at the infirmary seeing to their wounds and were likely being treated by none other than Brynwen herself. Had he gone, she would have seen to his stinging hands and legs, and lathered them with her Miracle Mix or any number of her sweet-smelling and effective ointments.

But no. Instead, he had been summoned to Helius's garden.

This was his first encounter with his many-great grandfather. Alone. *What will we talk about? Speaking of which, where is Helius?*

A slight tingling sensation started in his hoofs and shot up his spine. He spun around to find Helius standing at the side of the garden, regarding him. Beside him stood a three-legged table with a tray, pitcher of red wine, and two golden goblets.

"Padric, my lad." When Helius spoke, his voice was kind, lacking the disappointment Padric had expected. He did not know why suddenly it should matter so much to please this god whom he hardly knew. A god who had chosen another heir before him. No matter, he needed to remain strong, and not show any weakness.

"M'lord." Padric bowed, then placed his arms behind his back. He took care to hide his disconcertment as he stepped toward the youthful-looking god, being careful to keep his hoofs on the red stones along the path.

"Despite the outcome, you did quite well, I must say."

"Thank you, M'lord. I will tell my men you say so. Sir Warin is a substantial rival." *Rival sounds better than nemesis.*

"Come now, Grandson, do not be so downhearted. You have two trials left to prove yourself. Warin is a formidable fellow, but I have every confidence in your abilities to succeed. A nice, long soak in the bath house should set things a'right again. Many an hour have I spent in there, for contemplation and relaxation."

The uncomfortableness of his own sweat and stench came to the forefront of Padric's mind.

"And both of your teams fought admirably. I must say, you kept me in suspense from beginning to end! That lad with the winged shoes was a most pleasant surprise. I have not seen Mercury's shoes in ages."

Ah, Padric thought, *Herman is a descendent of the Roman god Mercury, messenger and herald of the gods.* "A soak in the baths does sound splendid," Padric admitted. Never had he been so thrilled by the prospect of a to visit the baths.

"A splendid idea. Our baths are the best, as you no doubt have already utilized. I will have the dryads pour rosewater for you."

"Please M'lord, do not trouble yourself on my account." *The last thing I want is to smell like a flower.*

Not seeming to listen, Helius clapped his hands together twice. "'Tis no trouble at all, Grandson."

A green dryad, who looked similar to Nalini, stepped out of the house and bowed.

"Rosewater for Sir Padric in the bath house, and the extra fluffy towels. Only the best for one of my grandsons." He grinned and winked at Padric as though sharing a secret.

The prophecy flashed across Padric's vision again, the urgency of the oracle Roana's words as fresh in his mind as the day they were first uttered. Padric blinked, and found the god's gaze resting thoughtfully upon him, his eyes glistening. It made Padric's palms itch for some reason. "M'lord, what troubles you?"

"You look so much like him."

"Like who, M'lord?"

"Ulysses. Before he was a peryton, of course. I can even see some of my grandson, Telegonus, in you."

"What do you mean by Ulysses being a peryton? Are we speaking of the hero, or the winged stag?"

Helius raised his eyebrows. "Ah, yes, sometimes I forget not everyone knows our world. You see, Ulysses the hero and the Ulysses you have met are one and the same."

Padric gasped. "What? But how? He was a mortal who perished thousands of years ago, was he not?"

"Ah, that is where the storytellers deviated, I am afraid. Homer always was one for the dramatic endings. But that is a story for another time, one you must hear from Circe. Ulysses is now a peryton, half stag and half bird, and has remained with us for centuries."

Nalini's discussion of loyalty came to mind. "I see, that explains some things, like why he became your spy."

"A spy only out of necessity, but he *is* a member of the family," Helius said adamantly.

"'A member of the family,'" Padric repeated, his voice edging on sarcasm. *What is this family's obsession with transforming other family members from one form to another? For starters, why did Circe trap Ulysses in the body of a mythical creature?* For reasons he did not care to express, it almost made Padric feel akin to the traitorous creature. They were both trapped inside bodies neither could shirk. True, Padric could change between centaur and faun forms, but he could not change himself back into his fully human form. It was one of the most frustrating things about this whole adventure.

Another memory struck him. Days ago, on the hill into Cataractonium, Circe had made an unexpected comment: *"From the moment I saw you, I knew you were special, that you were of my blood. You look exactly like Ulysses. You are my great-grandson, over sixty generations."* At the time, Padric thought little of it, but now he had a better understanding about his family's past. *It is strange to think that I resemble my ancestors after two millennia have passed. Were all the mythical texts I studied in reality historical? I have so many questions, it makes my head spin.*

"Speaking of family, M'lord, pray tell me about Ulysses's son, Telegonus, if you would. I know only what little there is of him from the stories."

The god's mouth pressed together, as though the memories were too painful. At length, he nodded. "My grandson, Telegonus, is a complicated youth."

Padric raised an eyebrow. "Is he not thousands of years old?"

"Yes, yes, but I always think of him as a child. He became immortal when he was seventeen and has always appeared so youthful. Some might mistake us for brothers." He chuckled. "When he was a child, he yearned to be just like his father, Ulysses, whom he had never met. He heard the stories of his father's bravery and cunning, and wished to be a warrior. For years, Telegonus trained and became a fearsome warrior. When he turned seventeen, he begged Circe's permission to let him go out to prove himself. He hoped to find his father, but I dare say you know the ending."

Padric nodded. He knew the story of *The Odyssey* well. Telegonus unwittingly killed his father with a poisonous spear. After that, he married Penelope, and Circe granted them both immortality, at which time he fell into obscurity.

"The very act unsettled my grandson. The first person he killed—or nearly killed—was his own father, at his own hands." He shook his head.

Padric recalled the red diamond-shaped mark over Ulysses's heart, one of his distinguishing features. "But how did Ulysses survive? That is something I do not understand."

"Circe rescued him just in time. Even though Ulysses survived, Telegonus felt immense guilt over the fate of his father, who was forever trapped inside a peryton's body. The poor lad was devastated for months. He barely ate or slept, and every night he relived the nightmare of the act. The guilt nearly drove him insane. Never again did he lift a weapon, not even to defend himself."

"Yet, he has managed to live this long."

"Indeed, though I know not where he is now." His voice wavered, and he paused to collect himself. "After forsaking the sword, so to speak, he became a scholar. It became his passion, and sometimes, his obsession. He studied under the best, including Socrates and Plato, Aristotle and Pythagoras."

"Telegonus sounds much like a friend of mine," Padric said.

"What is it? Did something happen to your friend?" Helius responded to Padric's change of expression.

Padric had not realized he was frowning. "Yes, he had to leave on urgent business weeks ago, and never returned," Padric replied. "He is also a great scholar and very knowledgeable about history and languages."

"Ah, he and Telegonus would have gotten along well. Pray, what is his name?"

"Gregorio Fiori," Padric replied.

Helius's smile faded. "Gregorio Fiori, you say?"

"What is it, M'lord?"

"That is a name I have not heard for a long time." The sun god staggered to the fountain and plopped down. "Gregorio Fiori. It cannot be.

Did you hear that?" He turned his head to the left, as though expecting someone to be there.

Padric peered at where Helius looked but saw no one. "Do you know him, M'lord?"

The god dipped his head. "Once, a few centuries ago, I knew a man named Gregorio Fiori. He was a friend of Telegonus's, who I thought long dead. How extraordinary."

Long dead? "Mayhap it is a common name, or a family name. M'lord?" Padric moved forward when the god's eyes glossed over. "Are you well?"

"What?" Helius shook his head. "Oh, *sic, sic,* do not listen to an old god and his ramblings." He patted Padric's forearm. "Mayhap soon I will show you my chariot—it is coming along nicely. Now, run along, and refresh yourself in the bath house. The day is still young, after all."

No, I cannot leave yet. I have so many questions. But the look Helius gave him was enough to quell Padric's onslaught of queries. *Another day, then.* He thought. *And soon.*

"I would like that very much, M'lord. And thank you." He bowed to Helius and turned, but not before a shimmer from the fountain caught the sunlight, nearly blinding him, and his hoof clipped the next steppingstone. Padric regained his footing and continued on his way.

As though their conversation had summoned him, Ulysses stood just outside the stone wall, bobbing his head expectantly, as though waiting for him. A twisting occurred in Padric's stomach, a warring of feelings at seeing the stag, or *peryton,* with his graceful antlers and the diamond-shaped mark over his heart. Contempt for leaving, yet compassion—or was it pity—for his long life of servitude. *He is like me. And yet not. What have you been through these many centuries trapped inside this body and serving the gods for the rest of eternity? Could this be my same fate?* This last thought sent a small spasm of panic to the pit of Padric's stomach.

To calm himself, he tried to picture what Ulysses the hero looked like compared to the winged creature before him. He tried to imagine Telegonus, and the correlation with someone hundreds of years ago with his old tutor.

His head spun with all the new questions that needed to be answered.

❧

Despite Padric's efforts to tell the peryton he could find his own way out, the stubborn creature shook its head and followed him anyway. Something in its eyes sparked amusement.

"I knew I forgot something." Padric and Ulysses were not two steps to the front door before he remembered. I did not ask about the second trial. Unless you know something, Ulysses?" he asked accusingly, knowing fully well the creature could not, or *would not* answer.

The peryton provided him with a blank stare.

Padric huffed. "I did not think so."

They re-entered the garden. Ulysses stuck to him like an annoying fly, but Helius was nowhere to be seen.

"There is not another exit from this garden, is there?" Padric asked.

Ulysses shook his head.

"Then unless he used magic to leave, he may still be here somewhere."

They moved inside the garden, circled the fountain, and stepped onto the path leading through the tall grasses.

Ulysses's ears perked. A moment later, Padric heard them too: voices.

Silently, they made their way toward the voices, avoiding treading on uneven stones, until they reached a vine-covered wall. Padric pressed his back to the wall and Ulysses made himself as small as possible—which was not very effective with the intricate horns upon his head, to say the least.

For some reason, the vines reminded Padric of his short but disturbing time with the succubus, Lilith. The memory of nearly losing his spirit and soul to the monster turned his stomach.

There, not two yards away, Helius sat on an ornately carved stone bench with his back to Padric. The god whispered Latin but with great animation, to someone standing behind a fig tree to his right. Unfortunately, Padric could make out only two words in the ancient language that made any sense—*currus...crystallinus*—chariot...crystal.

From the direction of the fig tree, Padric spied a flash like a reflection on metal. *What is that?* Padric wondered. He had seen a similar flash a few times before. Then he heard a whisper, almost too quiet to hear. He shifted his head forward for a better view of the second person.

His eyebrows knit together as he retracted his neck. There was no one else there. *Could I have imagined the second voice? Perhaps the leaves had rustled in the breeze.*

The god of the sun, rider of the fiery chariot, the great titan, was sitting on a bench and speaking to himself. The blood in Padric's face drained down to his hoofs. Circe had warned him about Helius's erratic behavior, yet hearing about it and witnessing it were altogether two different things.

Helius finished his sentence and paused, waiting for an answer. He nodded and shook his head as though listening to the response, then responded again in his one-sided dialogue.

A pang of pity barreled its way through Padric's insides. Barely did he know the god, yet seeing his mind deteriorate bothered him. It was as though he intruded on the privacy of Helius's illness.

Lost in his own thoughts, he almost missed the shift of the god's robes as Helius rose to his feet. Padric's hand brushed against the vines as he pushed himself from the wall, uncovering a statue in low relief, partially standing out from the wall: the body of a man with two faces, one looking forward, the other behind. The nose of the forward-facing part of the head had broken off with a jagged edge. *Odd. The rest of the garden was spotless with all the statues on display. Why would this one be hidden? Because of its imperfection?*

A stone shifted under Helius's approaching foot. Releasing the vines, Padric spun around. The exit was too far away for them to escape before Helius rounded the corner. Ulysses bristled his wings and nodded his head, encouraging Padric to climb on his back.

Revulsion sprouted in his chest. "No, I shall find my own way out."

Ulysses glared at him with piercing deep brown eyes. *Now, or we will be spotted,* he seemed to say.

Padric gritted his teeth. Unfortunately, he could see no other option than to obey. Without further hesitation, Padric leaped onto Ulysses's back. It took his breath away as the peryton leaped into the air, keeping close to the wall. It was very different from the rush he felt when being flung into the air by the Cetus. Before he knew it, they were several blocks away, hidden behind a small building.

Padric quickly dismounted, willing his heart to quiet down. His question for the sun god long forgotten, he contemplated his conversation with Helius, as well as the one-sided conversation he and Ulysses overheard.

Two faces. Padric's body jerked to a halt. "Two-faced. That is it."

The peryton gazed at him expectantly. Rushing to his many-great grandfather—stagfather?—he glanced around to be sure of their seclusion before speaking aloud, and that even under his breath.

"Two-faced. The statue of a man with two faces was Janus, the god of time." Ulysses nodded in agreement. "Nalini said something the other day, referring to *Dissimilis ille bifrontis deus*—'that two-faced god.' I thought she meant a deceptive god, but mayhap she meant Janus, since he has two faces." One face saw the future while the other one saw the past. "Then the question becomes, does Janus have something to do with Circe and Helius? She has not mentioned him even once."

Ulysses's eyes sparked.

Padric thought he understood. "Of course, you must have known Janus, too. By your expression, he must not have been your favorite person."

The peryton shook his head vehemently, *No.*

Interesting. He would have to speak to Nalini or Circe regarding what they knew about Janus, and why the god's relief was covered in vines, as though to hide its very existence. His stench from the morning's challenge wafted up to his nose. *But first, a bath.*

The peryton shook his head. *Not yet,* it seemed to say in response to Padric's unvoiced thought. Then he turned his head toward the entrance of the stone building, up a set of three steps.

"This is not the bath house." After another scan of his surroundings, he realized he had not passed this building perhaps once before, but what it was eluded him. "Where are we?"

Ulysses pressed his antlers against Padric's chest and lightly shoved him toward the entrance. "Fine, fine, I am going." Padric chuckled.

Padric shuffled up the steps. The stinging in his hands and legs renewed, reminding him of sliding down the column during the trial. *The trial we lost,* he thought regrettably.

The sound of a hoof clacking on stone made him halt. When he wheeled around, Ulysses had already taken flight into the sky. Padric could not help but wonder what spy mission Circe would send him on next.

"Wait, I believe I do know what building this is."

A small smile jerked his lip as he ascended the final step of the building.

CHAPTER 17

$\mathcal{B}$rynwen raced back to the infirmary after the outcome of the first trial. Excitement had run through her at seeing Talfryn and Padric in action, but she was disappointed by their loss to Sir Warin. She had seen Warin and some of his teammates at the tourneys in the previous years, and knew they would be formidable foes, but what she did not understand was how Padric's team had lost. Everyone around her seemed to believe Padric had taken the comb, but Warin ended up carrying it to the finish line. Something must have happened in the forest between the pond and the finish line.

With quick steps, Brynwen entered the ward. Only a few patients awaited her, suffering from broken or swollen appendages. However, she knew some of the trial participants from both teams would be making their way to the infirmary shortly, perhaps people she knew.

"Brynwen, how was the event?" The matron, Douse, stood in the doorway, the sincere question clear on her face.

"Oh," Brynwen blushed. "It was quite close. Sir Warin's team triumphed by a hair." She gave a quick synopsis of the trial, and Douse listened intently. Brynwen knew of Sir Warin's popularity among the people in Cataractonium. Maids whispered about his great strength and handsome features, as well as the feats he had performed, both before and since his arrival in the city. He won all the tourneys he participated in at home, which aggravated her cousin Leowyn to no end.

"How did Sir Padric take the loss?" Douse asked.

"He was disappointed, to be sure. But he still has two trials left, and I'm confident he can win."

"We shall see. Since you are back," Douse said, "would you mind making more lavender oil, and your wonderful mix? I believe we have all the ingredients here..."

"I will get right to it." Brynwen reached for some sprigs of lavender and the mortar and pestle and set to prepare her Miracle Mix in the little medicine preparation room.

Nessie greeted her with a twitter and fluttered around her head.

Brynwen laughed. The creature certainly knew how to cheer her up. "Yes, yes, I brought you the seeds you wanted." She procured a small paper packet. "Here you go, you little mooch."

The little bird crooned as she enjoyed the treat, chirping happily all the while.

She was in the thick of combining the oils together when a strange feeling came over her. Not strange, exactly. But—familiar. Warm, as though something missing had been put back in place.

Nessie perked up and tipped off her perch by the window then zipped out of the room.

Wiping off her hands on her stained apron, Brynwen stepped out the door. With quick steps, she rounded the corner from the doorway into the main ward and stopped dead.

He is here. Talfryn.

Her brother stood with his back to Brynwen with the other players from the trial surrounding a couple of wounded men. Nessie settled on his shoulder. In the middle of a conversation, Talfryn stopped speaking, his body rigid. He turned slowly. When he spotted her, a wide grin filled his face.

"Bryn?"

"Tal."

The next thing Brynwen knew, her brother had scooped her up in his arms and was swinging her around, a wide smile and laughter on his lips. She laughed too. Hot tears streamed down her cheeks.

When her feet finally found the floor again, she hugged him tight. "Oh, Tal."

Talfryn buried his face in her shoulder. "I thought I would never see you again. I thought you were...you were..." He gulped and pulled her arms off of him and gazed into her eyes. Tears stained his cheeks. He brought her in again and squeezed her tight, making her wheeze for breaths.

"I'm...fine." She managed to pull his arms from around her and stood at arm's length, still holding onto him, not wanting to let him go. "I was so afraid when you didn't come after a few days..." She couldn't finish.

He kissed her forehead. "Deep inside, I always knew you were still alive. Somehow. I can't explain it, but I felt it. When Cir—when I heard you still lived, I held out all hope. How did you survive?"

She pulled away. It was so strange, trying to talk about something she couldn't even recall, although she had been there. "Well, I don't remember much. I—"

"Cousin," came an excited cry.

A blond-haired young man with friendly blue eyes came up from behind Talfryn and hugged her.

"Leowyn," she responded in kind. "It is so good to see you. I looked all over this place, but couldn't find you."

"I've been mostly working inside the temple, lately. I had no idea you were here, or I'd have come sooner."

"It's no worry, you're here now," she said, her insides warm now that she had two people she cared about back. "You both did well in the trial. I'm so sorry you didn't win."

"So, you were there?"

"I wouldn't have missed it. And Padric?" She craned her neck around her brother's broad shoulder expectantly. The other young men from Padric's team were there, but not the lieutenant himself. She pulled her eyes away, sadness engulfing her. She had so much to tell him. And yet...how could she tell him she had lost the amulet?

Her brother laid reassuring hands on her shoulders. "He wanted to see you, too." She looked up into Talfryn's eyes, noting his dirty and bruised face. "There was something else he needed to take care of first. You will see him soon, though, I'm sure."

Leowyn and Talfryn introduced her to the others on their team. When the introductions were over, she examined the foot of the quiet young man with dark hair sitting on the cot named Rawlins. Padric had spoken of him before, as being one of his oldest friends. His face and arms were scratched and bruised, with dried blood caked everywhere—but nothing a little salve couldn't heal quickly enough. A thick purple and blue bruise encompassed the entire ankle. He winced as she prodded the tender flesh.

"No lacerations or breaks that I can see, which is good. I know something that will help soothe the pain, and help it mend quicker."

She returned a few minutes later with a fresh cloth, a bowl of water, and the completed lavender mixture. She wiped down his cuts and injured ankle with water, lathered oil on the wounds and bruises, then gently tied some bandages around his ankle. She instructed him to keep it raised, and to not walk on it for a couple of days. He would need to come back every day to check on its progress and receive more treatment.

"No need for all that." Rawlins's face turned red. "I'll be good as new in no time."

"You will do this if you want to keep your foot."

The sergeant tried staring her down, but Brynwen would have none of it. Realizing he wouldn't win, Rawlins promised to comply. "I'm not losing my foot after a little tiff with a blimey plant."

Brynwen couldn't help but laugh. Then she and the other healers tended to the wounds of the rest of the participants.

AFTER A FEW MINUTES, the infirmary door opened, and everyone became silent.

"It's about time," Rawlins said, his expression back to being unreadable. "Don't expect me to get up for you now."

Curious as to who entered, Brynwen looked up from Rawlins's foot; but in a sitting position, the newcomer was blocked from her line of sight to by the other trial participants. Talfryn and the young men she had already treated from his team, moved to the door.

A familiar voice cut through the others.

"All is well, I assure you," he said. "The Master merely wished to exchange a few words."

"Padric?" she said, heart leaping to her throat.

"Who else would it be?" her patient said grumpily.

He's here! I didn't think he'd come. What should I do? What should I say?

Forgetting her patient, she got hastily to her feet, barely registering the shout of pain from Rawlins as she smoothed her skirts and apron. Her feet were rooted to the spot, still unsure what to do with themselves.

It seemed like forever before the men finally finished questioning Padric and returned to gather around Rawlins's cot. Brynwen didn't think her heart or patience could take it any longer. The men finally released Padric from their queries.

Then his mossy green gaze rested on Brynwen. All the butterflies in her stomach released and did hundreds of backflips. The faun had never looked more alive. Despite the bruises and cuts along his torso and appendages, he appeared as she had seen him months ago, before Circe came into his life. Before her stood a true knight.

His smile took the breath out of her lungs. *This is getting ridiculous*, a tiny voice at the back of her mind said. As he approached, Brynwen tried very hard to get her feelings in check. She wanted more than anything to leap into his arms, to give him the biggest hug, but she knew propriety would not allow it.

Padric halted three feet from her, his expression bright.

"Brynwen," he said, standing straight as a stick. "It is so good to see you."

"Sir Padric," she replied with a slight curtsy, keeping her face down to hide her blush. "Thank you. You as well." *Why are we being so formal?* He hadn't been that formal since the first few days after he had been trapped under the tree near her family's farm.

Talfryn came up, wrapping his arms around both their necks, drawing them closer together. "See, I told you he'd come."

Taken by surprise, Brynwen mis-stepped and nearly rammed into Padric's chest. He caught her arm effortlessly, and Brynwen took a whiff of him. She was not sure what she'd expected, but he still smelled of himself, of leather and cedar, but mixed with the tangy scent of sweat and being outdoors. *Although, was that a hint of lavender in there? Where did that come from?*

Padric righted her and released her arm. The absence of his touch felt cold, like missing a coat sleeve in the autumn.

"Are you all right?" he asked.

"I'm fine, thank you." She hoped he didn't see her blush.

"Do you know what the next challenge is?" Talfryn asked, oblivious to Brynwen's discomfort.

Padric shook his head. "I did not have the chance to ask. We spoke of other things, one of which might interest you in particular, Talfryn."

"Oh? Regarding?"

"Ulysses."

Talfryn's mouth curled in disgust. "What about him?"

"Ulysses?" Brynwen asked. "How do you know him?"

Both Talfryn and Padric started. The latter leaned forward, his hands unconsciously taking hers. "What do you know of him?"

Her breath hitched at his warm touch. The sudden contact sped all her thoughts away, leaving her a stuttering mess. She hadn't realized how much she missed Padric until this moment. As though she had been holding her breath for weeks until he stood in her presence.

Finally, she found her voice. "He rescued me. Well, I don't remember much, because I hit my head and was unconscious for a while. But he saved Nessie and me when we fell from the cliff, and I woke up here." She indicated the infirmary, which looked the same as it had when she first arrived.

"Ulysses rescued you?" Talfryn asked, incredulous. He folded his arms across his chest, not believing what she said.

On the other hand, Padric's expression betrayed surprise. He brought a hand to his chin in thought. She nodded. "That's what I was told. I haven't met him yet to thank him, though. Why?"

"It's nothing." Talfryn shuffled his feet. Brynwen knew when he was hiding something, yet the thoughtful look he gave hinted that her news was a good thing. Maybe she would get it out of him later.

"Brynwen, you do not know how important that information is to us. What I gleaned from the Master may shed some extra light on matters. You see, Talfryn and I have met Ulysses before. He rescued us the very same night as you, yet we had no idea he aided you, as well. This brings what I have to say more importance."

"He rescued you too?" Brynwen asked, eyes wide. *What happened after he carried me away?* However Ulysses did it, her gratitude toward him had doubled.

"Yes, but we will recount that tale later."

Brynwen felt disappointed in having to wait, but she would ask them about it later.

Padric told them of Ulysses's relationship to himself and Circe and how he became a mythical creature called a *peryton*, as well as an immortal, bound to the god and goddess.

When he finished, Brynwen and Talfryn remained silent, soaking in the information. She hadn't officially met Ulysses, but she felt for him. Padric had only been a faun for a few weeks, whereas Ulysses had been trapped as a *peryton* for over two millennia.

Talfryn took it surprisingly well. He unwound his arms from his body and gaped at Padric. Finally, he nodded. "Yep, I can definitely see the family resemblance." He peered down at Padric's goat legs.

The faun rolled his eyes heavenward and sighed. "This will never die, will it?"

"Never," Talfryn agreed.

Laughter overtook them. Brynwen forgot about Padric's injuries until he winced.

"Sir Padric, let me see to your wounds."

"Please, Brynwen, you do not have to call me that," he said as she directed him to an open cot. Another healer took over the wrapping of Rawlins's dressings, and Talfryn went to check on his other friends.

"I do, in this place," she replied, remembering like a pin prick her place in society. She was a healer, a midwife. A peasant. She was considered a nobody, certainly no one Padric would entertain to court. He had noble blood, and she had nothing to offer him.

Padric's back stiffened, but he said nothing.

She quickly changed the subject as she lathered a helping of Miracle Mix onto the cuts in his hands. "Miriel and Isemay will be saddened to have missed you, but they should be in later this afternoon for their shift."

"They work here, do they? I had wondered what their occupations would be," Padric said thoughtfully. "Please give them my regards. Miriel will be most upset about missing me." His lip curled up.

"Furious," Brynwen agreed with a wide grin. She was privy to Miriel's semi-possessive friendship with Padric.

Her smile turned to a frown when she remembered her failure. It had weighed upon her heart for two weeks, and now was the time to confess. Disappointing Padric was the last thing she wanted to do, but he needed to know, and the sooner the better.

"Brynwen? What has you troubled?" he asked, green eyes cloudy with concern.

"Hmm?" she asked.

He reached for her hand as it mindlessly twirled her braid. Letting go of the braid, she let his warm hand hold hers briefly before pulling away with an inward sigh.

"I have a confession to make, and I don't know how to tell you."

"Then tell me. I shall not judge, I promise."

Looking anywhere but his handsome face, she came clean in a rush of words. "I lost the amulet. It must have fallen out of my pocket somewhere between the river and here, when Ulysses rescued me. Please forgive me."

With his uninjured hand, Padric cupped her chin and gently raised her head. "Do not fret, Brynwen. I could never be upset with you. If we were meant to find it the first time, then we shall find it again. Or mayhap we do not need it."

"But the prophecy—"

"I concede it is a setback, but sometimes these things cannot be helped." He seemed so calm as he spoke. All the while, her heart was pounding at her total incompetence at keeping safe the one vital piece they needed to stop Helius's weapon from destroying the world.

A little while later, Brynwen and the healers finished tending to the wounds of the remaining trial participants and sent them on their way. She loathed being parted from her dear brother and Padric so soon after being reunited, but they promised to see her soon.

"Go be with your friends. You deserve it. Oh!" she said, catching Talfryn's arm. In all the excitement, she'd almost forgotten to tell him. She lowered her voice to a whisper. "It was the most wondrous thing I witnessed earlier today: flying horses. I saw them and thought of you. How beautiful they were!"

Talfryn and Padric looked at each other, then back at Brynwen.

"Where?" they asked in unison.

"How many?" Talfryn continued. "What colors? Will you show them to us?"

"Woah, woah," she said with a laugh, holding up her hands in defeat. "I knew you would be excited, but not quite this much.

They were flying above Cataractonium during the trial. I never saw them before today."

"Nor have I," Padric said. "Are they at the stables now?"

"I only saw them flying in the sky, but that's as good a guess as any."

"Can we go to the stables?" Talfryn asked, practically bouncing up and down like an excited child asking for a sweet at the market.

"Of course," she replied. "How about we meet before breakfast at the stables tomorrow morning?"

"Perfect. Then I'll tell you everything. What a wonder you are, dear sister. I'll bring your satchel, too." He gave her another big hug.

Everything. What did I miss since we were parted? Whatever it was, she would find out tomorrow. That, and she would be reunited with her favorite satchel filled with her medicinal supplies. She'd missed it dearly for the past two weeks.

"Will you be joining us, Sir Padric?"

"Alas, it pains me to decline the offer," Padric said with a frown. "I am to meet with the Mistress first thing in the morning before training."

"I understand," she said, swallowing her disappointment. She had hoped, with the first trial over, he could have some time to rest, but knew it was unrealistic. What with two more trials to prepare for, as well as finding and destroying the deadly weapon before the solstice, he would have little time for anything else.

As she watched Talfryn, Padric, and Leowyn round the corner and out of sight of the infirmary window, Brynwen sighed, relieved they were safe. Alice, too. They were together again. At last, most of her heart had pieced itself back together.

PART II
WINGS

"Be strong, saith my heart; I am a soldier;
I have seen worse sights than this."
— Homer, **The Odyssey**

CHAPTER 18

June 7, AD 1356

Every day since arriving in Cataractonium, Talfryn had passed by the stables. The noises emanating from them sent a pang to his chest. How he missed his home, his grandfather and brother Samuel, his delinquent goats, Hay and Stack.

Now, he stood in front of the structure, Brynwen's satchel around his shoulder, waiting. The mangy, tan-colored dog yipped and spun in a circle by his feet when it sniffed at his pocket, he pulled out a napkin filled with food.

"All right, all right. Eat up, nosey. Ooh, that's a good name for you: Nosey."

Talfryn tossed the stray dog the last dregs of the evening meal he had managed to keep in his pocket overnight, even after being transformed into a hedgehog. Somehow, his clothes—as well as the food in his pockets—returned to him in the exact same state they had been in at sunset the evening before.

"Are you a spy, too?" he asked the dog. It must be a happy spy, at any rate, with all the treats Talfryn had given it over the past few days. He couldn't help thinking how glad he was that Ulysses was a spy, otherwise Brynwen would have died that night. Ulysses must have had a reason for leaving him and Padric while they were still recovering, so it was hard to keep a grudge.

Before parting ways, Padric had instructed him to find out what he could about the horses: which ones were to fly Helius's chariot, their dispositions, their favorite food, and so on. The food knowledge was for Talfryn's benefit. A little extra snack for the horses definitely wouldn't hurt to get their cooperation. *It worked with Hay and Stack, so why not for the flying horses?* The plan was to, somehow, keep the horses away from the chariot carrying the crystal weapon. If it couldn't fly, it couldn't go anywhere. Then they'd only have to worry about the crystal.

The stables were as logical a place as any to search for magical flying horses capable of hauling a chariot and the sun through the sky. They'd have to be heat-defying, so they didn't burn to a crisp, and have the ability to fly. *What exactly might a flying, sun-proof horse look like?* Brynwen didn't have time to fill in any details, so his imagination came up with all kinds of ideas, including horses with little chicken wings soaring on clouds.

"Fancy meeting you at the stables. Are you staring at them again?" Brynwen bent down to give Nosey a good scratch behind the ears. The dog flipped his tail in delight. Her hazel eyes became brighter as she chuckled at his antics, causing Talfryn's insides to bubble with joy. He still couldn't believe how fortunate he was to have his sister back, and he intended to keep it that way.

"Aye," he replied. "These stables are even bigger than anything in Chad or Derby. Here's your satchel. I had to use a few things." It was considerably lighter than when he dragged it out of the river, with much of its contents used to keep Padric alive after being stabbed by the mysterious cloaked man.

Brynwen took the proffered bag with a smile, as though greeting an old friend. She traced her fingers along its edges, then opened it to peruse the contents. "Thank you, I've felt lost without this." She placed it over her shoulder crosswise. Now she looked like herself. "Are we going in, or are we waiting on Leo?"

"I guess he's running late. If it were anyone else's stables, I'd walk right in—well, within reason. But Heli—the *Master's* stables? Now...that could get us into some mighty trouble."

She caught his eye and smirked. "Since when has that ever stopped you from satiating your curiosity?"

"Maybe I've learned to be more cautious." The look his twin gave made him blush. "Well, mayhap just one little peek wouldn't hurt...Leo's always late. What say we just pop in and out before he arrives?" Giving her a wink, he looked about, and seeing no one else around, grabbed his sister's hand.

"That sounds more like my brother." Then lowering her voice, she said, "Quick, while no one's around."

She's become bolder since we parted. I wonder what happened to make her so? He drew the tall wooden door open with the hint of a creak and stuck his head inside. A quick scan of the vast interior met with no impending danger. No stable hands meandered about.

"All clear," he whispered.

Pulling the door open another couple of inches, he let his sister and dog slink their way inside before following and closed the large door behind him.

Now that he stood inside, he gaped at the largeness of the place. Wooden rafters rose to meet the high roof. Grand in scale, the structure had at one time held hundreds of horses for the Roman Legionary corps, or so he had been told by Padric. Now, though, it housed a mere twenty horses of varying colors, a half dozen mules, eight cows, and a small flock of sheep. A feasible assumption made him think the sheep were what Nosey had been sniffing the day before. This morning they, along with most of the horses, were out grazing in the pasture beyond the stables. There were only a handful of animals still inside their stalls.

Nosey worked fast, determined to find something interesting as he put his nose to the ground and sniffed each nook and cranny of the stable. Every so often he raised a bark or low growl of delight.

They had only been looking around briefly when a shuffling sound in the center stall set Talfryn's heart racing. He shoved his sister into the closest open stall.

"Relax," she smirked. "It's only a horse scraping against its stall."

"Right. Only a horse. I wonder why it's still inside when most of the other animals are outside."

With caution, they peeked into each stall. Talfryn couldn't get over the feeling they were trespassing. After a moment, he felt someone staring at him. *Helius?* was his first thought. With great effort, he shook off the feeling. *No, I'm sure he's doing something more important than keeping tabs on me...I hope!*

Pivoting, he turned and found himself nose-to-nose with a dappled-gray horse with a cream-colored snout and mane, chewing merrily on a few strands of straw. "I beg your pardon, my good Sir...Horse," he said through red cheeks. Feeling sheepish at his impishness, he sauntered on after his sister.

"Found anything yet, Bryn?"

"Nothing interesting—you?"

"Nay, I..." As he passed an empty horse stall, he cast a glance inside and saw something curious. "Feathers?" *What are feathers doing in a stall meant for a horse?*

"You...feathers?"

"What?—nay—I mean, yea, I found some feathers in this stall. Great black feathers."

"Like a raven's?"

"Much larger than a raven. A little bigger than Ulysses's feathers."

Brynwen stepped up next to him and on her tiptoes peered into the stall. "I'm not completely certain, but they could be from the flying horses. They had long black wings."

"What about—"

Squeeeeeak!

"The door!" Brynwen said in a loud whisper. "Someone's here!"

CHAPTER 19

The din of many maidens giggling increased as the tall back door opened wider.

"This way." Yanking his sister's arm, Talfryn rushed backward toward the door where they had entered from.

"Tal—"

"Scratch that—this way. Excuse us, Sir Horse, might we share your stall?" He didn't wait for the horse's reply—an indifferent puff from its wide nostrils was all he received. "Our many thanks. " He shoved Brynwen into the small space.

"Oof!" She plopped down in the straw and gave him a hard look.

"Nosey," he hissed. At the other end of the barn, the dog's ears flipped up, and he happily came running to his new master. "Hush," Talfryn hissed again, shoving the dog into the stall half a second before the loud female giggles filled the stables.

Talfryn sidled in next to his sister. The stall was much too small for two people, a curious dog, and a horse.

To Talfryn's amazement, the giggles grew louder. All the maidens began speaking at once about something which excited them, though Talfryn could not catch many of the words. At first, he thought it was just his heart beating fast, but then he realized it was a mixture of

English and another language. *Latin?* He caught a few familiar words from church. *Yes, absolutely Latin.*

Besides their excited conversations, Talfryn heard the clop of horses and the sound of someone working, cleaning out stalls, dropping straw bales from the loft, and spreading straw throughout the stable. After the talking died down, one maid began to sing. Soon others joined in, in three-part harmony, and Talfryn thought it to be the most angelic singing he had ever heard. Even better than at St. Mary's or the York Minster.

Without being aware of it, he had released the dog and gotten to his feet to peek over the stall at the singers. He didn't even notice Brynwen's protests. Sir Horse bumped against Talfryn's rump in tune to the nymph maidens' singing. When Talfryn could see, his blood ran cold. *No!* he thought in dismay. *Why did it have to be them?*

The green skin and translucent dresses in blues, greens, and browns a half dozen dryads filled his vision. Without warning, his gut twisted in on itself. Then an overwhelming need to get out of the barn took hold. For some irrational reason, every time he saw a dryad, his stomach began to ache, and his brain yelled at him in an unnaturally high-pitched voice to *run away now!*

And yet....yet...he couldn't tear his eyes and ears away. Their siren song lulled him into a sense of safety and everything around him dissolved. As he watched, they were all cheery and worked at the same pace as their song, as if their chores had been created specifically for the music.

Why do all the mythical creatures have the best singing abilities? First Circe, now the dryads. Talfryn always lamented his tone deafness. The last time he tried singing, Brynwen and his grandfather threatened to disown him. Even the goats ran for the hills. His mother was the only one who had appreciated his singing—although he doubted it counted because she couldn't sing any better than a choir of cows on Tuesday. Sadly, he hadn't heard her voice, singing or otherwise, since the plague spread throughout Derbyshire over seven years ago.

He stared, completely enthralled in the music, when his eye caught something out of place. Something sharp pinched the inside of his leg, just above the knee. Shaking his leg, he ignored the annoying sensation. His eyes darted around the barn, but he failed to find it again.

There was another pinch, then the swish of Nosey's excited body rubbed against his leg. He batted Brynwen's hand away. He didn't have to look at her to know she scowled at him.

"What are you doing?" he hissed.

"Get down before they see us," she hissed back. "And help me with the dog."

"Just a minute, I saw something..."

Bump.

Avoiding stepping on the dog, Sir Horse's rump rammed into the twins, and their hips slammed against the side of the stall with a loud thump. In a panic, they both crouched down and scrambled back to the corner, striving to be as small as possible.

Now fully aware, Talfryn's fear of dryads—*dryadphobia?*—came flooding back like the River Trent in an April rainstorm.

"Do you have a weapon?" he asked Brynwen, frantically inspecting the stall for something—anything—to use for defensive measures. Staring at Sir Horse's leg, he wondered if he could pry off one of his horseshoes; first, without him noticing, and second, without getting kicked in the head.

"I could be wrong, but I doubt a sprig of lavender will work against a group of dryads. Unless they suffer from hay fever."

"You never know, they might," Talfryn replied.

Nosey, enthralled with the singing and thinking of the horse's antsy movements as a game, yipped and ran in and out of its legs. Sir Horse snorted and lifted its appendages in great agitation. Talfryn watched warily, afraid someone would get kicked in the face.

"Nosey, stop it," the twins cried softly. Together they stared help-lessly at the dog. Any moment they would be discovered.

"We have to stop him," said Brynwen.

"You distract him while I get his back. Then you grab his head. Got it?"

She nodded.

"And...go!"

The twins moved at the same time, in different directions. On his knees, Talfryn skittered along the ground, as Brynwen waved her arms and in a silent plea coaxed the dog toward her. Torn between bothering Sir Horse some more and obeying Brynwen, Nosey paused.

Talfryn pounced. He seized Nosey around the waist as Brynwen grabbed his head and neck.

Still believing it a game, Nosey growled and shook his head and hindquarters, lunging and bumping into the twins and the horse. *Please don't trample us to death, please don't trample us to death.* It might have been a humorous scene had they not been terrified for their lives.

A sudden bout of giggling halted their fight with the dog. The twins looked at each other, realizing the singing had stopped.

That cannot be good.

"Well, well, well," came a voice from above them. "What a pleasant surprise." The even tone she used made "pleasant" sound like scratching one's face with a piece of sandpaper.

Eliva.

Jumping nearly half a pace off the ground, Talfryn landed hard on his bottom, his heart pelting against his ribcage. All his muscles locked as he refused to look at her. He wished to be smaller than a piece of straw.

I am so dead! She'll finish me off right where I sit.

It was Brynwen who responded first. "Good morrow," she said as politely as she could muster. Releasing the now still Nosey, she rose to her feet, brushed off her skirt, and nudged Talfryn's rear with her foot as she did so. "We were just admiring the stables, weren't we, my dear brother?" When he failed to answer, her foot bumped his rear again.

At last, he finally peered up, his face crimson from embarrassment and fear. Sometimes, when he was in trouble, he could deflect its direness with wit and humor. This, however, was not one of those times. The fear which gripped him was irrational, and he knew it, but he would rather die than face them again.

Eliva stared down at him, her expression null, identical to the day they fought on the edge of Circe's lair. This, above all, unnerved him—he could never tell what she was thinking. While they fought, he had tried to disarm her with charm and humor, and barely received a twitch of her eyebrow to communicate her annoyance with him. It was like her face resembled a brick, for all his effort to crack her hard outer shell. Her skills with a polearm outmatched his with a hatchet, leaving him to die wallowing in a carnivorous bramble bush. His back had been raw and sore for days.

Ever since then, whenever a female dryad maiden came into view, fear took root that Eliva had come back to finish the job and his feet would automatically flee in the opposite direction.

Legs finally deciding to work, Talfryn launched to his feet. "Aye! Aye, good morrow, good lady—ladies," he said, noting how all the green maidens watched him in curiosity. He launched into a series of sharp bows of the head. Still unaccustomed to the inhabitants of Cataractonium, he bowed to every strange person he met. As a rule, this saved time—and his head. "Truly these accommodations are far superior to anything we have in Derby." *Oh. Why did I tell her where I live? How much more imbecile can I be?* He clamped his big mouth shut.

Eliva regarded first Brynwen, then Talfryn, in a deadpan. In monotone, she replied, "Undoubtedly. The Romans built many great things. Was our tour from earlier this week not sufficient? I would be most happy to show you the rest."

...and then lead me to a dark alley and murder me where I stand. No thank you.

The ensuing silence which followed could've filled a trough to the brim with water. It was then he realized he said "No thank you" out loud. His eyes rolled as he rehearsed his own eulogy in his head.

"What I mean to say was, 'No thank you, not today. Alas.' We must get to work now. Mayhap next time." He pushed his sister and dog toward the gate. Talfryn could have sworn he saw Eliva's eyebrow lift the slightest fraction, but the dryad merely obliged by opening the stall door and allowing the twins to exit with all haste.

After the stable door closed behind him, he breathed in the fresh, dryad-free air of the outside world, and a thought popped into Talfryn's head. "She didn't sing."

"What?" asked Brynwen, stopping alongside a red stone building. "Who didn't sing?"

He shivered. "From before. The thing that seemed out of place when they were singing. It was Eliva. She didn't sing a single note. The rest of the dryads sang with everything they had, like a light illuminating all the surrounding nature, chasing away the dark. But Eliva didn't glow—she just...was."

Brynwen furled her eyebrows in thought. "Not that I can claim to know many dryads, but does that seem so strange? Mayhap she doesn't have a pretty singing voice."

"Aye," Talfryn concurred, but the response lacked conviction. "Mayhap so."

"There you are," said a tall mop of blond hair rushing around the corner. *Leowyn*. "I looked all over for you two. I was running late, and no one was here when I arrived."

"Sorry, mate. We already went into the barn for a quick peek."

"And made some new friends." Brynwen gave her brother a sideways glance.

Talfryn's cheeks burned.

"We'll tell you all about it at breakfast. Come on." She wove her arms through both her brother's and cousin's. "Alice promised something extra special this morning."

At that, Talfryn's and Leowyn's stomachs growled, and all thoughts of the barn dissipated. Talfryn bowed deeply to his sister. "Then by all means, M'lady, lead the way."

CHAPTER 20

*P*adric sat on the large, soft cushion on the garden floor, eyes closed. Birds chirped. The fountain flowed. The flowers gave off a calming aroma. And yet…

"I do not feel any lighter," he muttered. They had been sitting in Circe's garden for hours. Despite the relaxing ambiance, he found little in the way of concentration.

"Hush, and let the air lift you," Circe said. Even with his eyes closed, he could feel her grin.

Again, he concentrated, but to no avail.

"Padric," Circe spoke calmly, her eyes still closed. "You cannot hope to figure this out without trying harder."

"M'lady, how can I sit here and meditate whilst I should be using the time to train? Neither the human nor the centaur inside me wish to be released, no matter if I meditate or hack at a tree. If I am to defeat Warin, I need to be out there. I cannot even train with my own men, because they are needed to build Helius's blasted temple."

"Oh, curse-breaker, you are getting upset again. Release your aggression, and—"

"I would feel better if I knew when the next trial is, and what it will entail. To be honest, the suspense is eating me up inside." Padric had already failed once, he could not do so again. He must win, for every-one's sake.

> *...Reclaim the amulet of darkest night*
> *To destroy the weapon of untold might...*

Except he had no amulet. He did not blame Brynwen for having lost it. If only he could believe what he told Brynwen about finding it again after finding it the first time. Likely, it dropped to the bottom of the river. Retrieving it now would be short of a miracle. His only hope now was to prevent Helius from being able to use the chariot. If he could not fly, he could not kill Apollo, and therefore the world. His second hope was that the cloaked man would never find it.

Circe huffed, an edge coming into her voice. "Alas, I know little more than you. *Pater* is being rather obstinate. For now, let us review your abilities. That is why we are here, after all."

Padric let out a long sigh. "Mayhap I truly am cursed."

"You are not cursed. You broke the two curses I threw at you long ago. When first I froze you and your comrades, what happened?"

Closing his eyes, Padric recalled his first encounter with the sorcer-ess. "I pictured myself being bound by chains and secured with a lock, then formed a key in my mind to free myself."

"And the second time, with the tree? You were a centaur, and?"

"I needed to be free from the tree, so I willed my body smaller. I was desperate to escape—yet, why I chose faun legs instead of my own, I have no idea. At the time, I was sure it was you who changed me, but since then I have learned those changes were my own doing."

Circe's eyes glinted. "I was as shocked as you when I learned what you had done that night. And pleased with your progress."

"But why can I not change at will? I want to be myself. I miss my original legs." *And not garnering unwanted attention from hundreds of curious and wary eyes.*

It did not help that, since Padric's and Talfryn's arrival in Cataracto-nium, Warin and his compatriots had started spreading rumors about Padric's legs, and his inability to become a human again. *'If he is a curse-*

breaker, why doesn't he change back?' Goat jokes, beast quips, the lot. With his enhanced hearing, he could hear the snickers behind his back. He ignored them as best he could, but still, they burned within him.

"Tsk, grandson. Do not give up hope. It is there, somewhere. We will get this, but you must want it."

"But I do want it."

She shook her head. "Yes, but there is something missing. I will continue to do more research to figure out how to unlock your human side. But for now, you must keep training in both mind and body."

Silence refilled the garden, and Padric did his best to concentrate for the rest of their session. The only thing remotely close to finding his inner self was his connection with his horse Firminus, whom he had absorbed the day Circe transformed him into a centaur. At first, when Padric was very stressed or afraid, his human and knightly instincts fought with Firminus's animal instincts within his mind. It was very disconcerting, but he had learned to control it.

When it was about time to go, Padric uncurled his stiff gray legs from the soft cushion. "M'lady?" He moved toward the wall where he and Ulysses had overheard Helius speaking with himself. "Before we withdraw, what can you tell me about this?" He pulled back the green vines to expose the two-faced god, Janus, revealing the missing nose on the forward face. "Why was this hidden, when all the other statues in the garden are out in the open and preserved?"

In the blink of an eye, Circe's skin lost its sheen, her impeccable hair appeared less kept. Years of heartache took a toll on her as she rose to her feet.

"How did you find that?"

Heat flushed up Padric's neck. "I stumbled upon it recently."

"Please, do not ask me about it." Her knees buckled.

"M'lady—" He reached out a hand to steady her. With careful strides, he guided her toward the fountain and deposited her gently on the nearest stone bench.

After a few minutes of silence, Circe looked up, tears welling up in her eyes. "Some things should not be remembered. He drove Telegonus away." She said the last so softly, Padric had to lean closer to hear.

"Who? Janu—"

"You look so much like my son, and like his father Ulysses." She cupped Padric's chin tenderly. "When you pulled back the ivy, for a moment I thought you were my Gonus."

"That is what I have heard." Disappointment hummed through him as Circe strove to change the subject.

"My father thinks so as well. You two would have gotten along quite well. I wish beyond everything he would return to me. To us. Then everything might be better. But for now, you are our hope."

"I will do all I can, M'lady."

"I thank you," she said with a nod. She twiddled her fingers in her fine blue dress. "You are a combination of both warrior and scholar. I must say, I am impressed with your knowledge of our world. *Pater* mentioned you have a friend who taught you?"

Padric's chest constricted. "Yes, he was my tutor for several years. He taught me Latin and Greek through reading old mythological texts—although now I suppose I can no longer call them 'myths.' Learning with him made everything so much more interesting than I would have ever imagined. He would adore everything about this place. From what I gather, he and Telegonus would be fast friends."

"You talk about him in the past tense. Did he die?"

He shook his head slowly. "Gregorio disappeared a short time ago, and I do not know what happened to him."

As lightning, Circe grabbed his arm. Squeezed tight. "What name did you say?"

Taken aback, Padric replied, "Gregorio Fiori."

She released his arm. Without another word, she disappeared in a puff of blue smoke.

Staring at the welt she had left on his arm, Padric wondered what had happened between Circe, Helius, and Telegonus. *And where did Gregorio and the statue of Janus fit into all of this?* Leaving with more questions than before entering the garden that day, Padric hurried to the training field for another thrilling afternoon of fighting large animals and fierce dryads.

CHAPTER 21

The next two mornings, Talfryn drifted to the stables with Nosey on his heels, crouched behind a bale of straw near the back entrance, and waited. Each morning, the female dryads ascended on the stables singing beautiful songs while they performed their morning chores.

He spied Eliva with them, melancholy as ever, whilst the others chattered and sang in merriment. But once, her eyes seemed to glisten as though she wished to join, but didn't, for whatever reason.

The third morning saw Talfryn in front of the stables, long before any of the dryads would be around. Unfortunately, neither Brynwen nor Leowyn were available to come. Brynwen had spent a long night attending an unwilling patient-turned-goat with a broken foreleg—or arm. Leowyn was tasked with helping stock the building site with more stone, since the first speck of daylight. Nosey was still sleeping, so it was just him.

Only a few ribbons of red and orange lightened the sky when Talfryn headed to the stables, the instant his hedgehog spikes diminished from his back. Wiping the sleep from his eyes, he made his way to the back of the stable toward the pasture. The sheep grazed in the green grass nearby, the flurry of their white coats moving en masse in the distance.

Perfect! he thought. *The rest of the beasts must be inside still waking up.* Leaping over a rough wooden post enclosure, he made haste to the tall stable door, drew up the latch, and ducked inside.

Upon entering, his senses were shocked by the smells and sounds of waking barnyard life, quite different from a few days before. Closing his eyes, he drew in a long, deep breath, taking it all in: the whiff of crisp straw covering the floor; the bales of yellow hay stacked in neat columns against the walls and in the loft; the horses of many colors and sizes shaking their manes to loosen the dust of straw from their backs; the snickers of horses and mules waking from their night's slumber, ready for a new day.

I am home!

This had always been his favorite part of the day. He loved entering his family's tiny barn in Chaddesden and being greeted by the just-waking animals, each so happy to see him. *True, their happiness at seeing me may have been because I'm the one who fed them on a regular basis, but no matter.*

His fingers twitched to pick up the nearest rake to begin the morning's chores. A stone in his stomach dropped to his feet as he realized how much he missed his family and the animals at home. Right now, he, his grandfather Eduard, and brother Samuel would have already eaten Brynwen's porridge and be headed to their chores in the fields. Talfryn hoped the two were still well, and that Hay and Stack didn't torture Samuel too much. Without a doubt, they were the most mischievous goats this side of the River Trent.

It took a few moments for the nagging at the back of his head to remind him time was of the essence. After all, the dryads could decide to arrive early to do their chores. With a heavy sigh, Talfryn shoved his shoulders off the tall door and carried himself into the stable.

According to Brynwen, the flying horses had long black wings. That would certainly coincide with the large black feather he'd found in the stall the other day. It made sense that, like Ulysses, Helius's flying horses would have wings.

Glancing into each stall as he passed, he noted the different horses, most of Arabian descent. They held their heads high and puffed air in his face, but they didn't seem in any way remarkable. He took note of the horses, giving a few of them names. Albers, The Frenchman, The Duchess, et cetera. As he moved along, he had the sudden, odd impression that someone watched him. Shoving it aside, he surmised it must merely be the bored, waking animals hoping for a bite to eat.

Halfway down on his return circuit, a pretty mare caught his eye. The color of deepest ebony, the beauty stood, legs straight, munching daintily on a bit of hay.

"My, aren't you a beauty?" He took in her fine qualities. "Of all the pretty lasses, you are the most fair."

The horse looked him straight in the eye and nickered. *Is she blushing?* Holding out his palm for her to sniff and become familiar, he glanced around her stall. Neat and proper. This was the stall where he and Brynwen found the large black feather. He didn't have to look far to realize the wings were attached to her. From her withers, sinewed muscles sprouted into powerful wings. He could only imagine how long they were, since it was too cramped in the stall to unfurl them.

He gaped in wonder, marveling at the magnificent mare. He began to wonder how many other normally flightless creatures could have wings. *What about goats or foxes? Now that's a scary thought—and many less chickens left to the poor farmers who thought their chickens safely nestled in their coops.*

The black beauty nudged his hand, pulling him from his thoughts. He smiled and stroked her mane.

"Nay, nay, my pet, I haven't forgotten about you. Alas, I don't have any extra vittles to give you this morn'. I've yet to have any myself." He gave her a quick scratch below her chin and behind her ears.

Time was running out, and he needed to finish his search. "I must be off, my lady, but I shall see you again soon." He gave her a grand smile, bowed, and moved along.

The next six horses were equally ebony in color and bore wings, all furled at their sides, still waking up. As he passed by, the winged stallion on the end stretched its wings out halfway. Talfryn's eyes widened at the magnificence of them.

Seven ebony horses with wings. Four larger than the rest. *Curious. Did the larger ones pull Helius's chariot? It would make sense. The horse-drawn carriages at home generally used horses of similar height, so why not these?*

Taking a step toward an empty stall, Talfryn heard a creak. At first he thought it was his own movement causing the sound, but he had touched nothing, and the stable floor was only dirt and straw.

Someone is here. In the rafters, from the sound of it. Drat, I knew it was folly to dally. Now it's going to cost me. Oh, how I wish I had my hatchet!

Is it Eliva, come to finish me off without witnesses? On their previous visit, she had allowed him and Brynwen to leave, but it could have been because other dryads were around. His grandfather, Eduard, would say Talfryn was a glutton for punishment, and maybe he was right.

As much as he wished to flee for his life, he resolved to get it over with once and for all. With a deep, inward sigh, and a giant knot twisting around his insides, he stood straighter, ready to recite his own last rites.

Then, nearly indistinguishable over the sound of his thumping heart, he had heard it: a giggle.

Eliva did not giggle.

It stopped just as abruptly as it had begun, but there was no mistaking the sound.

The giggle resumed, a haunting melody to his ears. *Not as melodious as the dryad maidens from before, but more innocent, like a child? A young lass, in this place?* And where was she giggling from? She sounded far away.

Suddenly, his stomach unclenched its hold around his insides, and he breathed again. He chuckled in relief. Pivoting on his boot, he looked around, but found no one in the rafters.

A third giggle rang out.

"All right," he said loudly, "what's so funny?"

The giggling stopped. "You act as though you've never seen a horse before."

"Oh, well, of course I've seen horses. My family owns one. I've ridden one, too." Recalling his first attempt at riding a horse. His hands absently moved to rub his bottom at the painful reminder.

"You only have one?"

"Aye." He turned to where the voice came from, but saw no one. Then the plop of a small body sounded directly behind him, next to the empty stall.

Spinning on his heel, he spotted the lass, standing squarely and looking at him with curiosity. Quite small, he thought, maybe about eight years old, with gangly little legs. And yet, her eyes showed an intelligence far greater than her petite size indicated. With that, she could have been nine or ten. The lass's green skin was a shade darker than the others he'd seen—it appeared she spent most of her time in the warm English sun. She wore the same blue and green outfit as her sister dryads, though disheveled by rough play, and sported short, uneven hair, as though someone had tried to cut it, but she ran off to play before the deed could be finished. Or she cut it herself. And yet, it suited the wildness he sensed within her. With an exception to Eliva, she differed from the other dryads, but it could also be her age, since the rest he had seen had reached—if not close to—womanhood. However, Padric had said Nalini was older than she appeared, making Talfryn wonder if this lass were older than she looked as well.

"One horse suits our farm just fine for now. But my brother Samuel hopes to someday have two horses to plow our fields."

"Plow fields? When do you get to ride them?"

Talfryn shook his head in disdain. "We avoid riding them whenever possible," was what he wanted to say, remembering his weeks riding the horses to Cataractonium. Instead he replied, "There's little time to ride them, with the amount of work we have every day. Besides, we've a cart for our horse to haul into town when we go to market."

"Sounds boring to me."

Talfryn pumped his fists on his hips. "Oh, well, I don't know about that. Sometimes the cartwheels get stuck in huge mud puddles on the road. Hauling them out can be quite an exciting time."

Eyes alight, the lass let out a giggle and took a step closer, hands clasped behind her back. "You are funny. My sister would like you."

Talfryn let out a chuckle of his own, and his body relaxed, leaning up against the stall containing the fourth winged horse.

"Does your sister love to laugh?"

"Oh no, but she could use some cheering up."

"Well, you should tell her..." his voice trailed off as his throat choked the sound out of him. *Sister...her sister was most definitely a dryad. And the singing nymphs would be here at any moment. Plus, he still had to grab a bite to eat before work, otherwise he'd have to wait until the evening meal.*

The black winged horse in the stall puffed out some air.

Shoving off the stall with a clatter, Talfryn glanced both ways down the stable's aisle, expecting Eliva and the others to come marching into the stables any moment. "I beg your pardon, miss, but I best be off. Work duties and all, you know." He hoped she couldn't hear the pounding of his heart banging against his rib cage.

"I'm no miss, sir. I'm called Thimble."

An odd name, Talfryn thought. *And yet, it suits her.* He bowed deeply. "Pleased to meet you, Thimble. And I am no sir. Call me Talfryn. Fare well, dear Thimble. I hope to see you again." With half a glance at the lass, he straightened and turned to go.

"Wait." Thimble took a timid step forward.

Pausing mid-spin, Talfryn held in the grimace he dearly wished to release. *They'll catch me again. Doesn't she know much how danger I'm in?*

She didn't speak, but stood there, hands still behind her back.

"What?" he asked in barely contained agitation. *If they see me again, their suspicions will be aroused, and they'll turn me in to Helius right quick. Maybe even now this child is a trap to lure me into staying. Not even Circe could save me from the god's punishment.*

Her eyes grew to wide, dark brown pools, frightened at his severe outburst. Even Talfryn was surprised at his own gruffness. *What am I turning into at this place?* Every turn was perilous, and pulled at his wits to no end. And here was this child, who only wished for a friend, and he was being harsh to her. Drooping his shoulders in defeat, he took a step forward, hands raised in supplication. "Please forgive me, Thimble, but I fear to be late to work. What is it you wish to ask of me?"

"Would...would you like to know their names?"

Talfryn blinked once. Twice.

"The winged horses. Or pegasi, we called them."

He couldn't believe his luck. She could tell him everything he needed to know about the horses, then he'd be able to keep them away from the chariot. "Oh, yes, I'd like that," he said, trying to not sound too eager.

"How about a bargain, then?" asked Thimble, emboldened by the hope of a new friend.

Talfryn eyed her with suspicion. "And that would be?"

"If you come to visit me every day, I will tell you the names of the pegasi. One name per day."

Oh, a clever one, she is.

"Seven visits," he said. "One name per day. And you'll not tell anyone I was here?" It seemed a bit ridiculous, seeking information from a child. But with only a week and a half left until Solstice Day, he needed to know about the horses, and she was all he had to work with. *But that would mean seven mornings without breakfast. That's a big no.* "How about four days, one for each of the biggest four winged horses." She nodded her head. "Then it's a deal." Talfryn bowed low to the ground a second time. "I'll see you tomorrow, then, to begin our grand stable adventure."

Thimble returned the curtsy, quite graceful for one so small. *And yet, she's a dryad,* Talfryn reminded himself. Grace seemed to befit them all, even the smallest and most gangly.

"And do bring your dog!" she called after him as he bustled through the great door on the cusp of the first notes of singing dryads at the other end. "He makes me laugh."

"Wait, how did you know I have a dog?"

"I know everything that goes on in my stables."

Talfryn left at a jog, hoping beyond hope he hadn't put his trust in the wrong child.

CHAPTER 22

"Where is your dog?"

No greeting. No welcome. I can play that game, too, thought Talfryn. "Nosey's busy this morning." If Talfryn had to guess, his new mutt friend was likely cowering behind a boulder to escape the lions. "And he's a nuisance to horse-kind."

"Indeed. Which is why he and you make me laugh," Thimble said.

"Well, there are three more days, so maybe he'll make an appearance by the end. Have you considered getting a dog of your own?"

Without so much as a crouch, Thimble leapt up and landed square on her feet on the top of the last pegasus stall. The action failed to incite any reaction from the horse or its neighbors, so it must have been used to her stunts. "Can't."

Talfryn raised an eyebrow.

"My sister says the lions'll eat it up."

No argument there.

"Come up here."

"I won't fit."

"Come onnn." Without losing an ounce of balance, Thimble clutched his arm and started hoisting him up. Talfryn was quite taken aback by the amount of strength she possessed. With much less grace than the little dryad, Talfryn clambered up the stall to sit beside her. To his amazement, the wooden gate held firm against its hinges. *No creaking or breaking at all. I could get used to this Roman architecture.*

"Besides, dogs are loud and may disrupt the Master, she says."

"Aye, they could at that," Talfryn agreed, "based on the dog. Some are quiet, while others bark at anything. At home, my dog Finn will bark at anything. Mostly to say 'come pet me.'"

"What other animals do you have on your boring farm?"

"My *boring farm*, as you call it, isn't so very big. We have two white goats, Hay and Stack, a horse named Paul, a cow named Bernita, and some chickens with not very clever names. A cat makes its rounds between the neighboring farms to eat up the mice. We usually see her a couple times a month. Come to think of it, she's probably at the farm right now, attacking poor, defenseless, hungry mice, and eating them up for breakfast. In exchange for her services, my brother'll be generous and give her a healthy helping of cream. At least, he promised to before he left. It's generally me giving the milk."

"Do you help the cat hunt?"

"Not very well. He usually glares at me when I try."

"I'd think that'd be much more entertaining than digging holes and planting seeds."

"I agree. When my sister and I were little, we would pretend we were her kittens and follow the cat. We would pounce on each other and on the ground. We even tried catching a mouse once."

"Then why do you do it?"

"What?"

"Why do you continue to be a farmer?"

"Well," Talfryn thought carefully. "My family has always been farmers. For more generations than I can possibly count. We've lived in the same cottage, in the same village, forever."

"But..."

"There is no but."

"Yes, there is."

Talfryn spared a thought for her words. "My sister did become a midwife's apprentice. But she still lives with us."

"But she's not farming?" Talfryn shook his head. "See? She changed. Why can't you?"

Talfryn stared at the little maiden. She couldn't possibly understand the way the outside world worked. "Look, I just can't go around changing jobs whenever I feel like it. I'm a penniless peasant and have responsibilities to my family." Despite his argument, she had a point. He'd always resigned himself to being a farmer, though he had no enjoyment in it. The small glimpse he had of being a mason was shattered with the coming of the plague. All he had to look forward to was backbreaking labor every day and little thanks for his work. His grandfather's back was crooked because of his years tending the farm. Most people in Chaddesden were in the same situation, remaining as they were. "I...don't know."

Suddenly, a thought swirled through his head. *Possibilities.* "My older brother Sam will inherit the farm. He is to marry soon, and will have sons of his own. He'll have little use for me then." It was something he had never considered—the future, and what it would look like. But so much had changed in the last few weeks. He had done many things deemed impossible only a short time ago. And yet, here he was. All because Brynwen rescued a wounded, cursed knight, turning their world upside down.

"You are incredibly perceptive for one so small. Mayhap you should be in politics."

Beaming, Thimble patted him on the back. "See. I told you there was more. What is a politics?"

Talfryn snorted. "'Something adults do but not very well.'" One of his father's old friends once said that and wasn't too far off the mark. "Well, what about you?"

"Me? Oh, I am planning on leaving this place, as soon as I can, and have adventures of my own."

"I might wait a while, were I you."

Thimble flashed a wary set of brown eyes at him. They seemed to cast sparks, and Talfryn half wondered if she was a child of Helius. Perish the thought he become the friend of one of his enemy's children. Padric did *not* need more dangerous family members to contend with.

Holding up a placating hand, he quickly stated, "You know, to stretch those legs out a bit. You will go farther in a day with longer legs. Now, can you tell me....What are you doing?"

Without warning, the young lass got to her feet to balance again on the stall door. Then without a further glance, she leapt up, higher than a little maiden her age should have any right to, and grabbed a hold of the lowest beam. The traveling acrobats that came through Chaddesden couldn't have performed the feat better or more gracefully. Maybe she could make it on her own.

Kicking her legs up, Thimble's feet landed on the horizontal beam, then she let her arms fall free. Imagining her plummeting to the floor, Talfryn nearly fell headlong off the stall door to catch her if she fell. But she defied him again, and stayed there, a mix of triumph and mirth on her face.

"See here," Talfryn scolded. "You nearly scared me to death!" Try as he might, he couldn't get his legs to cooperate enough to stand atop the stall and get her down. "Stop laughing and come down!"

Thimble halted, covering her mouth, her little body writhing in mirth. "Ooooh, you should see your face!" She proceeded to crack up again.

"So this is what it feels like to be Bryn, trying to keep me in check," he commented to himself. "What exactly are you doing up there, anyway?"

"Stretching my legs, of course!"

"Umm, I don't think that's how it works."

"Well, that's all I can think of. You should join me."

"I don't think..." Talfryn looked around for a way up without breaking his neck.

"There are handholds just there. And there." She pointed at two spots on the pole connecting two stall doors.

The farmer eyed the pole with a skeptical eye, feeling the ridges with his fingers. "Well, I—"

The sound of voices outside brought his attention back to himself.

His stomach twisted as he looked up. "They're here. I'm afraid I've overstayed my welcome." Scrambling down the stall door with a rough scrape to his arm from a splinter hanging from the wood, he peered up. "Can you get down?"

"Of course I can get down. Go." She flapped her arms at the exit.

"But—"

"Wait."

Talfryn skidded at the front door, his heart threatening to leave the stables without him.

"Pyrois is the leader."

"That's it?"

"Yes. Now go!" Thimble shouted.

As the oversized door closed behind him, the sounds of the dryads' giggles and musical humming echoed behind him.

CHAPTER 23

*H*is body over eighty percent submerged in the hot water, Padric squared his shoulders against the blue and white tiled wall of the vast public bath. The heat did wonders to ease his aching muscles. Nalini and a lion tag-teamed against him today, and it was all Padric could do to keep them at bay.

Nalini and the dryads had challenged him with different targets at archery practice, each harder than the last. Now all he wanted to do was rest in his darkened corner of the bath house for the last hour before sunset. None of the dozen other men, all in their undergarments, seemed to have noticed him skulk to the shadows of the pool.

It helped that Warin and his friends were pleasantly absent from the baths this time. Their incessant banter and laughing insults generally took away any hope he had of loosening his tight muscles.

His time to fulfill the prophecy drew nearer by the hour, yet he still did not have all the information. *What am I missing? The puzzle seems to widen with every moment.* Padric shook his head against the doubts. *I have a job to do, and that is all.*

Closing his eyes, Padric tuned out the drone of conversations around him, and allowed his mind to drift into oblivion.

"There you are," a familiar voice shouted.

The *plop* and splash next to him announced the addition of two more bodies into the heated pool.

Padric grimaced in displeasure, hoping against all odds that the voice had some other intended target.

"Is he asleep?" the voice asked.

"Oh, no, he's awake," said a deeper voice next to him.

Next time I must find a darker *corner.*

"What a coincidence," Padric said, his eyes still closed, "that we should all be in the same bath house at the same time." *And just before curfew, at that.*

"We've been looking all over for you." Talfryn crossed his arms. "Rawlins thought you were avoiding us."

"Mayhap I was. What can I help you with, gentlemen?"

"We discovered something really interesting today while working," Talfryn's voice rose a fraction in his excitement.

"This could not wait until the evening meal? I would really appreciate five minutes of quiet first." Padric kept his eyelids firmly shut.

"But..."

"Five minutes."

"Five minutes," Rawlins repeated evenly. Padric could sense his sergeant fold his arms across his chest, not relaxing one ounce in the water. *When was the last time Rawlins relaxed?*

"Fine," Talfryn said with a sulky voice. "I suppose it can wait. Bryn's the one who discovered it, and—"

"What?" Padric's eyes shot open.

"I knew that would get your attention," Talfryn said with a cheeky grin.

"You could have started with that."

"Do you hear that?" Rawlins asked.

"Sorry, it's my stomach," Talfryn replied. "I haven't eaten yet."

Rawlins frowned at Talfryn. "Nay, it was something else. A hiss."

"Like a snake?"

If it were anyone else, Padric might have said he imagined it. After all, bathers carried on conversations in various tones of dialogue and gestures, and the fountain in the center rained water into the pool at all times. But Rawlins was one of the most perceptive people he knew. Especially when it came to danger.

Now fully at attention as a hound on a hunt, all Padric's thoughts of relaxation—and Brynwen—vanished.

"There it is again," Rawlins said.

Pulling from his knight training, Padric slowed his breath, concentrating on the sounds in the bath house. As he inhaled, he could hear each drop from the fountain hit the water; the slightest inflection in tone from one of the men on the other end of the bath; the *plink plink* of water as someone excitedly slapped their fingers against the water's surface.

"I think I hear it, too," Talfryn agreed.

The hair on the back of Padric's neck rose when he heard it —hissss.

Where did it come from? None of the other people in the room seemed to notice anything amiss.

As silent as a feather, Rawlins waded forward through the water in search of the source of the hissing sound.

Every fiber of Padric's senses rose to high alert, tamping down the panicking animal part of his mind imparted by Firminus. This was no time to falter. Keeping his eyes on the water, Padric saw movement. "Talfryn, get a torch."

The farmer blinked, then hastened out of the bath toward the nearest torch resting in the sconce on the tiled wall. It squeaked in the hinges, but he finally freed it from its iron clutches. Returning to the water's edge, Padric reached for it.

Talfryn's eyes grew wide. "Rawlins!" His voice echoed off the walls and ceiling in the chamber.

All conversations ceased.

Padric whipped around just in time to see a small sandy- and white-colored snake with red stripes streak out of the fountain toward Rawlins, its impossibly long fangs bared, headed for his chest.

With the reflexes of a fox, Rawlins batted the creature away. It flung through the air with a screech and plopped into the water next to Padric.

Recoiling, Padric retreated two steps from where the creature splashed. *What was that?*

A high-pitched scream came from the other end of the pool. Then another, followed by more.

A dozen little green streaks shot out of the water, leaping from one man to another. A cacophony of screams, shouts, and splashing ensued.

"Everyone out!" Padric shouted. Those not battling small creatures scrambled toward the edges to exit the water and the building. Regardless of the danger, a few curious stragglers remained in the room.

"Where is it?" Talfryn asked. He lowered the torch to the surface to locate the creature.

"Rawlins, hurry," Padric urged.

Rawlins gave him the *What does it look like I am doing?* scowl. His right arm—the one that struck the serpent—hung limply at his side. He clutched his favorite dagger in his good hand.

Where did he hide that on his person?

"What happened to your arm?" Padric asked.

The sergeant's scowl deepened, if that was even possible, as he continued to glare at the water. "I don't know. I hit the snake and now my arm feels like lead. It won't move at all." As he spoke, a red spot formed on his forearm. Ignoring it, he dove into the water to aid the bathers in trouble.

Talfryn's eyebrows rose. "If the slightest touch will do that..." He gulped and continued to search the pool.

Padric was more than a little alarmed at the potential danger of such a small creature. *It is more than a simple snake. What is it?*

Following Rawlins's lead, Padric shoved off the wall after him. Something smooth slid against his calf. He kicked only twice more before his right leg gave out, dragging him down like an anchor.

Not now!

A flash of tan and red shot past Padric's arm, hissing all the while. *This is ridiculous.* In moments, he was reduced to hopping through the waist-deep pool at a snail's pace. *At this rate, the creatures will take out everyone before I reach the other end of the pool.*

Not to be forgotten, Talfryn ran around the perimeter of the pool, still holding the lit torch, his feet slapping against the cool tile.

As Padric approached the scene, he spotted Rawlins batting away serpents with his knife, protecting the men unable to exit the pool. To Padric's horror, some men floated in the water, their eyes closed. Hurrying to them as fast as he could with one good leg, he snatched up the closest man with long brown hair.

Thankfully, he still breathed.

Talfryn stood by the edge of the water, his eyes darting around, unsure what to do.

"Talfryn, stay there." Dragging the man over to the edge, he and Talfryn hoisted the unconscious man up and out of the water. Padric rushed to get another unconscious victim.

Miraculously, the creatures stayed away from Padric for the most part. Except for the one that slithered up his back. It tickled at first, then it felt like he wore a sodden woolen shirt dragging him down. He still had no idea where the little beasts came from.

Grabbing a third bobbing body lying amid the fray, another shout overtook the others. Glancing over, he spotted Talfryn staring face-to-face with one of the tiny serpents. It had taken him by surprise when it bounded out of the water and landed on the torch in his hand. Talfryn shook the torch to fling it aside.

"No, that will only anger it," Padric yelled at him, but Talfryn did not hear.

The serpent held on tight. Thoroughly angered, it hissed and bounded at Talfryn's face.

"Gah," he cried. The snake wrapped itself about his head like a sash. "Get it off!"

"Tal!" Padric cried. Holding onto the wounded man, he pushed off the ground. A heavy body slammed into him, its elbow catching him in the jaw, driving both Padric and his charge under water.

CHAPTER 24

*P*adric's jaw screamed as the heavy body shoved him to the pool floor. As he struggled with his attacker, flashes of fighting the cloaked man in the river bombarded his thoughts. *Cloak's strong grip. The dagger catching the moonlight. Blood flowing.*

A hand grabbed Padric's arm, and before he knew it, he was above water, spluttering and coughing. The vision of Cloak faded, and the bath house and its chaos returned.

Rawlins released Padric's arm, his forehead creased in worry. "No time for play," he said, then moving on to help someone else.

Padric was left stunned at Rawlins's behavior. Then he shook himself free of the notion and shoved his way to the edge so he could push the hurt person onto the tiles and help Talfryn.

Padric rushed out of the water and hurried Talfryn. A closer inspection of the creature showed it to have two tiny ram-like horns above its eyes. *But how can I get the creature off Talfryn's head without hurting either of us? One touch, and my arms will be useless like Rawlins's.* He would have to worry about that later, or Talfryn might end up injured even worse.

The little monster bit Talfryn's cheek with fangs like a viper, the latter releasing another agonizing scream.

Two ram-like horns and venom. That sounded like something he had read about...

Memories of paging through his tutor Gregorio's texts shot through his mind. He had made a point to study all the drawings of the mythical creatures within *Naturalis Historia* by Gaius Plinius Secundus, or Pliny the Elder. One such creature was a *cerastes*, which resembled these snakes, but larger. This must be an infant as it was no longer than his hand. It was born from the blood of Medusa in the Libyan desert. It was said that while eloping with Paris, Helen of Troy stepped on a cerastes's back and broke it, which caused it to move in a sinuous, crooked fashion. However, Padric could not recall exactly what the creature did, or how to defeat it, but it was in the seventh volume of Pliny's extensive collection entitled: *"Bestiae Periculosae,"* or "Dangerous Beasts."

Talfryn screamed again, bringing Padric back to the present.

"It's eating my face," Talfryn cried.

"Nay," Padric said, taken aback. This was quite surprising. "It is in fact licking your face."

"What?"

Talfryn opened an eye—the other being swollen by the cerastes's bite. After the first bite, it began to lick him as though he were its friend, or mother.

Now, how to pry the creature from his face? Padric picked up the torch from the ground. *Miraculously with all the splashing, it has not gone out.*

The cerastes's tongue halted, then it raised its head to peer directly at the torch as Padric brought it closer.

What?

He moved the torch around, and the cerastes's head followed. "Maaa?"

"I think it is following the light—or heat—source." *Because it is blind.* "An infant cerastes, looking for its mother."

"Me, ith muvwer?" Talfryn's tongue swelled to twice its normal size as he tried to speak.

"Talfryn, let me—"

The little creature squealed in delight. The noise filled the room and the flailing and shouting behind Padric ceased.

"Uhhh, Pawic?" Talfryn pointed over Padric's shoulder.

This cannot be good.

Slowly, Padric turned, heart pounding in his ears. All the infant cerastes stared directly at them—rather, at Talfryn with the viper latched onto his face. His chest constricted as it dawned on Padric that this must be the leader, calling its siblings to their mother. As one, they propelled themselves toward Talfryn.

A hand slammed on Padric's shoulder. "Come on." Rawlins helped Padric up, then Talfryn.

Padric scanned the room for a weapon or another way out—but the creatures barred the doorway. An unlit bronze brazier sat in the corner, next to a table piled high with white towels. If nothing else, he could give the others time to escape.

"To the brazier." Padric picked up the torch. "Help Talfryn, and I will catch up." Rawlins half-dragged Talfryn while Padric hopped on one hoof. They rushed past half-conscious men lying on the floor.

The pack of minute snakes bounded out of the water, their hisses more frenzied by the moment.

"Faster," Padric urged, glancing over his shoulder. A mistake, as he slipped in a puddle of water and landed flat on his face. His hip and rib smarted.

Rawlins paused and glanced back.

"Keep going!" Padric shouted. Easier said than done. Scuttling to his hands and one knee, he dragged his dead leg behind him, the torch still in one hand. The grout in the tiles grated at his palm and knee. The thought of becoming a centaur crossed his mind, to either run faster or stomp the little monsters to death. But three legs would be even less useful than one at this juncture.

A white form dashed from behind one of the far pillars and out the door. It looked like a man with broad shoulders dressed in a hooded cream-colored cloak. *Who is that?*

Hissssss!

Despite their small size and crooked movements, the creatures caught up to him quickly, only one slithering pace away. Picking up his stride, extending his lead another arm length along the slippery tiles.

Rawlins sat Talfryn down behind the brazier. The knight waved for Padric to hurry.

Closing the gap, Padric chucked the torch into the brazier. In two seconds it blasted fire into the air.

The scuffling of the cerastes skidded along the tiles. Their hisses faltered. Behind the safety of the brazier, Padric nearly collided with the wall in his exhaustion. With a final gust of power, he kicked over the brazier. It spewed sparking coals, incense, and ash across the floor.

His strength waning, Padric crumpled to the ground, taking in great gulps of air. *One moment, then I will get up.*

If this terrible plan does not work, all three of us will be completely paralyzed shortly.

Slowly, the cerastes wriggled toward the brazier, their long tails swishing behind them. They halted three tail-lengths away from the coals, a few brave snakes inching within a hair's breadth of the glowing embers. "Maaaa…" they said as one.

The infant on Talfryn's face peeled part of itself off, mesmerized by the fire, then scurried down to be with its siblings.

Good arm folded to his chest, Rawlins kept vigilant, not daring to take his eyes off them.

Now that we have the creatures all in one place, how can we catch them if we cannot touch them? Fear froze Padric's blood as it dawned on him: they could be paralyzed forever.

Groggily, Talfryn poked at the red, puffy blotches on his face. "Mm fash not fell too well."

"What?" Padric asked.

"No' fell too well."

"Towel? That is it! Rawlins, get the towels. We can capture them yet."

So intent was he on the cerastes, Rawlins had completely ignored the table piled high with white towels. Removing a handful, he tossed a couple to Padric. He threw one at Talfryn, but it just unfurled over his head and onto his shoulders. "Oooh, darkkk."

Moving his aching appendages, Padric crawled close to the cerastes near the brazier. Rawlins came up on the other side. At the count of three, they deployed the towels and scooped up nearly half a dozen in each, then knotted them tightly.

The pounding of a dozen feet echoed along the tiles of the bath house. Six dryads entered the room, including Nalini and Eliva, their polearms at the ready for combat. Circe followed close behind, her staff, as always, in her hand. She frowned at the sight before her: men lying by the pool with red splotches all over their bodies. A few were awake and groaning, while others remained still. A pang shot through Padric, praying they were only paralyzed like him.

"M'lady," Padric said, trying—and failing—to get up off the floor.

"Just in time," Rawlins said, the two "bags" of wiggling cerastes dangling from his uninjured hand. "M'lady," he added gruffly.

Circe studied the three rumpled men near the fallen brazier, embers still popping, and the two towel-bags tied with wiggling creatures inside. She smirked. "I see we missed all the excitement."

"Just another day in the bath house, M'lady," Padric replied. "A bath *and* adventure all in one visit."

"So I see. Ladies, please assist these fine gentlemen to the infirmary." She indicated the wounded men by the pool.

The infirmary? Padric's heart did a little dance. *Is Brynwen there today? Does she have any remedies for infant cerastes poisoning?*

"And as for you gentlemen…it would appear you have a story to tell." She gestured for a towel-bag, and Rawlins reluctantly proffered one of his. Closing her eyes, she handled the bag and felt the little moving bulges. Her eyes shot open. "Thank the gods these were mere infant cerastes instead of adults—otherwise, you would all be very, very dead. The adults are not as forgiving, for their very bite can be a death sentence."

Padric gulped. He was lucky to only have only gotten attacked on the leg and part of his back.

"Dedwy?" Yanking the towel from his head, Talfryn's face was barely recognizable, a reflection of terror and red rashes.

The goddess's gaze met Padric's. "Very deadly. But I am sure they are too young to cause necrosis or madness in any of you. These infant cerastes must have come from my father's collection of exotic creatures."

Padric's face paled. "You have a collection of exotic creatures?" First lions, tigers, and bears, then *Cetea*, and now cerastes. He was afraid to ask what other creatures resided in this collection.

"Yes, but they should be secure."

"Clearly, that's not the case." Rawlins's eyes narrowed.

"We will double the security." Circe clenched her staff with white knuckles. "What I want to know is how ever did they get in here?"

"I have an idea," Padric said under his breath, but he did not elaborate. The body type under the cream-colored cloak was too short to match Warin, but it must have been one of his followers. Padric's shoulders sagged. Without proof, all that remained was conjecture.

"Come," Circe said, mistaking Padric's actions as weariness. "We will patch you up so you can continue work and training on the morrow."

Talfryn huffed. "Fanwathik."

CHAPTER 25

June 12, AD 1356

"I admit, this isn't so bad," Talfryn said the next morning, his hair and arms dangling around his face. His tongue still felt a bit puffy, but at least he could speak clearly for the most part. The swelling in his face had mostly gone down, too.

After the incident in the bath house with the cerastes, Circe took him, Padric, Rawlins, and the wounded men to the infirmary. She'd mixed up a large batch of a smelly liquid consisting of daffodil, rue, radish-seed, cumin, wine, and calamint. She and her dryads had made sure everyone drank every drop of the foul beverage before allowing those who could stand to go back to their business. Brynwen would've made sure everyone had something sweet to wash it down with afterward had she been there—*and didn't Padric's shoulders droop a bit at that?* Talfryn had almost been sick while taking it, but after an hour it began to take effect. In the morning, he and the others affected by it were deemed well enough to get back to grueling work—*if one could call feeling exhausted, stiff, and like they'd spent a whole night at the ale*

166

house in their cups being well enough to work, then yes, he'd agree without question.

He was still unsure how she did it, but Thimble managed to talk him into joining her in hanging upside down from the stable rafters. Nosey, the lucky dog, stayed on the ground. Still a bit shaky, it took an incredibly long time for Talfryn to make his way up, and Thimble both encouraged and laughed at him the entire time. *The things I do for vital information to save the world.*

"Now that you've lured me up here, it's my turn to ask you some questions," he said. Despite his hopes, hanging upside down did *not* help any of his ailments.

She eyed him in amusement, a wide, toothy grin spreading across her face. "Go right ahead."

"Your name, Thimble. What does it mean?"

"When I was born, my sister gave one look at me, scrunched up her nose, and said, 'Ma, that mite is small as a thimble. Put her back so she grows bigger.' Well, my mother decided to keep me just as I was. and I'm still me. The name's stuck since."

"I'm glad you've grown a bit, if nothing more than to spite your sister."

"Oh, I'm still small for my years. But the best part of bein' small is I can fit into tight spaces."

"Mm-hm," Talfryn said. "Being small can certainly help with that." Having worked on a farm all his life, the muscles on his arms and shoulders got in the way more times than not. Especially when his pesky goats would get themselves stuck in tight spaces. He knew he had to get to work soon, so he changed the subject. "So, what do you think of the Master?"

"Oh, he's usually nice, a little quirky. But he's been acting strange lately."

"Strange in what way?"

She furrowed her brow. "He'd go to bed in a happy mood, then upset the next morning. And he can't stop talking about the temple." She rolled her eyes. "He's possessed."

"Obsessed?"

"Yeah, that."

Circe had told Talfryn and Padric about Helius's strange behavior for the last couple of years, but especially since December. Thimble's comments backed up what the goddess had told them on the hill overlooking Cataractonium.

Warming to the topic, she gave him a conspiratorial grin. "I overheard my mother and sister talking about it once. M'lady had to stop letting other gods visit. They made him get all worked up."

"I'd probably do the same thing. Which gods did she ban?"

Thimble tapped a finger for each god or goddess she listed. "Ummm, the one with the laurels in her hair—she's a little strange. And then the one with the wings on his shoes is kinda wild, mother says. Has a nice smile, though. Oh, then there's the one that's got these two faces, one looking that way—" She pointed forward "—and one backwards." With the other hand, she pointed behind her.

Isn't that the one Padric mentioned the other day?

"Ugh, he gave me gooseflesh. I was really glad when M'lady banned him."

"Why?" Talfryn asked, an uncomfortable feeling creeping in. "What did he do?"

"He didn't do much. Pretty much stayed with Master, but when he'd come out to visit the grounds, he'd walk around like he owned the place. Used nice words and smiled a lot, but something about him just felt… wrong. My mother says Master'd get upset whenever he left, and M'lady and her son'd spend days or weeks getting him back to normal. It was a bad time. But he hasn't been back in a while, so we're good."

Talfryn thought the two-faced god sounded a lot like Sir Warin: *walking around like he owned the place and boasting and smiling a lot. Could they be related?*

She continued. "But M'lady'd let Jupiter inside in a blink, if he'd come. He hasn't, by the way."

"That's a shame. I'd sure like to meet the god of war."

"No, silly, he's the god of lightning and Mount Olympus."

"Whew, that's a relief! Last thing I need is the god of war coming down here."

Thimble's eyes grew wide. "They're here."

"Jupiter? Oh. Already? It's only..." He reached up to the rafter beam, but the act made him dizzy. His blood had settled in his brain, making his thoughts sluggish. "Thimble, I can't get down." Each second he looked for a way down, his brain became more frazzled.

Out of nowhere, something dangled in front of his face. Squinting, he saw a thick rope.

"Climb down, quick." Thimble was already halfway to the floor. "Talfryn!"

"I'm coming." He tried to cling to the rope. *Now if I can just get my legs to work...*

"Oh, you're taking too long. I'll go distract them. There's a hole in the wall of this stall."

"You're telling this to me now? This might've been great information the other day."

She winked, and before he blinked, she was gone.

"Thimble? Fine, leave me all alone, with this tiny rope," he grumbled. *I'm going to break my neck, aren't I?*

Wrapping the rope around his wrist three times, he uncurled his knees from the beam. The next thing he knew, he was on the ground, wind cast from his lungs, and coughing up straw. A cloud of dirt and straw dust billowed around him.

"I'm fine," he wheezed. "Don't mind me."

Feminine laughter caught his ears.

Perking up, Talfryn remembered the dryads' arrival was imminent. *The hole. There's a hole....a hole, a hole... come here little hole... Ah!*

A hole in the wall led to outside and freedom. He stuffed his head through the hole, then his right shoulder, and then...nothing. His left shoulder was stuck. Each time he pushed forward, his arm and shoulder embedded themselves further into the wood.

Nosey barked from outside the other end of the stables. "Nosey. Good boy. Come here." The dog rushed to his master and immediately set to licking his face with his long tongue.

"Good boy," Talfryn repeated. "Now, I need you to go and get—I'm happy to see you too, boy. Now—I'm quite drenched, thanks boy—can you get help—stop, Finn—er, Nosey—*Nosey...*"

"I told you to get going," a small voice said. "And here you are, lazing around on the ground."

Thimble crouched down to scratch behind Nosey's ears.

"I did," Talfryn said, not able to lift his head higher than her small, shoeless, green feet. "I seem to be a mite..." he pushed with his knees and winced as his arm pinched on the uneven stable wall. "Stuck."

"I have no problem squeezing through this hole."

"See, this is what happens when you labor for a living: massive shoulders."

"That's why I won't be a laborer. I'll be a huntress or a—"

"Would you mind helping me a bit here? My arm's going numb."

"Fine."

"Mmmrghrhh."

"What?" Thimble asked.

"You're foot's on my face!"

"Sorry. You're too big's all. Can you go back in?"

"Soon I'll become part of the stables myself."

"That's only happened once."

"What?"

"Umm, never mind."

By her expression, Talfryn had a sudden fear for his life.

"We need another strategy," he said. "Do you have something for a lever or a rope or something?"

Thimble looked thoughtful for a moment, then she said, "No, but I have a lion!"

"A...what now?"

But it was too late, she was already zipping away from the stables.

"I hope it's not a real lion," Talfryn called after her. An abundance of sweat accumulated on his neck and forehead. "She wouldn't bring a real lion here, would she, Nosey?"

Nosey's tail wagged as if excited about meeting the lion. Then again, like Finn, Nosey was excited to meet almost anyone.

Talfryn and Nosey waited an incredibly long while. He was more than likely already late for work. Luckily—or unluckily—no one wandered around the side of the stable. If anyone did, he would be beyond mortified, but would still beg for help. Maybe not Eliva, though. Then, he'd just wish for a quick end.

Nosey was in the midst of licking Talfryn's face for the twelfth time when his large ears pricked up.

"What is it, boy?" Talfryn asked.

Then Talfryn heard it. At first it was soft, but it grew louder; a rustling inside the stable, in or around Talfryn's stall, if he had to guess.

It started as a low growl. It was higher pitched than a lion, tiger, bear, or wolf.

Heart hammering at his rib cage, and trying to be as small as possible, Talfryn whispered, "Nosey, I need you to help me out of here before I become someone's breakfast."

Nosey kept on licking.

"Useless dog..."

The scuffling grew louder. Then—

Poke!

Talfryn's eyes bulged as something touched his leg. *This is it. It's the end.* "Nosey, this is important. Tell Bryn I—"

Bump.

Something tapped his bottom.

Above his taxing heartbeats, he thought he heard whispering from the other side of the wall. Then another bump, but harder.

It was all he could do not to flinch.

Just get it over with! He was about to sob when a dozen sharp needles attacked his bottom.

"Gahhhh!"

The next thing he knew, he was sitting ten feet away from the stables, panting, and very sore around the bottom, waist, and shoulder. Later, he would find a fair number of splinters embedded in his skin, and Brynwen would have to remove each one with the smallest tweezers she could find.

"See," said Thimble, sticking her head through the hole Talfryn had escaped from. "Got you out in no time. Good job, Pandra."

A furry golden muzzle appeared through the opening by her face, sniffing at the ground and open air. A curious little growl emitted from it.

"What is that?" Talfryn asked, even as Nosey moved over to explore the golden muzzle.

"This is the lion, you silly. I'll be right back around." She popped her head back into the stables, the small lion following her.

When she emerged around the corner, Talfryn got a good view of her small lion friend, Pandra, waddling at her side. It was only a cub. *A cub.* His cheeks turned bright red. *As if things couldn't get any more embarrassing, I was rescued by a mite-sized maid and her lion cub. Fantastic.*

Thimble stopped a couple feet away, but the cub meandered to his boots and began sniffing. The excitement over, Nosey smelled the lion cub, then decided to join in the perusal of Talfryn's boots. *What is it with animals and my boots?* Talfryn couldn't help but wonder.

"Thimble, where did all the dryads go?"

"Oh, I may have told them I saw a mouse in the stable. You should've seen their faces. They won't be back for a good long while."

Huh, even dryads who thrive in nature are afraid of mice. "Even, um, Eliva?"

"Even her. Though she looked a mite suspicious. What is it with you and her?"

"Nothing," Talfryn muttered. "Well, umm, thanks to you and your friend for getting me out. I've got to get to work now." With care he got up. He wouldn't have time to get to the healers, but he felt his tunic and leggings, and none of the holes seemed to be too large or in humiliating places. It looked about normal for him. "Which pegasus is it today?"

"Eous, who loves to fly."

"Eous, eh? Great. I'll be back tomorrow, first thing." Two more days, then he'd have the information on the pegasi he needed, then he'd be done.

"First thing," she said with a wide grin. Talfryn felt a little trepidation for what excitement lay in store on the morrow.

CHAPTER 26

Eight stalks of lavender, and two sprigs of comfrey. Brynwen ticked off the items in her basket for the herbal recipe Douse needed. "That should do it," she said to Miriel and Isemay.

"Finally." Miriel stomped off.

They picked up their baskets of plants and herbs and made their way through the streets toward the infirmary. There were a few possible paths, but she liked going past Helius's temple-in-progress, where she could sometimes see Talfryn and Leowyn at work.

A few times since the first trial, she had spotted Padric from afar. Unfortunately, she couldn't watch his practices or go anywhere near him when he was training. It infuriated her to find out Padric and her brother had been to the infirmary after the snake creatures had attacked the bath house. Her shift had ended not more than an hour before their arrival for treatment, and she had missed them entirely. It felt unfair.

Maybe it's for the best, she told herself for the hundredth time. *Besides, he has to save the world.* A knight did not, as a rule, fraternize with healers and midwives.

She saw neither her brother nor cousin as they strolled by the temple. They were likely in the quarry on the other side of the construction site. A little disappointed, Brynwen had just turned her head back to the road when she heard a crash and some men cry out from within the temple.

The breath caught in her throat—what if Talfryn and Leowyn were in there?

Without hesitation, she rushed to the temple. She didn't know if the others followed her, but she had to find out if they were injured. Even if it was someone else, they would certainly need a healer or three.

Nearly getting blindsided by a cart laden with white stone, Brynwen barely let out a "sorry" before barreling her way through the crowd that had formed in the last few seconds at the temple entrance. As she entered, a huffing Isemay and Miriel behind her, she stopped short.

Helius stood in the back, at least twenty feet tall!

Her heart fluttered when, after a second, she realized it was just his statue—but its likeness to the god was incredible. Even with being an all-white statue, it seemed real enough to the actual god that if they both stood together, it might be difficult to discern which was which.

Why does the statue have to be so large?

Having never been inside the temple before, Brynwen took a moment to observe the room. Long, slender columns stood at regular intervals along the outer edges of the interior, with the exception of one, which it lay in pieces on the floor.

Two men lay sprawled alongside the fallen column, covered in stones and dust. If they had been standing two feet closer to the statue, they would have been smashed flat.

Miriel froze at the door.

"Miriel?" Isemay said. "Are you all right?"

"It's just so big," Miriel said, peering all around, her eyes wide. "I knew it was big from the outside, but never came in before."

"Come on," Isemay said, bustling by Brynwen and Miriel, all business.

Remembering herself, Brynwen followed the red-haired maiden inside. Three other people entered behind them.

"Benny," Brynwen said, turning around. She grabbed the arm of one of the young men she knew from Chaddesden. "Can you please keep everyone else outside so we can work?"

"Aye." He turned around to block the door to prevent the room from becoming overwhelmed with spectators. *Who knew how many would be helpful in a medical situation?*

As they worked on the wounded, Brynwen wondered about the temple. According to Talfryn, Helius's chariot resided on the roof. Only a handful of people were allowed up there, and it was guarded at all times. Not even Talfryn's friend, Jarod, who was designing the crystal weapon for the chariot, had been there.

What if I somehow found a way to get up to the roof? If I could see the chariot, then I can tell Talfryn and Padric about its specifics.

Brynwen took what she hoped were innocent enough glances about the large room, wondering where the stairs might be.

She almost missed them. Behind the overly colossal statue of Helius, in the shadows to the left, she finally spied a spiral stairwell. A tall guard stood in front of it, spear in hand, not moving. The clothing he wore was strange, at least not anything like what men wore in Chaddesden and Nottingham. Leather with padding, and sandals with straps that twisted around his calves like snakes. He had cropped hair nearly to his scalp, and didn't move an inch. She had seen a few men dressed like him around Cataractonium. The couple she had heard spoke in an unfamiliar language, and when they spoke in English, it was with a deep accent. *Where are they from? Padric would probably know.*

Great, I found the stairs—but how do I get past the guard? According to Talfryn, Circe had trouble finding a way to the roof, even if she could appear out of nowhere. *Was it because of these soldiers, and are there more on the roof?* She hoped to find a way up, if only to deliver *some* information to Talfryn and Padric. They only had a few days left before the solstice.

Instructing Benny to let others in to help clean up and take the men to the infirmary, she mulled over a plan of action. *What I need is a distraction.* Once the workers got everyone out of the rubble, they would begin cleaning up, and there was quite a bit to move. *That is it!*

"Miriel." She turned her attention to her friend. "Could you ask that guard over there if he would be so kind as to assist these men with lifting those heavy stones?"

"Guard? What guard?"

"The one in the corner, over there."

Miriel squinted at the dark corner in question.

"Oh…I had not noticed him there. He looks quite intimidating."

"Don't stare," Isemay hissed.

"Why should he want to help?" Miriel asked. "These men seem to be doing all right."

The workers struggled with the stones, grunting and heaving.

"That man looks quite strong and I'm sure would be of great help. Besides, I want to see what's up the stairs."

Miriel started to turn around again to look at the corner, but decided against it. "Fine, but you take my next infirmary shift."

"We usually work the same shifts," Isemay pointed out.

Miriel pouted.

"It's for Padric."

Her face lit up like a ray of morning sunshine.

"You should have started with that," Isemay said with a grin.

Miriel was quickly on her feet and brushing off her pink dress. From the floor, Brynwen could see how worn the hem had become after so many weeks of wear. She refused to put on the peasant clothing provided by the dryads and resorted to washing her gown repeatedly.

Miriel sauntered over to the guard, hips swaying in a seductive way only a young woman used to getting her way could utilize to her advantage. The guard never looked at her, but continued to stare straight ahead, as if he were a statue. *He is flesh and blood, isn't he?*

At last, Miriel came within a couple feet of him. Her head bobbed as she spoke.

Brynwen and Isemay strained to hear, while looking busy checking on the wounds which were as well mended as could be, but they couldn't make out more than a few words on the up-beat. The guard never looked at Miriel, never interrupted her, never batted an eye.

It's not working, Brynwen thought as her heart plummeted. *Now what are we to do?*

Miriel must have said the right thing, for the guard's eyes shifted suddenly, and he mumbled what sounded to Brynwen like a grunt. He pushed past the maiden and came over, set his spear on the floor, and assisted the others, his back to the stairwell. The workers ogled at him for a moment, then returned to their tasks.

Apparently these special guards rarely help. I'll have to ask Miriel what she said to the guard.

A self-satisfied grin plastered on her face, Miriel waved them forward. Without hesitation, the two healers gathered their belongings and slunk over to the stairs. With one last look over her shoulder, Brynwen followed the other two up the tight staircase until they were well hidden from sight.

"Mir, what did you tell him?" Isemay asked before Brynwen could.

The maiden in question smirked. "A maiden has to have *some* secrets, does she not?" She chortled silently as she climbed the stairs.

Brynwen raised an eyebrow at Isemay, who shrugged.

Padric certainly hadn't exaggerated when he said Miriel usually got her way.

They burst into laughter, trying to quiet themselves before someone came investigating as they ascended the stairs.

"What is this?" Miriel paused on a short landing with a wooden door on the right inner side of the spiral stairwell.

Brynwen scrutinized it. "It couldn't be more than a storage closet, at most. But it has a door knocker on it," she pointed out. Sure enough, it had a little golden sun door knocker just above Brynwen's eye level. *What is this doing in the middle of an infrequently visited stairwell?*

With a tentative movement, Miriel reached toward the door latch, but paused three-quarters of the way there.

Impatient to move on, Brynwen twisted the latch, but it didn't budge. "It must be locked."

"Oh," Miriel said with disappointment. "That is a shame."

They traveled up the staircase single file, but saw no more strange doors during their ascent. However, the climb seemed long, much longer than it should, considering the height of the structure. It appeared to be three-stories tall, but the climb felt like at least four or even five.

Breathless, Brynwen nearly struck her head at the abrupt appearance of the ceiling. "Wait," she called a warning to the others.

Isemay and Miriel halted on the steps below her.

"What is it?" Isemay asked.

Brynwen raised her hands to the smooth wood above her, painted white to match the stone surrounding it. Vaguely, it reminded Brynwen of the trapdoor in the mausoleum in Mamucium that had almost ensnared her, Talfryn, and Padric in its lower level forever. She shivered at the memory.

"The steps end abruptly into the ceiling, but there is a door." A bronze handle stood out near the top step.

"At last!" Miriel burst out and plopped down on her step in an unladylike fashion. It was as though she had never climbed a staircase before.

Brynwen touched the bronze handle and pushed upward, but the trapdoor did not budge.

Isemay joined Brynwen at the top, huffing. "Does it open?"

"It doesn't seem to want to budge," Brynwen said. *Nothing is cooperating today.*

"Perhaps there's a lock?" They both searched around every cranny of the door, but found nothing resembling a keyhole.

"There has to be something," Brynwen said. "We can't have come all this way for nothing. Wait, what's this?" She spotted a tiny hole, no bigger than a needle. A couple of scratches marred the wood touching the hole. "Could this be something?"

"I wonder." Isemay studied the tiny hole. "Mir, may I borrow a hair pin? I have an idea. Mir?"

Brynwen peered down to where Miriel sat, but it was empty.

Where did she go?

"Miriel?" Isemay said, raising her voice a little.

No answer.

Not good. Brynwen and Isemay rushed down the spiral staircase.

Down, down, down so fast Brynwen thought she would trip on her skirts.

"There she is." Isemay pointed. "Miriel, wait!"

Brynwen spotted the worn-out pink hemline. Miriel had stopped in front of the door with the strange sun knocker, but this time, the door opened for her. The blonde maid entered without seeming to hear her friends calling.

"Miriel, don't go in there," Brynwen said. She reached out to the maid, but her hand brushed only air. The door slammed closed behind Miriel.

No! Brynwen and Isemay banged on the door, no longer worried about their own safety from the armed guard below. Miriel was in trouble. *And I brought her here.* After another fruitless minute, they gave up.

"What do we do now?" Isemay asked.

"I don't know," Brynwen replied, her heart plummeting to her feet. "I wish I knew where this door leads, we could meet her on the other side." For some reason, the thought sent a shiver to her spine. *Where does it lead?* "We need to keep calm and think of a plan."

She closed her eyes and leaned her forehead against the white stone doorframe, wondering when the guard would come up and seize them. He'd probably take her and Isemay to Helius. She had heard of some of the punishments dealt to those who broke the rules of Cataractonium. Never had she thought herself a rule-breaker, but here she was. *Rule-bender? Sometimes, when I must be. This isn't helping me find Miriel.*

Pacing up and down the stairs behind her, Isemay paused and gasped.

A light breeze brushed against Brynwen's cheeks, and the stairwell seemed to brighten behind her closed lids. Opening her eyes, Brynwen couldn't believe what she saw.

CHAPTER 27

The door creaked open, sunlight streaming through as though it led outside. Birdsong emanated from within, welcoming them forward.

Eyes wide, Isemay stared at Brynwen. "I didn't touch it."

"Nor did I."

"This isn't a closet, is it?"

"I don't think so."

"Do we go in?" Isemay asked with a shaky voice.

Her tongue tied, Brynwen could only nod. She pushed the door open all the way to reveal a woodland path. Trees canopied the earthen floor, leaving room for daylight to shine forth through the foliage. The path led straight and faded in the distance. Bird chirps came from everywhere. A hare crossed their path ten yards away. But Miriel was nowhere to be seen.

How is this possible? The enchantments from the first trial were amazing. But here, a whole forest was hidden behind a door. *Magic,* she was discovering, *is everywhere.* The arena had been dangerous, but who knew what lay behind what she saw in front of her? It seemed harmless, but her instincts warned her against it twofold.

"How far does it go?" Isemay asked.

"I don't know," Brynwen replied. She winced, feeling like she knew nothing of importance at all anymore. Her insides warred with one another. The atmosphere was warm and inviting, but her heart raced as though she had just run around the entire compound of Cataractonium twice.

"There is only one thing we can do. Go in and find Miriel."

Isemay bit her lip, then nodded.

Brynwen grasped Isemay's shaking hand and, bracing themselves, they entered the woodland together. One step. Then two. She didn't know what she expected, but the scene remained the same as when she and Isemay stepped through the door.

What tricks has Circe and Helius left for us? Vividly, she recalled her encounter with the woodsmen and the man in the cloak, when she had fallen to what would have been her death if not for Ulysses. It was just her and Isemay this time, and she had to remain strong.

A loud crashing of leaves and cracking branches came through the woods to their right.

"Miriel?" Isemay asked.

Brynwen listened intently. Maybe it was her trepidation of the place, but something seemed off about it. "Does Miriel make a habit of moving through the trees at a run?"

"Not typically. Despite her loud proclamations, she's quite graceful. Never a toe out of place, by her mother's personal instruction."

"That's a no, then."

"Mayhap we should go back."

They spun around, but the door was gone. The forest merely went on and on in both directions.

"No," Isemay cried.

"Not that way." Brynwen grabbed Isemay's arm.

They dashed to the opposite side of the path and stumbled into the trees, halting behind a medium-sized tree trunk. Brynwen prayed they would not be spotted.

As the noise grew louder, Brynwen was convinced it wasn't Miriel stomping her way noisily through the trees. As it drew closer, her desire to run grew. She had lived close enough to the forest outside Chaddesden to know this was no human.

It seemed as though forever passed before a large boar burst out of the trees. It paused on the path, two huge tusks gleaming in the sunlight shining through the foliage. It scanned the trees, then continued through to the side of the path where Brynwen and Isemay hid.

Brynwen began to breathe easier, until a figure lunged out of the trees, her feet making no noise whatsoever. Many more followed, too numerous to count, each as silent as the first. The only sound was the occasional whisper of wind through their clothes as they dashed through the forest. There was no mistaking their light green skin and long, dark hair. Dryads.

It was another twenty heartbeats before the boar's noisy departure became but a silent—though frightening—memory.

"I suggest we walk faster," Brynwen said as they got back on the trail. "The songbirds stopped singing once the boar came toward us, but they have resumed singing."

"If this place wasn't so full of wild beasts, and we weren't looking for Miriel, I would say this was a pleasant trip."

"I agree." And yet, she simmered inside at failing to get up onto the roof to view the chariot.

They continued on, constantly surveying their surroundings.

They walked for a long time, the scene always the same. The occasional deer or hare bounded across in front of them. Cheerful birds swooped down from the trees. She wished Nessie were in those trees so she could find help, as she had found Padric and Talfryn.

Isemay sniffled, wringing her hands together. "If anything has happened to Miriel, I will be beside myself. I'm supposed to be watching her. I'm—"

"Don't fret, Isemay, we will find her." Brynwen hoped her voice sounded more confident than she felt. Inside, she was a mess, and knew Isemay was no better off.

They came to a fork in the road but didn't know how to proceed. The one on the left was dark and full of deep fog, while the right was light and airy.

Isemay shivered. "Miriel would never go down the dark path."

"I don't know who would choose that path," Brynwen replied.

As they walked down the second, lighter path, the birds' chirping sounded merrier, the ribbons of sun shining through the tree canopy were brighter. Brynwen's trepidation diminished. *What was I so worried about?*

"Miriel is probably fine." Brynwen's steps slowed. "We shouldn't have to rush at all."

"You know, I think you're right," Isemay agreed. "I could curl up under a nice tree and stay a while. She wouldn't want us to worry, anyway."

"Of course not," Brynwen said. "I should bring Talfryn and Sir Padric here. They would love it, and could use some relaxation."

Isemay hummed a melody Brynwen hadn't heard before. Soon, she began humming along. After a few bars, more voices joined theirs. A chorus rose from seemingly everywhere at once, all in harmony, in a language she did not understand. Soft voices, filled with happiness and light, love and laughter.

Brynwen couldn't help but listen, the song absorbing into her, and the last dregs of her trepidation and fear subsided.

The sound of splashing water came from down the path and to the left. A cool splash in the water sounded wonderful, given the heat. In fact, the urge to go toward the water grew more and more inviting the more she thought about it.

A small trail veered from the main path, and Isemay followed behind Brynwen. Giggling came from up ahead. Isemay giggled with them.

In no time, the trees opened up, and they saw a pool of water. Seven young maidens with immaculate light blue skin surrounded a large rock at its center. Upon that rock, with her golden hair flowing freely, sat Miriel.

CHAPTER 28

The blue maidens giggled; two brushed Miriel's hair with shell combs and tied beads and pearls into the golden strands; one held each of her hands; the rest fussed over Miriel in general.

Miriel giggled with them, relaxed and at ease.

Some of the trepidation Brynwen had felt before taking the fork returned. *These young maidens look like dryads, but why are they blue instead of green?* The creeping feeling of Lilith sent stabbings of fear to her stomach. *Is this a trick? Did they fall into another trap? This time she was the one being lured, and Padric and Talfryn had no idea where she, Isemay, or Miriel were.*

"Miriel?" Isemay asked, her eyes calm. "May we join you and your friends?"

"By all means, come in, Iss, Brynwen," Miriel said. For the first time, the nymphs looked at the newcomers. They smiled warmly and waved their hands in welcome.

Isemay leaned over to remove her shoes.

"No, Isemay." Brynwen snapped fully out of the spell. "Don't go into the water. It's a trick, don't you see?"

Isemay stared at her blankly. "I see my friend having a wonderful time in a cool, refreshing pool surrounded by friends. Why wouldn't I join her? Relax, we could both use the break, Brynwen. Come on."

"We need to leave. Miriel, Isemay, come on. Remember what I told you about Lilith?" Just saying the name made Brynwen cringe. *Only holy water stopped Lilith last time. Do I have enough for these devious maidens?* She reached into her bag for the half-empty bottle.

"Oh, Lilith?" asked one of the maidens combing Miriel's hair. "She is horrible. No taste at all, and much too forward for my liking." She scrunched her nose in distaste.

Brynwen nodded eagerly, stalling for time. "I agree, she has no…wait —no taste?" She thought of her brother, who was good looking enough for any maiden; and of Padric, who was handsome and perfect and strong and kind and—

The blood rose to her face.

"Padric, who is most fair, Danallis," Miriel said matter-of-factly. "Lilith at least had good taste in him."

"Ohhh," said Danallis, realization dawning on her. "You knew someone who was charmed by her wiles." The other maidens whispered and nodded in agreement, then sighed in sympathy. "We are sorry for your loss. I am sure he was a good man."

Brynwen shook her head vehemently. "Oh no, he—they—"

"They? The succubus seduced two men at different times? That must have been rough for you."

"It was at the same time. But they both survived."

All the blue maidens' eyes grew wide. In a flash, they stopped pampering Miriel and swam closer to the shore, their curiosity piqued.

Left alone on her rock, Miriel whimpered. "My new friends? Are you coming back?" She seemed unable to decide whether to stay put or follow them and get wet.

How is she not already wet? Brynwen nearly stepped back, but she did not wish to show them fear. *This must be a fear tactic of theirs.*

Danallis asked, "Will you tell us of this miraculous encounter with the vile Lilith, O brave Brynwen?"

"Oh, there isn't much to tell, really—"

"Tell us, please," they all pleaded. Even Miriel, who had deserted her rock, begged to be regaled again with the drama.

Brynwen wished to roll her eyes but thought it would be rude. *Maybe they aren't as bad as Lilith.* "Then you will let us go?" she asked.

"We will," they chimed in harmonic unison.

"We would also like to brush your hair before you go!" said another one. She especially ogled Isemay's unruly red hair as if to say: *I am up for the challenge!*

Brynwen looked to Isemay, for it was her life on the line as well. The be-freckled maid seemed to have come back to her senses, as she returned her gaze with clear eyes.

"If they can do something with this mop of a mess upon my head, *and* let us leave, then I am agreeable," Isemay replied.

"Challenge accepted," the nymphs chorused.

Brynwen nodded. "Then I agree." Gathering her skirts, she sat down on a dry spot on the bank to tell the tale, all the while keeping her hand near the little bottle of holy water, just in case.

Brynwen began the story of when they first saw Mamucium and felt something was off about it. In the night, both Talfryn and Padric had walked as though in a wakeful dream. She told of her meeting with the succubus named Lilith, and their subsequent fight with her, how she had splashed the creature with holy water, how Padric's final blow had finished the evil creature forever, and how the forest had healed and spoken to her almost immediately afterward.

Shortly into the tale, half of the blue maidens emerged from the water and eagerly set upon the three human maidens, their shell and wood combs sliding through their hair like magic.

Danallis's eyes glistened. "It is a truly amazing story. We will sing songs of your bravery and the defeat of Lilith, who was once our sister but no more."

"She was once your sister?" Miriel asked.

"Oh yes, many, many moons ago. It was a sad time for many of us naiads."

Naiads. I wonder if the name means water nymph. It makes sense.

Danallis continued. "The Roman legionaries and the human inhabitants of this isle, the picts, were at war. There was little love left in the world. Lilith—her name then was Axichis—turned her back on our ways and thought she could exploit the men into loving her to change the tide of the war. If any of them rejected her, she…well, they never returned home.

"It became an obsession with her. How many men she could seduce in as many days. And how many unworthy dead she could leave in her wake. Finally, our leader made Axichis leave. The last we heard of her, she went to the western shore, toward the Roman fortress Mamucium, and took the name Lilith."

"That is indeed sad," Brynwen said. "But she will no longer hurt anyone."

The naiads shook their heads sadly.

Brynwen hadn't realized the late hour. "We should go. That is, if you will let us."

"Of course. We are pleased to have met you, Brynwen the Brave, Miriel the Beauty, and Isemay of the Challenging Hair." Brynwen grinned at the titles.

A smaller naiad stood up, her incandescent dress of blues and greens shimmering in the light. Her hands were clasped behind her back.

"What is it, Rhetia?" Danallis asked.

"I may have some information for you, Brynwen the Brave. Miriel the Beauty told us the story of how you came to the place of the Sorceress. Of how Ulysses the Winged One brought you there, and all you went through. I was out one day, and saw the Winged One fly past very fast in urgency. Then minutes later, he retraced his path just as quickly. Something shiny fell from his back when he flew by the first time. The Voice told me to follow it, and I did."

Brynwen's eyes grew wide. *The amulet?* She could not believe her good fortune. "You found the—" She stopped herself before saying it aloud. "The artifact?"

Rhetia shook her head sadly. "I searched for hours and hours, but could find nothing. I have not found it these two weeks."

All elation deflated from Brynwen like a squashed berry. At least she knew it didn't get swept away by the river or her cloaked attacker. But if this naiad could not find it in two weeks, what luck did she have in finding it in another week? What if someone else found it first? "Why do you tell me this? How did you know about it?"

"The moment you walked into this clearing, I knew you were its owner."

But I am not its owner. Padric is.

Rhetia must have seen Brynwen's confusion, for she smiled. "This artifact, as you call it, is meant for more than just a single person. I see three tied to this one object."

A strange twisting swirled in Brynwen's belly. Not of worry, but a mixture of excitement and wonder at what exactly that meant.

"But how will I find it if you didn't?"

"Fate has brought you here to us. I see something to help you in its location. Small, white, and round."

"Something small, white, and round?" Brynwen frowned. More riddles. Another one always cropped up at every turn. "Mayhap it *was* fate, our meeting." *Or perhaps a bit of prayer.* She felt lighter than when first hearing the naiads' song. "Thank you, Rhetia. You have given me hope."

"One last thing." Danallis stepped forward. "Be wary of the wild nymphs. They do not like humans in their part of the forest."

"We almost met them earlier," Isemay said. "They were chasing a boar."

"Then that boar will be long dead by now. You must go, and quickly. Continue on the main path until you see the portal. It will take you directly back to the sorceress's fortress."

"But how will we know what the portal looks like?" Brynwen asked.

"It is slightly different for everyone, so there is no use telling you what I see. You will know it when you see it."

Great! Another vague answer.

"Thank you for everything." Miriel gave each naiad a hug.

Once the maids were released from being smothered by the friendly naiads, they followed Danallis's instructions, but it wasn't long before they began arguing.

Miriel crossed her arms. "She said to go straight until we find the portal."

"But the main path veers here," Isemay replied.

"We need to search for the portal," Brynwen added, eyes darting this way and that for the so-called portal.

They argued for several minutes, getting nowhere, when a loud crashing noise sounded behind them.

Isemay's eyes became round. "Is that the same boar?"

"I thought it was dead," Miriel said.

"The nymphs aren't far behind. I suggest we run and ask questions later." Brynwen dashed down the path, the other two on her heels.

Moments later, the boar crashed through the trees and onto the path behind them, not stopping this time. Brynwen didn't look back, but she felt the eyes of the wild nymphs turn from their hunt and bore into the back of her skull.

"Faster," Brynwen cried.

A spear flashed past her head. The nymphs gained on them. They were no match for the speed of the boar.

You will know it when you see it. What a terrible clue!

"There it is," Miriel yelled, pointing at a thick tree trunk straight ahead with a cluster of honeysuckle sprouting by the roots. She ducked as an arrow sped past, parallel to her arm as though pointing the way.

"It's just a tree," Isemay yelled.

"Follow me," Miriel screamed. She plunged headlong into the tree and disappeared. A bewildered Isemay followed suit.

Bracing herself, Brynwen rushed at the tree and plummeted the last five feet to the hard floor. She landed with a thud; the air shoved out of her lungs. Straw and dust flew up, choking the remaining air around her. Groaning, she sat up and looked around. The portal had taken them to the stables.

"Uh, Bryn, how did you get here?" A very bewildered-looking Talfryn and a green dryad child stood by a horse stall, staring down at the three maidens who had fallen, as though from the heavens.

Brynwen groaned as she attempted to get to her feet. "We had a delightful walk through the woods."

"Oh," Talfryn said, "is…uh, is that all?"

"Mir, how did you know that tree was the portal?" Isemay asked, stiffly helping the blonde maiden to her feet.

"Well, if you must know, the moss at the bottom of the tree was on the south side, and anyone with any sense knows it mostly grows on the north side of a tree. So, I figured that must be it."

"But I didn't see any moss, only honeysuckle," Brynwen said, confused.

"And I saw blue berries," Isemay said. "Danallis did say we would all see different things."

"Oh, right, of course," Brynwen replied. Well, I'm very glad you knew about the moss, Miriel," Brynwen said with a furrowed brow. *How does Miriel know that?*

Whatever the case, Miriel amazed them a little bit every day.

CHAPTER 29

June 13, AD 1356

The sky had been overcast all morning, and the weather did not help Padric's mood. Despite Nalini's assurance that it would not rain, the knight kept looking to the sky for signs of droplets.

Training in and out of the arena was brutal. After the first trial, Circe allowed Padric and Warin to train separately in the arena every other day. She gave them whatever training aids they required, but none of the other men were allowed to train with them, because they were needed to finish the temple.

Helius kept everyone so busy, Padric rarely got to see his friends other than at the occasional evening meal. However, by a happy accident, they were given leave to attend Padric's training session for one day. Normally only Ulysses visited, so Padric was thrilled to see Talfryn, Rawlins, Leowyn, Serill, and Byron with Ulysses. Aeron was elsewhere.

Instead, she sent dryads and her special animals: mammoth lions, the occasional brown bear, or wolves—each wearing leather armor. That was all well and good, except they did not train in sword play. Mainly

Padric had to defend himself from polearms, daggers, staffs, claws, and sharp teeth. To add to the strangeness, the only weapons he was allowed were the short Roman legionary sword called a *gladius*, a small round shield called a buckler, and a short bow. He already knew how to use the bow, but it took some time to get used to the other weapons. It heartened him to know Warin would be at an equal disadvantage, having also to learn to use the legionary weapons.

During his training, he narrowly blocked a massive lion claw aiming to rip out his clavicle. Stopping half a pace away, the lion, Hark, roared its annoyance, the strength and heat of the bellow buffeted Padric's hair in every direction.

"I daresay, it would displease your mistress should you kill me," he reminded the enormous cat.

Hark growled and batted a paw at him. Padric leapt out of the way with a grin.

"But that does not mean you should not try." If he were to fight Warin in combat, he would need to defeat him. Too many times had he triumphed against Padric and the other Derby knights in the tourneys at home. He had almost done so during the first trial. Despite his great size, Warin was fast. Padric's new set of faun legs gave him an advantage, but he did not know if it was enough.

Lunging with his *gladius*, he locked eyes with the lion. It ducked and swiped at his legs. Padric leapt and twisted in the air, out of its reach. They danced and struck out at each other countless more times until they both had cuts and bruises all over their bodies.

As the routine became familiar, Padric's thoughts wandered to the next trial. According to Circe, the second trial would occur soon. Unfortunately, that was all the information she could get out of the god. However, she did mention he was becoming more obsessed with the timeline of the solstice.

The not knowing frustrated Padric more than anything. As did his ability to transform into a centaur at will, despite Circe's lessons. It only worked when he found himself under extreme pressure, as when Brynwen and Talfryn were in danger from the woodsmen and the cloaked man.

The dance ended when the huge lion body slammed him to the ground. He wheezed in pain as the animal crushed his windpipe.

"If you kill him now, there will be nothing left to play with later," Talfryn yelled from the stands.

When Padric could breathe again, he sat up. The lion sat next to him on its haunches, quietly licking a paw, seemingly unconcerned about the training exercise—a common distraction tactic he had come to recognize. It was not yet ready to end the game, but neither was he.

"Ready for the next round, Hark?" Padric stood up, gripping his aching chest. Nalini and Brynwen would berate him for this.

They danced around the arena again, this time with Padric's mind focused and intent on defeating the massive cat. Remembering his training, he sought the creature's strengths and weaknesses. Similar to humans, creature had their own differences and styles of fighting. In time, he discovered how its forepaws and teeth were its obvious strengths, whereas its back legs remained on the whole defenseless.

He feinted to the right, then leapt in the air to land near Hark's hindquarters. The lion's tail swished as a useless defense. Padric slashed at the armored leg, slicing through leather and flesh.

It was nothing a healer could not fix, Hark did not see his logic. His eyes turned coal-black, and his deafening roar could be heard all the way to York. He backhanded Padric clear across the arena. As he hurtled through the air, the lion's roar echoing in his head, Padric realized his folly with remorse toward the animal. This was not how an officer behaved. With a crack, his head struck the arena wall, and everything went black.

Groggily, Padric opened his eyes. Even with several bleary blinks, his vision remained misty, but he caught a flash of auburn hair glinting in the morning sun.

"At last, you're awake," came her voice. Soft and gentle.

His heart nearly burst at the sound.

"You came," he managed to say through dry lips. He didn't even recognize his own voice. "You've come back to me." But he could not remember quite where she had gone to in the first place.

"Did you miss me?"

"Of course. You were lost—"

She shushed him, a smirk playing on her lips. Her eyes lit up the world, and his heart danced. "I was never lost. Mayhap you just didn't look in the right place."

"I looked everywhere."

"Did you?" She paused, her mouth drawn in a line. "You should get up."

"My head spins. I think I will remain here a bit longer. Will you stay with me?"

"Sadly, I have to go."

Panic caused Padric's hand to shoot up, and his fingers curled around her wrist. "Nay, do not go."

She tensed at his touch.

"Not until I tell you something important. How I feel." He raised up onto his elbow and lifted his free arm, aware as each movement sent sharp needles stabbing mercilessly at his entire limb. His fingers caressed her stubbly cheek. "Do not leave me again, my sweet. I could not bear it."

"Oh. Well, yes," her voice became deeper. "I suppose I should probably shave first after stone laying. I mean, what would the other fellows think if I showed up with a full beard?"

Padric started, then blinked several times. As his vision cleared, he spied Talfryn kneeling over him, grinning with pleasant amusement. Rawlins, Serill, Leowyn, Byron, and Ulysses completed the circle around him, each trying in vain to quiet their snickering.

Padric felt his cheeks heat. He was sure they shone as crimson as his Derby uniform.

The twins' faces and hair are so similar...did I dream again? He ran a shaking hand through his hair and winced. "I thought..."

"Oh, you should see your face." Talfryn laughed whole-heartedly, almost falling onto his back in hysterics. "Red as a beet." Tears gathered in his eyes, then pooled over his cheeks. He wiped them away with a careless finger. "I haven't laughed that hard in a while."

Padric wanted to beat his jovial friends senseless for letting him carry on, embarrassing himself. He punched Talfryn in the arm and shoved Rawlins in the leg, then managed to stand without tipping over. He glared at the farmer.

"You could have said something."

"I tried."

"You did not try very hard."

Another wide grin. "You're right...I didn't." Everyone howled with laughter again.

"You won't live this down, my sweet," said Rawlins with a rare grin.

"Not likely," Padric replied, flush forming anew. He sighed, finding himself grinning and laughing with them. Even Hark seemed to carry a sappy grin on his maw.

A HOT BATH had relaxed Padric's tight muscles after the long day of training. Although his muscles had relaxed, his nerves and impatience had heightened. When not training with the dryads and animals in the arena, he shot at targets with the huntresses. Those were interesting sessions. Eliva participated, though she said little. She mainly kept to herself and set her sights on the targets instead of friendships. Her aloofness and skill intrigued Padric, helping him understand a little better why Talfryn was uncomfortable with discussing their fight.

Training for what, he did not know, but he surmised there must be a fight of some kind, most likely at least once with Warin. Padric tried to think about the heroes' trials in the myths, but it could be any number of things: fighting monsters, solving puzzles, heroic rescues—anything. For the umpteenth time, he wished to speak with Gregorio. His tutor and friend could have helped him sort out the many intricacies of Circe's world. Alas, he could only hope the older man was still alive.

Standing on his balcony with Ulysses, he viewed the cloudy evening sky. All the young men in the fortress had settled down in their pens for the night. It made Padric's stomach turn every time they transformed.

"Ulysses, did you find out anything more about the infant cerastes?" Padric asked.

The peryton shook his head, his antlers nearly scraping the outer wall of the guesthouse.

"I did not think so."

They watched the evening in silence for a few minutes before Padric pulled out a stoppered vial from his pocket. It had been in Brynwen's medicine satchel when they retrieved it from the river. The vial contained five layers of Brynwen's favorite herbs entwined together. "Brynwen's Miracle Mix." He smiled, recalling Talfryn's name for his sister's famous brew. Thinking he would never see her again, he had kept it as a memento.

He longed to camp out in front of the infirmary, to wait up all night until she arrived in the morning. To tell her—

No, he still thought it unwise to call too much attention to her, or to Miriel and Isemay, who all worked at the infirmary. He could never forget his ever-present animal guards, who saw and heard all. There was no telling how Helius could exploit them, or what Circe might have told the god. Padric had already drawn Rawlins, and Talfryn, and the others into his circle with the first trial. Sighing, he leaned against the wall of the balcony beside Ulysses and the glass door. The blue curtains swayed gently with the breeze.

Nalini popped her head around the door. Startled, Padric reached for his sword—which was not there. *Old habits.*

"Oh." Nalini's eyes widened. "Sir Padric, Ulysses, I did not mean to startle you. I knocked, but no one answered. I came to ask if you needed anything, and to give you news about the second trial."

Padric pushed off the wall to face her, his heart racing at her sudden entrance. Like Rawlins, she had a knack for sneaking up on people.

"Nalini. Forgive me, I did not hear you knock. What is this about the second trial?" he asked eagerly. Ulysses stood quietly regarding Nalini, and dipped his head slightly.

She stepped onto the cramped balcony, forcing Ulysses and Padric to shift, and gazed out into the night. She kept her eyes locked on the horizon. "Well, it is not exactly news, but a supposition."

"And that would be?"

"The Mistress believes it will be quite soon."

"Soon as in tomorrow? The day after?" It was all Padric could do not to shake her by the shoulders and demand more answers. "Is that all she has to say on the matter, that it will be soon?"

Finally, Nalini spun to face him, her eyes sparking as they beheld him. "Yes. Every day she does her utmost to get anything about the trials out of the Master, but he keeps his secrets closer to himself than he does his own hand. However," she lowered her voice, "she has noticed him acting increasingly secretive and excitable around her, like he is planning something considerable. I have seen it as well, and I believe it to be true." The drop in her gaze told Padric all he needed to know about Nalini's worry for the god. She had known him a long time, long before he began making plans to kill Jupiter's son Apollo out of vengeance.

Any excitement Padric had felt a moment before fled. "Well, I suppose it is more than I had before. Please give the Mistress my thanks for this news."

Nalini nodded, then tilted her head to Padric, her lip turned up thoughtfully. "I know this is not how you imagined you would be spending your days." She took a step closer, eyeing the little vial in Padric's hand. On impulse, he moved it behind his back, hiding the vial from view. Though she seemed trustworthy enough, she had no reason to know what it was, or what it meant to him. "But you have coped well so far."

For some reason, Nalini's comment grated on his nerves. For what seemed like an eternity, Padric had been going through the motions of playing Helius's games, tolerating Warin's incessant bravado, training until his body was stiff and sore, all the while aware of the solstice's impending approach. All the fears and frustrations he had been keeping down burst from his mouth before he could stop himself. "Cope? I did not come here to cope," he raised his voice. "Or to be comfortable, set in such luxury, whilst my friends and countrymen wallow in pens and overcrowded dormitories below." He waved his arm at his rooms, then out into the night. "I am here to help my people, and nothing more. I will do what I must to gain their freedom. That is all I want." He also wanted to stop the weapon which threatened to destroy the world and return home. If he failed, there would be no home for anyone to return to. By winning against Warin and becoming Helius's heir, Padric would remain in Cataratonium for the rest of his life as the god's servant, away from everyone and everything he knew; away from his vocation of knighthood; away from the maiden who had stolen his heart. He gazed at the low clouds, yearning to see the stars, some semblance of familiarity, but not even they would cooperate with him.

"Tut," Nalini said, green hands on her hips. She dared another step closer to Padric. Now she was less than an arm's length away. "Certainly that is not all you want. You desire something for yourself, do you not?"

"I do not have the luxury of desiring anything for myself."

"Nor anyone?"

"I...nay, I cannot." *Can she read my mind?*

"But what about the one who made you the trinket?" She nodded at the concealed vial. "Something assembled with so much care would not be given away lightly. She would only give it to someone she cared for deeply."

Padric's breath caught and clutched Brynwen's vial to his heart. But she had not given it to him, did not even know he had it. He recalled the first time he saw it, how she blushed, her eyes lightening the darkened shrine in Mamucium. It seemed so long ago.

"I can see no way to be with her while my duty is here. And afterward, should I win..." He shrugged. "She will return home."

"Ah, so she is here."

Drat. Too much information.

Nalini turned away as though uninterested. Her finger drew a line across the horizontal bar on the balcony and gazed lazily down on Cataractonium. "What would you give to see her again? To be with her?"

Padric's cheeks burned.

Anything.

He shoved off the wall. "That will be all for tonight. Thank you, Nalini."

Her eyes glittered. There was more she wished to say, to know, but instead she bowed her head deeply. "As you wish."

Padric and Ulysses followed her into the living room, and she glided toward the front door. Just before grabbing the latch, she spun around.

"For what it is worth, it is nice to have someone care for you. Love is not a luxury, but a gift. You should cherish each moment while you have it in your young, mortal life." With that, the dryad slipped out the door, the latch clicking behind her.

Padric's legs gave out, and he stumbled onto the couch, his head sinking into a large overstuffed pillow. After a few moments of his heart ripping itself to pieces, he flung himself off the velvety plush couch and strode past a confused Ulysses to the ornate mirror hanging over the white stone fireplace.

"How can you be so foolish?" he asked the face in the mirror. "To even entertain the idea of this ending up in your favor? You know well that once you complete the trials, you cannot hope to be with her, even for a short time. You will belong to him. She deserves more. Someone who will always be there for her." He almost swallowed his tongue. *Someone like Jasper.*

Jasper, the younger brother of Leowyn, who proposed to Brynwen before she left with Padric and Talfryn on their journey. He seemed like a decent fellow and was sure to be good to her and make her happy. His heart plunged to his hoofs as he trudged to bed, though he could hope for little sleep.

CHAPTER 30

Talfryn's little hedgehog legs tried to keep up with the bigger and faster bodies of Hay and Stack. The goats zipped through the fields of Chaddesden, tearing up greenery and leaving destruction in their path. They left little bits for Talfryn to munch on, to his chagrin. Angry villagers, Dunstan and Uncle Walter among them, wielded pitchforks and shouted threats at him and the goats.

Other farmers surrounded the three creatures, pinning them amid of their own destruction. The little hedgehog didn't know where to go. He tried running through the giants' legs, but they cut him off at the last second. The shouting grew increasingly loud. Farmer Dunstan hefted the creature up into the air, put his face directly into Talfryn's, and yelled at the top of his lungs.

"Talfryn."

Startled, Talfryn opened his eyes wide. A scene of chaos filled his vision. The air was thick with trouble. Men stood all around, fists clenched. It took a second for him to realize he had been dreaming.

Jarod, mouth in a frown, had a wad of Talfryn's shirt clenched in his fists. Talfryn shrugged his shirt free of the calloused hands.

"Gerroff me, you blighter!" shouted a deep voice behind Jarod.

Not again, Talfryn thought with a roll of his eyes. *Just once I'd like to wake up to some peace and quiet.*

"I'm s-s-sorry, Jack," said the young water carrier, Simon, in a squeaky voice. "I d-didn't mean to..."

"Didn't mean to what?"

Thwack. Thump.

Sighing, Talfryn launched to his feet, Jarod beside him. He was just in time to catch Simon before he hit the ground. The lad must have gotten up too close to Jack this morning. Everyone tried their best to give the foul-tempered man a wide berth, whether in animal or human form, but it was difficult in the tiny pen. Jack looked and acted every inch the badger he became at night.

"You might want to sit this one out, mate," he told the youth, patting his shoulder. The timid lad gave a myriad of nods and slid behind Talfryn and Jarod, trying to look very small, like the mouse he became between sundown and sunup.

"'Ey, I'm not finished with 'im yet," said Jack with a sneer that didn't help his looks one bit.

"Oi, Jack." Talfryn grinned widely. "Lovely as the day is new, you are. Always ready with a smile on your lips and a song in your mouth." *Though I can't imagine anything melodic ever coming out of that codfish of a mouth.* "I see you've greeted young Simon here with a most radiant welcome of the sun's rays."

All activity hushed, everyone standing in a semicircle around them. Talfryn searched out which ones were Jack's friends. *This is a bad idea,* he thought, scanning for an out. *A really bad idea. Today Thimble is to tell me about the fourth winged horse. I have to get this over with fast.*

"I..." Jack's eyes nearly crossed. "Well, I just, umm, you know?" The man actually blushed.

"Just showing him where to catch the best rays of sunlight, is that right?" Talfryn asked.

"Yeah," Jack said, his confidence returning. "Didn't want him catching all the sun and whatnot."

"Oh, never forget the whatnot." Talfryn nodded at his fellow pen-mates. "That's the most important part."

Jack responded to the rebuke in Talfryn's voice. "And what about you, sniveling in the corner?"

The circular pen...with corners. Right.

"On the contrary, I can sleep anywhere. Even in the shady 'corner.'"

"Then why don't you take another nap?" Jack stepped forward, arms swinging.

Talfryn easily sidestepped the first swipe, but the second swung right behind it into his chin. His teeth mashed together painfully and before he could readjust his balance, the pen erupted into chaos. Men and lads shouted at one another as fists flew freely.

So much for getting it over quickly.

Jack was already moving in for another fist to his face. Talfryn blocked, and they locked arms. Jack was much bigger, and was the stinkiest man in the pen, perhaps in the whole compound. The woodsman, Jeffrey, had been ripe, but Jack's foul stench of sweat and unwashed body beat them all. *Apparently, he never takes advantage of the Roman bath house only a block away.*

They grappled, as much as possible in the tight pen, bashed on all sides by furious men. The Roman gods had stolen these men from their families, stripped them of their freedom, then cooped them up together for too long. And Talfryn found himself in the middle of it all.

Out of the corner of his eye, he spied Jarod and Simon trying to keep out of the fray, though Jarod exchanged a few punches when necessary. Simon was in the process of climbing out of the pen when one of Jack's friends grabbed him by the scruff of his neck and dragged him back into the pen.

A couple of men locked in a fistfight battered their way through the crowd. Their antics dislodged the upper hand Talfryn had finally gotten. He stepped back and tripped on something, and all four of them went down in a heap of arms and legs. A sharp pain issued through his entire body as his head cracked against the wall, with the weight of three fully grown men on top of him.

When the other three scrambled up, Talfryn remained on the ground. His vision was murky and he couldn't hear much. Someone grabbed his shirt and mumbled garbled words, but another batted his hand away. Something shifted under his legs, but it took too much effort to try seeing what it was.

He blinked, and it took a while before he could open his eyes again.

"Come closer, Jarod, I can't hear you from there." Talfryn's own voice sounded far away.

His friend mumbled something, but he still couldn't hear it. Then Padric's face whittled its way into his view. His mouth opened, but Talfryn heard nothing above the ringing in his ears.

His mind wandered to Thimble. She was going to be annoyed by his tardiness. "Tell her I'll be a little late," he said, then all went dark.

"TALFRYN."

He raised his arms, ready for Jack to pummel him again.

"Talfryn," came the voice again.

"Do your worst," Talfryn said. His arms felt heavy from blocking so many punches. "I can take it."

"Tal," said the voice a third time. This time she sounded tired.

She? With a bit of effort, he opened one eye. Nothing happened, so he tried to open the second eye, but it wouldn't budge. It felt like he'd been punched in the face and kicked in the head by a goat.

"Bryn?" he asked, his sister's worried face coming into focus. *What is she doing here, in the men's pens? No, not in the pens.* He was inside a building, and from the feel under his fingertips, he lay on his side on a cot. "How did I get to the infirmary?"

"Jarod and Leowyn brought you in. You gave me a fright, brother. There was so much blood, and you wouldn't respond to any of us."

The blood drained from his face as he recalled his fight with Jack, but he couldn't recall what happened next.

"Rumor has it you started a brawl." Brynwen raised an eyebrow.

Talfryn smirked. "Nothing I couldn't handle."

"Tell that to the bloody knot on the back of your head and your eye swollen like a red apple. Any harder, and you would have crushed your skull. You are one lucky farmer."

Talfryn's hand went automatically to the thick bandage wrapped around his noggin. Sore to the touch, he didn't prod it much. Vaguely, he remembered trying to calm Jack down, which backfired like trying to stop Stack from climbing onto the roof—a weekly pastime for the wily goat. How he wished he could go back to dealing with animals and plants instead of people. He would take the mundane over unpredictable humans any day.

"Hmm, now I remember. I tripped."

"Why am I not surprised?"

"No, I mean, I think I tripped over something or someone. I nearly had him."

"Who tripped you?"

"I don't know. But," a realization struck him. "What time is it? How long was I out?" He made to get up, but his head immediately swam.

Brynwen pushed him back down. "Oh, no. You're not going anywhere."

"But I have to meet—"

"It can wait."

"It can't."

"It certainly can." She gave him the healer's eye. He'd loathed that look since he was a child; first from his mother, now his sister.

"No." He tried to concentrate through the distortions in his vision and his throbbing head. He squeezed his eyes shut to stop the spinning. "I need to see my friend. It's important."

"You can see them tomorrow."

"It'll be too late then."

Brynwen sighed. "Tal, the instant you stand up, you will fall over. I've seen it before in patients with head traumas. Will you please listen to me?"

He wanted to. He would love to stay in bed all day and do no work, but this was important. Padric had given him the duty to find out about Helius's horses, and he couldn't let him down. Or the world.

Talfryn shook his head. *Worst idea ever.* He grabbed Brynwen's wrist, partly to get her attention, and partly for support as his stomach twisted, its contents barely staying down. "Bryn, I have to meet her." *I have to see her every day, or it's all for naught. I also have to admit I like the spunky little dryad. She reminds me a lot of himself at her age.*

Brynwen patted his hand the way she always did during the rare times when Talfryn was distressed. And like always, it calmed his roiling stomach.

It was as if she read his mind when she said, "A cup of chamomile tea might hit the spot. I just brewed a new batch. I'll be right back." She gave his hand a squeeze and stood.

When she disappeared through the door to the herbarium, he made his move. As much as he wanted a mug of her famous chamomile tea, he needed to see Thimble. *It may already be too late.* A quick glance out one of the many windows revealed the sun had moved closer to noon than dawn. Regardless, he couldn't waste his chance to learn more about Helius's pegasi. It could be the difference between life and death for them all. *Moving the chariot, or at least the horses, before the god could take them out to kill Apollo might be our only chance.*

Mustering himself, he shimmied his legs toward the end of the bed. However, when he tried to pull the blanket off, it got stuck under his foot. He tried throwing it off, but it got jumbled up all over his legs. Scooting toward the end of the cot, his elbow slipped off the edge. The next thing he knew, he landed in a heap on the cool stone floor, the blanket twisted around his body.

A loud groan escaped his lips before he could stop it. His head pounded worse than before.

He hoped no one had noticed, but a dark shadow appeared over him, blocking the light.

"I was only gone fifteen seconds," Brynwen scolded. Steam wafted up from the wooden cup she held.

A whole group of young women stood around them. His cheeks burned with their stares. His sister set the cup down on the bedside table, then stooped to pick him up off the ground. She was assisted by a maiden with so much wild, flaming red hair it nearly swallowed his whole head when she leaned over him. A beautiful blonde maiden in a pink dress held a basket of freshly-rolled bandages. She never touched him, only scowled. *Wait, I've seen her before somewhere.*

As they got him back into bed, Talfryn remembered two of the maidens from his previous visit. The redhead and blonde were Padric's friends, the ones who had been kidnapped by Circe the day Padric received his new set of legs. Isemay and Miriel Wilmot.

"I know, I know." Talfryn held up both arms to his sister when she opened her mouth to berate him. "I should have listened to you and stayed put."

Brynwen's eyes reflected her disappointment. "Thank you, ladies. I can take care of him from here."

The others left to tend to other duties. Brynwen was quiet as she straightened his blanket, her mouth drawn in a tight line. Talfryn hated those moments the most. They reminded him of his childhood when his mother would scold him for doing something bad, like taking a piece of bread before mealtime or bringing the goats inside the cottage.

"I'm sorry, Bryn. I won't try to get up again." *How can I explain without explaining why I need to go?* No one else knew he'd befriended Thimble. Besides, what would happen if Helius found out? Talfryn didn't want to tell anyone about it until he had all the information for Padric. And they were running out of time.

"Wait." He gave her an accusatory look. "Did you set a blanket trap for me? Oh, you did. Just like all your patients at home."

"How else am I to get them to stay in bed?" She smirked, but her smile faded as she leaned closer. "Is this to do with," she mouthed the name *Padric.*

He nodded.

"Can I meet this friend for you?"

Talfryn considered it. He nodded once, then grimaced. "If you would," he replied. In a lower voice he said, "It's my friend from the stables. You met her after your adventures on the forest path."

"Oh, that little friend. She seems nice."

"She is, and I don't want to disappoint her. Can you go right away? It may already be too late."

"I'll see if the matron will let me."

"And *then* will you untie me from this bed?"

"We'll see." She grinned.

THE NEXT MORNING, when he was released from the infirmary—after lots of begging his sister and the matron to let him go—Talfryn made his way directly to the stables, Nosey at his heels. The mutt had stayed outside the infirmary door all night. Taking careful steps, Talfryn removed the head bandage. He made it in one piece, but barely managed not to pass out when his head started spinning. Nosey helped nudge and guide him when he faltered. He hated to admit it, but the mutt was more helpful than his own dog Finn.

Fine, maybe I'm not ready to be released, but I have to find Thimble. Her being the last piece needed for Padric to succeed and all since we'd lost the amulet. Brynwen couldn't find her at the stables, and he feared the little dryad was mad at him.

"Please be there," he begged for the fiftieth time that morning. "Padric needs this information. And if we don't die in a few days, I'd rather not be a hedgehog every night for the rest of my life."

The stable door made its familiar little squeak as he pushed it open. Not finding any signs of the other dryads, he closed the door behind him. The winged horses remained in their stalls, which was good news.

He took a step, then heard a rustling in a stall near the other end. *Was that a person or an animal?* Nosey barked at the noise.

"Thanks for announcing our presence, boy," he said with a dose of sarcasm. "Thimble?" he called out.

The rustling stopped. A stall door opened, and out popped a dryad. Not a small, wild-looking maid with short, uneven hair, but a tall maid with long braided hair trailing down her back.

Eliva.

Talfryn's stomach plummeted to his feet. *She's going to finish me off now, and it will be the end. I should just leave. Yep. I'm out of here.*

But his feet didn't move.

"Ummm," Talfryn said rather unintelligently.

The hint of a smile raised Eliva's lips as she slowly sauntered toward Talfryn. *Oh, she knows how much she makes me squirm. Luckily, I don't see any polearms or other weapons on her. I really hoped there's nothing deadly hidden in her skirts.*

"Is, uh, is Thimble here?" he finally managed to ask. His head began to throb again, and he leaned against the closest stall.

Eliva shook her head, a frown forming on her lips.

"Oh. Can you please tell her I came?"

"Thimble won't be coming anymore."

Now his stomach rose to lodge itself in his throat. "Why not?"

"She doesn't wish to see you. She mentioned a broken promise and is very upset." She lifted an eyebrow.

It was as he'd feared. Palms up, he took a tentative step forward. "I can explain."

Eliva held up a hand. "Nay, she doesn't wish to hear it. Mayhap you do not understand the power of a promise."

"But I do understand. It's just…an accident happened and—"

"It is final." She sighed, looking bored. "I would suggest you don't return if you know what is good for you."

Oh good, we're back to threats again.

He gulped. "All right, I understand. Can you please just tell her I'm sorry?"

"I shall."

"And can I say one last goodbye to the animals?"

She paused, regarding him like he had two heads. "I suppose that would be acceptable."

*Why did I ask that? Now I have to go past her, and she's going to murder me and hide my body beneath the horse trough, and…*But when he passed, she did none of those things. He made his goodbyes to the pegasi and the other animals, just as he would have done at home. *I miss Hay and Stack and Finn. They're at home while I'm doing…well, not accomplishing much, by the looks of it.*

Darn the luck that made him miss one of the vital things they needed to succeed against Helius. No amulet and no pegasi. *If I would have just minded my own business instead of jumping into Jack's face, things would all be different.*

A thought sparked in his mind to ask Eliva about the last Pegasus's name, but he quickly decided against it. *What if she turns me in for conspiring against her master? No, I can't risk that.*

Saying a quick farewell to the animals, he hurried out the door. *There has to be another way to get the answers. Or else we're all dead.*

❦

THE SHADOW APPROACHED the knight in the shade behind the furthest building in Cataractonium, close to the training fields.

Is all prepared?

"Yes, every precaution has been taken and bribes have been secured. Our targets will not suspect a thing. I relish in seeing de Clifton's face when he comes across our surprise."

If he lives long enough to see it. Indeed, it would be a tragedy if he died before we can present him with his surprise.

"I'm counting on him to have his own Roman tragedy. And in front of his lady love," the knight finished with a sneer.

Mayhap his lady love will also be instrumental in manipulating him to our purposes.

"Now *that* would be a story worthy of the gods."

CHAPTER 31

June 15, AD 1356

*B*rynwen knew he would come into the infirmary sooner or later. A handful of dryad and human maids brought him in, surrounding him as though a delicate rose, fawning over every smile blaring the enchanting dimple on his cheek despite his limp. The other healers present what they were doing to gape at him, the brave ones coming close and asking what they could do to help as they led him to an empty cot.

Sir Warin had arrived at the infirmary.

Brynwen only wished he was someone else. Someone with mossy green eyes.

Isemay heard her sigh and smirked. "He is quite handsome."

"What?" Brynwen asked. *Was I staring at him? Nooo.* Begrudgingly, she replied, "Oh, yes. But it appears Miriel has already moved in for the conquest." Even as she spoke, Miriel patted the huge knight's forehead with a damp towel, batting her eyelashes all the while. Sir Warin appeared to soak up every moment of it.

Scowling in disgust, Brynwen continued to fold the sheets, jabbing the corners into each other and nearly bowling over Isemay. "Sorry."

Unfazed, Isemay regarded her friend. "In my thinking, I'd say you've set your sights on a different young man." She grinned from ear to ear, her freckles dancing on her cute nose.

"Not likely." Brynwen unfolded and re-folded the towel. "I have too much work to do to think about men." *Handsome men who rarely came to visit. Only one time when I was here. What use do I have for the likes of them?*

Isemay raised her eyebrow. "Ah-hah."

For the next half hour, while the band of healers worked on the cuts on his legs, which he disclosed were from a group of massive lions during training, he regaled them with stories of his knighthood and heroism. During these tales, Brynwen ignored him, uninterested in what he had to say.

Eventually Douse had to drag all the admirers back to work. Closing his eyes, Warin laid back on his cot and folded his arms behind his head.

"You," he called as Brynwen hurried past his cot on her own business. "Miss, hold on a minute."

Drat, she thought. *What does he want now?* Taking a breath, she turned and gave him what she hoped was a pleasant, unassuming smile.

"May I help you, Sir Warin?"

He produced the charming smile that made most maidens swoon. It was all she could do to not roll her eyes.

"What is your name?" he asked.

"Brynwen Massen."

"Brynwen." He said it slowly and thoughtfully. "You look familiar. Have we met somewhere before?"

Is this how he seduces maidens? "I cannot say, sir. I am from Derbyshire."

"Derbyshire." He frowned. "I thought mayhap you hailed from Nottingham. You have been to our tourneys, then?"

"A few here and there." *Or all of them.* "I must be getting back to work now." Although the patient load was light, he needn't know it. She curtsied and took a step away.

"Wait. I have seen you somewhere else. Where was it?" She could see the wheels churning behind his eyes as he tried to think. "I will get it, fear not."

Somehow, his last statement made her nervous. *What is he playing at?* "Well, when you figure it out, please let me know." With that, she hurried away to her other tasks, and for the rest of the afternoon, she tried to keep away from his cot, hoping he would leave. Much to her frustration, he merely lay there, conversing with the healers and patients, until she had to go past his cot again to clean up a vacant bed.

"There you are, Miss Brynwen. I have figured it out."

She cringed as he said her name, but when she faced him, she plastered on her friendliest smile.

"Ulysses the winged stag brought you in, and I carried you here, to the infirmary."

Brynwen's breath halted. "You did? I...I don't remember much about that journey." Only bits and pieces came to mind, of fur and antlers. None of them were of Sir Warin, unless they were of his large brown boots. "Do you escort all the new arrivals to the infirmary?"

"Only the pretty ones." He flashed his winning smile. Cocking his head, he continued, "Masson, did you say? No relation to the dopey farmer friend of Sir Padric's, I hope."

"What of it?" Brynwen had her guard back up.

"You set out with them, didn't you? And something happened."

Why is he asking this? "We got separated." The memory of following the false-Padric, her every word falling on deaf ears, rushed back to her. She had fallen for his ruse, and would never forgive herself for it. It had cost her brother and friend great heartache when they thought she'd died, and nearly led to their deaths as well.

"He lost you?"

"No. I..." She blushed and changed the subject. "Why did you take up the challenge to be the Master's heir? Do you think you can do better than Sir Padric?"

He huffed a laugh. "I *know* I can do better than that jester. I have bested him and his men single-handedly at the tourneys. And besides, my legs look better."

"Winning tourneys doesn't necessarily prove you're the best qualified to be a godly heir." She had to wonder. Circe discovered Sir Warin was one of her descendants through one of her children. *Could he have received a prophecy too?*

He shrugged. "Mayhap not, but it certainly can't hurt. Look, de Clifton was not here all these months. He doesn't understand what we have been through."

"Do you know what he and my brother have been through to get here?"

"Do you know how long I and the others have been slaves here? How many months we have toiled and labored, day in and day out while you lot lazed in the sun?"

The young man in the cot next to them shot a glance at Brynwen, shaking his head.

Warin lowered his voice. "We have suffered hardships."

She bristled at his words. "Is that what you think we did? Sat around and celebrated the fact that our friends and loved ones were taken from us? We searched every single day, Sir Padric more than anyone. He sacrificed everything to get here."

"So he can be the Master's heir? I know him. He isn't up to the task."

"That's the thing, isn't it? You don't know him. You can't understand what's at stake. This isn't just some wager to win fame and riches, to be the hero of the hour. It is much bigger than all of us." Padric's prophecy came to mind, and the dread drained the blood from her face.

He must have seen the fear in her eyes, because he shifted on his cot. "Is that what he's told you?"

"Brynwen," Douse called. "I need you."

"I'm coming," she replied then spun back to Sir Warin. "Mayhap, instead of assuming everything is about you, try to think about others for once. And for the record, my brother may not be a knight or have a cent to his name, but he is loyal and one of the best people I know. He knows who his friends are. Do you?" She left him with his lips shaped in a perfect "o" as he pondered her final statement.

CHAPTER 32

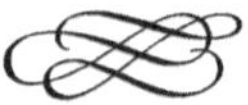

Clutching her basket the next afternoon, Brynwen perused the rows of freshly sprouted oregano in Circe's garden. She hoped to take a few sprouts for her own garden in Chaddesden, with the sorceress's permission, of course. The supplement would be a beneficial addition to her medicinal and food spice stores.

Brynwen carefully picked a few sprigs of oregano and reached for a handful of lavender. So engrossed was she in the abundant garden, she didn't hear the approaching footsteps until they were almost upon her. Startled out of her musings, Brynwen jumped, nearly ripping a couple of lavender leaves from their stalks.

She turned to discover the intruder, and spotted a young maiden with tinted green skin, her sheer dress swishing lazily in the light breeze.

"Oh, my apologies, I did not mean to startle you," said the maiden.

Brynwen released her grip on the plant and set down her basket, then brushed the dirt from her hands. "Not at all, you need not apologize. I was too engrossed in this glorious garden to hear your approach." *Haven't I seen her around before?*

The maiden smiled. "It is a grand garden, is it not? The Mistress insisted only the best herbs and vegetables be planted here. Sadly, she

"

could not get olives to grow here. The trees merely withered and died within the year, even though we tended them diligently."

"That is tragic," Brynwen agreed, although unfamiliar with the olive plant. "I have had my own share of disappointing plantings in the past." *Especially the year after my parents had passed away.*

The exotic maiden nodded knowingly and lifted an armful of empty baskets. "I have some plants to pick for the Mistress's cook. She specifically asked for cucumbers and a few choice spices."

"What is she making?"

"It is a delicacy to us, and our houseguests are dining with the Master and Mistress this evening. She wants them to have something exceptionally good before their second trial."

Brynwen nodded, but then caught the meaning. "Second trial? When will that be?" The solstice was only four days away. There was barely time for the last two trials to begin before then. And she still had not found the amulet, though she'd been looking for days among the grasses and trees around Cataractonium when she had the chance. Nor did she know what Rhetia meant by "something small, white, and round." She had practically ransacked her small pile of belongings for something white, but had found nothing of consequence beyond her roll of bandages and some linen strips.

"It will be soon." The dryad smiled serenely. Her eyes betrayed no emotion whatsoever. No hint of the trials to come, if indeed she knew what they were.

Perhaps it was time to take advantage of the locals for information. "What herbs are you looking for in particular? I can help, if you need. I have some time before I need to be back at the infirmary."

"That would be wonderful. I am Nalini."

"Brynwen." *So, this is the Nalini who Talfryn and Leowyn mentioned.* Returning to her knees, Brynwen picked what Nalini instructed, and they filled the dryad's baskets to the brink in no time, chatting all the while.

In the end, they filled five baskets, with enough food for about a quarter of the inhabitants of Chaddesden. As a rule, Padric ate light on the road. But she supposed other people would be at the feast Circe was preparing for his and Warin's benefit. A jealous pang issued through her chest, knowing she would not have a chance to see him during his meal, but Nalini would likely be there.

Brynwen suppressed a sad sigh. "Do you need assistance carrying all of this?"

"Alas, I did not think to bring a cart. Would you very much mind helping me carry them to the guest residence?"

"It would be my pleasure."

They balanced the baskets between them and walked toward the big guest residence. Brynwen could not believe her good fortune in meeting Nalini. *Perhaps I might chance a glance at Padric in the house. Maybe even have a word with him.*

CHAPTER 33

The scent of lavender and honey flowed through Padric's dreams. Overpowered them until he failed to recall what he had originally been dreaming. The scent brought about a soothing, calming effect, but it also filled him with longing.

He dreamed of Brynwen—her auburn hair, braided and hanging off her shoulder; hazel eyes, staring into his own. They stood in the ruins of Mamucium, holding hands, her face radiant in the sunlight. The lavender aroma washed over him anew, and he breathed in deeply, lost in her fragrance. Her lips parted and whispered his name. He took a step closer, trying to respond, but his mouth would not comply.

"Padric."

Darkness engulfed his vision. The dream was over, and his heart sank, but the scent lingered. He clung to it, willing it to stay, except it never faded. He had not imagined it.

Padric's eyes flew open and blinked rapidly to ebb the sleep away. Light came from his right. A shadow moved beside his bed. His vision cleared, and from the shadow emerged an arm and cloth. His eyes were drawn up the arm, alabaster in the candlelight, to the pale colored blouse and dark skirt, the bare neck, and smooth chin. The rest of her face was clouded, but a line of dark braided hair ran down her chest, almost to her waist.

A servant? Lavender filled his senses again, and he closed his eyes to absorb it. Struggling to see clearly, he peered up at her darkened face. His heart raced.

"Brynwen," he said softly, hopeful and yet unsure. *Could she be here with me? Do I still dream?* He reached up a tentative hand, then thought better of it and laid it back down on the bed. He stared at her face, willing the shadows to depart from her cheeks and eyes.

"It is me." She leaned over him. Her face passed into the candlelight, clearly revealing her high cheekbones and the flicker in her eyes as she smiled sweetly.

He struggled to sit, the pain in his muscles recalling the day's brutal training. He had only wanted a quick nap after the evening meal but must have fallen asleep.

As he rose to an elbow, he snatched up her hand, entwining her fingers with his. "I cannot believe..." His brain was too muddled for words. "I am so relieved to see you, but how do you come to be here?" he asked.

She giggled. "I used the door, silly."

"Nay, I mean..." He leaned back and laughed at his own sluggishness, wiping the sleep from his eyes. "I see that. But how did you slip past the servants and the wolf guarding my room?"

"I have my ways. A blacksmith gave me a brief lesson earlier. And," she swept a flyaway hair from her forehead, "there is more to being a farmer's daughter than milking cows." She lifted a glass, empty, save for the last droplets. His eyes widened in wonder. "No one was hurt, if you must know. Just a little drowsy."

Padric thought this a strange thing for her to say or do. "Bryn, why are you here?" He changed tactics when she pouted and squeezed her fingers. "I mean, I am glad you came, but it is dangerous. I cannot begin to imagine the consequences if you are caught."

Brynwen's face calmed, and she sat on the edge of the bed. "But I will not be caught. The rest of the household sleeps and I had to see you. You have gone through so much, I had to know you were well."

"As you can see, I am fine." He sat up and dangled his faun legs over the side of the bed, attempting to hide the wince of protest from the sore muscles.

He was very aware of how close Brynwen was to him, their shoulders almost touching. As much as he wanted her to stay, he knew she needed to leave for her own safety.

"Please Bryn, you must leave. Heli—the Master is very dangerous, and there is no telling what will happen to you should you linger long. I can escort you back downstairs to your dormitory, if you would like."

"But I want to stay." She traced the lines in his palm. "I have come all this way to see you. Even though you did not bother to search for me."

Stunned, Padric's mouth dropped open. "Nay, it was not like that. We searched all over for you. The river, the forest. When you fell—" The painful memory of her eyes crying for help before she disappeared over the cliff still haunted him. "Please Brynwen, I will always come for you. But it is not safe here. I ask you to leave for your own safety."

Brynwen looked up with a smirk. "My safety?"

He lowered his voice, though he knew it would not matter. "Helius has great power and knowledge. He can hear everything he wishes to hear."

"That is utter nonsense." She rested her head on his chest. Desire swept through him, and he had to gulp down his urge to kiss her. He was losing the battle, his fingers automatically combing through her silky hair.

"It is true. Please, let me take you back." He tried to push her off and get out of the bed, but Brynwen pulled back with such great force that he swung around and landed on his back across the mattress.

CHAPTER 34

Completely taken aback by Brynwen's great strength, Padric froze. She laid down next to him on the bed, holding his arm for dear life. "Please, Padric, don't make me leave. I wish to stay with you."

"Bryn, what are you doing? This is madness."

"Just hear me out." She released the pressure on his arm ever so slightly. "Please."

Padric tried to breathe normally and nodded. Brynwen leaned her chest and stomach onto his. With slow, seductive movements, her fingers caressed his cheek. The fingers she so deftly used to apply salves onto his wounds when they had first met; hands which had gently wrapped bandages around his body. Padric tried not to shudder at her touch, at her extreme closeness.

She whispered into his ear, "I want to be with you. This may be our only chance. Once you become the great champion, I will return home, but you will remain here. I want one night together."

The breath caught in his throat. Desire drew his face near hers, so close to those luscious lips. He had longed to kiss them for so long, and as he touched her more than he had ever dared, it was difficult to resist.

"Just one night," she repeated huskily. She leaned in and kissed him, first on the forehead, then both cheeks, and finally found his lips. He leaned in, but she pulled back and peered directly into his eyes, smiling knowingly.

His fingers caressed her cheek, cupped her chin. He breathed in the lavender and honey that lifted his soul every time she was near. She had a point. If he won the trials and saved the world, she would leave, which would break his heart all over again. This was no place for her, among Circe's court.

One night...He shook his head. He could not spoil her—for himself or for anyone else. She deserved so much more. His gut wrenched at the bitter thought. His mother and father had raised him better. *But she is so beautiful...Everything I want...My parents would be disappointed in me, of course. And her grandfather—*

Uttering a quiet sob, he gently pushed her away as his heart broke. "Bryn, no."

"No?" she repeated.

"No."

"Why not?" She sat up, flustered, then started fumbling with the ties at the back of her blouse. "Mayhap if I—"

Panic took over. Padric shot to a sitting position, grabbing her hands to prevent her from untying her clothes. "Please, Bryn. I—" He swallowed, his throat suddenly parched. "It is my turn to explain. As much as I want to, I cannot. I have obligated myself to Helius. If I win and stay with him, and you must go, would that be fair to you? If you were with child—what would you do? I would not be able to take care of you and the baby. I do not have the right to do that to you. Who will take care of you?"

"Grandfather and Talfryn—"

"Your grandfather wants to see you happily wed. Not to return home bearing the child of the man into whose hands he entrusted you. I gave him my word to keep you safe. Samuel and Talfryn will soon have wives and shall not desire the extra burden of a sister and her baby to care for."

"But we will be careful. We can take precautions."

A warning bell rang in his head, clanging and echoing in his eardrums. *What is she saying?*

He released her fingers, a waterfall of emotions and confusion engulfing him. But Brynwen scooped his hands up again in hers.

"We can run away together. You and me. We can hide where they will never find us."

"Before I complete the trials?"

She nodded vigorously. "I hear there is a little island off the coast of Africa that is very secluded. If we go immediately, we can find a boat to take us there."

Africa?

"Bryn, what are you saying? You would have us leave all these people to their fate? I cannot leave them to him. He will retain them as slaves for the rest of their lives, if they are not all destroyed first. I gave my word that I would complete these tasks or die trying. Would you have me break my oath? And what of the destruction that is to come?"

"I am sure he will release them someday."

"What of your brother, your friends? They will endure the same fate."

She looked away, suddenly seeming uncertain about her plan. "I didn't think about that..."

Deflated, he traced his thumbs along her slender fingers. "I know you would not leave them. You came with me to save them. I cannot understand why your sudden change of heart. Is it this place? Does it disagree with you so much that you would forsake everything and run away? How would we even escape?"

"I do not know what to think anymore. I am just so tired. There is so much work at the infirmary." She leaned forward again.

Padric pulled his face and shoulders away, which pained him even more.

"There is Jasper," he said hoarsely.

"Jasper?" She sounded perplexed, then curled her lip. "What about Jasper?"

"He is your beau, is he not? You should return to him as you are, pure. Perfect."

"But I don't want him. I want you."

"But are you not betrothed to him?"

Brynwen's face contorted in annoyance. "Forget about Jasper." She let go of him. "We are talking about you and me."

"I know he has feelings for you. He is a decent fellow and will be a good match for you. I cannot do anything that could ruin your reputation."

"Hang it all, Padric. I want you."

Padric was becoming annoyed. He folded his arms over his chest. "Why are you so adamant on doing this? Never have I seen you this forthcoming, other than in medicinal needs." Something else occurred to Padric. Something that had been at the back of his mind earlier. "Does not Talfryn milk the cow?"

"What?"

"Yes, I specifically remember Talfryn saying your grandfather is very superstitious, and believes the cow gives more milk to Talfryn than to anyone else in the family. So, he always does the milking. You said there was more to a farmer's daughter than milking cows, but you are not the one who milks them, are you?"

"It was a general expression."

He raised an eyebrow. "Was it?" He studied her face, but she betrayed no emotion. "Or did you merely recall it differently?"

She snapped back, "Well, I am too flustered. Forget it. It was a silly idea coming here."

"Nay," Padric said. *What happened?* She was acting peculiar, so unlike herself. "Mayhap you are under an enchantment. Is that why you cannot remember these things?"

Brynwen looked up at him. Anger and candlelight contorted her facial features. "First you wanted me to go, and now you want me to stay, and think someone jumbled my mind?" She stormed to her feet. "Well, I have had enough. Mayhap I *will* go to Jason after all."

"Jasper."

"Jasper!" She threw her arms in the air, making to leave.

"Wait," he said. *Something else is off. Not just the memories. Her great strength at throwing me onto the bed.* "Who are you really?"

Padric moved forward to grab Brynwen's hand as she scampered toward the closed door. He shook her arm. "Who are you?" he repeated, then yanked, forcing her to spin around. His eyes flashed, and she glowered.

"Why would you ask that? It's *me.*" She stepped closer and reached for his face with her free hand.

Padric caught the hand and held it. "You do not know who milks the cow."

"I told you, it was an expression. It meant nothing."

"You poisoned the servants."

"Just a small amount. They will be fine by morning. Mayhap a little groggy."

Padric furrowed his brow, not sharing her mirth. "And you would take precautions against having a child."

"Padric, those are trivialities."

"Nay, they are not. They are serious slips the real Brynwen would never do or say. Her conscience would not allow it. She would not milk the cow, because she wishes to please her grandfather's superstitious beliefs. She would never intentionally harm anyone. And she loves children too much to ever prevent one from being born."

The person masquerading as Brynwen yanked her hands away. "And what would you know about it? You are blind to everything going on around you. What about me—how *I* really feel?" "Stop this charade." Fear gripped his heart. "Tell me where she is. What have you done with her?"

The false Brynwen was momentarily flustered, then stood still and relaxed. "I concede. You win, Sir Padric de Clifton." More candles mysteriously lit up the room. Her voice became a little more husky. Her facial tone melted from white to green and her features jittered, then molded into a different person entirely.

Nalini stood across from him. Padric fell back against the wooden nightstand, almost toppling it over. "What is this?" he asked thickly, the deep hurt evident on his face. His arms hung limply at his sides. He had trusted Nalini, told her things he should never have divulged. *How could she betray me?*

"What have you done? Where is Brynwen?"

Nalini stood across from him. Padric fell back against the wooden nightstand, almost toppling it over. "What is this?" he asked thickly, the deep hurt clear on his face. His arms hung limply at his sides. He had trusted Nalini, told her things he should never have divulged. *How could she betray me?* "What have you done? Where is Brynwen?"

Nalini's face was smug, but her grin faltered. "She is unharmed. You have overcome the second trial, Sir Padric. A test of your honor as a man and a knight; to see if you would take advantage of the woman you love; to see if you can control your urges; to prove that you could set aside your heart's greatest desire and do the right thing. Fear not, your love is fine. Be grateful only your heart was wounded this time." The skin around her eyes crinkled in sadness as she glanced away.

Without another word, she spun around on her bare heel and fled the door closing silently behind her.

CHAPTER 35

Chest constricting, Padric dashed through the door with nearly enough force to rip it off its hinges.

He leaped past the startled half-asleep wolf outside the door, and practically flew down the narrow staircase, two steps at a time. His hoofs slammed on the ground at the bottom and he froze, nearly careening into Nalini's back.

She was in the midst of curtsying to a wide-eyed Circe and Ulysses. Circe gaped at her and Padric.

Recovering quickly, Padric grabbed Nalini's arm.

"Where is she?" he said through gritted teeth, chest heaving. Instead of answering, tears rushed down her cheeks. She yanked her arm free and flung herself down the hallway and out the front door. Padric rounded on Circe as the door slammed.

"What have you done with Brynwen?"

"Brynwen?" Confusion crossed her face.

"Where is she?"

Squeak!

For the first time, he noticed the hedgehog Circe held in her hands. It stared up at him with large hazel eyes.

Circe leaned back. "I assure you, I did nothing to her."

"Do not patronize me. Nalini did something to her, and she may need help."

The hedgehog barked.

"What did Nalini—ach," Circe cried and dropped the hedgehog. The quilled animal squeaked as it hit the polished floor, then scurried down the hallway to Padric's left. Shaking her fist in pain, the sorceress hissed. A dribble of golden ichor ran down her hand where the hedgehog had bitten her. "What was that for, you little rascal?"

But Padric was not done with the sorceress. "She is in danger." A dull banging reached his ears, along with the hedgehog's little claws scratching at a polished oaken door at the end of the hall. "What is that?"

The banging grew louder and more frantic.

Padric and Circe gaped at each other in astonishment, then rushed down the hall toward the hedgehog, Ulysses close behind. Padric reached the door first and tried the handle, but it was locked. "Stand back," he called to whomever was inside. Retreating a step, he bashed at the door with his shoulder, ignoring the ache in his arm.

"I have the key."

Ignoring the sorceress, Padric bashed the door a second time. It swung inward with a crash. The rodent did not wait for the others as he scampered inside the darkened room, nails tapping on the floor.

"Padric?"

The light from the hall fell on Brynwen as she stepped into view, her hair falling out of its braid and her skirt in rumples. Eyes glossy, she stared at Padric in confusion. His heart leapt. She raised a hand toward him and stumbled.

"Bryn!" Padric lunged forward and scooped her into his arms. Auburn hair fell about his arms as her head lolled to the side. *No!*

With a quick stride, he lay her on the couch and held her tight, breathing in her honey and lavender scent as he kissed her forehead. "Bryn, you are safe now." Light sparked behind him as Circe lit a candle. In the dim glow, he searched Brynwen's face for signs of scratches or bruising, but none were visible.

"What is wrong with her?"

Ulysses appeared next to Padric, his antlers filling the room. The peryton's reassuring presence tamped down some of the helplessness Padric felt.

Physically shaking, Brynwen clung to him for several heartbeats. "Padric, is it really you?" She reached up to cup his cheeks, then shaking her head, she pulled back and blinked hard. "Where did you come from? What happened? Where is Nalini?" She brought a hand to her temple and groaned.

Still concerned by her grogginess, Padric held her arms. "Bryn, what did she do to you?"

"Something in the tea."

Padric gasped. "Poison?" He turned to Circe in alarm.

The goddess shook her head. "Nay, but the tea was most certainly drugged. It appears my handmaiden wanted you out of the way, my dear."

A shadow filled the doorway as Helius materialized into the room.

"There you are, my champion," he cried with arms wide, gliding through the door in his violet night robes. "I have been looking all over the house for you. You have outdone yourself again. I am so proud of you." His grin spread from ear to ear.

Something heavy rattled inside Padric's chest. It burned inside until it started to boil in his veins. He lunged at the god, grabbing his robe in his fists, shoving him hard against the wall. "You are *proud* of me? You put me on display like a prize bull. What gives you the right to do that to me? To anyone? And what of Brynwen?" He pointed back at her. "Why bring her into this a'tall? She is innocent." Keeping his distance had done naught for her. He was such a fool for even trying it.

"I had to test you. Which you passed, by the way, with flying colors. Warin, on the other hand, did not fare as well in this trial." He shook his head in disappointment. "You have shown great restraint in matters of the heart and have demonstrated propriety, integrity, and loyalty. I must say, even Nalini would have fooled me had I not known her potion skills. I was impressed, to say the least. And the maiden was not hurt, so no harm done."

Padric's nostrils flared, and he released the god's clothes as though they burned his hands. "No harm done? Brynwen was harmed! This is not a game, sir. It is a shambles, a fraud, a hoax, all for your amusement. Were Nalini and I the night's great entertainment? Did you procure an audience to gape at us like at the first trial?" Lungs burning, he was dangerously close to striking the Titan.

A light shimmered near Helius's face, though he wore no jewelry, and he blinked. "Nonsense, it was all for the trials. I strategized every minute detail. The dryad had her instructions and performed them to perfection. Although she stumbled a bit at the end." He glanced at Circe. "I am sure you are appreciative that no harm came to your favorite servant."

Now it was Circe's turn to lash eye-daggers at the god. She gripped the small table until the wood groaned between her fingers. "Why would Nalini help you?"

Seeing he was not getting anywhere with his grandson or daughter, Helius scoffed. "Be realistic, Padric. You are young and will bounce back from this. Every mortal experiences this sort of thing at some point in their miserably short lives. Better to get it over with sooner rather than later."

The sorceress zipped around the table. "That is not fair, *Pater*. He should make his own choices, not be led by your whims of fancy." Her eyes grew wide. "Is this why you insisted on us all dining together this evening? So you could lure and drug this poor maid for your test?"

Padric whipped his head around to peer at her. "What?" Thinking upon it, Circe's guess made sense. Both Warin and Padric were present, and trying to make polite conversation with his greatest nemesis and immortal family member had been the most awkward dining experience of his life. The entire affair had been a strain on everyone but Helius, who seemed to enjoy his guests' discomfort. Padric finally understood. His hands shook at his sides.

A sigh escaped Helius's lips. "I see we are getting nowhere. Young man, it appears you need to let off some steam. I would suggest you take some of your energy to the training ground. It will help you prepare for the final trial."

Padric's eyes flickered. "And that will be when?" he ground out through gritted teeth. Little did he expect an outright answer.

The sun god inspected his manicured fingernails. "Oh, have I failed to provide that information?"

"The challenge is on the twentieth of June, is it not, *Pater?*" Circe asked.

A playful pout puckered Helius's lips. "Your humor has become quite stale of late, daughter. It must be the late hour. But no matter." He waved a dismissive hand. "You know me too well. Your final trial against Warin, young Padric, will be held at mid-morning on the twentieth, as Circe stated. All the masses will be in attendance to witness the announcement of my heir. Then the real festivities will begin."

"The solstice." Padric grimaced inwardly. *Of course it would be that day.* The prophecy rushed across his vision.

Did becoming Helius's heir really matter anymore? He had no amulet, no access to the chariot weapon. And only two days left until the end. *Two days.*

"When else, but to celebrate my feast day and the completion of my temple? I am giddy with anticipation."

Padric's eyes sparked as he beheld the father and daughter deities. "I do not suppose you will divulge any specifics?"

"Now where would be the amusement in that?" Helius asked.

"*Pater.*" Smoke circled around Circe as she fumed.

Helius's eyes grew wide. "Fine, fine. Padric, you will face off with Warin. Whoever wins will be my heir."

"I figured as much. How else would it end?" *Much like a duel to the death, I expect.* "Does Warin know?"

"He will be told first thing tomorrow."

Circe glared again.

"First thing, I promise."

Screwing up his face, Padric's eyes flashed in understanding. He would get no more from the god. Nor would he bestow any remorse for his actions, or inactions, this evening. This was not the Helius he spoke to in private the day of the first trial, the god who cared about his family and missed his grandson Telegonus deeply. This god had no remorse, no qualms about hurting others for his own amusement.

Resigning himself, Padric nodded and spun around to care for Brynwen. She was becoming more lucid and had raised her head from the pillow.

"And Padric, please do not take all your anger out on our lions. They do not deserve to be flayed alive," Helius chided.

Furrowing his brows, Padric turned back toward the god. A thought occurred to him, and he glared instead at Circe. "Did you know about this?"

A snort piped from the sorceress's beautiful lips. "I knew no such thing. Despite what you may think of me and those embellished ancient stories, I do not drug every single person I encounter. Now come, my dear," she said soothingly to Brynwen. "I have something that should be of use against your headache." A squeak drew her eyes down to the floor. In his haste to reach Brynwen, Padric had forgotten about the brown hedgehog, who was practically clawing at the poor maiden's skirt. It barked and squeaked frantically, cross at having been forgotten.

"You can come as well," Circe said to the little brown hedgehog. It barked excitedly and leaped into her outstretched hands.

Chest still heaving from his argument with Helius, Padric lifted Brynwen into his arms. She was lighter than he had expected. Without complaint, she rested her head at his neck and thought his heart would terminate right then and there.

Helius made to follow them out the door, but Circe lay a cautionary hand on her father's purple-clad chest. "Nay, you have done enough for today. Goodnight, *Pater.*"

CHAPTER 36

*H*er eyes closed tight against the spinning, Brynwen allowed herself to be carried by Padric as though she were light as a feather. They followed Circe down a set of stairs and then along a corridor, the air cooling the farther they descended. Brynwen's head felt clouded and her whole body shook. She rested her head on Padric's chest as they descended. His warmth radiated into her, and his scent of leather and cedar soothed her. She longed for it to last forever.

Her vision began to clear by the time they reached an ornate wooden door and entered a room that may have been a cave, lit by a dozen candles and torches.

There were several shelves and tables overflowing with spices, herbs, and jars of unusual specimens in the room. An entire wall was lined with leather-bound books, ranging in size from her forefinger to nearly two feet in length. On the parts of wall not concealed by crowded shelves hung ornate tapestries depicting heroes fighting ferocious monsters, men and women she assumed to be the gods, and one partic-ular god, presumably Helius, riding in his sun-chariot across the sky.

Two overstuffed couches completed the room, one in the corner, the other near the center of the room, and pillows and blankets were strewn everywhere. Circe halted in front of a table with a large metal bowl filled halfway with black, shimmery liquid. Brynwen's blood chilled at the sight. *Where are we?*

"My father will not hear us down here," Circe said. "I have placed wards against his fine ears. This is my own private room. Please, have a seat."

Padric set Brynwen down on the plush couch, then sat beside her and brushed the hair out of her face, his eyes searching for an ailment. It amused her how their roles had reversed. It was nice for someone to be taking care of her for once.

"Are you feeling any better?" he asked in a low voice.

Brynwen nodded and tried a smile. It was then she noticed the long slashes along his forearm. The claw marks were mostly healed, only the scabs remaining. She had heard he'd trained with lions and could only imagine what other recent scars he carried.

As the goddess perused her book collection, Brynwen realized they were sitting in the lair of the sorceress. She had them in her grasp and could do whatever she wanted to them. *But then why doesn't Padric seem more worried? He appears almost comfortable, as if he and the sorceress were old chums.*

Circe approached with the hedgehog in her arms. "If you are feeling better, you can hold him now. He has been fussing and fretting about you."

She interpreted the confusion on both of their faces. "Do you not recognize your own brother?"

Brynwen studied the squirming hedgehog, finally recognizing the hazel eyes. "Talfryn?"

A squeak came from the animal, and Circe plopped the creature into Brynwen's hands. Wide-eyed, she cradled the prickly hedgehog. She could not help but crack a smile as the fur around his eyes furrowed.

Circe placed a hand on her hip. "I was on my way to the guest house when I discovered this little fellow waiting with Ulysses at the door. I let them in just before Padric and Nalini came careening down the stairs. Your brother knew exactly where you were."

Snuggling him in her arms, Brynwen studied the little creature, still in disbelief that it was Talfryn, even though she knew what happened to him and the other men each evening. She did not mind his spines prickling her arms in the least. "How long did I sleep?"

"Hours, I should say." Circe moved to the bookshelf and peered at the numerous titles. "Nalini gave you a strong dose of sleeping potion."

"That's right. Tea with valerian root." She could still taste the bitterness of the tea in her mouth as memories came back one by one.

"Can you tell us what happened, Brynwen?" Padric asked.

Brynwen twirled her unbraided hair between her fingers as she berated herself for letting Nalini take advantage of her. She had seemed so nice. *I should have known better.* "Well, I helped Nalini find herbs this afternoon—it was today, wasn't it? Anyway, we brought them back to the guest residence and she invited me to tea. She said she had a special blend she wanted me to try. It had a strange flavor, but I couldn't place what it was, and thought nothing of it until I became drowsy. It was then I recognized the flavor I couldn't identify before: valerian root, which is a sedative. By then it was too late. When I awoke, I heard your voices outside the room and found the door locked." *And then the best sight I have seen in days crashed through the door to rescue me.*

Padric squeezed her hand, his eyes narrowing to slits. Brynwen could feel the anger emanate from his skin. "If she had hurt you, I…"

"Why would Nalini do that to me?" she asked.

Padric remained silent, his body stiffening beside her. The air seemed to grow colder in an instant. She suppressed the urge to shiver. "What is wrong? Padric?"

He ran an agitated hand through his curls. Finally, he brought up his gaze to hers. "I am afraid it was my fault. Nalini used you to get to me." He shifted his eyes away, rubbing the back of his neck.

She clutched his arm. "Did she hurt you?"

"No, not exactly."

"Then what happened?"

The faun turned his face to Brynwen's, brushing her hair back. "What matters is that neither of us came to harm." His lips touched her forehead, and her heart fluttered. But when she raised her gaze to him, his eyes did not spark. Something had happened. Something he did not wish to discuss. A dark part of her was annoyed with him for keeping secrets from her. But the concern in his face was genuine, so she pushed away the feeling. It was his to tell, whatever Nalini did.

Talfryn fussed in her lap, trying to gain her attention.

"Oh, Talfryn! Thank you so much for finding me, 'little' brother.'" She grinned widely as the hedgehog's needles rose up and down in irritation. His little nose wiggled, and she couldn't help but laugh at his helplessness.

"I think you want some attention, Tal," Padric said, a smile spreading on his face. "But woe to those who wish to pet you. Ouch." His laughter was music to Brynwen's ears. She hadn't realized how much she had missed his smile and laugh.

A shadow passed over them, and they looked up at Circe. "If you are all done making merry, I have a draught for your headache, Brynwen. Drink up."

Hesitating, she took the proffered drink in a metal teacup. "What's in it?"

"Camomile, hyssop, and something else to counter the effects of the sleeping draught."

"Something else?" Brynwen gulped.

"Just drink it," Circe demanded.

"She shan't bite." Padric smirked.

Furrowing her brow, Brynwen stared at the faun, and in a low voice asked, "How can you trust her after all she has done to you? To all of us?"

"It is a long story. I am not sure how much Talfryn has told you, but Circe is not as much to blame for everything as we thought. She is my grandmother." Brynwen eyed him skeptically. "Well, my many-times-great grandmother. Sixteen generations? Her father, Helius—who is my very-great grandfather—is behind everything. Circe was merely a pawn in his hands."

Was a pawn. "What is she now?"

"Someone we can count on, who wants to stop Helius as much as we do. We have no other course but to trust her." *For now, at least,* his eyes finished the thought.

Somewhat mollified, Brynwen sipped the drink with caution. Finding it actually tasted rather pleasant, she finished the cup in no time. She had just set the cup down when a soft grunt blew the hairs of her neck. She nearly jumped out of her shoes.

"Ulysses," Padric exclaimed with a smile. He bounded up and patted the stag's long furry neck.

Brynwen stared at the animal, her eyes wide, unbelieving. "This is Ulysses?"

Circe walked around her workbench. "Where are my manners? Brynwen, meet Ulysses. He is a peryton." The sorceress said this as though Brynwen knew what she meant. "He has been looking forward to meeting you officially."

"Yes, of course he has," she said unconvincingly. "Ulysses, it is an honor to finally meet you. It is you I must thank for rescuing me that day."

He gave a bob of his head.

"I have heard many wonderful things."

His eyes crinkled in what she took as a smile.

Padric got up and found a brush to comb the beast's fur near his right wing. Ulysses snorted happily. "Ulysses is also a blood relative," Padric explained.

That had Brynwen's attention. "Let me guess, your very-great great uncle."

Padric blushed. "Close. He is also my very-great grandfather."

The peryton huffed.

"Nay," Circe said to the animal, "you do not look a day over six hundred." The goddess approached the large stag and placed a loving hand upon his muzzle. The serene gaze she bestowed the creature gave away more than Brynwen could comprehend. In return, the stag moved into her touch, caressing at the same as time being caressed. Its great antlers moved fluidly, never once touching the beautiful woman standing next to him.

Brynwen watched the pair in wonder. With a blush, she realized she had been staring and glanced away. Suddenly feeling sleepy, she laid her head back on the couch and closed her eyes.

WHEN SHE AGAIN OPENED HER eyes a few minutes later, the headache had gone. *That is a magnificent potion!* she thought with a grin. *I must request the recipe from Circe.*

Padric was still brushing Ulysses's hide, so she looked around. She recognized many herbs and other ingredients on the shelves. Many of the jars contained specimens whose disturbing nature she would rather never see or mention ever again: eyeballs crammed into jars filled with a purplish liquid, dried bird's feet, rat tails. Someone with a weaker constitution might have passed out from fright.

Then she came to the books, putting to use the letter skills her mother had taught her. Perusing the tomes, she pulled out several, but many were in Greek or other languages she could not read. Her eyes were getting tired when one in particular drew her attention. Inspecting the faded black spine, there was nothing special about it. Her fingers tingled as she dislodged it from its place and opened the worn bound leather book. When she first peered at the text, the letters appeared to be in Latin, but then she blinked and could understand the words in English. She thought it odd, but the thought withered after what she found written there: illustrated descriptions and recipes of herbal and plant remedies and lore.

Glancing over several recipes, she stopped at one for treatment of apoplexy. It listed most of the ingredients growing in her garden. Only one item did she not have, but the hand-drawn picture next to it was a cluster of white snowberries.

Padric came to glance over her shoulder and his eyes grew wide. "Bryn, this is in Latin. How can you read it? Hold on, I have seen that berry. I shall return post haste. Do not move." He squeezed her arm tenderly, then dashed upstairs.

When he returned, he handed her a small cloth bundle tied with a brown string. "I found them the night we were attacked. My intent was to bring them back to you. Even when I thought you were dead, I could not bring myself to throw them away." He could not conceal the scarlet in his cheeks as he pulled out a vial with a variety of differing colors. "And this fell out of your satchel, and I kept it safe for you."

Brynwen chuckled at the vial. It seemed so long ago when she had made it, and Padric had first seen her experiment. "I see you like it. Please keep it, I want you to have it."

"But—"

"No buts. It is my gift to you." Her stomach fluttered as she said it. She focused on the cloth bundle in her hand.

"Thank you, I will persevere to keep it safe." He gave a little bow, his eyes bright, and she thought her stomach would fly away.

It took everything to concentrate and keep on task. With delicate fingers, she untied the string, drew back the folded cloth, and gasped. A handful of little white berries lay inside the cloth. Small, white, and round. Just like the ones in the recipe for apoplexy, as well as what Rhetia the naiad had described.

"What is it?" Padric asked in alarm.

"These berries, they might be the key to finding the amulet."

His eyebrows knit together as he contemplated her words. "How do you mean?"

Brynwen told him of her encounter with the blue naiads in the forest and what their seer, Rhetia, had said.

"They do fit the description. But how do they work?"

"That is what I must discover. Thank you for these." She placed the berries in her satchel, then planted a kiss on his cheek. She enjoyed the way his cheeks and neck bloomed with crimson.

"You two should get some sleep," Circe said from behind them, a cocky grin on her face. "For tomorrow is another long day."

"Yes, M'lady." Brynwen curtseyed. She scanned the recipe one last time, willing herself to memorize it before replacing the book back on the shelf. She struggled to let go of the binding, as though in the process she would lose a piece of herself.

"Of course, young midwife, you may borrow the book," Circe said, approaching. "May it come in handy for you. And Padric, if I do not speak to you before the trial, I wish you all the luck in the world." The sorceress gestured for the three guests to depart.

Brynwen's heart raced when a green house dryad entered the room, but it was not Nalini. The young dryad was there to chaperone Brynwen to her dormitory.

Ever the gentleman, Padric saw Brynwen and her hedgehog brother to the pens and her dormitory and wished them a good night. The faun held her hand for an extra heartbeat, then she watched his silhouette as the dormitory door closed, barring him from sight.

Now, peering at her new prizes in the moonlight from the dormitory window, *how to find an amulet of obsidian.*

CHAPTER 37

June 19, AD 1356

*P*sst!

"Did you say something?" Talfryn asked Jarod as they walked toward the food hall. It was the day before the Solstice, or Death Day as Talfryn wanted to call it.

"I didn't say anything."

"Must've been my stomach. I'm starving."

Psssst!

"Well, your stomach must be echoing, because I hear it coming from the stables."

"Are you sure?" Talfryn asked. "Because—"

Psssssssssttt!

"What could it be?" Talfryn asked.

"Could be rats."

The stable door was cracked open, and Talfryn thought he saw a dark head pop out for half a second. Why was she here? "Hmm, yes, it's a big rat, all right. Save me a seat." *I might as well get this over with.*

Peering around, Talfryn shuffled toward the stables until everyone in his group passed by.

The familiar animal and straw scent hit him as he opened the door. He breathed it in, reminiscing of home, family, and his goats Hay and Stack causing mischief. If all went well, he could go home again soon.

He opened his eyes and spotted the little green maid with short, uneven hair staring up at him, hands behind her back. She looked much the same as the last time he'd seen her.

"What are you doing here?" he asked.

"You stopped coming to the stables," Thimble replied matter-of-factly.

"I stopped because I heard you didn't want me coming around anymore."

"That's no excuse." Thimble folded her arms across her chest, a pout growing on her lips.

"It kind of is, though."

She glared at him, and he glared right back. Before Talfryn could give in, her shoulders sagged.

"Well, Mother doesn't want me to see you anymore. She thinks you're a bad infulse."

"Bad infulse? Is that a type of illness?"

"No, you know, *infulse.*" She waved her arms around as though it would drive the point home.

"Oooh, influence?" Great, Padric was rubbing off on him now with his learned words.

"That's what I said: influnce. It miiight have slipped how I'd used a lion to get you out of the barn."

He put his hands on his hips. "It just slipped out, eh?"

"Well, I mean, it was hilarious, and I had to tell someone. So, yeah. Oops."

"Right. So, if you're banned from seeing me…"

"'Banned' is a much better word than 'influnse'—"

"Then why am I here, Thimble? I don't want you to get into trouble on my account."

Peering intently at her feet, she poked a green toe at the straw. "I made you a promise."

"I thought I broke my promise by not coming."

"You did. But I didn't hear about your accident until a couple days later. My mother and Eliva thought I didn't need to know. I heard there was an alt—alter—alternation…"

"Altercation?" *Sheesh, where are these words coming from?*

"Yeah, that. Altercation in the pens, but didn't know who. I'm glad you're better, by the way."

"Thanks, me too." Aware of the time, Talfryn peered at the door. He wondered how long until anyone noticed he was missing. He only had a few minutes to eat before his shift at the temple began. "I hate to rush you, but…"

"Right." She snatched his hand and dragged him down the aisle. They stopped in front of the black winged horses. "You know the ones I told you about before? I made a song about them."

"A song?"

"Yeah, I get bored sometimes and make up songs. Now listen."

Like all the other dryads he had met, Thimble's voice was as sweet as honey when she sang. Her song included the first three horses she told him about before, plus the final one, stopping in front of each of the four larger pegasi in turn:

> *Pyrois the fiery one*
> *Leads the horses all day long.*
>
> *Eous, he who turns the sky*
> *Loves nothing better than to fly*
>
> *Aethon is the blazing one,*
> *She is the wonder of the sun.*
>
> *Phlegon, burning one so bright*
> *Fills the sky with eternal light.*

When the song was over, a tear fell from Talfryn's eye. It was so sweet, and Thimble sang with everything she had.

"Stop crying," she said, hands on her hips and rolling her eyes. "Now recite it back to me."

"All right."

She thankfully let Talfryn recite it back to her, without singing, a couple of times until he, for the most part, remembered it.

"Pyrois is the leader of the group. Eous likes flying through clouds. Aethon loves looking at the sun and compliments, especially about her mane. And Phlegon is the burning one and has a big sweet tooth."

"Bravo!" Thimble shouted and clapped excitedly.

"Well, thanks for everything." He shook her hand. "I won't be able to stop by tomorrow because of Solstice Day, but I probably could the day after." *Assuming we're still alive.* "Will you be at the final trial?"

"No," she replied sadly. "My mother won't let me go. It's not fair."

"I'm sure she has her reasons." He veered away from saying she was too young to see anyone fighting to death. That topic never went over well.

"Well," she said, "I hope Sir Padric wins tomorrow. You better go, they're here. And whatever you needed the pegasi's information for, I hope it comes in handy."

He grinned. "Oh yes, I'll have Sir Padric singing it in no time."

PART III
SOLSTICE

*"The difficulty is not so great to die for a friend as to find a
friend worth dying for."*
— Homer

CHAPTER 38

June 20, AD 1356

Padric had already inspected his quiver and all the arrows and sharpened his *gladius* to a fine edge on the grinding stone in the corner of the changing room, but he would check them again. The leather jerkin fit snugly around his torso and shoulders, yet was miraculously easy to maneuver in. Made with fine craftsmanship, he almost hated to wear it, knowing it could only be ruined with the day's events. The *manica*, a leather sleeve, covered his left arm and joined the *galerus*, a leather shoulder guard. However, he refused to wear the leg *greaves*, as they would impair his movements and didn't fit on his goat legs very well.

Taking a final look at the weapons, he handed them off to a dryad to take to the arena field. He was as ready as he would ever be.

The prophecy and the doom it promised once again flashed across his vision.

...To destroy the weapon of untold might

> *And rescue those of whom you seek*
> *Ere the sun attains its highest peak.*

So many thoughts and questions whirled around in his brain, it made him dizzy. The breakfast Circe had practically shoved down his throat threatened to come back up. All the people trapped in Cataractonium were counting on him to win. The overwhelming responsibility weighed heavily on him. *If I lose, what would happen to them? Will Sir Warin be able to destroy the weapon and free them? Will Helius keep his word and set the mortals free?*

A burst of noise down the hallway caught his attention. He turned toward the familiar voices. Rawlins, Byron, Serill, Leowyn, Aeron, and Talfryn clambered into the changing room and surrounded the champion.

Rawlins leaned with his casual calm against the wall and inspected Padric's fighting attire. A low whistle escaped his lips. "That is quite an outfit. Think the captain'll get us all matching sets when we return home?"

Despite everything, Padric found himself laughing with the others. "I suppose it is a bit ridiculous." He was still reluctant to wear the armored cap. Made specifically for his head, the helmet sat on the bench, with holes for his horns to stick through.

Talfryn picked up the helmet and studied it. "I suppose this is the only metal armor you get to wear." He set the helmet back on the bench.

"Lucky me."

Padric regarded the knights and farmer. He lowered his voice. "You all know what to do?"

Each one nodded gravely.

"Perfect. Then all we need to do is wait."

Everyone turned as a set of antlers poked through the doorway.

Padric's chest constricted. "It is time." He turned back to his friends. "Make sure you find good seats. I hear the arena is packed."

"Aye, Lieutenant." The knights saluted. Rawlins's eyes sparked in anticipation.

Padric smiled, hoping this was not the last time they would see each other. "At ease, gentlemen." He lifted the helmet and followed the already retreating Ulysses through the door.

Remember to breathe.

❧

ALICE'S BABY came two hours after dawn.

The newborn's healthy cries filled the infirmary. Neither the human nor dryad healers in the infirmary left once Alice began labor. They all wanted to witness this new life entering the world.

Brynwen could not have been more proud of her cousin. Alice was utterly exhausted, having been in labor all night, but she seemed to find extra energy as she held her little daughter in her arms and showed her off to everyone present.

"She is perfect," Alice said. She could not keep her eyes off the baby. Even when Brynwen tried to coax her to sleep, the new mother refused.

Brynwen was exhausted, along with Isemay and Miriel, whose voice was hoarse after singing dozens of songs to calm Alice over the course of the night. "You must rest at least for a little while. We promise to watch her." Brynwen's heart burst with love for the infant. Her blue eyes, her tiny fingers and toes, everything was perfect about her.

At the same time, the experience was bittersweet. Brynwen knew this might well be her last important action on earth, for if Padric did not stop the weapon in time, Alice's baby would only have a few hours of life. Happy ones for mother and baby, but then there would be nothing left.

Brynwen had not found the amulet, and it was almost time for the trial. She had searched everywhere while holding the berries, and even prayed to the Lord for guidance in its direction, but it never appeared. Rhetia must have been wrong about what she saw that night, or the berries were just normal snowberries, only good for pies and apoplexy.

"No buts, you need to get some rest now." Isemay smiled down at mother and baby. Alice nodded, and Isemay scooped up the newborn, however, moving the baby from her mother's warmth brought on a bout of crying. The tears broke Brynwen's heart.

"Hush, little one," Isemay cooed. "Your mother is right here."

"I have something that might help soothe her." Brynwen rummaged through her satchel to find the jar. "I made a concoction of lavender and chamomile oils for the baby. It's in here somewhere." Unfortunately, she hadn't had time to go through her stock lately. Removing a few jars from the satchel, she placed them on the table next to Alice's cot until she found the one she was looking for. "Here you are, little one." She proceeded to rub the oil over the baby's neck and chest with gentle strokes. In no time, the infant settled down in Isemay's arms.

As content as could be under the circumstances, Alice closed her eyes.

"You are a marvel at herbs and oils," Isemay said.

"She always has been," Alice replied, her eyes still closed. "Even when we were children, she always knew what was needed for an ailment."

Heat crept up Brynwen's face. "I learned from my mother and grandmother, that is all."

"Sure it is," Alice said with a grin.

A little while later, as Brynwen helped clean up the infirmary, Douse picked up the jar of snowberries Padric had given her.

"Brynwen, where did you get this?" the matron asked.

"They came from the forest between Mamucium and York."

"Interesting." Douse studied the berries some more and shook the bottle. "What do you have them for?"

"For research," Brynwen said, not willing to divulge any additional information.

"Research into what?"

"What is so special about these snowberries?" Brynwen asked. *Why is she so interested in them?*

"These are no snowberries. Or at least, not ordinary ones. This variety only grows in certain parts of England. They are plentiful on the continent, but here..." She gazed at them in wonder.

Brynwen bit her lip, trying to decide if she could trust her. It was a risk she would have to take. "I need to find something, an object, and those might be the key. Would you know how to use them?"

"I have seen it done, only once, but I do not have the ingredients. Only the Mistress might have what you need."

"The Mistress?" *What a fool I've been, not asking the one person in the room the night I received them. Instead, I had merely gone to bed and wasted days on a fruitless venture.* She glanced at the sun's location through the window. Almost mid-morning. She would have to hurry to catch Circe before the trial began.

༄

THE CHEERING of the crowd intensified as Padric strode down the torch-lit hallway to the arena, Ulysses at his side. The sun shone bright at the end of the tunnel. He took another deep breath, heart pounding, and calculated the strategies for his fight with Warin on the other side of the light.

"Wait!"

His breath hitched. Spinning on one hoof, he beheld Brynwen running toward him. Without hesitation, he darted to meet her, leaving the peryton staring after him. A spark of amusement flicked from Ulysses's eye.

When she caught up to him, they embraced. The scent of lavender and honey enveloped his senses, along with something else, something new. He could hold her for hours and years and never have enough of her. His heart twinged as he realized he might never have the chance to hold her again.

If Warin kills me—no, I cannot think it.

"Bryn. You came." His hand stroked the hair on her head.

"I am so sorry I'm late. Alice's baby arrived not long ago. I had to help her."

Padric pulled back just enough to peer into her eyes. Dark circles surrounded them, yet they were alive with wonder. "Of course, that is grand. And how are the new mother and child?"

Brynwen returned the smile, bright eyes reflecting the torchlight. "They are both well. The baby is beautiful."

Padric returned the smile. "They were—are in good hands. Take care of them, Brynwen."

The midwife probed his eyes. "You will be there to see them. You will."Her eyebrow raised knowingly. "And remember to breathe."

At that, she reached up and pulled his head down to meet hers. The gesture was so swift, he nearly buckled over. Their lips met, and the world vanished. It was just the two of them, together.

When the kiss ended, both gasped for breath.

Brynwen's eyes sparkled. Then she patted his chest. "If you die, I will kill you."

"Suddenly I regret giving you knife lessons." He gave her a wry smile, recalling the nearly disastrous first lesson she had received a few weeks prior.

Brynwen laughed and wrapped her arms around him again. "Please be careful," she said into his shoulder.

Padric held her for another heartbeat before replying. "I will do my best." He choked out the next sentence. "If I do not make it—"

"But you will."

He pulled back to hold her arms sternly. "Promise you will be happy, even without me."

"Nay, I cannot promise that," she said. Padric opened his mouth to protest, but she silenced him with a finger to his lips. "Padric, do not talk this way."

"Bryn..." Giving up, he shook his head and smiled.

All too soon, something nudged his side. He lifted his head to find a large set of antlers a hand's breadth from his face. He sighed inwardly. "I come, Ulysses."

The immortal peryton cocked his head to the side as if to say, *You are going to be late,* then continued down the hallway to the open arena.

Padric took a deep breath. Brynwen squeezed his hands. "Fight Padric. Fight with everything you have. I know you will beat them. I know it. May Christ keep you safe."

He stared into her hazel eyes, the flecks of green outshining the brown, rimmed red from fatigue. "With you and Him on my side, I will be victorious. I still have a few tricks up my sleeve." Giving her hand a final squeeze, he grazed his lips across her fingers, memorizing every inch of her. Then with great effort, he tore his gaze away, and followed the peryton to his destiny.

&a.

THE TASTE of Padric's salty lips on Brynwen's lingered even as he moved down the wide hallway to meet his fate. Her heart lurched for the man she loved. She finally had to admit it: she loved Padric de Clifton. "Lord, please protect him."

Maybe she shouldn't have kissed him, but she was glad it had happened, and would do it again in a heartbeat. She just prayed it wasn't the last…

Then something strange happened. His back to her, Padric moved down the hallway with deliberate strides. With each step, his resolve seemed higher, shoulders and back straighter, and height taller. She could feel it, his confidence lifting him. And then, his legs became human, enshrouded in brown leather trousers to match his fighting gear.

She blinked, and everything was returned to a few moments earlier, his legs curved and covered in furry gray hair. But his shoulders remained high. Wiping at her eyes, she wondered if her tiredness contributed to illusions.

"If you are finished ogling your swain, I will show you to your seat. You are to be a guest of honor."

Brynwen spun on her heel at the sound of the singsong voice. Staff in one hand, Circe placed her other hand on her hip. Her cerulean dress hugged her body, emphasizing every curve. Brynwen's surprise quickly changed to a wide grin. "Well, there you are, M'lady. That saved so much time. I thought I'd have to walk all the way around the arena."

Circe's eyes narrowed to slits. "What do you mean?"

Brynwen retrieved the jar of snowberries from her satchel. "We have a job to do, and no time to waste."

CHAPTER 39

The crowd cheered from the stands as Padric and Ulysses ambled into the arena. The scent of warm, fresh sand greeted him. Everyone was there, and all eyes were on Padric. *Wonderful.*

Sir Warin entered from a tunnel at the opposite end of the arena looking every bit the Roman gladiator. He wore a similar leather tunic, *galerus, manica, greaves,* and sandals with straps that wove halfway up his ample calves.

Following directly behind Ulysses, Padric's hoofs kicked up dust from the sand as he marched forward. With shoulders back and, he hoped, a blank expression, he halted next to the peryton mere feet from the edge of the arena wall closest to the emperor's box. A handbreadth away stood two unfinished wooden tables, each laden with various Roman-era weapons including a *gladius*—short sword, a buckler—small round shield, a bow with a quiver full of arrows, a set of *pugio*—daggers, a net, and a small mace.

About halfway up the audience sat the god Helius on his throne. However, for the first time since Padric's arrival in Cataractonium, the seat to Helius's right was empty. *Where is Circe?*

Sir Warin met Padric below the emperor's box, and they nodded courteously to each other. Padric considered trying one more attempt at apprising Warin of the impending catastrophe during the solstice. How in less than an hour, they could all die. As much as Padric despised and mistrusted the knight, he wondered if Warin would really want the world to end. *Would he help me stop it?*

Padric shifted his gaze upward to the Roman god raising his arms for silence. Despite his missing daughter, he seemed in perfect control of the situation as the audience settled down.

Helius's voice projected across the arena. "Welcome to one and all. Today we celebrate the completion of my temple. This would not have been possible without the intrinsic aid of each and every one of you. And though your prayers to me and my daughter at the various shrines littered around the fortress could have been utilized at a greater capacity, we prevailed nonetheless." He paused for emphasis. Padric held back a snort. Images of the whips descending on the builders' backs would haunt his memories for a lifetime.

"In celebration of its timely completion, I have prepared a treat for you. For the right of my heirdom, two challengers shall face off in combat. Our first challenger, Sir Padric de Clifton of Derbyshire, lieutenant of the first rank and my many-great grandson, will fight our second challenger, Sir Warin Ingram of Nottinghamshire, lieutenant of the first rank and also my many-great grandson." He waved an arm toward each knight as he introduced them.

"Challengers," Helius continued. "The rules of this challenge are three. First, you may use two weapons of your choosing. Second, you may fight with whatever means you see fit. Lastly, you will engage until one of you is utterly vanquished."

The last words rang around the arena, ending in an ominous silence.

Odd choice of wording, Padric mused. These Roman gods took everything seriously. But then again, things had not much changed in regard to war and power in Padric's own age.

The peryton's antlers shook ever so slightly. The nervous energy Ulysses gave off affected him enough that Padric had the urge to pat and comfort him.

"Sir Padric De Clifton, Sir Warin Ingram, do you accept these terms?"

Both knights accepted without argument.

"Choose your weapons."

With another quick scan of the weapons, Padric chose the *gladius* and buckler. He took the opportunity to check the straightness of his blade and the sturdiness of his shield. After so many things going wrong lately, he could not risk yet another setback. Any inaccuracy could mean his death.

Warin chose the mace and net. To display his abilities with each, he swung the mace overhead several times, the air swooshing each time it passed around. The crowd cheered and whistled at the display.

Padric held in the desire to roll his eyes. He could imagine Talfryn's response to Warin's antics and smiled.

Helius nodded. "Stances."

Padric spared a glance at Ulysses. "If anything happens to me, please protect my friends."

The peryton gazed into his eyes, unblinking. Padric could practically hear the winged stag saying, "I shall. And you shall triumph, grandson." Then Ulysses spread his wings, crouched on his haunches, and rose into the air. His wings caught the breeze to land in the emperor's box next to Helius.

The warriors moved to the center of the arena. Once there, Padric drew the *gladius* from the sheath on his back and gripped the *buckler's* handhold tight. While stretching his taught neck, he observed his opponent's posture: shoulders square, legs apart, chin thrust forward and up. The perfect setup for intimidation.

The prophecy raced in Padric's mind on endless repeat, warning him of the danger to come. He glanced at the sun's position. There was scarcely any time remaining.

"Warin, let us put aside our differences and part as friends."

Warin seemed to consider the proposal, his eyes turning to slits. "Oh, I do not know. I rather like being nemeses—keeps things interesting."

"Ready," Helius announced.

"Last chance to withdraw, de Clifton."

"I offer the same to you, Sir Warin," Padric said with a grin.

"Go!"

Gripping his sword tightly, Padric stepped into a slow arc with Warin, neither taking their eyes off the other. The moment seemed interminable.

"Shall we begin?" Padric asked.

"After you."

"I insist."

"Very well," Warin said. "May the best *man* win."

"Clever."

But Padric did not let Warin move first. They launched at each other simultaneously. Padric thrust and ducked as the mace swished past his face. As Warin spun, the weight of the mace pulled him down. It smashed into the ground, sending up a cloud of dust.

A quick kick to his rump sent Warin sprawling.

He leapt up with a growl, face red.

Perhaps not the best way to start a fight, Padric thought with a grimace.

They circled again, and this time Warin lunged first. Padric parried the mace, but the buckler got swallowed in Warin's net. It clattered to the ground.

Round they went, swiping and jabbing. Padric got knocked to the ground countless times. As they moved, Padric looked for an opportunity to retrieve his small shield. If he got hit with the mace, it would do irreparable damage to his body. But with every moment, they seemed to get further and further away from it—as though Warin planned it that way. Padric could only dodge the spiked weapon so many times. The only way to get to Warin was in close range—but the taller knight would have a similar problem with Padric.

"There's something I have been wondering." Padric parried another swipe with the mace, which clipped his horn and jarred his head. *Too close!*

"What?" Warin responded gruffly.

"How did you get the cerastes into the bath house?"

Warin threw up his net in defense. "I don't know…what you mean."

Better now than never.

Stepping in, Padric thrust toward Warin's stomach, the larger knight twisted his net around. Rolling under the net, Padric came up behind

Warin. He swung and nicked Warin's side, just enough to draw a thin line of blood. As Warin spun around, eyes gleaming, Padric leaped and rolled for the buckler. He brought it up just in time for the mace to smash into it. Bits of wood splintered off the side and into their faces.

A sharp pain lanced up Padric's arm. Wincing, he shoved at the mace, but Warin held firm.

A deafening trumpet blast filled the arena, followed directly by the screams of every person in the stands. Padric's ears rang with the sound of the trumpet-blast. The mace lifted, taking the shield with it.

"What is that?" Warin asked, peering up at the stands, a look of horror on his face.

Padric followed Warin's gaze and all the air left his lungs.

Easily one and a half times taller than an average person, and twice that in length, the monster had a human male face with long ivory horns affixed to its head. Instead of human hair, a brown and gold lion's mane flowed in wild wisps, followed by the sleek golden neck and body of a lion, which connected to massive, deadly paws. Instead of a short tail with a tuft of fur on its behind, a thick stalk of black armor reflected in the sunlight. Curved plates of polished armor curved up its back. But what really disturbed Padric was not the strange long tail itself, but what resided at the end. A black ball covered in spikes, much like a mace —a scorpion's tail—flailed every which way. An iron manacle encompassed each paw with links of chain dangling from them, as though they had been ripped from the floor or wall.

Is that a...a manticore?

The monster crawled around the top of the stands, causing havoc among the crowd. It chased and swiped at innocent people moving too close to it, batting them away like rag dolls.

Another unnatural trumpet blast emanated from the large human-like face. Angry spikes flew from its tail toward anyone within range, striking and injuring multiple targets at once. Its enormous paws pounded people around the stands, and its tail smashed into the stone like it was nothing. A group of armed dryads ran toward the monster, their polearms ready for combat. The manticore dispatched a handful of them with a single swipe of its paw.

According to Roman mythology, one touch of a manticore's spike point was lethal to any who touched it. *But where did the monster come from?* Then Padric remembered Circe mentioning her father's exotic creature collection...

Oh. Padric gulped back the lump in his throat. *We are so dead.*

CHAPTER 40

Brynwen coughed as the cloud of blue smoke dissipated around her. They were back in Circe's basement workshop in the guest residence, everything exactly as she had seen it a few days before. She swiped at it to clear the air. It did not smell like smoke from a fire, but more fragrant, as though several exotic spices had been mixed. *How did Circe get used to that?*

"Hand over those berries." Circe wasted no time.

A prickle of trepidation overcame Brynwen. She wondered if Circe would betray them or take the amulet for herself. *Don't be silly, Padric trusts her. But should he?* Unfortunately, she had no choice. Circe had helped her the other day when she didn't have to. Praying it wasn't a mistake, Brynwen handed over the jar of berries.

"Good. Now, find these ingredients for me." Circe rattled off a list of ingredients while Brynwen scrunched her nose at some of the items. She only hoped she had heard each item correctly, as she launched for the overfilled shelves of jars and boxes. Some items were normal, such as sage and witch's bane, while others were obscure: a rat's spleen, a beetle's antennae, and three raven tail feathers.

"How long does it take to make?" she asked.

"Only a few minutes. Gathering the ingredients for scrying takes the most time." Circe plopped the berries into a marble mortar and proceeded to crush them with a matching pestle.

Brynwen piled the items she procured from the shelves onto the table beside Circe. She peeked at the large scrying bowl, which still held dark liquid. She wondered what else the sorceress could see in it. *How much of our adventure with Padric and Talfryn had she witnessed before our arrival at Cataractonium? Or Padric's trial?*

"You forgot the lamb's breath."

"I don't know what that is."

Circe rolled her eyes. "And you call yourself a healer." She glided over to the shelf and plucked a jar filled with a whitish liquid.

"That looks nothing like lamb's breath."

"It is a lamb's breath mixed with equal parts summer rain and a fern. Now for the fun part," Circe gave Brynwen a conspiratorial smile. "I need you to crush these in the order I say."

Brynwen raised an eyebrow at her.

"Trust me, there is an order to everything."

"As long as we can find the amulet, I'll do whatever you ask."

"Good lass." Circe busied herself with reciting a lilting chant over the scrying bowl while mixing in the ingredients.

Unfortunately, there were no windows to see the sun's position so Brynwen couldn't know how Padric fared in his trial or whether Talfryn and the men were successful. She found herself tapping her foot on the floor. *How long is this going to take?*

"It is ready," Circe announced.

The contents of the scrying bowl swirled, a conglomeration of colors, bright and dull mixing together. Strangely, it reminded her of the jar of colored sand she had mixed weeks ago. As she stared, the colors swirled faster and faster, making Brynwen dizzy, and she thought she would lose herself in its chaos.

The liquid in the bowl lightened and slowly, as though looking through a cloud, and a picture floated to the surface.

Circe grinned. "I think it worked."

CHAPTER 41

The sane part of his brain screamed to *run, run, run away.* Nevertheless, with an intense amount of willpower, Padric pushed down the panic that threatened to consume him.

"Everyone, calm down," Helius shouted from the safety of the emperor's box.

The screaming crowd brought Padric's thoughts into focus. His friends were in there.

"Warin, we have to stop it," he called, but the tall knight only gawked at the huge beast, his eyes round with terror.

"Warin." Padric shook his shoulder. "Those people need our help."

The physical contact finally wok Warin from his stupor. He nodded blankly, then a swift resignation came over his features. "Let's go."

Padric leapt effortlessly over the eight-foot wall. He turned to offer a hand to Warin, but the knight was already hauling himself up with a loud grunt. Giving Padric an *I don't need your help* look, he raised his leg over the top of the wall.

Eliva and some other dryads ran down the stairs toward them, polearms in hand.

"What can we do?" Eliva asked. Four dryads stood beside her.

"Eliva, you and the war-maidens should help Warin get people to the exits."

"Of course," Eliva said.

"No," Warin said. "I can fight. I have friends here, too."

"Fine." A rush of relief flooded Padric at not having to do this alone.

"You can do this, Curse-breaker," Eliva said, then she and the dryads rushed off.

"Should we flank it?" Warin asked.

"That is as good an idea as any."

The manticore tooted another deafening trumpet blast as it launched a set of deadly spikes toward the dryads and populace. A handful of people were hit.

"*No,*" Padric cried, watching in horror as they went down. His chest threatened to cave in with despair. The manticore was turning the event into a massacre. Those innocent people were dead or would be shortly. People who had been taken from their homes and families, only to endure an even worse nightmare. *How is this happening?* The monster's rampage needed to stop. *Now, before anyone else dies.*

"We need to draw it away from them," Padric shouted over his shoulder. "I will draw it down toward the arena and you go in for the kill. But be on your guard, its spikes are deadly."

Warin nodded. "You've fought one before?"

"Not exactly."

"What does that mean?"

"I've read a bit. Now go."

They split up and flanked the creature. It took no notice of them until Padric beat his *gladius* against his buckler repeatedly. "Over here," he called.

The manticore turned its head toward Padric, its razor-sharp claws gleaming in the sunlight. Those claws could shred a man to bits, but he would gamble that they were not poisonous like the barbs in the tail. He also expected the fur over its hide to be tough, much like the armored tail. Padric squared his shoulders, adjusted the grip on his *gladius* and buckler, then lunged forward.

He leapt into the air and raised his *gladius.* The manticore's deadly claws scraped against the round shield, sending splinters everywhere. As he landed, the faun swung his *gladius* down on its arm. The blade struck below the elbow, but glanced off the tough fur. No cut, no blood.

The legend is true.

Before he could ruminate on it more, the manticore growled and smashed its powerful paw into Padric's shield, sending him sprawling down a handful of stairs. It swiveled its rump, and the spiked tail hurtled toward Padric's head. Before he regained his balance, the spines shot out from the tail directly at him.

CHAPTER 42

An exclamation escaped Padric's lips as he dove out of the way. Two spikes brushed against his jerkin and the fur on his legs. Two more skidded across the shield, leaving steaming scars on the wood. Most of the spikes skittered along the ground; some sank into the stone at an angle, shaking to and fro from the impact.

Padric's heart thudded hard, threatening to rip out of his ribcage. *That was too close.*

He glanced over and saw Eliva and the dryads making progress as they assisted the crowd down the exits. He thought Nalini joined them but could not be sure.

"Any time now, Warin." Padric glimpsed the tall knight smashing his mace into the manticore's armored tail. It bounced off without leaving even a dent. Warin bared his teeth and grunted.

"Working on it," came the gruff response.

The barbed tail quivered, then a volley of spikes darted out of it toward Warin. He dove out of the way just in time.

Then the two knights struck both sides of the manticore, causing it to growl and swing wildly in frustration.

Glaring at Padric, the manticore opened its mouth wide to release its anger in its horrible voice. A stone the size of Padric's fist crashed into the monster's head. The creature barely acknowledged the assault. It growled—much as a lion—and met with another stone to the cheek. Then one to the chest.

"Your voice is just awful, mate," Warin yelled from a short distance away. Narrowing its eyes, the creature pounced at Warin, but the knight was quick, and already making his way down the steps toward the arena. The monster followed close behind, swiping its massive paws at him. As Warin jumped from the ledge into the arena, the manticore's claws sliced at his back.

Warin cried out and toppled over the edge in a frantic flip, arms flailing as he fell.

"Warin!" Padric shouted as he followed them.

The manticore leapt over the edge. Bounding after it, Padric rolled on the arena floor. He grimaced as the gritty sand burrowed into his skin. Coming to a stop, he peered over at the manticore looming above Warin. The knight lay in a heap against the arena wall, unmoving.

A pang of regret ripped through Padric's chest for his rival. *Is he alive?*

Adamant on making sure its prey was dead, the manticore brought up a mighty paw and crashed it onto Warin's side. Padric's chest tightened as he witnessed the brutal attack on the knight's body. Despite their differences, Warin did not deserve such a death. Padric needed another weapon to stop the beast, as neither sword, mace, nor shield were a match for the manticore. Its hide was too tough. *What else can I use to defeat it?*

The monster landed another blow. Padric winced as he heard the crack of bone. Shooting to his hoofs, he took off running, willing the centaur inside of him to emerge. He pulled deep within himself. *Warin needs help.* But nothing happened.

Come on! he willed it again, then sunk deeper in concentration. His mind cleared, and at last it answered. The pain of the shift lasted but a moment, then he was running on four legs. Despite the situation, a grin broke out on his face. *I can do this.*

Padric charged straight for the manticore. As the monster raised its paw into the air, Padric smashed into its shoulder. It was like ramming into a boulder. Both manticore and centaur crashed to the ground.

His shoulder throbbing, Padric rose to his four hoofs. The manticore lifted its hulking mass slowly, eyes practically glowing as it studied Padric with his new set of legs.

By this point, the only people remaining to watch were Helius, Ulysses, four nymphs keeping guard, and about fifty people, either brave or foolish, on the far side of the arena. *Why are they still here?*

"Come on," Padric said with a wide grin. "I do not bite…much."

He barely brought the *gladius* up before the manticore charged at him. It was all Padric could do to parry and thrust, concentrating on his four legs not getting entangled together.

They locked gladius and paw. Padric held his own, glaring up into the creature's wild red eyes, when—

His heart nearly stopped. Those eyes, he had seen them before.

Light exploded in his vision as a heavy paw backhanded his rib cage, and the feeling of weightlessness took over his body.

CHAPTER 43

After what seemed an eternity, Padric crashed to the ground, his head bouncing off the sand; the air puffing out of his lungs. A groan escaped his lips. Every part of his body screamed in agony. The smell of sand and his own blood reached his nostrils, nearly made him gag. *Am I dying?*

The trumpet blast sounded different, something akin to a wail. Padric opened his eyes to find the manticore pawing at its face, dark blood oozing down its cheek.

"It bleeds?" Padric asked in wonder. *Perhaps it can be defeated after all.*

Unamused, the manticore glared at him with wild red eyes.

The eyes. Despite their redness, he could not shake the feeling of having seen them before. *But where?*

The manticore lunged in earnest, swinging its tail in a wild arc, eager to rip out his heart. Padric rolled away from the spikes, their deadly points scraping against his leather jerkin. Its strong paw smashed Padric onto his back on the compacted sand, the black manacles and chains clinking with the movement. Padric struggled against the creature, but its weight only allowed him to wriggle some. His *gladius* lay on the ground out of reach. His chest began to tighten, and not only from the pressure placed by the massive paws.

Stop. Think. Padric paused, working out how to escape, lessons from training as a squire and knight resurfacing. They seemed so long ago.

The bleeding face could be a weakness, but what else? Its belly? He thought of dozens of possibilities when a tingling sensation tickled his neck. A silver shimmer Padric had not noticed before ringed the manacles. *Magic. What magic resides in those manacles?*

The manticore snarled and bared three rows of razor-sharp teeth. Its breath filled his nostrils; the mingling stench of carrion and sweat was enough to make him gag. Its familiar, menacing red eyes glowered down at him. Padric bit back the mounting terror as the beast's teeth came for his throat.

A large sandaled foot appeared out of the corner of his vision.

"Not yet, he's mine," Warin exclaimed. He lunged at the creature with both the *gladius* and mace.

Padric could not believe it. "You are alive." Some of the tightness in his chest lessened. For once, Warin was a welcome sight.

"Took a little nap. Feeling better now." Warin's blows glanced off the tough fur. "How do we kill this thing?"

"Its face is vulnerable. Mayhap the stomach."

The manticore roared and struck out at Warin, its remaining forepaw adding additional crushing pressure to Padric's chest.

"Not helping," Padric muttered.

Padric's eye caught the light reflecting off something gold at the manticore's neck: a thin gold chain. *Why,* he wondered, *would a manticore have a decorative gold chain around its neck?*

Try as he might, there was no shaking the significance of the manticore's necklace. How strange to see the thin chain hanging around its thick neck, protected by dense golden fur. A curious realization dawned on him; the chain was identical to the one Gregorio wore. The chain which precariously held the tutor's heavy pendant.

But no, it could not be the same—could it? How did it get Gregorio's chain?

The manticore lowered its rows of teeth toward Padric's face, its intense red eyes piercing his own. The image of a set of brown eyes exactly mirroring the monster's caught in his throat. The gold chain, the eyes— "Nay. *It cannot be,*" Padric said aloud. A wave of nausea flooded over him. *"Gregorio?"*

What sick game is this? He shut his eyes as its hot, rancid breath swept over his skin and bounced around in his curls. Thick, yellow saliva oozed out of its mouth and onto his face. He grimaced at its warm touch, reminding him of far worse things he had seen of late.

Padric kicked out with two hoofs, while Warin struck its chest with his mace. Startled, the human face of the manticore retracted its teeth a fraction and let out a whimper. It was just the release Padric needed. His elbow jutted up into the monster's jaw. It released its hold on his chest, trying to regain its balance.

"Again," Warin instructed.

They struck its chest again, hearing the crunch of a cracked rib. When the manticore rose, Padric took the chance to shimmy away.

The manticore's scream curdled Padric's blood. He cringed on the ground, hands over his ears to muffle the excruciating sounds. *Are we killing Gregorio?*

When he opened his eyes a moment later, ears still ringing, his faun legs returned. Warin was on his knees, hands over his ears, face contorted in agony. The manticore's tail slashed around. Deadly spikes flew everywhere, landing harmlessly on the ground until they let loose in Warin's direction.

"Warin!"

Padric bolted over to the knight and shoved him out of the way. When the barrage halted, Padric rolled to a stop. Sharp pain slashed through his chest like a serrated knife, making him gasp. Daring a glance down, he cringed at the large red streak sliced through the leather. Crimson blood trickled out of the wound. It burned like fire through his body to his very core.

The manticore struck with an intensity which only a berserker could encapsulate. Warin stepped in and deflected its paw with jarring force. They grappled together, Warin holding his own.

Padric picked up and gripped his *gladius* tightly, arranging his fingers carefully along the handle. He paused for breath, ignoring his aching body.

The manticore's powerful manacled paws swiped at Warin. It let out a trumpet blast of frustration and knocked Warin to the ground.

"We cannot kill it." Padric turned to the large knight.

"What?" Warin screwed up his face in confusion. "You're joking."

"This is no ordinary monster. It is my friend Gregorio Fiori."

"He's not acting very friendly to me." Warin batted away another paw.

"He must have been transformed somehow. Regardless, we cannot kill him."

"Then what do you suggest we do, oh Knowledgeable One?"

Wracking his brain for a quick solution, Padric hobbled over to the discarded net lying on the ground. An idea formed in his mind with quick precision.

"We need to remove the manacles. They are magical." He had no idea if that would change Gregorio back, but he had to try.

Warin discarded his broken *gladius*. "Hand me the net. I'll distract it this time."

He nodded and tossed the net at Warin's feet. "Scatter when I say the word." Steeling himself, Padric rushed at the manticore's tail. He hacked at the spiked tail once. Twice. Thrice. The tail jerked in agitation, and the manticore wailed.

It grew angrier when Warin caught its paw in his net, letting loose another deafening trumpet-blast. Nevertheless, Warin refused to let go. "Hurry up!"

The spikes shot out of the manticore's tail with a vengeance. Padric pounced out of the way, running in a small circle toward its front side, as the beast left a line of deadly spikes sticking out of the ground.

"Run," Padric shouted, the spikes hitting the dirt behind him.

Warin dropped the net and fled.

Padric tucked and spun, directly over the manticore's netted and manacled arm. Spikes surrounded his twisting body, swishing past his nose and grazing his clothes and the fur of his legs.

They also struck the manticore itself. Another wail came from the creature as two spikes impaled its forearm, dead center of the left-paw manacle. In a frenzy, the creature shook its injured appendage and bucked, trying to shake off the poisoned spikes. It yelled what Padric expected were curses against his person. He watched in horrific awe as the manacle and surrounding fur sizzled. Then the shimmer diminished from both manacles. As one, they disintegrated into ashes in front of his eyes and mingled with the arena sand. A sudden wind swooped in and scooped up every trace of both manacles.

The monster collapsed onto its side and writhed in the sand, howling in agony. Its trumpet-scream was loud enough to wake the dead. Pure pain ripped through Padric as a direct result of the ear-splitting trumpet blast and spike wound. He swayed, and it was all he could do not to curl up in the fetal position.

Delirium grabbed at him. The remaining crowd's craze had simmered to a buzz, and the manticore's appearance seemed to meld into something else. Its fur chafed and fell away in great clumps. The scorpion tail waggled and diminished, as did the size of the lion's body, its toned muscles deflating to skin and bone. Its deadly claws retracted into human fingers and nails. The creature's entire body reduced to the size of a man, a wiry youth, no more than seventeen, with dark curly hair. Upon his person were a dirty, rumpled tunic and brown trousers with a faded scarlet cloak.

It was the same outfit Padric's old tutor wore most days.

"Gregorio?"

CHAPTER 44

"This is the place?" Brynwen asked, peering around her. The place Circe set them via her blue smoke appeared every bit as pretty as the place the scrying bowl targeted. Tall green grass, birch trees, and a small stream filled the area around her. A lovely scene, worthy of wall space in the Wilmots' painting gallery back home. However, like the contents in the bowl, nothing stood out to indicate the amulet's presence. "It couldn't lead us directly to the amulet?"

"That would be too much to ask of the spell, I am afraid," Circe replied. She held her staff in one hand, the scrying bowl in the other. "A ten-yard radius is the best it can do."

They wasted no time in attacking the plants in a mad dash to find the amulet. The sun drew closer to noon every moment, closer to the solstice.

How difficult can it be to find a gold ring with an obsidian stone? Quite difficult, actually. "Please, amulet of obsidian, Padric needs you," Brynwen muttered. She remembered Rhetia's message. "We all need you." Out of her satchel, she retrieved the two berries that hadn't been crushed for the scrying bowl.

Circe put a hand to a birch tree and closed her eyes. "I cannot feel the amulet's magic. But it must be here. The spell never lies."

"What does that mean?"

"It means the amulet is guarded by a cloaking spell." She spun to look at Brynwen, her eyes intent. "Quick, what exactly did Rhetia say to you about the amulet? The wording is important."

Brynwen pondered her question, then said, "'It is meant for more than just a single person.' She saw three tied to it."

"Three…you, your brother, and Sir Padric. Alas that not all three of you are here now. Do you hold something from each of them?"

"Padric gave me the berries, and Talfryn…"

"You are twins and share the same blood."

"Is that enough?"

"We shall see. Take the berries and hold them in your hand." Circe cupped Brynwen's hands between her own, and chanted:

O fructus terrae
Audi precem nostram dirissimam:
Duc nos ad cupiditatem nostrorum cordium.

O fruit of the earth
Hear our prayer most dire:
Lead us to our hearts' desire.

Circe repeated the chant two more times, but Brynwen noticed nothing untoward at first. Then her eyes grew wide as the berries in her hand began to glow. Something tugged at her hand, yet there was nothing there. An invisible force directed her hand to the left.

She glanced up at Circe in alarm. "What's going on?"

"Do not fight it. Let it pull you along."

Reluctantly, Brynwen stopped struggling against the pull and let it lead her. Followed by Circe, she rounded a boulder and hopped over the small stream, passing over tiny fish swimming in lazy lines, ignorant of the strange situation Brynwen found herself in.

I am doing this for Padric. The tug led her to a birch tree and stopped. The white berries nearly fell from her grasp, it was so sudden. "It stops here."

"Do you see it?" Circe rounded the tree but found nothing.

"It's not here." Brynwen's heart sank. *Are the berries wrong? Does my blood do nothing but confuse the berry-pull? This is my last chance at finding the amulet. If it isn't here, what am I to do?*

She glared at the tree trunk, blaming it for wasting her time. Then she remembered something. "Unless..." Raising her gaze up the birch's trunk, she peered intently into the fully-bloomed foliage. "No wonder I couldn't find it."

"Amazing. It must be stuck on a branch."

Brynwen took a step to the side and saw a spark of gold on an uppermost branch. She pointed up. "There. Can you get it down with your magic staff?"

Circe grinned. "Sweeting, this is your adventure. Our time grows short, so I suggest you begin to climb."

As if on queue, the ring moved. It began to descend the tree, brushing against leaves and branches on the way down.

"Wait, it's coming down," Brynwen gasped. "I thought you said—"

"It is not me."

A squirrel popped out of the foliage onto the trunk and paused. The gold object in its mouth reflected in the sunlight: the amulet of obsidian.

"Now what?" Brynwen asked.

"Begging might help," Circe replied.

I hate you right now.

The squirrel bolted down and around the back of the tree. *I really hate you right now!* Brynwen thought as she gave chase.

CHAPTER 45

Looking both ways down the deserted street, Talfryn slowly opened the door to the stables.

"This is too easy," Rawlins complained. "There's no one around."

"There's never anyone around," Talfryn reminded the sergeant.

"That's true," Leowyn agreed.

The massive door creaked open like usual.

Rawlins snuck in first, then Byron, followed by Leowyn, Talfryn, Serill, and Aeron. Talfryn's heart thudded against his chest. *This is it. Time to save the world.* There should be plenty of time to retrieve and hide the pegasi before anyone came to fetch them for the chariot.

Silently, Rawlins indicated for Talfryn to lead the way.

With quick steps, Talfryn made his way to the stalls. However, the stalls for the four pegasi were empty.

"The pegasi are gone!" Talfryn exclaimed. *Darn the luck.*

"What?" Rawlins growled. "You said they'd be here."

"Well, they *should* be here. Mayhap they're outside in the back."

But there were no horses, flying or otherwise, out in the back pasture.

Talfryn berated himself. They had discussed coming earlier, but if the pegasi were discovered gone too soon, a search party would have been sent out to find them.

"It looks like we're going to have to think of something else," Leowyn said. "They must have taken the horses to the temple early."

"Then what are we waiting for?" Talfryn asked. "Let's go get them." Going to the temple was the last thing he wanted. There would be plenty of guards watching the place, and there were only six of them. That was barely enough to make a decent distraction.

They hurried back toward the arena on the way to the temple. Someone shouted when they drew near to the arena's entrance. It came from the direction of the temple.

"Talfryn!"

"Jarod," Talfryn waved, recognizing his red-bearded friend. "What's wrong?"

"I need to tell you something." The jeweler caught up to him, chest heaving from the exertion of running. "We've got a problem."

"We know, the horses've already been taken," Talfryn replied.

"Yes, I saw two men leading the four winged horses for the chariot into the temple a little bit ago." He looked at the farmer and knights. "But that's not the only problem. It's finished."

"What's finished?"

"The last piece of crystal. I made it precisely as the Master instructed. They laid it in place in the chariot just after dawn. I know you've been asking about it."

Oh no. "That means..." Talfryn's stomach lurched.

"What? " Jarod asked.

"It means we have to hurry before the whole place is decimated, if Padric doesn't win." Talfryn hadn't shared anything about Padric's prophecy to Jarod, but he had hinted to his friend that the crystal was extremely dangerous.

The knights' faces blanched. They knew about the crystal, but hearing it again wasn't very pleasant.

"What?" Jarod asked with wide eyes. "What do you mean?"

"No time to explain. But we have to destroy the crystal and get the horses away from the roof."

Jarod's face paled. Rawlins caught him before he fell. "It's my fault," Jarod lamented. "I tried to stall, as you asked, but the Master's servants can be very persuasive." He rubbed the small of his back.

"Nay," Talfryn patted the man's shoulder. "You were only doing as you were told. That's all any of us did. Heck, I helped install the lovely white stones on the side."

"Your best work yet," Leowyn confirmed.

"Anyway, Jarod, you need to get out of Cataractonium if you can. Go to the tall hill to the southwest." Even mentioning the hill where he and Padric had first encountered Circe and her warrior dryads sent a chill up his spine.

The jeweler hesitated, likely churning over his options. "Nay, I helped make this thing. I should help stop it."

"It's up to you." Rawlins shrugged. "We need to hurry to the temple and get past the guards."

"Right," Talfryn said. "There's no time to lose."

"Where d'you think yer going?" came a voice from the arena entrance.

Does everyone know we're outside? Talfryn wheeled around to find Warin's friends approaching, Herman in the lead, his repaired winged-sandals in hand.

"It's none of your business." Rawlins stood to his full height and placed his hands on his hips. Talfryn wanted to call the pose: *casual death.*

"Oh yeah?"

"Off with you lot."

"Oh, no," Herman said, his face only inches from Rawlins's. "You're not telling us what to do."

The din of dissidence grew in crescendo on both sides. Knuckles cracked in anticipation of the chance for a brawl. The tension between the two groups had grown over the past two weeks, and now they had their chance to battle it out.

"We don't have time for this," Talfryn protested, but no one heard him. He shoved his way through the crowd until he finally made it to where Rawlins and Herman were staring daggers at each other. "Stop it.

We have to get to the temple, or we'll all be dead soon. I don't know about you, but I don't feel like dying today."

"What are you talking 'bout?" Herman asked with a sneer.

Leowyn whispered to Talfryn, "Herman and his friends want a fight. Why not give it to them?" He turned back to Herman. "Have you ever wondered why hardly anyone can go to the roof of the temple?"

"Because there are guards protecting it."

"Right. The Master is building a big weapon, and it'll be bad news for us if he uses it. We could use your help in stopping it."

The men around Herman began to murmur amongst themselves, discussing their options.

Talfryn tapped his foot. This was going nowhere fast. "You want to fight? Then let's put your skills to good use." Talfryn looked Herman straight in the eye, then spun to face the rest of his group. "Care to make some mischief and destruction of the temple, lads?" A sly grin crept up his cheek.

Herman blinked. "But we just finished building it. It was a pain to build." He peered back at his friends, and they each shrugged. He gripped the laces of his winged sandals. "Aye, we're in."

A gleam caught Rawlins's eyes. It made a shiver run down Talfryn's spine. *I do not ever want to be his enemy.* "That's the kind of talk I like to hear," Rawlins said. "I know where they store the weapons."

"After you." Talfryn gestured to the knight. "Let's sack some Rome."

TALFRYN CROUCHED behind the bush next to Leowyn and Rawlins near the foot of the temple. The bush was rather too small for three people to hide behind, but so far none of the temple guards had noticed anything out of the ordinary. Serill and Byron crouched behind nearby bushes, while Aeron and Herman's group were sent to the other side of the temple. Jarod remained behind a small statue of a goddess no one knew. No one even knew if she *was* a goddess. There had been some disagreement as to who would go where, until Rawlins stared everyone down and gave the orders. They obeyed without comment.

"What happens after the guards are taken out?" Rawlins asked.

"We need to get to the top of the temple and destroy the chariot and crystal," Talfryn answered, looking up. "And take the horses away, too."

"He means, do you have a plan?" Leowyn said.

"Oh. Leo, I'm making this up as I go. First, how do we get around them?" Talfryn wondered aloud. Human guards, all dressed in leathers and sandals, surrounded the outside of the temple. *Good thing Herman and friends came along to even out the numbers a bit more.* What really interested Talfryn and the knights the lack of dryads helping to fill the guard ranks. *They are fully capable of the task, so why use human soldiers?*

Leowyn's eyes followed the guards' movements. "And who knows how many are inside."

"Leave it to me," Rawlins said, straight-faced. "I'll dispatch the three on this side, then give the signal for you lot to move in. Make a direct path to the stairs inside. Don't wait for me, I'll catch up."

"Don't hurt them too much," Talfryn said.

Rawlins huffed. "Your concern is noted."

As Rawlins slunk away, Leowyn leaned closer to Talfryn. "Some of the men in the unit call him the Fox. You'll see why in a moment." He gave a signal to the bushes where Byron and Serill hid.

The farmer blinked and lost sight of Rawlins. He began to panic that something awful had happened to him, but heartbeats later, the knight appeared by the northeastern side of the stone building. With catlike grace, he was upon the lone guard standing watch on the corner. The Derby man performed a choke hold before the guard could react. The man struggled in vain briefly, then his eyes rolled up into his head and his body went lax. Rawlins slowly lowered the unconscious man to a sitting position against the temple wall.

Hands on hips, he began to yell at the unconscious guard. "Oi, what do you mean by sleeping on the job?" He shook a fist in the air. "I should report you."

The remaining guards, distracted by Rawlins's outburst, called out in protest.

That was the signal. Byron, Serill, and the others had their weapons out and rushed at the unsuspecting guards, both outside the temple and in. Too late, the sentries realized their mistake and fought back, but the Derby and Nottingham men had the element of surprise on their side.

Talfryn and Leowyn, followed by a nervous Jarod, made their way slowly through the crowd of fighting bodies. A few times, they got knocked over or had to strike out against one of Helius's guards for a few seconds. Talfryn rather enjoyed having the chance to bash an enemy or two over the head.

It was tight getting inside the temple, but the three of them made it. Talfryn spun around, and his jaw fell. He had not been inside the temple for two days. All the building materials and scraps had been removed and everything shone, immaculately. The white stone was practically blinding through the high windows. A huge statue of Helius stood near the back, nearly twenty feet high. The likeness was so realistic, Talfryn feared it might come to life and crush them with its massive feet, but thankfully, it remained motionless.

"Come on." Appearing at their side, Rawlins shoved Talfryn out of his thoughts.

"Right. Let's go."

They passed Byron and Serill inside, each holding their own against the temple guards. Herman zipped around the temple, to the consternation of the enemy. Talfryn, Leowyn, and Jarod made their way up the circular staircase, with Rawlins taking the rear. Like the York Minster, the stairwell was narrow, steep, and winding; they could only go up single file.

A crash followed by a confusion of shouts carried up the stairwell. Talfryn hesitated, but Leowyn and Rawlins urged him to continue. A howl echoed up the chamber. Claws scraped against stone. Another howl and heavy breathing, this time much closer. *Not human.* Talfryn's heart thudded in his chest, and he picked up his pace. *How many steps are in this place?*

Last in line, Rawlins scowled and brandished his sword. "Keep going. I'll take care of this."

The cousins didn't argue as Rawlins pivoted and withdrew down the stairs. Worried, Talfryn tripped up the steps, and Leowyn crashed into his back. Gasping, he waited until Leowyn righted himself.

"These blasted steps," Leowyn said. "Helius's architect should have been fired."

"It wasn't me," Jarod said indignantly.

Talfryn snorted, then tried to ignore the throbbing in his shins as he took the next steps. "We're almost there. Do you think Rawlins took care of whatever it was?"

Another roar carried up the stairs. Leowyn urged them to ascend faster.

Talfryn's heart sank right before the sudden slanted stone ceiling halted their progress abruptly.

"A little warning would have been nice." Leowyn rubbed his nose where it had connected with Talfryn's head. Then he followed Talfryn's gaze upward.

Directly above, a white, wooden trap door blocked their way, a bronze handle jutting from the wood. It was just like Brynwen said it would be. "Bryn wasn't kidding about the stairs' abrupt end."

"It's like magic," Jarod said.

Talfryn gave a dry laugh. Bracing himself, he wrapped his fingers around the bronze handle. It had been locked when Brynwen tried it a few days before, but he prayed it was open. With all the chariot preparations taking place, it would be a pain to have to unlock and lock it repeatedly.

Leowyn put a hand on Talfryn's shoulder, halting him. "Do you think the roof is guarded?"

"There's only one way to find out." He inhaled deeply, mumbled a quick prayer to his Christian God, and pushed on the door.

CHAPTER 46

Sunlight shone through the crack of the trap door to the temple roof. *Success!* Talfryn pushed up another inch, and it creaked noisily.

He winced. "Isn't this place new? It shouldn't be creaking already."

Leowyn glared at him. "Are you really worried about that at a time like this?"

"Lads," Jarod said with agitation.

"I'm just saying." Talfryn peeked through the crack. No movement outside. He pushed the door up further and cringed as it continued to squeak, slowly revealing the bright blue sky and a slanted roof, the shiny new tiles glistening with the sun's rays. Talfryn blinked a few times to clear his vision, but still no one approached them.

He shoved the door open the rest of the way and propped it up with a three-foot stick lying next to the opening, then hopped out of the hole, followed by Leowyn and Jarod. Together, they walked into the blazing sunlight on the slanted roof. With not a cloud in the sky, the sun blazed down on them mercilessly. He could feel a kind of energy in the air, much like an approaching thunderstorm.

Talfryn surveyed the area, his eyes landing on the umber tiles placed evenly on the slanted roof. He and the others had to watch their step, so they didn't end up slipping and falling to their deaths. Just behind the trapdoor, a white-stoned platform stood another couple of feet taller than Talfryn and measured the length of the tower. Directly in the center of the platform was a set of white stone stairs to match the rest of the building's architecture. At the very top resided Helius's gilded chariot.

The chariot's gilt frame covered a curved wooden body, carved by master craftsmen. The wheels were perfectly symmetrical, also gilt in pure gold. Painted on the side facing Talfryn, flames stretched and curled around a stunning red-orange sun—Helius's emblem.

Tied to the brilliant golden chariot, four black pegasi skittered at the banter of the pair of men holding their bridles. Neither man had noticed the newcomers below. Talfryn and his companions ducked and placed their backs against the platform before they could be noticed.

"That's not how you bridle a horse," said one of the men on the platform.

"It is too. See, like this," the second one argued.

"Nay, that's all wrong."

Jarod whispered, "The weapon is on the chariot."

The sparkling piece of crystal Jarod had crafted and placed perfectly to Helius's specifications would give Helius the power to destroy Apollo, and then, inadvertently or not, the world.

"Of course," said Talfryn. "And those two are barring our path." He glanced up at the sky again. *Almost noon. Great.* He hoped there was still time to break the weapon and get the horses away, and that whatever was down in the temple didn't disturb them before that. Or, to be honest, if it would refrain from coming onto the roof at all, that'd be most preferable. He wondered how Rawlins, Byron, Serill, and the others were doing against whatever was down in the temple with them.

Talfryn studied the structure again. "Jarod, your crystal is the key. If we can remove it and destroy it, it can't do any harm, right?"

"Right. At least, that's the theory."

"Great, I love theory. Then I'm going to need you to persuade those men to come down here. Can you do that?"

"I can try."

"Then head on up. We'll cover you."

Jarod nodded and ascended the staircase. When he was over halfway up, Leowyn put a foot on the bottom stair to follow. A sound came from the stairwell, rattling the trap door on the tiles.

"Rawlins?" Leowyn asked hopefully.

The sounds stopped for a moment, then a howl emerged from below.

"I guess it found us," Talfryn said. *Whatever it is.* The hairs stood up on the back of his neck.

"Guess so." Ever the knight, Leowyn took his stance. Talfryn tried in vain to copy him, but lost his balance on the slanted roof. He settled for holding his hatchet high above his head instead. The cousins gripped their weapons as a large gray head emerged. Its wolf-like fur had matted tufts, and it had mangled ears, one of which was pointed, the other partially ripped or chewed with the top half hanging limply.

Talfryn gulped. "Definitely not Rawlins, then. You brought reinforcements, right?"

"I thought *you* brought them."

Talfryn snorted.

The creature glared at them, heaving and emitting a low growl between huffs.

"It..." Leowyn licked his lips. "It was nice seeing you again, cousin."

"Likewise. Let's vow to never do this again."

"Deal."

Emerging from the stairwell, the shaggy wolf was twice the size of an average dog. Its eyes were dark as the blackest pitch. Three yellowed, saw-toothed protuberances sprouted from its forehead in a vertical line, one much longer than the other two. Five or six other spikes made of the same bone substance stuck out of its back. Its mottled fur shone in different shades of gray; splotches of fresh and dried blood dotted its coat and bone horns.

Sweat trickled down Talfryn's neck. *Are Rawlins and the others dead?* His body shook at their loss, and the hand holding the hatchet went clammy.

"Is that supposed to be a unicorn...or...a...a wolficorn?" Talfryn lowered his hatchet a fraction. "I thought unicorns were pretty, not ugly." He was beginning to wonder if they had any *normal* animals in Cataractonium. The creature cast its spine-chilling gaze upon him and growled deep within its throat.

"I think it heard you," Leowyn said. "Don't look intimidated. It will only encourage it."

"Umm, I don't think it needs much encouragement." Talfryn was pretty sure the creature could smell the terror emitting from him.

Without warning, the wolficorn leapt directly at Talfryn. Reflexes working, he swung the hatchet sideways. It sliced the air in front of the wolf, the momentum taking Talfryn with it. He bowled into Leowyn. They landed on the hard roof in a heap and slid down two feet.

Disentangling his limbs from his cousin, Leowyn jumped to his feet. When the wolficorn snapped at him, Leowyn lunged for its snout. The wolficorn plunged again, and he sidestepped out of the way, bringing the hammer down on its side. The monster yelped, then trotted away.

"I think it's toying with us," Leowyn surmised.

"No jest," Talfryn said. "Mayhap we should ask it nicely to go away and leave us alone."

Leowyn kept his eye on the monster. "Go ahead. I'm not stopping you."

"Thanks, Leo. Always the diplomatic one."

"I get it from my mother's side."

"Figures."

The three stared at each other for a few tense heartbeats. Finally, Leowyn spoke. "Mayhap we should rush it."

"I hate that idea."

"Or we could just let it attack us and gobble us up on the spot."

Talfryn considered their options. "I hate the first idea less now."

"Good. On three."

"Just like old times." Talfryn let out a breath. "This time, however, the monsters are real."

Leowyn counted to three, then the cousins dashed at the splotchy creature and shouted their childhood war cry at the top of their lungs. A memory flashed in Talfryn's mind of their adventures enacting the same thing, with trees in the forest as their enemies. This time, however, the enemy fought back.

Talfryn and Leowyn separated, Talfryn veering to the left and Leowyn to the right. They simultaneously swung their weapons at the wolf. It ducked and swiped its sharp horns at Talfryn. The jagged horns ripped through his leggings and sliced open the skin and muscle on his thigh, scraping against the bone. Talfryn cried out and landed hard on his side, his hatchet skittering along the roof tiles well out of reach. Heat seared up his leg and through his spine. Talfryn lay panting, unable to move from the acute throbbing.

Leowyn spun on his heel. In an instant, he charged the wolficorn again. The beast lunged as the knight ducked and rolled, swinging his hammer up at the beast's leg. They fought hammer and claw, ducking and swinging. The creature buckled and whimpered, backing away a few steps. Leowyn spared a glance at his cousin.

Talfryn saw the shift in the wolficorn's stance too late. "Leo, watch out—"

The wolficorn ran full force into the unsuspecting Leowyn and rammed its head into his abdomen. The knight flew into the air toward the front of the temple and crashed to the roof, the streaks and droplets of dark red blood left on the tiles a sharp contrast with the white stone.

"Leo—" Talfryn's heart caught in his chest. *No, no, no, not Leo, not Leo, not Leo.* A strangled sob emitted from his throat, tasting the bitter salt from his tears on his lips. He was going to be sick.

The wolficorn halted and panted, as though half expecting Leowyn to get up, but the young knight didn't move.

When Talfryn managed to tear his eyes away from Leowyn's body, the ugly wolficorn's ears twitched. Its huge head pivoted, fresh blood coating its facial horns. With slow, deliberate motions, it turned around, all the while staring into Talfryn's eyes, a glimmer of crafty delight upon its blood-spattered face.

Desperate to get away from the wolficorn, Talfryn stumbled to his feet on shaky legs. His injured leg gave out after two steps, and he toppled over, scraping his knee on the rough stone. The wolficorn took another couple of slow steps, savoring the kill, while Talfryn pulled himself together enough to get up again. He managed to stay on his feet this time and hobbled along the tiled roof dragging his leg behind him, each step pure agony, every shuddered breath a sob for his cousin. He'd never make it to the hatchet before the monster killed him—but he had to try.

CHAPTER 47

The wolficorn gained on Talfryn. Were the creature not laughing at him the entire time, he mightn't mind as much. Maybe he'd be less terrified.

"Just get it over with," he muttered under his breath.

His leg ached something fierce, and with each step, it cooperated less and less. Just a few feet away from the hatchet, his injured leg spasmed and gave out. He sprawled to the ground in a heap. Panic staunched any plan he'd had as he scrambled forward.

I won't see Bryn again, or Samuel and Grandfather. I've even let down Padric. The creature was only six paces away. With desperate fingers, Talfryn crawled, dragging his bleeding leg, scraping his calloused hands into the rough tile, and finally getting a grip on the hatchet handle. Even from a distance, the creature's hot breath slithered up Talfryn's neck, making his spine tingle.

The hideous wolficorn stopped at Talfryn's feet. Nostrils flaring, it breathed in his fear and sweat. *Savoring the moment,* Talfryn guessed in disgust. "Come on, then," he said with gritted teeth. "Make it quick."

A crash sounded across the temple roof. Talfryn chanced a glance around the wild beast. Rawlins heaved himself out of the trap door. A large, deep red hole gouged his left shoulder. Gone was the usual impassive expression. In its stead, an angry scowl had formed. Hate. Revulsion. All the things Talfryn felt for the monster were reflected on the knight's face.

Rawlins took determined strides straight for the wolficorn and was upon it before it could turn completely. He slashed and hacked with his sword and a dagger. The wolficorn returned the favor with sharp claws and bony horns. Talfryn could only look on in amazed horror.

Without pausing, Rawlins managed a glare at Talfryn. "Get on with it."

The command shook Talfryn out of his stupor. He got up and hobbled toward the platform stairs. With a deep breath, he prepared to climb, bad leg or no. The roars of the creature from behind set him off, and he put a shaky foot onto the first stair. Slowly he climbed, willing his leg to cooperate with each painstaking step. *I have to do this.*

Heart racing, he glanced back at Rawlins and the wolficorn. Rawlins's seemingly lazy attacks drove the beast wild. However, the knight was quickly tiring from exertion and blood loss. He deflected another blow by the skin of his teeth, then plunged forward. The creature backed up in defense.

Jarod quickly descended the steps. "I'm coming," he called to Talfryn, keeping an eye on the wolficorn's movements. He grabbed one of Talfryn's arms and hoisted him up with a grunt.

Next, Byron's brown head popped up through the stairwell onto the temple roof. Without hesitation, he joined Rawlins to fight the beast. *Where are Serill and Aeron?*

At last, Talfryn and Jarod reached the platform. "Piece of cake." Lying to himself was the only form of encouragement he could manage; trying not to remember how high he was off the ground, and even more, avoiding the vision of himself falling off the platform and landing face-first on the earth. His whole body was covered with sweat. He glanced up at the sky again and cursed. *Time is short. Really short.*

Mounted on the top-fore of the chariot lay the crystal. Cut into a geometric shape about the size of Talfryn's palm, at least twenty dazzling colors emitted off its sides at every angle, much like the rare diamonds he had glanced at the Derby market. But this precious stone was mesmerizing in its delicacy and dimension. A true masterpiece. Heat radiated from the crystal, as though it took heat directly from the sun itself—which made sense for Helius, god of the sun. *Where had Helius gotten such a gem?*

"Jarod, this is marvelous work."

"Thanks. Too bad it's being used for evil." He ripped off a sweaty strip of his own shirt and tied it around Talfryn's wounded leg.

Talfryn turned his attention to the two horsemen, who could have been brothers with long, dark hair. They stared down at the fearsome wolficorn, their hands shaking with fear.

"You need to leave now," Talfryn told the men through gritted teeth.

"But the creature will kill us," the one with longer hair said.

"Rawlins and Byron are distracting it. Go while you can."

That was enough for the men, who fled without a word, leaving Jarod and Talfryn behind.

"You should have asked them to help us first," Jarod said.

Talfryn berated his own stupidity. "I suppose that would have helped. Too late now. Come on."

"Now what? Most of the team is indisposed."

Talfryn shaded his eyes with his bloody fingers. "You take care of removing the crystal. I'll hold the horses so they don't get startled and run you over."

"What about your leg? You can barely stand."

"I'll manage." *Somehow.*

Not entirely liking the idea, the jeweler pursed his lips. "Fine, but we'd better be quick. The Master will be here soon."

Talfryn cringed at the honorific. A quick glance at the cloudless sky revealed the sun nearing dangerously close to full noon. The air suddenly became thick with a wild, nervous energy, raising the hairs on the top of Talfryn's head. The sun's rays radiated off the crystal, its heat both intolerable and blinding. Trails of sweat poured down his neck and back in rivulets.

His bad leg protested greatly as he hobbled over to confront the four skittish pegasi. One would think that, after carrying the sun around in the sky for thousands of years, they'd be little afraid of anything, but apparently, a scary wolf-thing with bones sticking out of its body was enough to terrify even the most stalwart of creatures.

The winged horses, he'd learned from Padric, were attached to the chariot by a central pole, or trace, fastened to the chariot's front prow. The mare closest to him whinnied anxiously and the others shared her sentiment.

"Shh, shh," he soothed, brushing her black nose with his fingers. "We are going to get you out of here." He batted his brains for the names of the horses and quickly hummed Thimble's song—the one thing he could remember in the hurried moment. "Pyro—Pyrois, Eous, and...was it Anthony? No...Aethon and Flagon."

The middle male horse huffed indignantly.

"Sorry, 'Phlegon.'" Talfryn stifled a snort. *Who knew horses could be so sensitive about name pronunciation?*

The mare on the end, Aethon, seemed the most frightened. He continued to speak to her in gentle tones—though his heart beat anything but gently—and forced a smile. "Are you 'the fiery one' or 'the blazing one'? You seem not a bit like the 'burning' type to me."

She snickered and he thought she blushed.

"Ah," he said, "of course. Your 'blazing' beauty has enraptured me, Lady Aethon." He bowed his head regally.

Her head bobbed shyly.

Leg throbbing, Talfryn suppressed down on the pain and the urge to lie down as he chatted with the pegasi, during which time he was nearly kicked when guessing wrongly over whose name meant "he who turns the sky"—Eous. They were finally at a point where they did not completely cower at the slightest noise. However, Jarod still had nothing to show for his efforts except angry curses toward the gods of jewelry and a completely intact crystal.

"I will return presently," Talfryn reassured the horses. "I'm just going to check on my friend."

He limped over to Jarod, the man's blazing red hair completely wet and sticking up in several places. His gray tunic was slick with sweat.

Jarod wiped his brow with his forearm. The back of his hand was bright red, as though sunburnt. "It's much too hot. It feels like I am standing directly next to the sun. I can only work on the mounting for a few seconds before I have to jump away to cool my fingers. Raising his hands, they both appeared deeply sunburnt and were starting to blister.

Talfryn regarded the brilliant crystal and reached for his hatchet. "I can have a go at it."

Sweat flicked off damp hair as Jarod shook his head sadly. "I'm sorry, Talfryn. I'm afraid you'll get no farther than I did. I don't know what else to do, and we're running out of time."

Talfryn grumbled. "The thing we should have done in the first place. Fly it out of here and hide the chariot where Helius can't find it."

"But where is that? Can't he appear anywhere at will?"

"I don't even know. The horses may be able to leave Cataractonium, but I don't know if we can. Mayhap we can at least fly it around the compound until the crystal cools off and isn't as potent."

Jarod eyed him skeptically.

"We've no other options at this point."

"Fine."

"Get in the chariot while I..."

A faint realization tickled his ear; everything around him had gone silent. The sounds made by Rawlins, Byron, and the wolficorn fighting and shouting were void.

In a blink, Talfryn's blood went cold. He didn't have to turn around to know the wolficorn lingered a few paces behind him. Jarod's petrified expression said it all, his body completely rigid. It wasn't hard to picture the creature observing them with a menacing gleam in its black eyes, saliva dripping from its putrid mouth. Talfryn stifled a shudder as he stilled, hearing the wolficorn emit a disturbing chuckle.

Razor-sharp claws scraped against the stone stairs. It was all Talfryn could do not to cringe. Daring a glance back and down, his heart sank as he spied Rawlins and Byron lying prone on the roof, either unconscious or dead. Pushing down overbearing dread, Talfryn pivoted on his heels to face the wolficorn. Ignoring the searing pain running down his leg, his mind worked fast for an escape route—at least for Jarod and the horses.

"I don't suppose you'd want to come back in about five minutes, Sir Wolficorn?" asked Talfryn.

Ignoring his query, the creature sprang. It bounded up the final four steps with ease, growling with grizzly mirth at the top step. Jarod fumbled for his hammer but Aethon's frantic rump knocked him to the ground.

The wolficorn leapt past Talfryn and landed right where Jarod had been a moment before, inches away from the closest pegasus. As he moved, Talfryn swung his hatchet at it, but it dodged the blow.

Rounding the chariot, Talfryn's bad leg tripped over the wheel, sending him sprawling into the basket of the chariot with a crash. Bright stars engulfed his vision as he slashed blindly at the wolficorn, scrambling to get away from it, and ended up cornering himself in the chariot. He kicked, and the wolficorn's teeth nearly snapped his good leg in half.

"Talfryn!" Jarod cried.

The wolficorn hesitated and looked up at the jeweler on the platform.

"Nay!" Talfryn cried. "Jarod, stay away—get off the roof. I'll take care of it."

"Nay, I won't leave you. The crystal—"

The wolficorn made to move toward Jarod.

"Just go!" Talfryn yelled as he jumped up and swung at the beast's paw. He wasn't going to lose another friend on this roof. A clawed toe flew off past its ear, then the wolf retreated a step and faltered with a yelp.

"Aww, sorry about the toe. But, you know, I think it's a good look for you."

Leaning back, Talfryn bumped against the crystal, then cried out in shock. He rubbed his rear, having forgotten about its extreme heat.

The snarling wolficorn butted its ugly snout into him. The force knocked Talfryn from the front of the chariot and seared his forearm.

He landed hard on his back onto the draught pole. Startled, the pegasi reared up and took off at a sprint. In a frenzy, they launched off the platform and into the wide air. Talfryn reached out and grabbed the first thing he could find: a horse's tail. Then the chariot dipped, heading downward at an alarming rate. Talfryn wasn't sure if he let out a maidenly scream as they hurtled toward the ground or not.

CHAPTER 48

Gregorio—a younger version of the man Padric knew, or a spectacular likeness—lay before him on the sand of the arena. Except for missing the white streaks in his dark curly hair and the few "scholarly" wrinkles, he could have been Gregorio Fiori's twin, or son. The youth lay on the ground, eyes closed, shuddering feverishly as though experiencing a nightmare.

"Gregorio?" Padric knelt on the ground beside him, completely disregarding the pain each movement brought his chest.

The young man's eyes snapped open. After a few heartbeats, his lips parted, but no sound emerged. He cleared his throat once. Twice. "Padric," he rasped. Then, with a weak grin, said, "I knew you would find me."

Warin came over in a stupor. "This is your friend?"

All Padric could do was nod. The two poisoned spikes remained lodged in Gregorio's arm, turning the skin and veins around them a sickly green. He needed medical attention immediately. Padric felt the fire in his own chest from where the manticore's spike had struck him and realized they both did.

As though the universe heard his thoughts, two plumes of smoke, one purple and one blue, appeared directly behind Padric. Helius stormed out of the purple cloud directly before Circe vacated the other, followed by...

"Bryn?" Padric gasped.

"Padric!" she cried, falling to her knees and wrapping her arms around his neck. Shooting pain rent though his chest. "I saw the last few minutes of your fight—what's wrong?" She drew back and her eyes immediately fell to the wound on his chest. A frown marred her beautiful face.

"'Tis nothing," he replied, though a cold dread filled his stomach.

"This isn't nothing." She swept her fingers near the scratches. "We need to patch this up before it gets infected."

"*Mater, Avus,*" the young Gregorio said. *Mother, Grandfather.*

Padric spun around. Circe and Helius knelt by Gregorio's head, holding him up.

"My son." Circe stroked his brow. "What has happened to you?"

"Son?" Padric asked, startled. *What does she mean?*

"Who did this to you?" Helius asked with thick voice, ignoring Padric's question. A tightness pinched his facial muscles as he regarded the youth. "They shall feel my wrath."

Brynwen tore her eyes away from Padric and interjected, "But first, M'lord, we need to remove those spikes from his arms. He and Sir Padric both need immediate treatment."

Without a thought, Helius ripped them out of the youth's arm, wincing as steam rose from his palm. Red welts covered his hand. Brynwen moved in to inspect the oozing wounds. *What is this creature that even the gods can be harmed by it?*

"Who is he?" Warin asked.

Everyone seemed to have forgotten about the large knight. He looked worse for the wear, with deep gashes on his arms, legs, and leather jerkin, and superficial scratches on his face.

Circe regarded Warin with mild curiosity. "He is Telegonus, my son."

"Telegonus?" Padric stared, incredulous. Earlier conversations with the deities came back to him, of how much their son loved learning, craved it, and how much he sounded like Padric's tutor Gregorio.

Because they are one and the same person. It does explain why he knew so much about mythology.

"I do not understand this." Warin placed his hands on his hips.

"Nor do I," Brynwen said.

"It appears," Circe said, "that our Telegonus has been masquerading around England these past years as Padric's elderly tutor, Gregorio Fiori. But why, Telegonus?"

"It is a long story," Gregorio-Telegonus said. "I shall tell you later. First, Padric, the hour has come."

"The hour," Padric said numbly. With all the excitement, he had nearly forgotten about the crystal and the chariot. The sun was almost at its zenith.

He nodded, and wondered how Talfryn, Rawlins, and the others fared with hiding the horses. It could already be over, and all might yet be won. He had perhaps one more chance to halt the proceedings.

Padric peered at Helius. "M'lord, you cannot go to your chariot."

"Why ever not? It is mine, and I have waited a long time for this day. As much as it grieves me to leave one so precious for a short time, I have work to do."

In the sky, from the direction of Helius's temple, a team of four black winged horses led the sun god's chariot over the arena. Even from a distance, however, it was plain that something was wrong. The pegasi flew erratically, dipping and speeding with each movement. Something large occupied the chariot seat, and something else...

"Tal!" Brynwen cried, launching to her feet.

Even with the horses' great speed, he could tell someone was hanging from the chariot. *But how can Brynwen be certain it is Talfryn?*

"My chariot!" Helius leapt to his feet. "What are they doing to my chariot?"

Brynwen trembled as she clutched Padric's arm. "Padric, he's in trouble!"

"I will retrieve him," he replied, gripping her arm for reassurance.

"But you're hurt. You can't go."

"I must."

Trembling, Brynwen glanced from him to the flying chariot, gaining distance from them with every second. "Then here. But please be careful. I need you both to come back to me." She thrust a small object into his hand.

"Go, I've got this," Warin said to Padric. He stepped toward the god, his face set in determination.

Without answering, Padric picked up his discarded weapons and whistled for Ulysses. Padric leapt on the peryton's back. He sent a quick nod to Brynwen, then Ulysses spread his wings and they took to the sky.

❦

IF NOT FOR his present circumstances, Talfryn might have enjoyed the cool breeze brought on by the pegasi's quick departure from the roof.

Nearly jostled off the trace bar affixing the chariot basket to the horses, Talfryn braced his feet against the chariot guard and clenched the coarse hairs of the horse's tail with everything he had. The horse—Eous or Aethon, he thought—whinnied in protest and bucked at him, narrowly missing his head. Heart in his feet, Talfryn repositioned himself more sturdily, his back still on the draught pole, hanging on for dear life. *In good news, I still have his hatchet. Now, if I can get back into the chariot, I can fly the contraption away from Helius and beat the prophecy. Easy.*

As they soared over the arena, an angry snarl came from the chariot bed.

"Oh no," muttered Talfryn with a gulp. Somehow, he had forgotten about the wolficorn. Unfortunately, the winged horses' quick takeoff hadn't jostled the wretched creature from the chariot as he'd initially thought. From the sound of it, now that it had one less toe, the wolficorn was more adamant on finishing off Talfryn than ever before.

Bloodstained horns slowly poked over the wall of the chariot, then an ugly gray snout sniffed the wind, followed closely by a pair of black bloodshot eyes, which ogled him with merciless ferocity. What felt like a two-ton stone lodged itself in Talfryn's throat. Trying to swallow, he almost ingested his own tongue, and was nearly sick all over himself. If he hadn't been frightened before, he was completely scared out of his wits now. He had nowhere to run. Falling to his death would almost be preferable to being clawed and mangled by the creature.

He licked his lips. "Nice wolficorn," he yelled over the wind. "Mayhap we could look for your toe and sew it back on. My sister is a wonderful healer."

Not amused, the wolficorn leaned over the edge, careful not to touch the hot crystal. *Smart creature. It learns fast.* It swiped at him and gave the impression it was toying with pouncing either on him or one of the horses.

"Go ahead and try it." Talfryn gripped the hatchet handle with his free, sweaty hand. His resolve was finally up.

With a quickness he hadn't seen before, the wolficorn leaned halfway out and clawed at Talfryn's stomach. Its sharp claw ripped at the wind-whipped fabric of his brown tunic. He prepared himself for the worst but felt no pain. Relief flashed through him as he swung the hatchet, also missing the creature. It disappeared back into the chariot bed, continuing to growl in a furious fashion.

Curiosity getting the better of him, Talfryn craned his neck for a better look. Forgetting his bad leg, he shifted his foothold on the chariot. That was the first mistake, as his bad leg had lost feeling again. His footing slipped, and his boot struck against the chariot with a loud bang. Quickly, he regained his balance with one hand.

The beast raised on its haunches in the chariot, its back to him, ears pricked.

Now's my chance. "For Leowyn!" Talfryn cried. Tears fought to flow anew as he launched the hatchet at the wolficorn's exposed back.

The monster wailed as the blade sunk into its flesh, narrowly missing the spine. Through the ratty fur, its neck muscles rippled, and its roar almost toppled Talfryn from his precarious perch on the draught pole.

What should have been a death blow only enraged the beast further.

"Why aren't you dead?" Talfryn asked, indignant. "That throw would've killed anyone else." *It's too stubborn to die.*

In answer, the wolficorn clawed at the chariot in its haste to turn, and in the process chipped off a layer of the golden paint on the side. Helius's sun was now marred and took on the appearance of a mangled rabbit.

Talfryn almost felt sorry for the creature until its terrible eyes locked onto his. Then, in a fit of rage, it gripped the chariot's front rail, its paw sizzling on the hot crystal.

"Why don't you stay inside the chariot?" Talfryn was running out of ideas. "It's much nicer in there than it is out here." *Please.* Talfryn froze in place as the creature sought footing to climb over the chariot toward him.

In one leap, it was on Talfryn, its heavy paws crushing the air out of his chest—likely dislodging a rib in the process. Talfryn screamed as a back paw landed on his wounded leg. The wolficorn's ghastly jaw snapped in his face, barely missing his nose. The impact jarred the pegasi, and they bucked the chariot wildly. The force made Talfryn crack his head on the draught pole, and the horsetail ripped out of his hand, leaving only a couple strands entwined in his fingers. With nothing to hold onto, he and the wolficorn slipped from the pole.

Talfryn felt as though his brain remained aloft while his body and the wolficorn free-fell through the sky. He watched with uncaring eyes as the wild and scarred creature slashed and swiped fruitlessly at the wind. Arms and legs spread wide, Talfryn slowly gained distance from the desperate wolficorn. He dared not look at the ground—at his ending. *At least Leo's murderer can't escape his fate.*

His head, ribs, and leg screamed in excruciating agony. Each pounding of his heart felt like a mallet on his wounds. *At this point, smashing on the ground into a million pieces would be welcome.*

The last thing he remembered were two glaring bloodshot eyes promising sweet, sweet vengeance.

CHAPTER 49

*B*rynwen's skirts were still bristling from the wind created by Helius's black winged mare as he took off into the air after Padric and the golden chariot. He left his children and Brynwen behind, coughing on the dust generated from the hurried flight.

Warin lay flat on his back and groaned. A charred handprint marred his leather jerkin where Helius, in a rage, had pushed him with his power.

Circe cursed beside her. "Insufferable man," she muttered at the sky, crossing her arms. "Never has he listened to reason. It might already be too late to stop him."

When Padric and Ulysses flew after Talfryn and the chariot, an unladen winged horse was already on its way to claim Helius. How it knew to come from the stables, Brynwen couldn't say. Circe and Warin had tried to stall the god, asking him to think it over, but he merely waved an impatient hand at them. Warin had gotten between Helius and his horse, upsetting the god enough to act against his own grandson before launching into the air.

"It is up to Padric now," Gregorio said.

Brynwen blinked. Even though Padric had explained everything, Brynwen still had a hard time comprehending it all. It made her head spin. She just hoped he could save Talfryn from that monster, and not die in the process.

Circe began pacing, kicking up sand every few steps.

"Can you not help them?" Brynwen asked with wide eyes.

The sorceress shook her head. "There is some sort of protective spell around the chariot," she explained. "*Pater* is paranoid to the point of obsession. If I step anywhere near the contraption, I will become ill for hours. I have tried everything, but my father used a strong spell. I wonder where he learned of it."

"Could he have broken into your den?"

"My wards would have sensed it. Nay, something else is at work. Something sinister. I have felt it all along."

Something else nagged at Brynwen. "What was that creature in the flying chariot?" *With Talfryn.* "Where are they headed?"

Circe hugged her arms to herself, and her brows knit together. "It is something I have not seen for centuries. An *aeternae.* It is a fearsome beast of prey, appearing as a wolf with bones protruding from its body."

From the ground, Gregorio cleared his throat. "They kill almost any living thing for sport, even if they are not hungry. The old legends say a bone grows on its back for each kill it has made."

His words shook Brynwen to the core. "Then Talfryn—"

"Is in grave danger, yes. But Padric is on the way."

"And Leowyn and the other knights?" she asked. "They were supposed to be on the temple roof with Talfryn to get the chariot. They may be hurt or..." She gulped down the bile rising in her gut. "We have to help them."

"I must help my son first," Circe said. "Manticore venom is deadly, even to you."

Brynwen's stomach constricted at the news. She had only seen the last few minutes of the fight before Padric and Warin overcame the manticore. *If even an immortal could perish from its venom, what about Padric?* She had placed the amulet in his hand before he took off to help Talfryn. *Is it enough to protect him?*

"I am fine *Mater*," Gregorio replied, but his face was pale and the veins of his wounded arm were green.

"Nay, your arm needs attention before—"

"Nay, the prophecy is more important than me. These men have risked their lives. I want to give aid where I can."

"We need to go now," Brynwen insisted. "They need our help."

The sorceress regarded Brynwen and her son, then nodded solemnly. "Help Sir Warin up."

Hearing his name, Warin roused and grabbed his chest as he sat up.

"Sir Warin." Brynwen knelt next to him. "Can you stand?"

The knight hesitated, then nodded. He took her proffered hand and together they rose.

"Ready," Brynwen said to Circe, and braced herself for her fifth harrowing ride through the smoke in as many minutes. Everything vanished in a cloud of blue smoke.

WHEN SHE STUMBLED out of the cloud, she was unprepared for the temple's slanted roof and listed to the left. Warin latched onto her arm before she could fall and roll over the clay tiles to the ground.

"I will never get used to that," she complained.

Gregorio chuckled. "The first few times can be quite unnerving."

"Can you transport that way, Signore Gregorio?"

"Alas," he said, "I was not gifted with such an ability."

Brynwen was about to respond when she spied the prone figure on the front end of the roof, recognizing his blond hair immediately. "Leowyn." She neared him and stopped. "Nay," she said, daring not to acknowledge the dark red river next to him, under him, on him. "Nay, nay, nay." Her eyes did not deceive her. There was no way he could have survived.

The breath caught in her throat, choked her. "He can't—can't be dead."

"Brynwen." Circe's hand yanked her around, wisps of her usually perfect blonde hair falling about her face. Dark circles began to form under the sorceress's eyes, making her appear older, almost human.

"You may want to say one of your Christian prayers for him."

"But—"

Circe shook her head. "I am very sorry, but there is little we can do for him now. However, there are others that need help. We must hurry."

Even though she felt sorrow beyond words, no tears came as Circe led her away from Leowyn. She could only berate herself for not getting there sooner. *Perhaps I could have helped him if I had come with him and Talfryn and the knights, instead of being swept off by Circe to retrieve the amulet. If only I had found the amulet sooner.*

"It will do no good to brew over his death," Circe said, reading her thoughts. "The creature that did this, the *aeternae*, would have run you through as well. Take a look at these men."

Warin took her hand, his big palm gentle as he held it. "My deepest condolences. He was a worthy warrior."

"I thank you," she managed to whisper.

She looked to Circe. Shaking the anger, sorrow, and frustration from her mind, she shoved the feelings deep, deep down, and followed the goddess to where Gregorio stood over two prone knights: Sir Rawlins and Sir Byron. A fourth man, Jarod, sat next to Byron, his feet braced against the tiles. Jarod's clothes were disheveled and drenched in sweat, his red hair standing straight up like grass.

Byron was awake, cradling his left arm while Jarod spoke to him in hushed tones. On his other side, Rawlins lay still, his dark complexion ashen and clothes torn to tatters, but breathing. The gaping hole in his shoulder looked serious, and he had lost a great amount of blood. Despite this, his normally serious expression struck her as serene—happy in the face of death. *Almost Viking-like,* Brynwen mused.

"Gonus," Circe said to her son, "sit down before you fall and topple over the roof." Gregorio thought to argue, then obliged without comment. He plopped down with weariness on the roof tiles next to the wounded men. Circe turned to Jarod. "Tell me, did the *aeternae* do all this damage?"

Jarod regarded the goddess with uncertainty. "That wolf-thing? Aye, marm. You see, it came out of nowhere and attacked us unprovoked."

"The *aeternae* needs no provocation. It will attack anyone, anything. It is a born predator. Many times it has killed for sport. I would liken it to a man in that regard." She leaned over Rawlins to check his wounds. His pale cheeks and blood loss concerned her.

"Jarod, thank you for watching over the knights," Brynwen said as she knelt between the two injured men, while Circe knelt next to Rawlins. "Where are the others?"

The young red-haired man shuddered. "There are more wounded down below. Many are your men, Sir Warin, but some are dead."

Byron's voice wavered as he said, "The way the creature killed them..." He shook despite the June heat.

Brynwen's throat constricted. *Worse than what had happened to Leowyn?*

Circe pursed her lips. "I feared as much. The healers are on their way as we speak."

"I need to check on my men," Warin said, his hands in fists. He pivoted and moved to the stairwell by the chariot platform.

Byron's complexion was pallid. A score of cuts and bruises accompanied his tattered and bloody cream-colored tunic. Many of his injuries were superficial, but the one on his arm appeared serious. With her gentle touch, Brynwen examined the appendage, taking care to inflict the least amount of pain possible. After a thorough examination, she applied a generous helping of her healing mix to his arm, then wrapped it in a fresh bandage. "Hold pressure here, Byron, and we'll see to your other wounds when we reach the infirmary."

As Circe leaned over Rawlins, checking his wounds, his eyes popped open and he shot to a sitting position—clamping his fingers around her throat. It happened so fast, no one could have prevented it. The force flipped Circe flat onto her back. Her staff fell out of her hand. Mouth set in a fierce scowl, Rawlins squeezed. A sound like a horse's shriek escaped Circe's throat. Taken unawares, she was powerless against him. Desperate fingers clawed at his hand and arm, leaving red welts but to no avail. Only moments ago, Rawlins's condition had been closer to that of a specter; now his firm grip proved otherwise.

Gregorio and Brynwen shouted and launched for the knight's arm, but it was locked around Circe's throat in an iron-clad grip. With each moment of panic, the goddess's complexion paled to blue. Her fingers and eyes sparked with energy aimed at him, but fizzled out as she grew weaker.

Why isn't she defending herself?

"Rawlins, she isn't the enemy," Brynwen pleaded, but he heard none of it.

Teeth gritted, beads of sweat ran down his forehead. The young man's eyes were utterly crazed. His total focus was locked on Circe, but Brynwen discerned with certainty that it wasn't the sorceress he saw. It was the creature. To him, the fight with the *aeternae* never ended.

With a shout, Warin dashed back to them. Both he and Jarod pried Rawlins's fingers off, one by one. Byron could only gape in helplessness.

Freed, Circe inhaled deep, gasping breaths. However, this only enraged Rawlins. He thrashed and threw his arms out in anger. "I will kill you!" he shouted repeatedly. They shoved him down onto the roof and pinned his arms to his sides.

Her words having little effect, Brynwen let go and peered around for another way to stop Rawlins from hurting himself or anyone else any further. Reaching into her satchel, she brought forth a second jar of the ointment she had made for Alice's Baby. "Rawlins," she said in a firm voice. "The fight is over and the creature is gone. Circe is *helping* us." As she spoke, she scooped out a generous amount onto her fingers and applied it to Rawlins's grimy forehead and cheeks with swift efficiency.

After a few more moments, the knight's eyes flickered. He began to weaken.

"It was a valiant fight, my friend," Warin said. "Come, we will celebrate with much wine and feasting."

Whatever grip the fear and pain had on Rawlins, it dissipated quickly.

"Rawlins," Brynwen said, stroking his bloody scalp. She placed her other hand on his good shoulder. "Rest now—you have earned it. You have prevailed against the creature and protected all of us from its wrath. Now, let us take care of you."

He blinked, lifting his head enough to squint into Brynwen's eyes. Then with a shudder, he passed out.

"Whatever possessed him to do that?" Gregorio wondered, voice shaking, gaping at his mother.

Circe's voice was deep and raspy as she spoke. "A knight's defensive protective reflex. An exceptional knight—" she coughed, "—will fight to the death."

Gregorio continued to eye Rawlins warily, though he slept. "In that case, I would not wish him as an enemy."

Brynwen grinned solemnly. "Nay, I should say not."

Circe cleared her sore throat. She smiled faintly, then found her staff and rocked unsteadily to her feet on the uneven roof.

"The chariot's protection spell," Brynwen whispered to Gregorio, who studied the goddess. "It is still affecting her, isn't it? Is that why she couldn't defend herself against Rawlins?"

"Lamentably," Circe said rather impatiently, trying to regain her composure. "It appears I am in your debt, young men and woman." She waved her hand. A puff of blue smoke swirled over the roof tiles before her. When the smoke cleared, a brazier holding a large bowl sat perfectly content on the tiled roof, as though it had always been there. Everyone glanced with curiosity inside the bowl, its black liquid splashing above the rim and then back into the dish without losing a drop.

"Shouldn't we depart, then?" Brynwen asked in earnest, eyeing Circe's scrying bowl.

"You can take these men down to the other healers. I will watch from here."

"Here? asked Jarod. "Why not at the infirmary?"

The sorceress glared at him.

"If we are not all dead, and if they come back," whispered Gregorio, "they will return the chariot to this roof."

CHAPTER 50

*A*ir and wind rushed past Talfryn, whipping hair into his face. He declined to open his eyes—refused to let the beast and ground be the last things he saw before he died. He couldn't bear to watch the beast catch and maul him to death.

"Talfryn."

He squeezed his eyes shut. The throbbing in his head intensified.

"Talfryn."

No.

"You are safe now. Well, safer."

There was no mistaking that educated voice. He cracked open an eye. "Padric?"

Worry knit his friend's brows. "You about gave me a heart attack when you fell."

"It wasn't my idea," he replied at last.

"Nay, I suppose not."

Talfryn opened his eyes wide. His heart plummeted as he noticed they were still soaring through the sky. Peering down, he spied green grass rushing past below them. A snaking road kept up with their pace. Bumps of lush greenery and trees flashed by. No buildings in sight. They were no longer in Cataractonium.

Finding himself sitting on Ulysses's back, the wind whistling past the peryton's antlers, Talfryn wondered how he'd gotten there. Dizziness came over him. He became terrified of falling again and clutched the fur on Ulysses's neck. He had the notion of holding onto an antler for better support, but thought better of it when he pictured being pitched back into the cloudless sky. The action only made his leg ache worse.

Finally, he regained some of his composure. To his immediate left, Padric clasped the reins of the four pegasi as though born for it. Wind rippled through his curls, the thrill of flying lifted his expression; and despite all the blood, cuts, and bruises all over him, he looked like a Roman emperor—or what he imagined a Roman emperor might look like. Padric was definitely Helius's heir.

"How did you get both me and the chariot?" Talfryn asked.

The faun grinned. "It would seem you have an admirer among the horses. The moment you plunged from the chariot, she dragged the other horses and chariot down after you. Then I scooped you up, jumped into the chariot, and placed you in Ulysses's care."

Talfryn stared at him in shock.

"'Tis true. You should give her a golden apple after a rescue like that."

"She certainly deserves one," replied Talfryn, peering in wonder at the end horse, Aethon. She neighed in agreement.

"Good shot, by the way," Padric said, pulling Talfryn out of his thoughts.

"Lucky shot." Talfryn's heart thudded, agonizing over Leowyn's lifeless body left lying on the roof. Not to mention the wolficorn's vengeful eyes after the hatchet struck its mark. "Is it dead?"

"I would imagine so, with the speed at which it plummeted to the earth. Honestly, I was more worried about rescuing your hide."

"Thanks for that." Talfryn swiped his unruly brown hair out of his face. "Did you beat Warin?"

"Not quite," Padric replied.

Talfryn squinted. "Explain."

"We ended up fighting against a manticore—a monster—together."

Talfryn's mouth dropped. "What?" *They worked together?*

"But we did not kill it, either. It was Gregorio, who is also Telegonus, Circe's missing son."

Talfryn's mouth couldn't drop any further. Two improbable things had happened at the same time. *Does the universe wish to make me go mad?*

"I know how it sounds, but 'tis true." Padric gave a brief, extraordinary synopsis of what had transpired between himself, Warin, and the manticore-Gregorio-Telegonus.

"I see," Talfryn said, not really seeing at all. "Then what do we do now?"

Eyes on the horizon, Padric shook his head. "Not we. You and Ulysses will return to the arena. I will take the chariot as far away as possible and hide it. Or hope it loses its power before Helius can harness it."

Talfryn bristled, indignant. Even Ulysses gave a little huff.

"Nay," replied Talfryn. "We aren't leaving. You'll need all the help you can get. Ulysses agrees with me."

"I can manage."

"Padric," came a voice from a short distance away. "Splendid job in retrieving my chariot for me."

Padric nearly dropped the reins in his surprise.

"Thanks to you, Champion, both Telegonus and my chariot are safe." Atop his black-winged mare, Helius swooshed to the side of the chariot to Padric's left.

"M'lord," Padric said hastily and dipped his head. He should have known Helius would follow him, but to his relief, the god did not seem to have overheard his conversation with Talfryn. "Sir Warin helped a great deal with Telegonus's rescue, and it was Talfryn who defeated the beast in the chariot on his own."

Padric grinned at his friend's blushing cheeks. "Ah, well, you know..." Talfryn rubbed the back of his neck.

Helius pried his eyes away from Padric, as though noticing Talfryn for the first time. The sun god scrutinized the farmer. "Well done, lad. There are not many who could defeat an *aeternae*." Then his eyes darkened with another emotion: worry. Padric had to concentrate to hear what the god muttered, "How on earth did it and the manticore escape the pit?" as though talking to someone directly next to him.

Padric thought he saw a silver spark and shimmer to Helius's left. He blinked and the shimmer vanished. He had seen the shimmer on multiple occasions—not gold, like the rest of Helius's jewelry, but more like diamonds. It was always near the god, and always appeared when he became silent or thoughtful. This was the first time Padric drew close enough to Helius when it happened, to tell for certain it was not an accessory, but something external. *What could it be?*

Discarding the thought momentarily, he asked about Helius's question. "What is the Pit?"

"The Pit." Helius scowled. "I see I cannot keep much from you, my grandson. It is a cavern at the edge of Cataractonium. Deep, deep down inside is where the *aeternae* and a number of other extremely dangerous creatures are housed. These monsters have not seen sunlight in eons. Even Circe is not aware of all that is housed there. Over two score of keepers guard it at all times. They were handpicked. The best. There is no way the creature could have gotten past them."

"That thing is *yours?*" Talfryn asked, mouth agape.

"And the manticore, Telegonus, was kept there as well, was he not?" Padric asked with a chasm in his stomach.

"To my shame. But only for a few weeks." Helius lowered his head, shaking it sadly. "I honestly knew not that it was Telegonus. Hold," he said, scrutinizing Talfryn. The shimmer appeared by the god's ear again. "How came you to encounter the *aeternae*—and *on my chariot?*" His gaze pierced Talfryn like a sword. The farmer crouched low on Ulysses's back, his hands urging the peryton for a quick escape.

"I...I was nearby when the creature attacked. It was already loose."

Helius raised a skeptical eyebrow. "We shall see. Come Padric," he said, looking upward to the sun. "We will finish this once and for all. Apollo shall die, and Jupiter will suffer. We must make haste to prevail upon the sun's power."

Padric cursed inwardly. *How was he to distract the god? He even tried to press at Talfryn and Ulysses to escape while they had the chance. Now what could he do?*

"We will come with you," Talfryn offered with a grin. "As an escort."

Padric shot daggers at his friend. Talfryn merely grinned wider.

"Splendid idea," replied Helius. "Then you may write of our victory, young man. A story you can tell your grandchildren, Padric."

"Marvelous," Padric replied dryly.

"Give me the reins, grandson."

"I cannot."

Helius cocked a brow.

"I wish to drive longer, sir. Since I was a boy, I have longed for the chance." It was not untrue. Sometimes he had daydreamed about flying, but never imagined in his wildest dreams it could ever be achieved.

Helius laughed heartily. "As you wish, lad." A cloud of purple burst around him, then it rose from the horse's back and Padric had to step to the right to make room as Helius burst out of the cloud in the empty space he had made. "But first—"

Padric glanced at Talfryn then flicked the reins. The horses shot forward, leaving Helius's smaller winged horse in their proverbial dust. The god clung onto the chariot walls for dear life.

A rush filled Padric, stealing the air from his lungs. *Oh, the freedom of flight! What would I give to fly as oft as I wished?* The wind rippling through his hair. It surpassed anything he had ever experienced before. The only downside being the heat radiating from the crystal. A mini-sun, practically in his face.

Ulysses and Talfryn kept up with the chariot as Padric coaxed the four horses to pick up speed. If their wings could travel all day and night lugging a chariot and the sun, a little extra momentum should not harm them overly much.

Yorkshire came into view. One could not miss the wall ringing the entire city and the megalithic Minster cathedral. The cathedral had been the turning point in his adventure. There, he had been given hope and his faith back.

They only had a few minutes left, at best. Already, he could feel Helius's strength grow beside him. Even as his own chest began to burn. *Dearest Lord, once more, I plead for the strength to finish this.* With a flick of his wrist, the pegasi were urged to veer to the right toward the safest place he could conjure up: due west to the sea.

Still laughing, Helius's eyes sparked golden sun rays. The chariot curved heavenward; the horses leading them toward the sun at a silent command from their true master. *The Charioteer.* Seething, Padric realized his stupidity at thinking he could control the situation. Of course the horses were being drawn to the sun, along with its namesake god.

Helius eyed the crystal with an insatiable hunger. "It is time." Pure power radiated off the god as his body absorbed the essence of the crystal. His fingers twitched as they extended with anticipation, the crystal humming and the sun's yellow and orange rays swirling in a vortex directly above it. A small ball of energy transferred to the space between Helius's fingers.

In an instant, an explosion erupted before Padric. His eyes beheld an engulfing fire. People screamed in their death throes. Land, sky—everything burned.

Roana's vision. The vision ceased as quickly as it began, jolting him back to reality. Once again, endless blue sky extended before him, foliage and roads below, dark pegasi pulling the chariot, and Helius, Talfryn, and Ulysses to either side. He gasped, releasing the breath he had been holding, and drew a shaky hand through his hair as a splitting headache started.

Helius peered at him with worry. "Padric?" Again, the silver star appeared near his ear, but Helius batted a hand at it.

"It is nothing," Padric said, shaking his head. "All is well." He could feel Talfryn's stare burning a hole in the back of his skull. His chest burned with a fierce intensity, almost to distraction.

The silver shimmer caught Padric's eye yet again. This time, he thought he saw an eye and a mouth. He wondered if the manticore's venom had given him hallucinations.

The god grinned, showing all his white teeth. "Excellent. The first thing we shall do is make a visit to Apollo and relieve him of his charge."

"What shall you do when Jupiter comes seeking revenge?" Padric asked and looked at the place which had shimmered next to Helius moments ago. Now it came to him. The eye, the mouth, it resembled a statue he had seen recently. One with two faces and a chunk of nose missing from one side. A statue whose likeness caused strife within his celestial family. Padric dared to hazard a guess as to why it was missing that nose. *Two-faced. Deceitful.* "What do you think, Janus? I see you hovering over there enjoying our discussion. Would you care to contribute?"

CHAPTER 52

a hearty, deep laugh broke out to the left of Helius, accompanied by a white shimmer rippling like a frosty blanket. From this, a body materialized in the shape of a man, outlined entirely of dazzling white stars. It reminded Padric of something between a constellation and a stained glass window. The transparent man sat atop what appeared to be the Pegasus constellation, keeping pace with them as wispy clouds and blue sky passed through him. In another moment, their outlines filled in, and in no time a man with a smooth head of black hair and a goatee, adorned in a juniper green outfit and white cape sat on a white flying stallion. Padric scrutinized the man. There was something familiar about him.

"My," the once-starry man said with a broad smile, "your grandson has some astuteness, Helius, does he not? And what an eye. Well met, young Padric de Clifton. And your friend Talfryn, of course." He did not acknowledge Ulysses, a slight Padric did not fail to miss.

Helius beamed. "Forgive me. Padric and Talfryn, this is Janus. The Roman god of beginnings, time, doorways..."

"And endings," Padric finished. It made sense now: Janus planned to destroy the world. This was not merely a case of a despondent god seeking revenge for his lost son. Another god was actually encouraging

Helius's erratic behavior. In all likelihood, Janus planted the seed of discontent. After all, the chariot was a gift from an unnamed friend.

"What?" Talfryn asked. Then realization dawned on his face. "Pleased to meet you, M'lord."

Roana's prophecy blazed across Padric's mind, persistent to be noticed.

"Sir," Padric turned to Janus, "how long have you been colluding with M'lord Helius?"

"Nigh on eighteen months, I should say."

Helius grinned. "It was I who asked him to return to help me with this project. During the latest eclipse, a vision came to me—the answer to why my son Phaethon perished all those years ago. I made the connection that Jupiter did not end his life to save the world. Nay, it was to remove me from the picture in order to make way for his own son, Apollo. The vision showed me how to be rid of Apollo once and for all so I might return. It was glorious. I could not call on Janus fast enough."

Padric contemplated the story. The eclipse had occurred six months ago, but Janus had admitted to being around longer. "Is Circe aware Janus is here?"

A frown drew Helius's lips down. "Janus asked to avoid her. They had a heated argument years ago. Well, many arguments. Janus merely wished to avoid her being cross, so he enchanted himself from her. I enjoy his company and was pleased to oblige, as much as it grieves me to keep the truth from her."

Padric ticked a finger against his thigh. That explained what Circe had told him about her father's recent behavior: always distracted and speaking to himself.

Talfryn cleared his throat. "That still seems unfair."

Padric gave him a withering look, and Talfryn bit his tongue.

Instead, Talfryn asked, "Where did you find this lovely crystal? I haven't seen its like before."

Janus studied his manicured nails. "I came upon it during my travels in China. When Helius told me of his plans, I decided he was in more need of it than me."

Ah, there it was. The clincher.

"He even had the chariot built to go with it." Helius clutched his friend's shoulder warmly.

"M'lord," Padric said to Helius in hopeful nonchalance, "may I have a word in private?" Janus grinned knowingly and bowed deeply, then coaxed his horse to fall back a few paces. When the dark-haired god was out of ear shot, Padric leaned in closer. "Does it not worry you how he suddenly reappeared after so many years, and completely avoided your family?"

"He is a god of many traits and abilities. What he does is his own business," Helius replied.

"Yes, but why show up now?"

"I called upon him."

Truly, Padric did not believe this. At least if he did, he was not in his right mind at the time. "But can you trust him?"

The god bristled. "Of course I trust him. He is my oldest friend, whom I have known for centuries and has always had my ear. What is this about?"

"Does it not strike you as odd that he happened to have the crystal on hand?"

"He probably gave you the manticore, too," Talfryn added jokingly.

Helius furrowed a brow as he regarded Talfryn. "He did, at that….Or rather, he gave me the name of a handler who dealt in such things. They captured it, and I was willing to pay handsomely and keep it safely locked away to prevent it from harming anyone."

"Ah," said Talfryn. "Janus is most generous and connected."

"To my reckoning, too generous and connected," Padric replied.

The sun god's face paled. "No. Janus had no idea the manticore was Telegonus. He could not have."

"Can you know that for certain?" Padric asked. "It seems rather grand timing, your grandsons fighting each other to the death. Taking two of your heirs out of the way."

"Nay—"

"When did you purchase the manticore?"

Helius started sweating. It was the first time Padric had ever seen the god in distress. "It was less than a month ago."

"That was the last time anyone saw Gregorio—er Telegonus," Talfryn interjected. "We found his campsite at Mamucium."

"Helius," Janus said from behind the chariot, "these young striplings are endeavoring to pit you against me. Would you believe them over your oldest friend?"

"I," Helius stammered, rubbing his temples. "I do not know what to believe anymore. Please tell me these charges are false."

Padric shook his head. "Circe saw through him years ago and forbade him to return, did she not?"

Janus crossed his arms lazily. "She is a meddlesome brat."

"Do not speak so of her," Helius uttered. This was the man Padric wanted to see, not the spoiled child he had played since Padric's arrival in Cataractonium.

Padric glared at Janus. "M'lord, ask Janus what he gains from this venture. I know I am all ears."

Talfryn nodded.

Poor Helius was a muddle of emotions. His oldest friend's loyalty and reputation were in question, but the accused man himself appeared unaffected by any of it. At last, Helius asked, "Janus, did you know the manticore was Telegonus?"

"What a silly question."

"Answer me, Janus. After all we have been through, I demand a straight answer."

The goateed god grimaced, tapping his fingers along his arm. "Verily, you are quite thick sometimes, Helius. Even these children figured it out. Circe was wise to ban me from your presence. Nevertheless, she lacked the foresight to put up wards against me." He snorted.

Helius gasped. "Janus, you would not—"

"Oh please."

"He was grieving!" Talfryn cried. "How could you take advantage of someone who was grieving?"

"For over two millennia? Spare me. My ninth child was mauled by a lion, but I mourned his loss for a mere half a century. Children die. It is unfortunate, but we move on." He shrugged.

The more Janus spoke, the more Padric disliked the deity. Discretely, he gestured for Ulysses and Talfryn to fall back, and hopefully make a distraction.

Out of the corner of his eye, he watched them glide behind the chariot toward Janus's back. Stopping short of the god, Talfryn gave an odd expression and began to speak to the back of Janus's head. The farmer introduced himself. *What is he doing?* Then it clicked in Padric's brain: *two faces.* Talfryn was speaking with Janus's second face.

"What is it you desire?" Padric finally asked of Janus. The crystal grew warmer with each passing minute. He spared a glance over the pegasi's shoulders. *How far away is the ocean?*

"I already have it," Janus replied. "Helius's power." With that, he raised a hand and a wooden staff appeared. It was not as grand as Circe's, but equally impressive, with runes etched along the shaft. In a heartbeat, the staff glowed, visibly pulling energy off of Helius. "I was going to have you do the honors of removing Apollo from his position, but it looks like I must do it myself."

Helius's eyes widened. "Janus, nay!" Channeling his power, the sun god drew more energy into his orb, intensifying the heat twofold, then launched a series of sun bolts at Janus.

Pulling his staff in front of him, Janice's piece of wood took the brunt of the attack.

"Cease," Padric cried to Helius. "That is exactly what he desires. He is absorbing your power. "

"I am unable to release it," Helius responded, eyes squinting as he struggled with the orb. No sooner had he said it, than the energy radiating from the orb slunk its way over to the staff of its own volition, as though the staff needed only one taste of the power to control it thereafter. The runes began to glow in earnest.

"What are you doing?" Helius could only gape with wide eyes. "Stop this at once. Janus—our plan!"

"Did you really think it was *your* plan, old man?"

Padric caught Talfryn's eye, and they acted simultaneously. Padric reached for Helius's arm while Talfryn pounced at Janus's back.

Giant sparks emitted from Helius's orb, sizzling and striking at Padric's arms and clothing. It was all he could do not to scream in agony as what felt like lightning ripped at his flesh. Dropping the reins, he lunged across Helius toward the staff. "Get away from him!" The might of the sun's power surrounding Padric took him completely by surprise as the blast struck him square in the chest. With an agonizing exclamation, he hurtled over the front of the chariot.

CHAPTER 53

Screaming inwardly from the pain searing throughout his entire body, Padric's ribs cracked against the chariot's draught pole. His hand caught the chariot wheel, and he dropped his body to dangle there while he fought to catch his breath. He was well aware of the chariot dipping and groaning with his added weight on this side.

Shouts and shuffles took place above. A blood-curdling shriek, and then nothing.

Helius! Taking in the direness of the situation, Padric steeled himself to climb back into the chariot. He had to stop Janus from killing Helius and going through with his plan. He scarcely looked up in time to view a spectacle of swirling purple cloth descending from the rear of the chariot. From the fabric, Helius's hair and appendages emerged. With quick reflexes, Padric hooked a hand around the god's elbow.

"M'lord!" cried Padric as he and Helius swung from the momentum. The muscles in his arms were near the buckling point. Ulysses nose-dived directly in front of them, flaring up Helius's violet robes as he rushed past with a screaming Talfryn on his back.

When they stopped swinging, Helius's head hung limp. The two dangled precariously from the axle for a few intense heartbeats, the strain in Padric's muscles nearing their end. "Helius?" Still nothing.

The peryton circled below once and retraced his route back up to the chariot. Padric caught the spark in Ulysses's eye, as well as the terrified and windswept expression on Talfryn's face. He almost laughed at the situation.

Arms exhausting at an alarming rate, Padric called to Helius one more time. *"Avus!" Grandfather!* His voice felt hoarse, but he sighed with relief when the god at last stirred. *"Avus,* listen carefully. You must go with Talfryn and Ulysses. They will catch you. Do you understand?"

The deity managed a feeble nod and mumbled something.

"What?" Padric asked.

"You must destroy it," Helius said louder.

"How? The crystal is too strong."

"With my last ounce of power, I overcharged it. You must hurry. There is precious little time."

With haste, Ulysses moved under the pair and Padric dropped Helius into Talfryn's arms. The god suddenly looked small compared to the farmer's well-built frame. "We will take care of him," Talfryn said gravely.

It was all Padric could do to nod. The rest of his strength would be needed to climb back into the chariot.

A bolt of sunlight seared downward from the chariot. It zapped the tip of Ulysses's antlers and cascaded down toward the ground. The struck piece of antler burst to instant ash. The peryton squirmed and darted another couple of feet away.

Blinded by the sudden brightness, Padric nearly lost his hold on the wheel.

"Enough," Janus's voice bellowed from above. "You have already lost."

Another bolt zipped past them. Talfryn's face became ashen as he glanced about for more lightning bolts.

Why does Janus not come down and smite us? "Get to safety," urged Padric.

Talfryn shook his head with a mischievous smile. "This is the safest place to be."

"Of course," Padric realized, "Janus must direct the horses upward and mustn't leave the chariot unattended. This could come to our advantage."

A third bolt shot down, this time near Talfryn's wounded leg, and Ulysses veered again. Talfryn whispered something to the peryton, who nodded and winged his way upward. Talfryn grabbed a hold of Padric's hoof and pushed up. Understanding his friend's gesture, Padric allowed the aid with untoward gratefulness. Steeling himself, he reached up with a sweaty hand and managed to seize the draught pole and swing the other leg up to catch a hoof over it. With a nod, he bade Talfryn release his grip.

"Finish it," Talfryn said as Ulysses listed left and away from the chariot. "And watch out for his second face!"

Helius lifted his head again, eyes on the chariot. "The crystal."

Lightning bolts followed them as Ulysses narrowly dodged each strike. Janus crowed in amusement, his booming guffaw grating on Padric's last nerve. Now that he was alone, a weight came upon him. Unsure if it was weariness or the altitude, Padric began to wheeze. He clung on long enough to let the dizziness subside and catch his breath. *What would I give for another winged animal at this moment?* The chariot dipped with a bit of wind, and Padric's body jolted. Heart pounding, he paused to calculate Janus's exact position.

"A question, sir," Talfryn called out, his voice changing direction as no doubt Ulysses was on the constant move to avoid blasts from Janus's staff. "Do you and your other face ever argue?"

"What?" came a melancholy voice. It was much different from the confident voice Padric had encountered a few minutes before.

"And," Talfryn continued, "do you argue out loud, or inside your heads?"

"I really do not think—"

"Which leads to the next question. Who is the victor of the majority of the arguments?"

"Well, that would be…ach, will you kindly stop moving so I can blast you to oblivion?"

Padric cracked a smile before his attention was drawn to the matter at hand. The anticipation of being near the power source a second time caused his insides to tremble. *No fear,* he urged himself. *Not now, when it is so close to being finished.*

Finish it, Talfryn's phrase repeated in his mind. He pulled himself up to a crouched position on the pole brace at the front of the chariot. After one last glance at the sky, he sprung up and pivoted, drawing his *gladius* from his back in the same movement. The sword shot up and arced down toward Janus's head, into the eyes of the second face.

The god of time was faster than Padric expected. Janus shifted a half step and the *gladius* passed harmlessly through the air where he had been standing a moment before, crashing into the side of the chariot.

Padric's arm hair burned as it came dangerously close to the crystal. *Finish it. Finish the crystal.*

The horses neighed wildly as Janus shook the reins. "Care to endeavor once more?" Janus turned his head and the second face—*or the first face?*—turned and spoke with a wicked grin. "I guarantee you will not wish to trifle with me again."

Recovering quickly, Padric replied, "Nonsense, I could fight all day."

"Then by all means." Janus tapped the staff on the chariot bed. It sparked something fierce, dazzling Padric. Retreating a step, his hoof slid along the draught pole, and his knee banged hard into the chariot guard. Janus took the opportunity to swing the staff. Padric parried, the staff sparking as it slid harmlessly along the metal weapon.

In an attempt for flare, Janus twirled the staff above his head, giving a roar of triumph. "Do you really think that will do any good against my new power?" In a snap, the top of the staff was engulfed in an array of orange and yellow flames. Janus shifted uncomfortably, wincing as the fire singed his eyebrows.

Padric smirked. "You cannot contain the power, can you? That is the reason you needed Helius."

"I daresay I have enough to bring you and Apollo to your knees, and the sun as well." Janus laughed again. A bead of sweat glided down his forehead.

"Not if I can help it."

Padric sprang into the chariot, forcing Janus to bump into the side of the chariot bed. Steel met staff as they sparred despite the close quarters. Side-step, thrust, and jab.

Is it me, or is it getting hotter? How far were they from Apollo now? His mind whirled, wondering how he could destroy the crystal before then if he had to fight Janus the entire time. Fatigue overcame Padric, brought on by the combination of the heat, the venom, and the continued fight. He made a clumsy swipe at Janus and regretted it immediately. His eyes grew wide as the staff arced down toward his head.

CHAPTER 54

*P*adric dropped his *gladius* and caught the staff in his hands. The shock of the staff's power jolted through his body and nearly sent him to his knees. He could feel the sun, its very epicenter at his navel. But instead of elation like what Helius experienced with the raw power, all Padric felt was scorching, blinding torment burning him up from the inside out. Tearing him apart.

The next thing he knew, he sat on the bed of the chariot, his back against the contraption's wall. He felt roasted and spent. Even the palms of his hands were black and charred. His *gladius* was gone, likely falling toward the ground.

Janus stood over him, gloating. "You are no match for me, lad. While I appreciate your valor and cleverness, I am afraid I cannot let you live." He raised the staff to bash in Padric's skull.

Wheezing through the pain, Padric pooled all his strength. Years of military training flashed through his brain within a heartbeat. Words his father said, regardless of the reason—life or vocation—soared through his brain, overtaking the words the Oracle had implanted in his mind.

Breathe.

Take in all aspects of the situation.

Act.

If he failed, he would let down his father and all the men in his unit. Brynwen and Talfryn. Miriel and Isemay. The entire world. His family would perish, completely oblivious to the reason they had died.

The amulet. In all the excitement, he had nearly forgotten about it. Once Brynwen handed it to him, he had slipped it into his pocket, and there it remained.

"Why are you doing this?" Padric queried, stalling for time. The low hum from the crystal sounded through his head, nearly to distraction. He bit his cheek to stay focused and retrieved the ring from his pocket. "Why destroy the world?"

His hair whipping in the wind, the two-faced god explained, "It is time to start over. A rebirth, if you will." He pushed at the staff. "I have seen the future of this world, and it is not in my favor."

That is it? Crimson anger coursed through Padric's veins anew. This god before him wanted to destroy the world because he did not like his prospects; had made people suffer to change his own life. *Are all the gods depicted accurately in the stories, and as selfish as Janus?*

"Helius was your tool all along." Padric felt profoundly sorry for his great-grandfather. "You exploited his pain and anger. You kidnapped Telegonus and turned him into a monster, hoping we would kill each other. For a false friendship, you would destroy everything?"

A new determination rippled through Padric; a strength pulled from deep within. A tickle. A tremor. Whether from his own power or his horse Firminus, he did not know, but his hoof collided with the god's shin. Janus winced, crashing into the opposite end of the chariot.

Slipping the ring onto his ring finger, Padric shot to his hoofs. Before Janus could react, Padric belted his elbow into the god's forward face. The deity's head whipped backward, his grip on the staff faltering. Padric yanked the staff from his hand and the sun's might intensified two-fold. *How does Janus stand it?* Without showing any more weakness, Padric twirled the staff and pummeled Janus in the shoulder. The strike hammered the god down, his bottom striking the chariot bed with a thud.

Janus sat on the floor in a daze. It was all Padric could do to not bash his head in on the spot. Instead, he inhaled deep, throbbing breaths. *How much time do I have left?*

He regarded the fallen god. There were so many things he needed to know, yet they remained cloaked in mystery.

"What was Warin's part in this?"

Janus shifted, rubbing at his sore jaw. "He was to keep you distracted while Helius and I finished with our plans. It worked, did it not?" He grinned wickedly at his own cleverness. "I must say I was surprised at your working together to defeat the manticore. Alas, I had so many plans for the creature, a lifetime of torture for his insolence against me. Me!"

"Telegonus broke your statue, did he? He saw you as the threat you are to his grandfather and lashed out."

"It took years to hunt him down, but when at last I captured him, it was a thrill to see him squirm. But then you came into the story, distracting Helius from our project. You cannot know how furious I was when you failed to fall for the dryad disguised as your maiden love."

Padric brought the staff closer. "Do not speak of her."

The god raised his hands in surrender. "You could join me. We could start over afresh."

Are you out of your mind? Padric wanted to shout. Instead, he could not help but think how Talfryn would respond and said, "Start over before breakfast, or how we met? Frankly, I would prefer breakfast, as it did not sit well this morning, much like this conversation."

The two-faced god burst out laughing. Wiping the sweat off his face, he said, "Oh, we could indeed have fun. Think on this—would you not change the world if you had the power? There are many evil things out there which we can bring to a standstill."

Padric paused at that. *Change men's hearts? What if I could? Certainly, I know many bad people, but I also know so many more who are good. Would I change them?* "Nay," he retorted. "The world may not be perfect, but it is what we have. Not everyone is evil, inherent or otherwise."

Janus guffawed. "You Christians. So full of hope and faith in your God. He is no better than the rest of us."

Padric swung the staff down toward Janus's head, but halted an inch before it could split his nose in half.

"My *Christian values* have more substance than your genocidal conjecture." Twisting, he smashed the staff over the crystal with all his might.

"Nay. You fool!" cried Janus, throwing up his hands. He scrambled to his knees and covered his face with his arm.

The staff snapped in half. The overlarge jewel cracked and fizzed. Sparks, shards, and splinters shot off, stinging and pinching Padric's skin.

The two-faced god stared at the damaged crystal. "I wanted to kill you from the beginning, you know, but Helius was confident he could sway you to our side." Janus barked a cruel laugh. "You think you have won, but not yet, young champion," he scoffed. "Mark my words, there will be a reckoning. And next time, you shan't win."

"Rather arrogant, are we not?" Padric raised a brow.

Janus merely harrumphed. "You should get that looked at." He indicated the painful abrasion on Padric's chest. An insincere frown pinched his lips. "Manticore venom is no ordinary insect sting." With that, the god snapped his fingers and melted away in a cloud of green smoke. The laughter from his lips reverberated in the air, then fizzled out like a thin vapor, but the laugh echoed in Padric's head much longer.

Suddenly, the whole chariot jolted and shifted. Within two heartbeats, they were flying horizontally with the ground, then it tipped down toward land. The reins had fallen over the side during their scuffle.

Beyond the damaged crystal, Padric spied Talfryn sitting atop the pegasus Aethon, guiding the chariot back to Cataractonium. Padric slumped against the chariot wall and laughed in relief. "Talfryn," Padric called, "I could kiss you!"

"But what would my sister say to that?"

Despite the pain of moving any part of his body, Padric laughed wholeheartedly for the first time in a very long while.

Astride Ulysses, Helius was awake. His eyes glowed with rage when he spotted Talfryn. "What are you doing to my pegasi?" he shouted.

"Resetting your course, of course," Talfryn replied, chuckling into the wind. "They concurred heartily."

The crackling of the crystal caught Padric's attention. It hummed and sparked at a disturbing rate. His heart raced in time with the sparks. "Blast, we have no time. Tal," he said, raising his voice. "Take us over the sea."

"Got it. Hold tight!" With a word, Talfryn directed the horses to swerve down and to the west.

Cataractonium passed beneath them. Pulling himself wearily to his hoofs, Padric calculated his options. To save the horses and themselves, he would have to move fast. The humming from the crystal escalated, causing greater and greater heat and bodily discomfort, and making it difficult to concentrate.

"Keep them steady," he called to Talfryn. The farmer waved a hand in understanding.

With the last of his strength, Padric clambered over the chariot guard and stepped onto the draught pole. He balanced and felt for the pin ring that connected the pole with the pegasi. Finding the ring, he twisted, but it refused to budge. He turned both ways, but nothing.

The pounding in his head intensified, until it was almost unbearable.

"Padric, hurry," Talfryn called back. "It's going to blow!"

Padric did not deem a reply necessary as he retreated to the chariot and grabbed one half of the staff. He jabbed mercilessly at the pin. After the second jab, it clicked. With one swift movement, he twisted, releasing the pin, and leapt onto Phlegon's back.

Talfryn kicked Aethon's sides. The crystal made one final *tink* sound, then exploded with fiery abandon. The god, humans, and pegasi screamed in chorus as the world burst into pure white.

CHAPTER 55

Scarcely did Padric remember the return to Cataractonium or the touchdown on the temple roof's platform. He vaguely recalled Talfryn telling a joke regarding exploding chariots and fiery horses, but the sun remained in the sky. The sky remained blue. Besides the chariot, nothing else exploded.

The world had survived.

With a passing thought, he wondered if Apollo ever came to realize the small margin his life came to being forfeit.

Talfryn was first to dismount and limped around the platform. Ulysses had already landed, and Helius slipped to the ground with a thud. The once glowing sun god was completely drained. Sitting in a huddle of his purple robes and hugging his knees, he appeared less regal, more like an agitated, exhausted teenager.

Brynwen ran one step ahead of Circe and Gregorio-Telegonus and reached the top step of the platform first. The healer embraced Talfryn, each talking over the other—Talfryn insisting he was in fine shape despite the gaping hole in his leg; Brynwen believing no such thing. It might have been more comical to Padric if he himself were in better shape.

Circe and Gregorio helped Helius to a sitting position. The sorceress caressed his cheek and even laid a kiss to his brow. It was the most affection Padric had ever seen from her.

Padric remained seated on Phlagon's back. The horse nickered, longing to be free and have the extra bushel of apples Talfryn had apparently promised him. In fact, all the pegasi became antsy after the rough ride. Each of Phlagon's movements made Padric want to either vomit or pass out. Both were likely outcomes. Once the sky cleared of smoke from the smoldering remnants of the chariot, all the pain he had pushed deep, deep down erupted to the surface. There was not one muscle or organ that did not scream whenever he made the slightest move. And the burning in his chest where the manticore's spike had scraped skin—it felt very *wrong*. It seared like nothing else, straight to the bone; festering to his very core. He dared not look at it for fear of its having eaten through his entire chest cavity.

Taking a fresh gulp of air, he prayed that everyone would leave him alone for a few minutes to collect himself to be more presentable—

"Padric!" Brynwen cried.

He winced involuntarily as her hand landed on his knee. "Bryn," he said, a little more breathily than he would have liked. Squeezing her hand was all he could manage.

"Padric, I called your name five times just now. Where did you go?" She was worried for him, and had every right to be, but somehow it made him feel vulnerable, again.

"Nowhere. I am the epitome of health—it looks worse than it is." He patted her hand for emphasis.

She slipped her hand from his and placed it on her hip. "If you are so fine, then I would like to see you come down from that horse." She raised an eyebrow expectantly.

The slightest movement felt like pins stabbing his chest. He grimaced involuntarily. "I prefer to stay mounted at present. How fare my men?" he asked instead. It had made him heartsick to learn the fate of Leowyn and other fighters by the *aeternae* from Talfryn. Even though he had not been there, Padric felt a failure to them, by not being there to fight beside each of them in the end.

Padric shuddered and peered over Brynwen's head, but had difficulty seeing much beyond the platform as dark spots crept into the corners of his eyesight. *There is quite a bit of movement...or is the roof moving?*

She shook her head. "With care, Rawlins and Serill will pull through. Warin took them to the infirmary right away, but Byron and Aeron wanted to wait for you."

"They are alive?" Padric asked. A huge feeling of peace washed over him.

"Lieutenant." Aeron's voice carried, trudging up the steps of the platform. Talfryn, Byron, and Jarod limped up after him.

Some of the tightness in Padric's stomach loosened, and he released a sigh of relief. Rawlins and most of the others still lived. *But Leowyn...*

"Lieutenant," Aeron and Byron said together when they reached the last step, their faces grim. A deep cut ran across Aeron's forehead, and several red lacerations sliced through his tunic. "I tried to stop the beast, but it knocked me out cold and dragged me into a grove of trees."

Padric smiled at the dark-haired knight in empathy. "It is good to see you in one piece, Aeron. Byron. You did your best. That is all one can ask."

"But Leowyn, and some of Warin's men didn't make it."

Padric swallowed and nodded solemnly, his chest constricting. "We will mourn their loss for all time."

"Go to the infirmary with Jarod," Brynwen instructed with a soft voice. "We will be there shortly."

Padric's vision blurred, and he blinked several times. The burning in his chest constricted his movements as he tried to think of what to say. "Bryn, I—" Another wracking pain stabbed at his chest, doubling him over. He vaguely heard Brynwen scream, then there was nothing but darkness.

CHAPTER 56

Thank Brynwen tore into the infirmary's little medicine closet. With quick abandon, she collected dried herbs and ointments of all colors in her arms, placing them in a surprisingly tidy row on the table by the infirmary's largest mixing bowl. All her favorite herbs. The best of the best of the herbarium's stores. She stared at each item, willing them to reveal which would work, which would save him.

On the way to the infirmary, Circe explained the dangers of manticore venom: the green substance oozing from the gash; the black veins protruding from the wound, searching for the victim's heart. The goddess had witnessed someone die from it millennia ago. There had been no available antidote then.

But Brynwen would find an antidote. *There must be one.* She lifted the pestle to start grinding dried rosemary when the sorceress's lilting voice spoke from the door. "How can I help?"

Brynwen spun and merely stared at Circe in disbelief.

Circe crossed her arms and barged into the room. "Padric and Telegonus are in equal danger. If there is an antidote, we will find it. Together." Her lips pursed as she peered at the collection of bottles and plants on the table. With deft movements, she rearranged and replaced a handful of Brynwen's chosen ingredients with others from the shelves.

"You barely helped me find the amulet." Circe had made her chase a squirrel to fetch the wretched thing, for all the good it did him. "Why should you help now?" Brynwen's hands itched in irritation. She hated to admit it, but some of the herbs the goddess chose were better than her original choices. Others were, well, rat tails and raven feet were among the very last ingredients Brynwen would ever add to anything.

Circe hissed under her breath. "The amulet was your quest, and I could barely interfere. And those currently injured are my own son and grandson."

"But Gregorio is immortal."

"Immortal in longevity only. He can still be killed by mortal means." She noted Brynwen's confusion. "He was not born immortal. I granted him immortality after he nearly killed his father. Long story—" she added, seeing Brynwen's questioning look. "He has a stronger tolerance for the venom because of being a demigod and my gift of immortality; but it will eventually kill him. Slowly and painfully." Brynwen heard the waver in Circe's voice and decided to refrain from asking more questions about it.

"Then where do we begin?" She gestured to the array of possible medicines.

"Where you left off will do."

The corner of Brynwen's lip turned up and she picked up the mortar and pestle. "We will start with some rosemary."

"Drink it, Padric, please," Brynwen coaxed a few minutes later, dismayed at Padric's scrunched nose. On the neighboring bed, Gregorio sat up on propped pillows, Circe fussing over him in the same manner.

"What is in this?" Padric asked, his cheeks blanching as he gazed into the cup of dark, murky liquid. "It smells revolting. Why would you make something so vile?"

"Only when the occasion arises." There was no way she would reveal what main ingredient Circe plopped into the elixir. It turned her own stomach. She nearly retched several times during its preparation.

The room, filled with wounded men from the fight at the temple, moaned in equal displeasure. Padric's men, Warin and his men, as well as several of Helius's soldiers were present.

"Byron," Rawlins groaned from the other end of the room. "Put your blasted boots back on. They stink like rotten eggs."

"It's not me," Byron protested.

"Not even the goats would drink that," Talfryn's muffled comment came from the bed on Padric's right side. Half his face was covered with his white blanket. "And they are *never* picky."

A snort escaped Brynwen's lips involuntarily. Her brother could always lighten the mood. "You honestly don't want to know the ingredients. You will call me a wicked witch."

Lips pale to an icy blue, Padric managed a smile and chuckled lightly. She so adored the sparkle in his eye when he laughed. Her heart froze when she thought he might not live to smile again.

"I sincerely doubt you could ever do anything wicked." He gazed at her intently.

To hide her blush, she indicated a little table holding a tray with a pitcher and two glasses. "I brewed fresh tea to wash it down with," she said. "Same for you, Signore Fiori." Gregorio's expression perked up at that. So, he had heard of her tea as well.

Circe pouted at her son. "You always drank your medicine as a child. Why do you reject it now?"

Gregorio's cheeks flushed. "Well," he stammered, "because I would pour it out when you looked away."

"You what?" Circe asked, wide eyed.

"Did you never notice how the rhododendron wilted periodically?"

"I...oh. That explains so much." Circe sighed.

"That is not reassuring," Padric muttered.

Regardless, Brynwen's pleading eyes must have swayed him, for Padric swallowed the vile concoction in one gulp, very nearly gagging two-thirds of the way down. He didn't stop to take a breath. After gorging down half the pot of tea afterward, he lay back on his pillows in utter exhaustion.

Gregorio and Circe watched the spectacle in shock. Then Circe glared at her son, and the youth downed his own medicine without further comment.

After a few minutes, both men's status remained the same: cheeks and forehead sallow. The rings around Padric's eyes were dark and deep like bruises. His magnificent curls hung dark and limp around his temples. Even the horns on his head seemed wilted. Brynwen knew expecting anything to happen after only a few minutes was next to impossible. These medicines took time. Unfortunately, time was not on their side.

Circe was unwilling to use magic. Brynwen had mentioned it once, but the sorceress ignored it bluntly.

"Do I look so very bad?" Padric asked with the hint of a grin. "Is a chicken foot growing out of my nose?"

"Oh. Nay." She realized she had been staring at him and smiled. "You look better. Truly." His humor almost seemed better. *Or is that only desperation speaking?* She gave what she hoped was a genuine smile, then looped shaking fingers around her braid, swirling the hair over and over. He covered her hands, making her look at him.

"Bryn, please do not lose your hair over me. Whatever happens..."

"Nay, do not talk like that." Brynwen launched to her feet and began to pace. "It has to work. It has to."

"We can try something else," Circe said. "Perhaps it needs more arrowroot. Or elder flowers or crows feet." She rattled off a list of things to try.

"There is one more option," Helius offered. In all the confusion on the temple roof, Brynwen had almost forgotten about the sun god. After what had happened, she had essentially refused to look at him, leaving Circe, Douse, and Isemay to take care of his ailments.

Pillows stacked behind his back, Helius sat in a bed on the other side of Gregorio, eyes sunken, yet still handsome in his rumpled purple robe. His main complaint was weakness and a relentless headache. And by the way he looked to his grandsons, a strong case of guilt.

Circe's head shot up.

"Nay."

"It is a risk, but it could work."

"*Pater*, do not ask it of me. I vowed to never do it again."

The room temperature lowered several degrees. With a puff of air, the goddess launched to her feet and stomped out of the infirmary in a puff of flowing blue skirts.

"This is all my fault." Helius shifted to the side of the bed and stood on unsteady feet. He watched his daughter's retreating form disappear, then turned sheepishly to those remaining in the room. "I have brought this on all of you. But I will make amends." Then he followed Circe out the door.

❦

JUST LIFTING a hand to scratch the itch on his nose left Padric breathless. The thought of sitting up was exhausting. His mind grew groggy, but sleep eluded him. So many thoughts and nightmares swept through his mind. The imminent departure of hundreds of people from Cataractonium. The return of everyone to Chaddesden and other cities and villages. Everyone's lives moving on. Except for him. He would either be soon dead or doing Helius's bidding for the remainder of his days.

A pang of regret filled his heart, for not saying goodbye to his family, for not having the chance to live the life he had worked so hard to achieve. But he fought to push those feelings away. It was better this way. Brynwen would be free to do whatever she wanted. Even if she did not marry Jasper, her prospects and knowledge had grown so much since he had first met her. She would be fine on her own.

A conversation in hushed tones buzzed to his ears. The group of healers thought he slept and did not hear their discussion—their fears regarding the manticore venom. Miriel voicing the question: "Why did the amulet fail?"

Why did it fail? But...did it fail? I should have died outright from the full blast of the sun-staff when I grabbed a hold of it. Any mortal would have died given the same circumstances. The amulet must have shielded him from being fried alive. What other explanation was there? A sudden urgency fell over him—*where is the amulet now?*

"You are awake." Warin stepped into Padric's vision. Bandages were wrapped around his ribs. "I have been wanting to speak with you."

As usual when Warin was around, Padric's defenses came up,

340

building a wall. But Warin held up a hand. "What you did today, first with the manticore, then with the chariot, well…" A flush of crimson rode up his neck. "I wished to say well done. I don't know if I would have done the same."

Padric was taken aback by Warin's admission. *Have I heard right?* It was a few moments before he could think of an appropriate reply. "We worked as a team, you and I, against the manticore. And together we saved Gregorio—Telegonus. You might have done the same given similar circumstances."

Likewise, if not for the aid of Helius and Talfryn, he might not have been able to stop Janus, but Padric was too tired to say any of this out loud. "I am sorry you lost some good men in the fight with the *aeternae*."

"As am I for your men. They all fought bravely."

"That they did," Padric agreed solemnly.

Warin's mouth set in a line, and he remained silent for some time before adding, "Say, neither of us won the third trial. We were interrupted."

Talfryn popped up next to Warin. "I think Padric won, because he drove the chariot."

"I would agree with that," Gregorio piped in from the other side of Padric.

Padric tried to chuckle, but it came out as a cough. "Mayhap we can have a rematch. If it has not been cancelled, the tourney should be coming up soon."

"It is a deal." Warin shook Padric's hand, gently this time. "It should be in Nottingham this year."

Padric drifted off as Warin continued to speak about the tourney and going home.

PADRIC CRACKED open his eyes and stared blankly at the ceiling, trying to tamp down the wretched pangs brought on by the venom. When he blinked again, from behind drowsy lashes, hazel eyes peered into his own. The breath froze in his lungs.

"Padric." Brynwen smiled at him, though it did not quite reach her eyes. Her hand slipped into his, and it was warm; he had not realized how cold his own fingers were until then. Brynwen's other hand swept up past his cheek, and deft fingers combed through his hair, patting down unruly curls around the horns.

Miriel and Isemay stood behind her, each holding a pitcher and bowl; both trying without success to appear cheerful. It alarmed him how quiet Miriel was. She was always so bubbly and all smiles.

"I have another tincture for you to try," Brynwen said in a soothing voice.

The very thought of the previous drink made his stomach turn. He shook his head, which made the room spin, creating two of everyone.

"Please. It will taste better this time."

Her pleading eyes stabbed at his heart, and at last he relented. "If you say," he managed to mumble. Indeed, it was not altogether horrible, and he drank every drop.

To his other side, Ulysses appeared, wings tucked tightly to his sides, and antlers taking up the rest of the space between the cots. Haunches on the floor, he rested his head on the bed near Padric's leg. Padric stroked the peryton's head a few times.

Attempting to relax on his cot, Gregorio appeared little more than an apparition. His normally bright, studious eyes were glossy. Despite his youthful appearance, he resembled a man even older than the Gregorio whom Padric had known the last few years. He could only imagine his own appearance. *Manticore venom at its finest. Would the venom have had a negligible effect on Gregorio if he had remained a manticore?*

The question that had been nagging at Padric all day suddenly became an urgent need to understand. "Gregorio," he said with a scratchy throat. The tutor looked up. "Why did you hide your appearance under the guise of an older man?"

The teacher grinned weakly. "Who would hire a youthful man as a prodigious educator, with knowledge of several languages and subjects, when he appears to have barely been weaned from his mother's milk?"

It made sense. Only years and years committed to learning could have produced the vast amount of knowledge Gregorio had acquired. A youth of no more than seventeen would have been scoffed at and turned away on his heel. Or given a much thinner salary.

"I see your point."

"Yes, well. But I knew who you were the moment I first laid eyes on you. You look exactly like my father, Ulysses, when he was less...furry," he explained with a grin.

Ulysses raised his eyebrows. Padric could sense a grin from the peryton.

Gregorio continued, "I knew then that you were the one to help *Avus*. To help all of us."

Padric was beginning to understand. "You left home not because you were cross with Helius or Janus, but to help your grandfather."

"Precisely. However, at the time I did not know how ruinous it was to become. I visited home often. As *Avus* grew worse, I did more research. I took more journeys away from Derbyshire. That was when I met Roana, whom you have also met, by chance. She was young and gifted and had many dreams and visions concerning the future. Longing for someone to confide in, she described to me her recurring dream: a nightmare that would wake her, completely drenched in sweat; one where the world was consumed by a never ending fire. I had a strong hunch about their correlation with one another."

"That was when you discovered the existence of the amulet of obsidian."

Gregorio nodded. "I became obsessed. However, I knew not where to begin the search. My only clue was that a Roman legion had it at one time in Britain, but it was lost centuries ago. Every time I thought the answer was in my grasp, it eluded me yet again. I imparted some of this knowledge in your studies, though gave no direct information to you. Thus, believing someday you could uncover the puzzle and help us."

"You could have told me outright."

"It was for your protection." Gregorio shook his head. "At any rate, would you have believed me? The last few months, when Mater was collecting slaves in Chaddesden and Derby for the tower construction, I hid myself from her with the use of my amulet." He touched the blue stone on the side table. "I was a coward, I admit it. At first, I thought Mater was coming after me. I was not ready to face her or Avus. But then, I discovered someone else was looking for me, someone nefarious. I knew it was something to do with Roana's vision, but also the amulet of obsidian. Honestly, I would have told you the night I left Chaddesden —found a way to convince you to help—but they were right behind me. I ran, desperate to elude them and find the amulet, thinking perhaps I could save Avus after all. But I misplaced my amulet, and they followed me all the way to Mamucium, where I discovered the location of the amulet. However, before I could obtain it, they overpowered me."

"By Janus?"

He shrugged. "I suspect so. They divulged no names, and yet, they knew everything about me. They brought me to their hooded master, who turned me into the manticore, then sold me to Avus. If I lived or died, no one would be the wiser."

Miriel's eyes were wide with wonder. "You mean all this time we had a god in our house, right under our noses?"

Gregorio smiled at her. "Nay, Mistress Miriel. Not a god." He explained to her the differences of godliness and mere immortality.

The infirmary door flew open. Circe stormed back in, vexation flowing off her body in rivulets, and harried by an adamant Helius. "This one time," she said, jabbing her hands onto her hips and giving her father a withering look. Then she turned to Gregorio and Padric. "There is a way to save you. Both of you."

CHAPTER 57

$\mathcal{P}$adric gaped at the gods. *If Circe has a solution, why does it sound less pleasant than the two tinctures I have already tried?*

Gregorio looked from one god to the other. *"Mater?"* he asked. "You are not considering what I think you are."

"We are out of options, Telegonus." It still threw Padric for a loop every time Circe or Helius called Gregorio his given name.

"What is the cure?" Miriel burst out. "Can you save them or not?"

Brynwen's grip on Padric's hand increased, mercilessly squeezing all the blood from it.

Circe eyed the maiden as though she would find pleasure in changing her into a tadpole, then gave a nod. "Of sorts. There is no known cure for manticore venom; however, healers of old made no light attempt to find one. Like a snake, the beast itself grows the venom within it, and each manticore has different chemistry than the next. The venom evolves with each offspring. Even if Telegonus's manticore body had been alive for centuries, we would have gleaned no hope of an antidote from it. The creatures are unapproachable. When dead, their corpses rot away to dust almost instantly, their venomous glands drying up like desert sand.

"However, there was one other time when I was able to save a life."

She indicated Ulysses, who raised his head from the bed. "Ulysses lay dying from a lance tip laced with venom. To save his life, I transformed the venom into a substance that was then dissolved harmlessly within his blood stream. But in doing so, his mortal human body could not handle the change. He faded, even as the venom was deemed harmless. His body structure and chemistry had to transform as well. Only his mind remained intact."

Brynwen let out a breath and glanced at the peryton. "The change is...permanent?"

The sorceress frowned. "It is. My powers are not attuned to the healing arts but more to animal transformations. And on occasion, the gift of immortality."

"And you?" Brynwen turned to Helius.

The sun god shook his head sadly. "Alas, I have been of no use in the healing arts, unless they are attached to the benefits of the sun's uplifting and healing rays. Excellent for the skin, in moderate quantities. But poison and venom?" He lowered his head.

With bleary eyes, Padric squinted at the red spot on Ulysses's chest. "But your gift left a mark."

Circe nodded. "Unfortunately, Ulysses has retained a permanent blemish. A reminder of his one-time mortality, and that not all sorcery is perfect, even in immortality."

"There is always a price," Gregorio finished.

Brynwen stood on shaky legs. "There is no other way?"

"None that I know of, nor that would come in time, at least. If we are to do this, we must act quickly." She turned to Padric, then to Gregorio. "If you die, your body is forfeit to my powers. Should you choose this, you can name the animal form you desire. Ulysses chose the stag for its swiftness and grace. I bestowed him with the form of a peryton, for his greatest wish was to fly. And they are quite easy on the eyes, are they not?" A forced smile raised her lips.

A kind of panic tugged at the back of Padric's mind, and he could not breathe. Whether from the effects of the venom, or the insanity of their idea, he was not completely sure. Gregorio's face was even more ashen than before. He squeezed Brynwen's hand to get her attention.

Leaning over Padric, Brynwen's eyes studied his face. "Will you?" She nibbled her lower lip and took a breath. "Will you do it? She can save you." A tear raced down her cheek.

I can live...but everything will change....

He would have little choice but to leave her, or vice versa, now or later. With a gentle caress, he wiped the tear away from her cheek. "And if I break her spell as I did the others? I could die regardless."

"But maybe it won't break. Could you change yourself back into a human or faun afterward?"

Both Padric and Brynwen turned their heads to Circe in expectation. Gregorio and Helius were interested in her answer as well.

The goddess took her time considering the answer. Finally, her hands clasped together so tightly the knuckles turned white, and she answered. "It is entirely possible that you could reverse the spell, I am afraid. Unfortunately, there is no way to be certain, and no other sorceress could make it here in time to try their spells."

"Nay."

The answer came out of his lips before he had truly thought it over. But the answer was right. Felt right.

"What?" Brynwen and Circe said at the same time.

Brynwen frowned. "But Padric—"

He rolled his eyes, a painful feat, and repeated, "Nay." Attempting to sit up, his body was too heavy. "I will not do it. I will not forfeit who I am. What I have so far achieved in my meager life. If I die in this form, as a faun on this day from manticore venom, then so be it."

He felt rather than saw the glare Brynwen gave him. His body squirmed under her scrutiny. The power she had over him—it scared him more than anything. And he longed for more of it. *But not like this.*

Everyone in the room stared at Padric in astonishment, and he glared right back. He would not falter, not in this.

Brynwen gaped at him, face stony. "I need a moment with him," she said to the room at large. "Alone."

The Roman gods nodded and spun to set their weary sights on Gregorio.

Brynwen sat on the edge of the bed, but merely held his hands for several silent moments. The blue fabric of the blanket made her muslin dress and patchwork apron stand out. Padric looked her over feverishly, trying to remember every detail about her. Every hair in her braid, every freckle. The brown flecks in her irises.

"You must do it," she said. She looked away then and returned to worrying her bottom lip. "Mayhap we can find a way to change you back later."

Reflexively, Padric pulled his hand up to her face and gently brushed his thumb over her lip. "Bryn, stop."

She scowled and pulled from his touch. "Why?" Then, lowering her voice so the others could not hear, "Why would you do this, when you have the chance to live? How can you possibly give that up?" Another tear ran down her cheek. "How can we go on? How can I?" She choked up.

Padric resigned himself. *How can I even explain it?* "Oh, Bryn." He caught the tear on his index finger. "I want to live. I really do. But even if it did work, how can I change completely into an animal, knowing full well I can never communicate with anyone the same way? With those I care about, those I love? My family, friends, and acquaintances. I would become a true stranger to everyone. Never again would I be able to protect anyone in the same manner. I would never be able to touch anyone the same. To hold them, to...to love them.

"When I look at Ulysses, I can see how much he misses being human. After all these centuries, he has retained his memories of being a man, of love and loss. His immortality eats at him. And he can never again touch the women he loves so much. Not in the way he wants." He could see how much Circe was still affected by his change, even after more than two thousand years. Two lovers doomed to be forever parted, in essence.

As a knight, as a man, Padric had so much to look forward to, but as an animal? "I could be immortal, Bryn, and be free to roam wherever I wish, with whomever I wish. Yet everyone would grow old and die around me, all my family and friends. I have loved my life. Being a knight has its own merits and challenges, and if I can never be a true man again, then so be it. I gave my life to others. I only wish there was more time, Bryn." He placed her hand on his heart. "For us."

Utterly exhausted, he leaned back into the pillow. Her fingers caressed his wan cheek, his hair. "It's unfair," she said after a few heartbeats. "You are a good man."

"Half-man," he corrected.

Again, the glare. Her cheeks flushed, temper flaring. "Padric, do not sell yourself short. I have only known you a short time, but you are more of a man in any form than almost anyone I have ever known. You are honest and loyal to a fault. No matter what form you take, you are always true to yourself. The way you command others—they follow you, do you know that? There is not one man in this room who would not follow you to the grave. They risked and sacrificed their lives today because they believed in you. And so do I. You would do the same for any of us. That is what I love about you."

His breath caught at her speech, and he looked up at her in surprised wonder. *She really feels that way?*

She leaned in closer. "For selfish reasons, I do not want you to leave me. I couldn't care less what form you are, man or animal. I have watched you near death so many times these last weeks." She paused to gather her thoughts. Another tear flowed down her cheek. "But, I understand why you cannot do this. I wish there was a potion I could make to fix this, to fix everyone. I pride myself in my ointments and herbs, but despite my best efforts to save you, you are dying before my eyes."

Padric blinked away a dark spot from his vision. "Who is selling themselves short now?" He winked. At least, he tried to wink, but his whole face spasmed instead. "You mix medicine as though born to it. And your tea? It is perfect; I have never had its like. You have a gift, Bryn, a true gift."

She hugged him. Every single wound upon his person screamed in outrage, but he welcomed the pain as he breathed in her sweetness: lavender and honey.

Brynwen pulled back and apologized profusely. Brushing away

another loose strand of his limp hair, she teased, "You could survive Helius's sun blast into your body, but a little venom will kill you?"

He shrugged. "No one is perfect."

"Helius will not be pleased. You made an oath, after all."

"I could have sworn upon the River Styx, but not much good that would do me."

Brynwen looked away and wrung her hands in her apron. her somber eyes raised to meet his. "Mayhap you should have."

GREAT SPASMS THREATENED to overtake Brynwen's body. She urged herself to take a deep breath, then another, then willed resolve to take over. She would not let this break her. *Not now.*

A scared and hobbling Talfryn followed her into the medicine room. She didn't fail to notice him wince with every step, his leg heavily bandaged. "Bryn," he tried to reason with her for the umpteenth time. "You cannot save everyone."

"We've already lost Leowyn, and soon Gregorio. I can't lose Padric too. There has to be a way to save them."

"Leowyn was not your fault."

His eyes glistened and her heart wrenched at her own careless words. "Mayhap not, but it wasn't yours, either." She crossed the two steps between them and embraced her brother, her whole heart going into the action.

Heart? Releasing Talfryn, her eyes scanned the shelves, looking for something she missed, anything that could solve this problem. But there was nothing. She had tried it all.

"If anyone can find a cure, you can," Talfryn encouraged.

Circe had sworn there was nothing left in the herb garden which wasn't already in the infirmary or her workshop. Feeling entirely helpless, Brynwen's chest constricted, getting tighter and tighter until finally she couldn't draw another breath. She knew an extreme attack of anxiety when it came on, and it was taking over completely. She hadn't had one in years, not since the plague took her parents.

"Breathe, Bryn." Talfryn rubbed her back, trying to calm her. "Take deep breaths. What would Mother have done?"

She closed her eyes and imagined their mother, her dark brown hair and ready smile. Most of what Brynwen knew about herbal remedies had been passed down from her mother, and her grandmother before her. Mother had always had the answer. But instead of calming her, Talfryn's usually helpful quip only annoyed Brynwen further. "Mother cannot help us now. She is dead." She shoved off her brother's hands and banged a fist against the workbench. "She is very, very shriveled up and slain by that horrid, useless plague."

A fiery rage consumed her, and she swept her arms over the workbench, knocking everything onto the floor with a resounding crash. Glass bottles and stoppers, baskets and bowls, loose herbs and pasty ointments were all sent to the floor in heaps, puddles, and shards of color. Circe's recipe book landed on the floor with a thud to an open page.

"Feel better?" Talfryn asked.

Brynwen let out a huff and crossed her arms. "Loads," she said sarcastically. Then she covered her face with her hands. "Oh, what have I done?"

"That's my lass." Talfryn rolled his eyes. Circe and the other healers rushed to the door to see the commotion. The goddess's blue skirts blew into the room. "Not all those ingredients grow on trees," she said as she surveyed the room. Then she turned to the healers. "Do you not have better things to do?"

Almost instantly, they separated and went about their business.

"My my, you have a rage about you." Circe smirked.

Brynwen snorted. She knelt down to place the loose but still-dry herbs in a basket while Talfryn swept. In another minute, she spied the open book on the floor, and with a sigh picked it up. Anger reignited in her chest. "You are of no help." She began to slam it closed when a title caught her eye, one she somehow hadn't seen before.

Anti-Venom. There were a couple others in this book, but somehow she had missed this one. Without a second thought, she poured over the ingredients. Read it a second time.

Something tickled her leg. The broom swept up to her skirt. "Come on, sis. No sleeping on the job."

"Wait, Tal. I may have found something."

"What?" Talfryn and Circe asked at the same time.

"This page," Brynwen said. "*Anti-Venom*. How didn't I see it before? It calls for rosemary, hyssop, a few other things we have in here, and the tears of a...a cal-a-drius."

"A what now?" Talfryn asked, taken aback.

"A *caladrius*."

Talfryn paused, leaning against the workbench. "Circe, back on the hill, didn't you say that Nessie is a *caladrius*?"

"Come to think of it, I did," replied the goddess. She pinched her nose in irritation, then smacked her forehead. "What a fool I am. I have been so wrapped up in finding a potion or magic, I forgot about the blasted *caladrius*."

Brynwen jumped to her feet. "We must find her before it's too late."

Forgetting about his lame leg, Talfryn dashed into the other room. After a few moments, he hobbled back into the herbarium. "She's not in there." He stuck his head out the little window by the workbench, put his fingers to his lips, and whistled loudly. "Nessie!"

Brynwen's heart had never pounded any harder than it did at that instant. But time passed and nothing happened. The little white bird didn't fly through the window.

"Nessie!" Talfryn cried out the window, like a fool. "We need you."

"Please," Brynwen begged. Her hands turned white as they clutched the workbench.

Within seconds, the white bird swooped in with a rush of feathers, twittering all the while. "Good lass," Talfryn exclaimed excitedly, patting her gently on the head. "Who is my best lass?"

"Place her near the bowl," Circe directed. Together, she and Brynwen placed the ingredients into the bowl while Talfryn held Nessie. Then without instruction, Nessie hopped from his hand and onto the bowl rim. She fluffed her white feathers, blinked twice, then submitted two tiny tears to the concoction.

"We must hurry," Circe said, stirring the bowl, then pouring part of the mixture into another bowl. "The tears dry up faster than water in the desert. Then it will be useless."

Circe called all the healers to quickly take a small portion and smear it on the fiercest wounds of any patient who needed it most. After she and Brynwen had taken a share for Padric and Gregorio, the rest of the healers dipped their spoons into the precious mixture.

Brynwen rushed out the door, praying to God that she was in time to save both men.

As she worked the mixture into Padric's wounds, everything else around Brynwen ceased to exist. He was all she cared about. Much which occurred after that was a blur of rushing around, pacing, and praying.

At last, Brynwen plopped down in exhaustion in the chair between Padric and Talfryn's beds. His complexion was less pale after a couple of hours, but the knight remained unconscious. She glanced over to Gregorio. His chest rose and fell evenly in slumber. He fared little better. Helius hung his head in shame as he sat in the chair between his grandchildren. Circe sat on the other side of Gregorio, and even Warin stopped by a few times to see if there was any improvement.

Staring at the god, the thorn Brynwen held in her heart for Helius shattered. He was devastated by his own actions. Raising his head, he caught her scrutinizing him. Unable to avert her gaze, he shrugged his shoulders. "I am a fool. After all these centuries, I still cannot save my own family. I allowed a madman into my home and let him take over my mind."

Brynwen knew she should keep silent, keep her mouth shut, but in the end, she found her voice. "We all make mistakes. All of us. It is what you do with the results that mark the measure of the man, or god, you are."

A small smile raised the corner of Helius's lips. "It is kind of you to say." He peered at the sleeping Padric. "Thank you, my child." His eyes sparkled, and Brynwen knew he meant it. "I must confess something, and it might as well be to you. While Padric and Warin are both my grandchildren and true champions, there can only be one heir. That is Padric; both Circe and Ulysses saw it from the first, as did I the moment he entered Cataractonium. Despite this, Warin had a good chance of becoming my heir should he prove himself worthy, and if Janus had his way, Warin would be my heir now."

And we would all be dead.

"Padric," she said, leaning over him. "Did you hear that? You are the charioteer's heir."

She almost missed it, but Padric's eyes fluttered, then cracked open.

"Padric," she breathed, not allowing herself to hope.

With all her might she tried to hold it in, for the healers, for the gods, for her own propriety. Finally, her resolve broke, and the tears flowed down her cheeks freely in a flood of joy and exhaustion. Heart full, she laid her head on his chest and cried without restraint, soaking his bandages with her tears.

When the tears at last dried up, the physical and emotional exhaustion had led her to a deep, dreamless slumber.

CHAPTER 58

$\mathcal{B}$rynwen cracked her eyes open groggily. Sleep eluded her, only because of a sharp twinge between her shoulder blades. In an attempt to move, she found her muscles were stiffer than an old piece of leather. At last, she sat up slowly, rubbing her neck and shoulder where they had rested on the cot. The sun had risen, and no one had woken her. She was slightly incensed at that.

Brynwen spread her hand upon the empty cot, gliding her fingers along the sheets. Confusion swelled in her brain. Then worry nagged and twisted at her stomach. Visions of the worst things happening flashed through her mind. *What if he died right after I fell asleep, and they took his body out and buried him? Nay,* she pleaded, *please do not be dead.*

Even if he did rise out of bed on his own, he would still be weak, even if the ointment had healed his wounds. A quick peek around the room revealed no sign of him. Jumping to her feet, she rounded the row of cots holding her sleeping brother and the remaining knights. None of the other healers, Alice, nor her baby, were about.

Then a sound came from the lavatory. *Strange,* she thought, *it sounds like a horse.* Her heart lodged in her throat. Casting her eyes about for a weapon, she found a large wooden spoon with the remnants of an ointment on it. *Perfect, perhaps I can give the assailant a splinter and then heal the cut with the ointment.*

With caution, she snuck to the door, and with excruciating slowness, turned the latch. Standing over a little wooden table and basin of water, a man wearing a pair of dark brown trousers peered into a tiny tarnished mirror on the wall. A razor moved toward his chin below wet, curling hair. He was stripped to the waist, revealing muscular arms and a thin torso. Three long, faint scars ran down his left arm and back. Draped over his shoulder hung a blue towel which matched the curtains of the small window. But what really surprised her was the chestnut horse, standing directly next to the man, intently watching him. As though it, too, contemplated a shave.

Face flushing, she grabbed clumsily for the door latch. "Oh, I beg your pardon." She swung the door half closed before realization dawned on her. Heart leaping in her chest, she thrust the portal back open, and it banged against the other wall.

The horse remained in the same spot, but its head swiveled around and gazed at her with curiosity. Somehow it seemed familiar.

The young man turned around, a curious expression on his sodden face.

Padric. He was transformed.

The faun legs he had sported the last several weeks were gone. In their stead, beneath those trousers, were human legs and human feet. Even the horns atop his head were gone. She was so used to his appearance as a faun, she hadn't recognized him at first.

But how?

Padric stood awkwardly, razor still in his hand. One stubborn drop of shaving soap remained on his otherwise immaculate cheek. Around this, his cheeks resumed their normal rosy hue. Gone was any trace of the illness which had only a few hours ago consumed him. His eyes were bright, as green as ever. An indeterminate time passed as they gaped at one another.

Is it really you? "You're up," she said, deadpan.

He flashed his mischievous smile, the one that made her toes curl. "That I am."

"You know, someone should teach you proper instruction on the use of a shaving blade. You missed a spot, just there." With gentle fingers, she rubbed his soapy cheek.

"Mayhap if someone were to give me the proper instruction, I might thrive in its undertaking."

"Mayhap."

More silence. Then he exhaled.

Heart beating erratically, Brynwen didn't know what else to say. A sudden shyness came over her, and she couldn't bring herself to look at his face. *Am I dreaming? Is this a ghost come to haunt me, to plague me with what might have been, for the rest of my days?* Of their own accord, her feet started moving toward him, with slow, deliberate steps, as though they knew what her heart desired most of all. They stopped mere inches from his, and his body grew rigid. Even this close to him, Brynwen still could not get over the fact that Padric was hoofless. Her eyes rose from his ten toes to his scarred torso.

"Are you a ghost?" she dared to whisper aloud, "Or do I dream of how you would be?"

With tentative gentleness, she raised her hand to the pink horizontal scar on his chest from the manticore venom. From left to right, she traced two fingers slowly along the scar, which was now a faint reminder of how close he had come to death. Yesterday, she had treated the black wound with green substance oozing from it, but today it looked as though months had passed since its healing.

Then her eye fell on the scar on his left side, where the mysterious cloaked man's knife had plunged and nearly killed him. This scar too, she traced, smiling at Talfryn's uneven stitching. The thread from the stitches was long gone, but the marks left behind by the needle remained visible. *His skin is smooth. Toned. Real.*

Padric's empty hand cupped her cheek with utmost delicacy. "Bryn." The spell broke. All of a sudden, she was in his warm arms. When at last she let go, holding him at arm's length, his mossy green eyes bore into hers.

Gently as ever, his hands stroked her cheeks, her hair. Her heart nearly burst at the contact. "You are so clever and beautiful." His voice was thick with emotion. "I knew you had it in you...your own magic."

"But I don't have magic. I—"

He kissed her, deeply, cutting off whatever she might have been ready to say, and she returned the gesture with the same enthusiasm and passion, not wanting it to ever end. The thousands of thoughts and questions swirling around her head dissolved into the void. When at last they came up for air, they were completely breathless, their foreheads resting against each other.

Then she remembered the horse in the room and cast a curious glance its way.

A chuckle arose from Padric's grinning lips. "Firminus does not mind in the least."

"Oh, fine then." She punched him in the arm.

"Ach!" Padric jumped back in surprise and rubbed his shoulder. "What was that for?"

"For nearly dying on me." She tried to keep a straight face while glaring at him.

"But not for lack of trying. It was difficult to do with you making a racket and attacking me with ointments and tinctures."

"Well, I had to get your attention somehow."

"I should say it worked."

She grinned, feeling the heat flush her cheeks. "But just one thing," she asked. "How?"

"How did I transform back?" he asked with a gleam in his eye. He huffed and drew his hands through his rapidly curling hair. Water droplets scattered everywhere. "Early this morning I awoke and felt much improved. Whilst everyone slept, it gave me the opportunity to think. Even though Apollo and the world were saved, I was could not keep the people in my charge from harm." He shuddered, crossing his arms across his chest. "I thought...I thought if I was a better leader Leowyn and the people in the stands might have survived. Fewer people would have been hurt. My heart ached with the weight of it all. The guilt. As yet, I did not deserve to have my previous life restored. Nothing would ever be the same again.

"But then I knelt and prayed this morning, thankful for the Lord's help, yet still lost in sadness for all who perished. As though whispered directly into my ear, advice I had recently received from a wise young woman came to me." He swept away another loose strand of auburn hair from her forehead. "She told me I can be whoever or whatever I wish to be. To trust myself. Truly, it is a hard lesson to learn you are not invincible and you cannot expect to change an outcome or save everyone. The answer is not adapting physically, but mentally. Circe had said I broke her curse long ago and should have been able to lose my animal form at any time. The problem was not with magic, it was me. Here." He pointed to his head. "All along, I was afraid to be myself, for how could I live with my many mistakes? It was then I discerned that, regardless of what physical form I take—human, centaur, or faun—it is still me in thought, word, and deed. I am all these things, and all these things are me.

"And this maiden," he said, caressing her jawline with his thumb, "accepts me for who or what I am regardless."

"It took you long enough to come to that conclusion."

Padric shrugged. "I am a stubborn man." He chuckled and leaned in for another kiss.

A celebratory handclap came from the open door. Startled, Brynwen spun around. Talfryn leaned against the door, leg no longer bandaged. Brynwen's cheeks flushed in embarrassment.

Talfryn grinned. "Well, well, that made for quite the entertainment this morning. What say you, crew?"

A few heads popped around the door: Rawlins, Byron, Isemay, Miriel, and Gregorio. They all feigned mild indifference, except Miriel, who clapped her hands together in delight.

Without missing a beat, Padric spun on his heel toward the horse. "Firminus, are you quite finished using the water-wardrobe?" The horse nodded in affirmative, and Padric smiled wryly. "Then our time in here has concluded." Giving Brynwen a knowing look, he squeezed her hand. "It is all yours to clean up, friend Talfryn. Oh, and we march out in one week."

Brynwen burst out laughing at Talfryn's startled expression.

Together, she and Padric sauntered out of the little room with six pairs of eyes gawking at them in wonder.

CHAPTER 59

One week later, June 29, AD 1356
Cataractonium, England

The dryad servant halted amidst the wide courtyard of topiaries and native flowers. Circe's grand house loomed directly ahead of Padric, Talfryn, Brynwen, and Warin, its white exterior extending up and wide, with grand pillars stretching along the front from ground to rooftop. Despite having been there for weeks, Padric had not dared to marvel at its beauty before this day, because he felt that admiring them would be akin to giving in to the Roman gods; giving in to defeat.

It will never resemble the gardens of Chaddesden manor, Padric thought with a pang.

The servant stood an arm's length apart from Padric and the others. With some regret, he became aware that he had not seen Nalini since the end of the second trial. He understood she had been under Helius's orders to seduce him, and as much as he disagreed with her methods, she had, in fact, helped him to better know his own heart. For that, at least, he hoped to thank her someday.

From the grand house emerged Helius and Circe, followed closely by a still-young-looking Gregorio. The pair of gods appeared immaculate in their morning robes: Helius in his standard royal purple, and Circe in cerulean. Gregorio's red cape had been laundered, mended, and draped regally around his gaunt shoulders. It heartened Padric to see his tutor had healed as fast as himself with Brynwen's antidote. The tutor grinned warmly at his pupil.

"You are looking well, M'lord," Padric remarked, taking in Helius's appearance. Indeed, Helius was much improved from the afternoon of the solstice. His eyes were clear, and his youthfulness became even more pronounced as he beamed widely at the little group. His maniacal tendencies were all but gone.

The sun god clapped a hand on Padric's shoulder. "I have you and your friends to thank for that, and for rescuing Telegonus. It is a great gift to have him back."

"M'lord," Padric and Warin said together, and bowed.

Helius continued, "I cannot discern how I ever let Janus get into my head so deeply. And to think how much Circe had ventured to warn me on this very subject. I was a fool."

Enslaving these people was wrong as well, Padric wanted to include, but held his tongue. *Who knew if it was really Helius's idea or Janus's? Nonetheless, now was not the time to broach the subject. But soon.*

Straightening her shoulders, Circe gave her father a withering glare. "At least you found sense in the end, and Padric fulfilled the prophecy. Young man, you must keep that amulet safe. You three have a destiny around it together, I can sense it." She looked at Padric, Brynwen, and Talfryn in turn.

With a crushing foreboding, Padric nodded. Wetting his lips, he asked, "What shall we do about Janus?"

The sun god pursed his lips. "He is in the wind. The dryads say there is no trace of him anywhere within twenty miles."

"Mark my word, he will return," Padric said. "And with a vengeance. We should find him before he tries something else."

"What will he do?" Brynwen asked.

Combing his fingers through his hair, Padric glanced near the sun. It still surprised him when no horns grazed against his fingers. "A more significant question is: why attempt to destroy the whole world? What does he gain if there is nothing left?"

"Enough," Helius said, clapping his champion on the shoulder and casting a warm smile. "That is for another day's worry. You, my children, are prepared for the journey home?"

"Yes, the civilians in the first group are ready to depart, M'lord," Padric replied.

"As are the second group, M'lord," Warin said.

"Your room is ready for you when you return, Padric," Circe said, smiling with warmth. Padric noticed how bright her face appeared, with the strain of her many spells now gone.

"I thank you." Padric shuffled, his feet not yet accustomed to wearing boots. He had forgotten how his toes squished in his socks. "I shall return presently, once I see the caravan out of Yorkshire."

Helius shook his head. "Nay, you will be on that caravan."

"What?" The twins asked simultaneously.

Padric knit his eyebrows. "M'lord, perhaps I misheard you?"

"You heard correctly, grandson."

"But I am to remain here. My oath—"

"Is to serve me at my will. I cannot have you going around challenging each of my daughter's animals all the time. My will is that you should return home until I summon you. For now, ensure everyone is returned to whence they hail."

The knot that had clenched in Padric's stomach released itself. "I thank you, M'lord. Most heartily." He grinned at Brynwen. She mirrored his sentiments, and his stomach fluttered. *Home. All of my inner prayers had been answered. How can I ever repay the Lord for his good fortune?*

Talfryn patted Padric jovially on the arm. "I am sure we can find room for you in the caravan somewhere."

"You are welcome to ride in our caravan any time," Warin said gruffly, as though granting Padric a favor.

Padric smiled and gave him thanks. It was still difficult to encounter Warin without animosity. *Will that last through to the next Derby-Nottingham tournament?*

Brynwen squeezed Padric's other hand tightly, hazel eyes bright, glowing with the good news. He swallowed down his urge to kiss her on the spot.

"Gregorio," Padric said, regretfully prying his eyes from her, "will you return with us?"

"Alas, there are some things I must take care of here first. And see what more I can discover about Janus. I will return within a fortnight or so. Until then, would you mind ensuring my two little brats of pupils keep up with their studies?"

Padric cracked a smile. "By all means."

Then Helius put his arm through Padric's and led him away from the group. "Stay close to that fine maiden of yours. She has a wicked way with the tongue and is quite the catch. I would not make her wait for you forever."

Ears on fire, Padric diverted the subject. "But Grandfather, why change your mind about me staying?"

Helius studied his grandson in silence. "Please, call me *Avus*. I like the sound of that. It is because you are very young Padric. And I, who have lived many millennia, forget how quickly time passes for mortals. You deserve happiness as long as you can."

Padric hesitated. There was one more thing heavy on his mind.

But it was Helius who brought up the subject. "And nay, I will no longer try to maim Apollo or anyone else...Unless I get my hands on Janus, then I can make no promises."

"I do not blame you in the least. And the temple?"

"No more slaves. Upon the life of my *mater*."

Satisfied, Padric nodded. "That is well."

The god released Padric and slapped his arm in a friendly gesture. "Now hurry up, your sergeant is becoming impatient."

Padric laughed and held up his hand in salute. "As you command, M'lord."

Home. He could almost smell it. He returned to the others as Circe and Gregorio finished a conference with the twins. When Brynwen reached out to clutch his hand, her smile and warmth calmed his racing heart.

Talfryn turned to Helius, his mirth all but gone. "M'lord, what of the wolficorn—er, the wolf creature?"

"Ah yes, the *aeternae*. That infernal beast is on the run. Nevertheless, some of my best trackers are trailing it, Nalini among them."

"And what will you do when you catch it?" Talfryn was physically trembling, which was justifiable, considering it had nearly killed him.

"It will have to be destroyed." He sighed. "I should have destroyed it long ago."

After what it had done to the men fighting in the temple, Padric did not argue the point.

"How did the *aeternae* and manticore get out in the first place?" Warin asked. "I heard there was an investigation into it."

Circe pinched her lips together, then answered. "Yes, we discovered that a few of the guards were bribed. However, after interrogating them, they could not reveal much information as to who bribed them other than that it was a man who stood in the shadows."

Padric shared a look with Talfryn and Brynwen.

"The cloaked man?" Talfryn asked.

"I do not know," Padric replied, "but he hired the woodsmen in the same way when they came after us and the amulet."

The twins nodded.

Circe gave her winning smile to her grandson. "Stay out of trouble, Padric. You know how to contact me should you need me. Sir Warin, you are a strong knight and have all my thanks for your help these last months. Young Talfryn, you are braver than I gave you credit. And Brynwen, remember what we talked about." Brynwen blushed and nodded.

Padric and the twins gave quick gratitude and darted out of the courtyard before the gods could change their minds.

"Oh, and Padric," Circe called out. He halted, fear gripping his throat. "I will tell Nalini there are no hard feelings."

Grinning at her uncanny mind-reading, he called back a thank you, then hurried to his rooms in the guest residence to pack his things. He was going home.

❧

PADRIC LED FIRMINUS, fully blanketed and saddled, to the head of the line where his unit was taking order. Warin and his unit took charge further down the line. Despite the joviality Padric felt toward going home, he faltered. He had finally begun to understand Circe and Helius, and it felt strange to leave them. Shaking his head, he knew not why he felt the sudden melancholy. It was only the feeling that it was too soon to leave them on their own

There also had to be a way to tell his own father, Garrick de Clifton, about their family lineage. But there were several days of travel ahead to think about that.

"It's about time you got here." Rawlins approached, something resembling a smile, or a smirk, spreading across his face. With a blink, Padric thought the sergeant looked reminiscent of a fox. Surprisingly, Rawlins still wore the sling on his arm despite his many protestations against it. *Brynwen must have had a word with him about it.* "I suppose Talfryn and Brynwen told you the news?"

"Aye," Rawlins replied. "So, the old dodger is letting you off the hook for a bit. He must be getting soft."

"Mayhap. He will summon me again when I am needed."

"When will that be?"

"No specific date, but I hope not for a long time."

"Good, then let's get going." Brynwen swept a finger along his arm in quick flirtation.

Padric tried to stifle the heat in his cheeks, but Talfryn glimpsed it and snorted.

"Talfryn!" a young voice called.

The farmer spun around just as the little dryad, Thimble, barreled into him for a hug. "There you are. I was afraid I wouldn't see you again before we left. Where have you been?"

"We've been busy. My sister had to go hunt the *aeternae*, and my mother kept me busy with chores. I just snuck away."

"Glorfidia," someone called from over the hill. The dryad's eyes widened, and she ducked behind Talfryn's legs.

"Glorfidia? Is that your real name?" Talfryn asked in wonder.

"Only when I'm in trouble," she replied. "Well, I'd better go. I'll see you soon?"

Talfryn knelt and gave her a big hug. "Of course. Be good for your mother until then."

"I will." Thimble dashed off with a wide wave to Talfryn and the rest of the train.

Everyone assumed their positions in the caravan. Rawlins deferred the lead to his lieutenant, then moved with Byron, Serill, and Aeron to the sides. Alice rode a horse, her newborn baby cooing in her arms.

Brynwen approached as Padric positioned Firminus at the lead of the column. "Where should I be? With the healers?"

"You can ride with me, sitting pillion."

Brynwen put her hands on her hips. "I am perfectly capable of riding on my own horse."

Padric glowered back. "It is not a question of your ability to ride a horse. We are low on mounts."

"Well, then, I do not need to ride a horse. I can walk perfectly well."

"What if your feet tire?" he asked. She paused and he crossed his arms. "Do you wish to ride with me or not?"

Brynwen scowled again. "Padric. We have had this discussion before."

From behind Padric, Talfryn chortled. "This will equal miles and miles of entertainment."

EPILOGUE

June 29, AD 1356

From atop the hill, the Shadow observed the caravan of mortals setting out to leave Cataractonium.

Well, and so the shapeshifter lives. The Master will be pleased. Then it shrugged. *He has other things in store for him and his friends.*

As it watched the progress of the caravan, the shadow felt another presence in the vicinity. Someone else watched the spectacle below. With slow, deliberate steps, it crossed the underworld barrier through the browns and grays of the middle world, as it called it, to a nearby hill where a black-haired witch materialized next to Circe. The blue-clad goddess seemed to expect the woman's sudden appearance.

The Shadow melted into the shadows of the hillside to observe.

"Well, well, well, dear sister," said the woman. "It appears your little shape-shifting demigod managed to succeed after all."

Circe smirked. "Jealous at my ability to handle situations?"

"Hardly. At least *I* did not swear on the River Styx."

"Oh, let us not go over that again. That is the mountain under

Olympus now. Why have you come, Pasiphae?"

"I am anxious about Janus. The god has remained quiet for some time, and only reveals himself now. What is he truly up to?"

"Nothing good, I am certain," Circe replied. "At the moment, I am more concerned about the missing *aeternae*."

"It is more than that, Sister. Do you not feel it? Something is brewing in the air. Something erroneous, just beyond our reach. Whatever it is, Janus is not the only one of whom we should be wary. Olympus seems more disinterested with matters than ever before."

Circe's lips pinched into a thin line. "I have felt the same, but prayed it was only my imagination."

Pasiphae shrugged. "Helius was not the first to be affected, and I doubt very much he is the last."

"You are not suggesting?"

"I know nothing for certain, but it smells strongly of old magic."

"That does not make me feel better." Circe paused in thought. "If we could send someone in to take a look."

"I know just who to send," Pasiphae said without hesitation.

Circe rolled her eyes. "Not Pavla."

"No one will suspect her. Besides, who else is better equipped for the task?"

A sigh escaped Circe's lips. "If she fails, then all is lost."

"Then she shan't fail."

If the Shadow could have smiled, it would have. As it was, the edges of what was taken for a mouth twitched at the ends. Slinking back through the dark recesses of the fortress, the Shadow now had intelligence its master would be most interested to hear posthaste.

There will be much to prepare for our success. My man on the inside has his work cut out for him.

The End

The adventure continues
in book 3:
Perilous

A WORD FROM THE AUTHOR:

Thank you for taking the time to pick up Treacherous!

If you have a moment, I would really appreciate it if you would take a couple of minutes to leave a review on your favorite booksellers and social media sites. Reviews help authors find new readers and receive feedback about their works.

To receive alerts about Rise of the Charioteer series, sign up for my newsletter at: susanlaspe.com

AUTHOR'S NOTE

Cataractonium was a real Roman fortress to the northwest of the walled city of York in England. After the Roman Legion abandoned Europe in the fifth century AD, they left the fortress to the elements and the populace of the area to use as they pleased. Over the centuries, the villagers and farmers used the stones from the walls for building materials of homes, bridges, and walls. While upgrading the A1 highway in Yorkshire in 2013-2017, the discovery of part of Cataractonium's wall and artifacts resulted in a large-scale excavation of the area surrounding it.

Did you know all the wolves were almost completely driven out of the British Isles nearly one thousand years ago? King Edward I ordered the extermination of wolves in England in AD 1281. By the end of the fifteenth century, wolves were all but extinct in England, with some surviving in Scotland until the eighteenth century.

Regarding medieval knights: In my story, squires became knights at a younger age. Historically, a page became a squire at age sixteen, and dubbed a knight at twenty-one. However, because of the Bubonic Plague, which ravaged England from summer 1348 through December 1349 AD, many of the populace perished, including knights and soldiers. It would be safe to assume the need to replace them would be a priority in many places, especially large cities. As a result, the knights in my series became squires earlier, at age fourteen, and knights at eighteen, to make up for the need for a lord's or city's security. There is no evidence that this occurred, but I don't think it would be completely out of place during a time of need such as this.

ACKNOWLEDGMENTS

Words cannot describe how crazy it is that I have written and published two novels! But I couldn't have done it without great people to help guide and encourage me along the way.

Kelsey Gietl, thanks for helping me brainstorm and go over covers, writing, and marketing strategies, as well as all the time spent in "writing sessions" where we talked for hours and hours instead of putting more than five words on the page. You are the Merry to my Pippin.

Anne Poelker, you helped shape the characters into who they are today. Padric, Brynwen, and Talfryn are now way cooler than they were when I began this series.

My wonderful husband Mark, who was patient as I disappeared into the office to work on book stuff and kindly read my books even if you would rather play computer games. You are the Rory to my Amy.

My awesome beta and advance reader (ARC) teams: Rachael Johnston, Kelsey Gietl, Jen R, Kirsten Wright, Carla Varner, Christine Emnett (and yes, she *is* related to the Rohirim!).

To Patric Tebeau for taking the painstaking time to translate all the Latin text in my books. Having not taken any language classes in a long time, one forgets how much work goes into figuring out verbiage based on context, gender, and number!

My dedicated editor, Sarah Everest, who spent way too much time clearing out all the millions of "that" and "for a moment" from the novel, which I had thought very important at the time.

And although I know he'll never read this in a million years, to musician James Arthur for inspiring a scene in my book with your song "Say

You Won't Let Go." That song resounded in my head every time I thought about, worked, and reread that scene.

To you, reader, for taking a chance on me and picking up my books. I appreciate you!

And last but certainly not least, to my Lord and Savior, Jesus Christ, who is my All in All.

ABOUT THE AUTHOR

Susan has loved watching television and movies, reading, writing, and art since her earliest memories. Her push to create her own stories was influenced by Grimm's Fairy Tales and the Percy Jackson book series, as well as a love of history (one of her favorite subjects in school). Treacherous is her second published novel. When not working or writing, she can be found doing one of too many craft projects or playing board games with her husband in St. Louis, Missouri.